D1171377

WHAT PRICE VICTORY?

WORLDS OF HONOR #7

WHAT PRICE VICTORY?

WORLDS OF HONOR #7

DAVID WEBER

with
Timothy Zahn & Thomas Pope
Jane Lindskold
Jan Kotouč
Joelle Presby

BAEN

A Baen Books Original

Baen Publishing Enterprises
P.O. Box 1403
Riverdale, NY 10471
www.baen.com

ISBN: 978-1-9821-9241-9

Cover art by David Mattingly

First printing, February 2023

Distributed by Simon & Schuster
1230 Avenue of the Americas
New York, NY 10020

Library of Congress Control Number: 2022050409

Printed in the United States of America
10 9 8 7 6 5 4 3 2 1

CONTENTS

TRAITOR

Timothy Zahn and Thomas Pope

PROLOGUE

Cutler Gustavus von Tischendorf was eight T-years old when he had his first space battle.

Though in retrospect, he realized it probably wasn't actually the first such battle he'd been in. He had vague memories of his mother disappearing for hours at a time while he floated in zero-gee in their cabin, listening to rumblings and thuds and occasional shouts from the passageways beyond. Afterward, when all was quiet again, his mom would come back into their cabin, and the deck would slowly become a deck again instead of just another bulkhead. Sometimes his mom would then go out again and not be back for another few hours, but sometimes they went off to the wardroom to eat. There was laughter and loud talk at those times, and he always got an ice cream sundae before his mom took him back and tucked him in for the night.

But it wasn't until the Battle of Jorgan's Star that Cutler finally learned the whole truth.

His mom was a *kapitän* now. That meant their cabin on *Schreien* was bigger than the ones on their previous ships. But it also meant that the cabin had a small set of repeater bridge displays that let Cutler see what was going on.

And it was glorious.

The rumbling was autocannon fire as the ship defended itself from incoming missiles. The thuds marked the launch of *Schreien's* own missiles in response. The shouting was men and women swimming rapidly through the passageways on their way to fix equipment that had failed or to reroute power or sensor lines.

Finally, it was over. Cutler had kept track as he watched, and by his reckoning his mom and *Schreien* had destroyed three whole enemy ships.

And sure enough, an hour later, he got his ice cream sundae.

"Did you watch the battle from the cabin?" his mom asked as he dug into the bowl.

"Uh-huh," Cutler said. "It was really cool. We got three of their ships, right?"

"Three ships were destroyed, yes," she confirmed with a smile. "But we didn't do it all by ourselves. The other ships helped, too."

"Oh. Right." Vaguely, Cutler remembered other ships being in the battle. He hadn't paid much attention to them. "Was Uncle Gustav's ship one of them?"

"Oh, yes," his mom said. "His ship is *always* one of them. And always the best one."

"I don't think so," Cutler said firmly. "*Schreien's* the best. Because *you're* the captain."

"Well, thank you," she said with another smile. "I'm glad you think so." Her eyes shifted across the room—"Pablo?" she called.

"Yes, *Kapitän* Jen?" a swarthy man Cutler remembered seeing around the ship said, coming over to their table. He shot a smile at Cutler. "How you doing, *Kapitän* Jen's son?"

Cutler bristled. He hated when people on his mother's ship called him that. Almost as much as he hated it when they called her *Kapitän Jen*.

But she didn't notice, or else didn't care. She launched into some stuff with Pablo that was way too technical for Cutler to understand. "Yes, Ma'am," Pablo said when she'd finished. "I'll get right on it."

"Thank you," she said. She almost always said thank-you to people.

Cutler wasn't sure he liked that. He'd heard Uncle Gustav order people around, and he was a lot more firm and a lot less friendly sounding.

And they called him *Admiral Anderman*, not *Admiral Gustav*.

"Trouble?"

Cutler blinked. His mom was looking at him, her forehead wrinkled a little. "How come they call you *Kapitän Jen*?" he asked. "I don't think that's very polite."

"Oh, they're polite enough," Jennifer assured him. "The thing is, when politeness and protocol are fighting practicality, the practicality—"

"What's practicality?"

"Practicality is doing things the practical way," his mother explained. "Being efficient. Making sure you get to the result you want in the simplest way that works. In this case, *Kapitän von Tischendorf* takes"—she paused, her lips moving—"seven syllables to say. But *Kapitän* Jen takes—?"

Cutler did a quick count. "Four."

"Four," Jennifer agreed. "A little over half as many. Besides that, *von Tischendorf* is a bit hard for some of the crew to pronounce. So I just told everyone to call me *Kapitän Jen*. You see?"

"Uh-huh," Cutler said. But he still didn't like it. A *kapitän* should be respected, not called by her first name. "But when *I'm* a *kapitän* I'm going to make them call me *Kapitän* von Tischendorf."

"When *you're* a *kapitän*?" Jennifer asked, raising her eyebrows. "You want to command a ship like this?"

Cutler looked around the wardroom. Of all the ships he'd been on, this was the one he liked the best. He liked it even better than Uncle Gustav's battlecruiser *Seydlitz*. "Not a ship *like* this," he corrected her. "I want *this* ship."

"Ah," she said. "Well, you know, there's a lot of work to captaining a ship. And a lot of study and learning first. Are you ready to spend your whole life that way?"

Cutler looked around the wardroom again. "Yes," he said firmly.

"Good," his mom said. "Then finish your ice cream and let's go."

"Where are we going?" Cutler asked. He stuffed in the last two mouthfuls, wincing at the momentary brain freeze.

"Forward Weapons," she said, getting up and picking up his bowl and spoon. "Commander Pablo is going to tear apart one of the autocannon."

She leveled a finger at him. "And *you*, *Kapitän* Jen's Son, are going to watch."

I

"*Bayern* to escort commanders," *Großadmiral* von Tischendorf's voice came over *Schreien*'s bridge speaker. "Call in ready."

Cutler waited until the vanguard leader and each of the two flank leaders checked in with confirmations. After that, it was his turn. "*Schreien* reporting ready," he called.

"Thank you," the *Großadmiral* said.

Mentally, Cutler shook his head. There she went again—and a *Großadmiral* now, too—still thanking people for doing nothing more than their jobs. And probably still letting her senior officers call her by her first name. At the very least, he could hope it was *Großadmiral Jen* now.

Though if he wanted to get *really* technical, it was *Großadmiral Jennifer von Tischendorf von Tischendorf*. Gustav Anderman had always been amused by their family name, not just because of how incredibly German it was, but also because the "von" part made it sound like a relic of nobility from pre-Diaspora days. A few years ago, when Gustav started really leaning into his obsession with the Old Prussian leader Frederick the Great and began handing out titles and lordships, he'd decided to double down on the von Tischendorf name and also make it their title.

Cutler's mother took it as a sign of affection for her and her son. Cutler himself wasn't so sure it wasn't just Anderman laughing to himself.

"Everyone stay sharp," the *Großadmiral* warned. "We're getting some gravitic signatures from behind T-116."

Cutler peered at his display. Sure enough, someone lurking behind one of the larger asteroids in the distance ahead had lit off a wedge. Right on schedule, the Tomlinson Security Force was coming out to play.

For all the good it would do them. Andermani Naval Intelligence had already done a complete workup on the Tomlinson forces, and they weren't in the least bit impressive: two frigates, five corvettes, and an unknown but probably small number of remote-operated missile batteries on some of the larger rocks of the asteroid zone the Andermani task force was currently decelerating through.

And with those seven defenders facing a battlecruiser, two heavy cruisers, two frigates, three destroyers *and* one of Gustav Anderman's incredibly powerful battleships, the Tomlinson force was going to be less than a speed bump on the way to teaching President McIntyre that destroying an Andermani heavy cruiser was *not* a good idea.

Especially when that battleship was the flagship of *Großadmiral* Jennifer von Tischendorf von Tischendorf.

"Getting telemetry signals," Cutler's sensor officer announced. "Probably sending to one or more local missile batteries. Jamming now."

"Acknowledged," Cutler said, glowering at the displays. Sitting back here in the three-ship aft screen, he could certainly disable the Tomlinson missile batteries. But that was about *all* he could do. Where he *should* be was near the center of the formation, between the battlecruiser and his mother's battleship, where *Schreien's* sophisticated EW suite could draw enemy attacks away from those high-value targets and then neutralize them with her heavy antimissile systems.

The problem was that there were three more warships in the TSF's collection: a frigate and two corvettes, warships that the ANI report said were currently undergoing repairs. But that was a conclusion, not hard data, and *Großadmiral* von Tischendorf was too good a commander to put her full trust in even expert extrapolations.

Hence, *Schreien's* position in the aft screen. If the TSF had managed to get the frigate and corvettes back to operational status, they might hide them out here among the asteroids to pop out behind the Andermani force and attempt to throw some missiles up their kilts. Such an attack would be a long shot at best, given that the Andermani were still racing away from such a theoretical ambush and those theoretical missiles, which would give the *Großadmiral* plenty of warning and enough time to pitch wedges against them. But it *was* possible, and the *Großadmiral* wanted to make sure *Schreien* was there to foil any such backstabbing attack.

"*Trakhener* and *Drachen*, decrease deceleration fifty gees," the *Großadmiral* ordered.

The two commanders acknowledged, and on Cutler's tactical the frigates' icons began drifting forward of the main group. Now that contact with the enemy had been made, the admiral was sending the flanking ships ahead of the force to hopefully sniff out any surprises the Tomlinson defenders might have planted up there.

For whatever good it would do them. In a few hours—a few days at the most—Tomlinson would cease to exist as an independent nation.

They had only themselves to blame, of course. Gustav Anderman had never intended to create an empire out here. He'd been perfectly happy to take over the struggling colony world Kuan Yin, rename it Potsdam, find a solution to the genetic plant problem that was killing the crops and starving the colonists, and accept their gratitude in the form of being proclaimed king.

But not everyone had been so pleased with the planet's regime change. Seven T-years after Anderman's arrival, Ronald Devane of Nimbalker had allowed one of his vassals, Baron Sigismund, to raid the New Berlin system. At the time, the prevailing theory among Cutler's circle of friends and fellow officers was that Devane had known what was happening to the Kuan Yin colonists and had a solution, but had deliberately withheld it in the hopes that everyone would die off and he could pick up some new real estate at bargain prices. Gustav's arrival had ruined that plan, and so he was going to call out the upstart and see what he was made of.

On paper, at least, the plan looked reasonable. Nearly a quarter of the Liegnitz, Ltd., officers and spacers had chafed at the prospect of settling down on Potsdam, and had been permitted to take their ships and return to mercenary life elsewhere in the galaxy. Many of those who stayed were rotated from shipboard duty to civilian police and ground security forces. Looking at the resulting "official" size of what was then the New Potsdam Protectorate Navy, Devane had clearly concluded that Gustav's fighting strength was almost nonexistent.

But numbers were only half the story. Devane should also have looked into the tales of Gustav's fighting skill and checked out Liegnitz's success rate. He hadn't, and as a result was forced to watch as his world was annexed barely a T-year later. Three years after that, New Berlin and Nimbalker were formally redesignated as the Andermani Empire, with King Gustav now Emperor Gustav.

That should have been the end of it. The Empire's other neighbors should have taken the hint and steered clear of New Berlin. Certainly

Gustav wouldn't have made any further trouble on his own. Even before his coronation he'd told his closest friends, including Cutler's mother, that he had no interest in further expanding his new empire.

But Hereditary President Trudy McIntyre of Tomlinson was rotten at taking hints. There had been tension between the Tomlinson and Nimbalker systems dating back well before Gustav arrived on the scene, and McIntyre wasn't the type to let a change in management interfere with a good feud. Six T-years after Nimbalker's annexation she sent three frigates to attack the heavy cruiser SMS *Sirene* in Nimbalker space, destroying her and her entire crew.

To no one's surprise, except possibly McIntyre's, Gustav took it personally.

Which was why today, eight T-months later, *Großadmiral* von Tischendorf and the battleship *Bayern* had arrived to deliver an ultimatum: McIntyre would surrender herself, and the remainder of the Tomlinson government would cede control of their world to the Andermani Empire.

There was no *or else* included in the message. Cutler was pretty sure no one on Tomlinson needed one.

Maybe this would be the end of it. Once Tomlinson had been dealt with, maybe all the other small nations out here would leave the Andermani alone. A few hours, a few days at the most—

"Contacts!" the voice of *Trakhener's Fregattenkapitän* Rosten came suddenly from the com. "Six contacts, bearing—"

"Wedges!" Cutler's tactical officer snapped. "Six wedges forward, three each starboard and portside."

"All ships, pitch one-eighty positive," *Großadmiral* von Tischendorf ordered, her voice as glacially calm as always. "*Trakhener* and *Drachen*, return to flanking positions. Aft screen, stay sharp for an up-the-kilt ambush. *Schreien*, increase your missile battery jamming if you can."

"Aye, aye, *Großadmiral*," Cutler said, eyeing the tactical. The six unknowns were clearing the edges of the oversized asteroids they'd been lurking behind, about midway to the TSF ships the Andermani force had first spotted in the distance. The plan had probably been for the first group to act as decoy, holding the Andermani forces' attention long enough for them to sweep past the lurkers, whereupon the latter would swoop out of hiding and put the Andermani into a pincer.

But thanks to *Großadmiral* von Tischendorf's caution, the lurkers had been spotted before that could happen. The Andermani force was now bearing down on them, alerted and in the proper attack formation to quickly deal with the threat.

There was only one problem. Even if the *Großadmiral* had been right about the missing TSF ships being functional again, that only added up to three extra ships.

So why were the Andermani facing *six* wedges?

And then, the ship IDs came up on the tactical, and for a frozen heartbeat Cutler found himself staring in disbelief.

The ambush force wasn't the missing frigate and two corvettes. It was, instead, a full squadron of six corvettes.

Six corvettes.

Someone on *Schreien*'s bridge swore softly. Cutler couldn't blame him. There had been no indication of additional warships in the Tomlinson system: nothing the task force had seen, nothing that ANI had heard even a whisper about.

But they were here. And all six were charging toward the Andermani force, toward *Bayern*'s forward screen and toward *Bayern* herself.

"Here they come," *Großadmiral* von Tischendorf's voice came over the speaker. If she was startled at the size of the unexpected attack force, it didn't show in her voice. "All ships: cease deceleration on my mark: *mark*. Aft screen, hold position."

Cutler hissed out a silent curse. *Hold position.* In other words, stay back where he and his two companions would be completely out of the battle.

That was insane. *Schreien*'s whole reason for existence was to be out there in the open where she could draw off the attacks that would otherwise be directed at *Bayern*. But his admiral had given him an order, and he had no choice but to obey.

Unless he saw an additional threat that needed to be checked out. Or even just *suspected* there was such a threat.

"Pitch twenty degrees positive and move us up one hundred kilometers," he ordered. "I want to be able to see behind that asteroid ahead to portside."

"Twenty degrees positive, up one hundred kilometers," the helm acknowledged.

"*Herr Flottillenadmiral?*" Cutler's XO asked quietly.

"The asteroid in question is large enough to conceal another corvette," Cutler told her. "I want to make sure nothing sneaks up behind us." And in the meantime, once they reached their new position they would be fully clear of *Bayern*'s wedge, allowing the Lorelei lure of *Schreien*'s EW signal to hopefully draw away some of the attacks the corvettes were about to launch.

"Yes, Sir," the XO said.

"Missile tracks!" the call came from CIC. "Incoming—*Gott im Himmel!* There are *twenty-four* of them. Repeat: twenty-four missile tracks."

Cutler stared at the display, his brain momentarily refusing to accept the evidence of his eyes. Twenty-four missiles—four from each attacking ship—was insane. A typical corvette could barely control half that number.

Which meant these corvettes were anything but typical. Modern corporate ringers, beyond a doubt.

And with that salvo came terrible danger. Even with *Bayern*'s forward screen and flankers running at top efficiency, twenty-four missiles were almost certain to overwhelm their defenses. One or more of those missiles were going to get through.

And their target was certainly going to be *Bayern*.

His mother's ship.

"Helm, get us in there," he bit out, tearing his eyes from the tactical long enough to start running some numbers. "*Leipzig, Danzig*—hold position. Watch for additional attacks." At full acceleration, once *Schreien* was at the new position he'd specified . . .

The XO got there first. "We're not going to make it, Sir," she murmured. "We're still in *Bayern*'s impeller shadow. There's nothing we can do about that salvo."

Cutler ground his teeth. "Then we'd best make sure we're there for the second, hadn't we?"

He sensed her wince. "Yes, Sir."

Schreien was still moving to get clear when the salvo hit.

The result was as bad as Cutler had feared. The forward screen took the brunt of the attack, with the heavy cruiser *Bretagne* blazing into scrap with the nuclear fire of missile strikes and the even brighter starfire as her ruptured reactors exploded. The destroyer *München* survived, but the attack took down her wedge, forcing her to fall out of formation and head for the hyper limit as best she could. The battlecruiser *Rossbach* also survived, but suffered two near-misses which neutralized her forward sensors and missile launchers and likewise knocked her out of the fight.

And *Bayern* . . .

The battleship was tough. Tougher than most people who'd never faced anything bigger than a battlecruiser realized. The single missile that got through her defenses would have destroyed any other warship. But *Bayern*, while severely damaged, survived the blast.

But it was only a respite. With the forward screen and *Bayern's* own defenses gone, the attacking corvettes had a virtually clear field for their next salvo. Only the flanking frigates were still in position to counterattack.

They were doing their best. Both ships had pulled in closer, trying to bring *Bayern* into the protective shield of their autocannon. Simultaneously, they were throwing their own missiles as fast as they could at the enemy.

But it wasn't enough, Cutler knew. Each of the Andermani frigates could only control two missiles, and even if by some miracle all four of them found their targets that would still leave two corvettes ready to throw another eight missiles at their undefended prey.

Bayern's only hope was for Cutler to get close enough to draw that second salvo to himself.

And then, he spotted something. A telltale flicker in *Bayern's* nodes, a clear sign that they were about to go.

Again, he quickly ran the numbers, keeping an eye on the readouts of *Bayern's* wedge and nodes. Another flicker, and then a third. The battleship's last gasp . . . and possibly also her last hope.

"Change vector," he snapped, keying the new course over to the helm. "Execute at once."

"Ah—" the helmsman hesitated, peering at the numbers.

"Execute at once!"

The helmsman twitched violently. "Aye, Sir."

"*Herr Flottillenadmiral*—" the XO began urgently as *Schreien* leaped forward.

"Yes, I know," Cutler cut her off. "Don't worry. *Bayern*'s wedge will be gone well before we're in danger of intersecting it."

"Sir, that's an assumption," she countered. "And if it isn't gone—"

"Then we die," Cutler said harshly. "What's the matter, XO? Are you afraid of death in the line of duty?"

"I'm not afraid of death, Sir," she said stiffly. "But I have no interest in dying for no reason."

"The reason writhes in pain in front of you," Cutler said, just as stiffly. "*Bayern*, and however many of her crew still live. Without us, all of them will die. With us, some may yet survive."

"And if you're wrong, not only do they die, but so do all of us."

Deliberately, Cutler turned back to the tactical. "I'm not wrong," he said. "Make sure all EW systems are operating at full efficiency, and prepare missiles and autocannon."

They were ten seconds away from crossing wedges with *Bayern*, and Cutler was starting to wonder if he might indeed have made a mistake, when the battleship's stress bands gave one final flicker and vanished.

Leaving the battleship helpless . . . but also leaving the enemy corvettes open and vulnerable in the distance ahead.

"Stand by missiles," Cutler said coolly, permitting himself a small smile as the tac lit up with the tracks of the corvettes' second salvo. "Autocannon ready. Flank ships, prepare a full salvo on my signal. As soon as this attack has been dealt with, we take the battle to the enemy."

※ ※ ※

It didn't work out that way. In the end, Cutler had no choice but to take the task force's remaining ships and abandon the field, leaving the twisted hulk of *Bayern* and an unknown number of survivors behind.

But it wasn't over, he knew. There would be a day of reckoning. And it would come very, very soon.

II

"Flottillenadmiral von Tischendorf?"

With a start, Cutler looked up from the flag-draped coffin resting beneath the soft lighting. To his surprise, he saw that he was the only one still sitting in the room.

A young ensign stood at the side door, her face and body language radiating discomfort for interrupting a senior officer at a time like this.

"Yes, *Kadett*?" Cutler kept his voice calm and civil. What had happened wasn't her fault, after all.

"Your pardon, *Herr Flottillenadmiral*. His Excellency has called for you. He requests your presence at the Palace at your earliest convenience."

In other words, immediately. "Understood," Cutler said, standing up. He gave his mother's casket one final, lingering look, then headed toward the ensign. "You have a car?"

"Yes, Sir," she said. "If you'll come this way, please?"

She headed down the hallway at a brisk walk. Cutler followed, his heart starting to pick up its pace. Maybe, just maybe, Uncle Gustav had finally made his decision.

The military funeral home was only a few blocks from Sorgenfrei Palace. Probably set up that way on purpose, Cutler had often thought, given the Emperor's long association with warfare and violent death. The car covered the distance in less than a minute, the ensign dropping him in the courtyard with instructions to meet the Emperor in the audience room. Cutler climbed the wide steps, passed between the pair of two-meter-tall *Totenkopf* Hussars standing their silent watch on either side of the door, and went inside. He walked through the Marble Hall, pausing along the way to briefly pat three of the greyhounds who bounded over to greet him, then passed into the audience room.

Cutler had wondered if Uncle Gustav would be alone. He wasn't. There was another uniformed man in the room, his back to the door as he talked quietly to the Emperor. Gustav looked past him as Cutler walked in and beckoned the newcomer forward. "*Guten abend, Herr Flottillenadmiral*," Gustav boomed out a greeting. "May I once again offer my condolences on the passing of your mother."

"*Vielen dank, ihre Exzellenz*," Cutler replied politely as he walked forward. The other man half turned—

Cutler felt a stirring of cautious excitement. It was *Vizeadmiral* Gottlieb Riefenstahl, commander of the battlecruiser *Faust*.

And it didn't take a genius to figure out why he was here.

There were quiet reports that Gustav was forming a new military unit, Wehrkreis II, which would focus on the slowly expanding Andermani Empire with the battleship *Liegnitz* as its flagship. The rumors—and, really, basic logic—also suggested that Riefenstahl was going to be promoted to admiral and put in command of the force. What the rumors *didn't* say was who was in line to be his flag captain.

Riefenstahl was here, talking to Gustav. Cutler had been summoned into their presence.

It was always risky to connect speculative dots. But in this case…

"She was an excellent officer," Gustav continued as Cutler reached the proper place in front of the Emperor and bowed to the proper angle. "And an even more excellent friend."

"Thank you, Your Excellency," Cutler said, fighting against the reflex to say *Uncle Gustav* instead. He'd been twelve when Gustav told him not to call him that in public anymore, but the reflex remained.

He straightened up from his bow, giving his Emperor a quick once-over. Most visitors, even those who should be more discerning, saw mainly the archaic King Frederick the Great garb and powdered wig that Gustav had been outfitting himself with for the past thirty-three T-years. Most of the visitors who got past the clothing stopped again at the Emperor's piercing gaze. Only a few could see past both of those to the face of the man itself.

And only a *very* few, like Cutler himself, could see how that face had changed over the past few years.

Years, hell—he could see how Gustav's face had changed over the past few *months*. The Emperor had been shaken by Tomlinson's unexpected and unprovoked attack. Shaken and furious both. The whole reason he'd settled down on Potsdam in the first place was that he was tired of the constant battles of a mercenary's life. He'd come here hoping all of that had been put behind him, and that he would finally find peace.

It hadn't worked out that way. And people like Cutler, who'd grown up with the man, could see how rapidly he was aging.

Of course, Gustav *was* eighty-six T-years old. Even someone who'd held off old age as well as he had couldn't hold it off forever.

Which wasn't to say that there wasn't still a good deal of fire behind that lined face. McIntyre had found that out the hard way. The Second Battle of Tomlinson had followed the first by only a few T-months, with the Andermani forces this time under the direct command of Gustav himself. In the intervening months McIntyre had received three more of the fancy corporate corvettes that had caused *Bayern*'s force such grief, reinforcements that had been of exactly zero use against Gustav's force of twin battleships plus much of the rest of the Andermani fleet.

The results had been quick, inevitable, and thoroughly decisive. The Tomlinson Security Force had been utterly demolished, the sole survivor being a frigate that was undergoing maintenance at the time. The victors had plucked a few survivors from their ships, subsequently trading them for the handful of *Bayern* crew that the TSF had rescued.

And, of course, for the bodies that had been recovered.

Gustav had made arrangements to tow *Bayern* back to New Berlin, but there was little hope that she could be repaired.

"I've been studying your tactics at First Tomlinson, *Flottillenadmiral* von Tischendorf," Gustav continued. "I've also been considering your requests." He raised his eyebrows, those piercing eyes flicking from Cutler to Riefenstahl and back again.

Cutler nodded, again trying to suppress his growing excitement. If Riefenstahl was promoted and given *Liegnitz*, that would also leave *Faust* in need of a new commander. The only question was which of the two possible positions Cutler was about to be offered.

Both had their advantages. Serving as flag captain of the *Leignitz* under Riefenstahl would probably let him see more action than sitting on a battlecruiser whose sole job was to orbit Potsdam and keep the capital safe. On the other hand, there was a lot to be said for the prestige of having his own battlecruiser.

Besides, given the current trend of political rumbling in neighboring star nations, there was every chance that even the Home Fleet ships would get out for some exercise every now and then. No, he would be content with whichever post Gustav offered.

And the Emperor *would* offer one of them. Because Cutler *deserved* it.

Not just because he was ready. Not even because Gustav had been promising him a major command for at least five years. He deserved it because *Großadmiral* Jennifer von Tischendorf had been one of Gustav's absolute best officers since before Cutler was even born. Legacy alone—honor and gratitude alone—dictated that Cutler get one of those positions.

And if Emperor Gustav was anything, he was a man of honor.

"Before I address that, though," Gustav said, "I want to speak to you about the maneuver that saved *Bayern* and the last remnant of her force from total destruction."

Cutler felt himself grow a little taller. Legacy, honor, and gratitude were all well and good. But ultimately, it was ability and ingenuity that Gustav prized above all else. Gustav's own genius was why Liegnitz, Ltd., had been the best mercenary group the galaxy had ever known, and why the Andermani Empire would last forever.

"It was, and I say this with all respect and deliberation—"

Cutler suppressed a smile. Gloating was unprofessional, especially in front of his Emperor and a senior officer.

"—possibly the most foolhardy maneuver I've ever seen."

The rosy glow vanished. Had Cutler heard him correctly? "Your Excellency?" he asked carefully.

"Not only did it endanger both *Schreien* and *Bayern*, but also the other ships of the task force," Gustav continued. "If *Bayern*'s impellers hadn't collapsed, you would have instantly destroyed both ships. Furthermore, the loss of *Schreien* would likely have strained the task force's remaining resources to the point where none of the ships would have survived."

"But, Your Excellency," Cutler protested. "It worked. It *worked*."

"That it did," Gustav acknowledged. "But the fact that it succeeded does not alter the fact that it was untested, untried, and extremely dangerous."

"Your Excellency—" Cutler broke off. Gustav's mind was clearly made up. And if there was one thing his mother had hammered into him, it was the fact that once Gustav Anderman made up his mind, the decision might as well be cast in battle steel.

"Having said that," Gustav continued, ignoring the choked-off protest, "the situation you found yourself in has highlighted a possible flaw in our battle doctrine. *Vizeadmiral* Riefenstahl has formed a group from the Academy to study the issue, including experts from both engineering and tactics, particularly as regards the positioning of EW warships within a formation. I would like you to lead that group."

"Yes, Your Excellency," Cutler managed.

So there it was. No *Faust*, no flag captain of *Liegnitz*, and a kick downstairs to the Academy.

Was *Schreien* also being taken away from him? "About my current command . . . ?"

"For the moment, this study group will be your only concern," the Emperor said. "Officially, you're still *Schreien*'s CO, but your XO will oversee her repairs. Once your report is in and *Schreien* is ready to return to duty, we'll discuss your future assignment."

"Yes, Your Excellency." So much for honor and gratitude and loyalty. "Will there be anything more?"

The Emperor's eyes narrowed slightly, as if wondering whether Cutler's brusqueness constituted an insult. "No, *Herr Flottillenadmiral*, I believe we are finished," he said. "You'll report to *Konteradmiral* Chun Kao-ni at the Academy tomorrow at oh-nine-hundred. He'll assist you in assembling your study team."

"Yes, Your Excellency," Cutler said. He gave the proper bow, to the proper angle, because *someone* ought to show proper respect today. Then, turning his back on his Emperor, he strode through the door.

Trying very hard not to let his anguish and simmering rage show. There were, after all, *Totenkopf* guards at the door. No doubt watching him closely.

✳ ✳ ✳

The guards closed the door behind von Tischendorf, and Riefenstahl suppressed a sigh.

The man didn't get it. In fact, as near as Riefenstahl could tell, he'd missed the point completely.

Yes, his maneuver had been foolhardy. *Yes*, it had risked the entire mission. By all logic and probability the outcome should have been a completely destroyed task force, whereas if von Tischendorf had simply accepted the loss of *Bayern* and the other ships and broken off after that first devastating salvo, he might have saved more than just *Schreien* and two of the other ships. And *yes*, it was the Emperor's right as sovereign, as well as his duty as overall Navy commander, to point that out.

But the fact that the Emperor had recognized that von Tischendorf had found a flaw in standard combat tactics and wanted him to take the lead in building new doctrine was an incredible compliment.

Von Tischendorf didn't see it that way. He'd come in here fresh off his mother's memorial service, fixated on claiming *Faust* as if it was his by divine right. That wasn't how the Navy did things.

But his mother had been one of the Emperor's closest friends and confidantes, and von Tischendorf himself had grown up calling their sovereign *Uncle Gustav*. He clearly felt like the universe owed him.

Which wasn't how the universe did things, either.

"Have you seen the latest report on the corvettes' missile control package?" the Emperor asked.

Quickly, Riefenstahl shifted his mind from spoiled military brats to the more immediate problem at hand. "I skimmed it, Your Excellency, but haven't had a chance to give it a proper study," he said. "The approach seemed unorthodox but intriguing. Probably Solarian League, but it's possible some researchers at PFT came up with it. Either way, we'll want to follow up on it."

"Agreed," the Emperor said. "I've sent out enquiries. We shall see what they uncover. A question, *Vizeadmiral*: Clearly, the first use of this telemetry system should be on our warships. But it occurs to me that a scaled-down version could perhaps be added to our freighters."

"An interesting suggestion, Your Excellency," Riefenstahl said, running the possibilities through his mind. Six T-years ago, in the wake of the Nimbalkar annexation, the Emperor had decreed that all Andermani freighters would henceforth be armed. Two of those freighters were already in service, with *Lenz* nearly completed. "I doubt we'll want to load that many missiles on a single freighter, but the system would certainly allow control of two missiles at a time and likely give the captain better and longer control of them."

"My thoughts exactly," the Emperor agreed. "I'll call *Konteradmiral* Popovich and have him suspend *Lenz's* final construction work until the telemetry group has finished their analysis."

"Yes, Your Excellency. Would you like me to handle that?"

"Thank you, *Herr Vizeadmiral*, but I'll see to it," Gustav said. "I haven't spoken to Yuri for a long time, and it would be good to renew acquaintances." The Emperor's lips creased in an almost melancholy smile. "So few of my old friends still remain."

He lifted a hand, and the reflective mood lifted. "At any rate, you already have enough work to do. I'll let you get to it."

"Yes, Your Excellency," Riefenstahl said again. Bowing, he turned and headed out of the audience room.

Four of the palace greyhounds were milling around the Marble Hall as he entered, and he paused for a moment to make sure each of them got a pat and chin scritch. He could understand the Emperor's melancholy and sense of loss—Cutler's mother had been just the most recent of many, many of his old friends who had passed on.

But where others might look at that increasingly empty glass and yield to sadness or despair, Gustav Anderman instead turned those memories into a determination to make sure that the men and women under his command would never unnecessarily lose their own friends and colleagues. And when they did, that those losses would not be useless or in vain.

Tomlinson had learned about that determination the hard way. Maybe the Andermani Empire's other neighbors would take the hint.

But he doubted it.

III

"Very good, Sir," *Korvettenkapitän* Ludmilla Golovskina said briskly, making a final note on her tablet. "I'll add these to the official report." She looked up and gave Cutler a cheerful smile. "And then, I believe, we'll be at an end."

"So it would seem, *Frau Kapitän*," Cutler agreed, eyeing her with a set of decidedly mixed feelings. Golovskina had come into the project late, a full two weeks into the study, substituting for an officer who'd had to withdraw due to a family emergency. At the time Cutler had been angry at the potential delay and had nearly asked that she be dropped and that the group simply go on as it was, one member short.

But she'd been faster on the ramp-up than he'd expected, doing much of the catch-up work on her own time. She also proved herself smart and capable, offering fresh ideas and new twists on old ones in the group meetings, and showing a flair for composition and wording as the official report took shape. In fact, much to Cutler's surprise, she quickly became his favorite member.

But now the project was coming to a close. It had been decidedly successful, with the group coming up with new suggestions for EW ship deployment in a variety of situations, as well as how those ships could support and be supported in turn by the rest of a formation.

Whether Emperor Gustav would accept any of them into official Andermani doctrine, of course, was another matter. For years, off and on, the Emperor had been writing what he claimed would be the definitive text on space warfare strategy and tactics, and it was quite possible that once the book was finished Gustav would consider the matter set in stone. Hopefully, Cutler's report would be in time to make the final version. "Any idea how long it'll take to make the additions?"

"I'll have them for you by tomorrow morning," Golovskina promised.

And then she'd be gone, reassigned to a ship or another ground station, and he'd probably never see her again. A smart, capable officer, and the closest he would ever come to her again would be exchanged nods in passing. "You really don't have to do this on your own time, you know," he said. *Or we could work on it together*, a small part of his mind added.

Sternly, he stifled back the suggestion. "Tomorrow afternoon will be soon enough."

"Thank you, Sir, but I have nothing else to do tonight," she said. "And I'm anxious to see how His Excellency receives it. Hopefully, he'll be pleased."

"Hopefully," Cutler agreed, feeling a sour taste in his mouth. After kicking Cutler off his ship for this little exercise, Uncle Gustav had damn well *better* be pleased.

"So what will you do next, Sir?" Golovskina asked. "If I may be permitted the question?"

"Of course, *Frau Kapitän*," Cutler assured her. "The simple answer is that I don't know. The Emperor said we would discuss my next assignment after we delivered our report."

"Really," she said, sounding a bit taken aback. "I see."

"Is that a problem?" he asked.

"No, Sir, not at all," she hastened to assure him. "I was just assuming that with the new weapons upgrade you'd be returning as *Schreien*'s commander. With a long-overdue promotion, of course."

"That would be up to the Emperor," Cutler said, frowning. Granted that his XO was the one in charge of *Schreien*'s repairs, it was still odd that she hadn't at least taken a moment to call him with the news of an upgrade.

Unless Cutler *wasn't* going to be returned there. Had that decision already been made, only no one had bothered to tell him? "Where did you hear about new weapons?"

Golovskina shrugged uncomfortably. "I have a friend who works at the shipyard," she said. "Forgive me, *Herr Flottillenadmiral*. I shouldn't have spoken."

"No, that's all right," Cutler said. Maybe Gustav was finally catching up with the rest of the galaxy and upgrading the Navy's missile launchers. "What's *Schreien* supposed to be getting? A new cell launch system? Railguns?"

Golovskina made a face. "No, Sir, at least not from what I've heard. It looks like *Schreien* will be getting the new RW5 twin-arm launchers."

Cutler stared at her, his gut curling tightly around the remains of his lunch. *Schreien* already *had* a pair of twin-arm launchers. Was Gustav really going to just replace those maintenance nightmares with newer versions of the same? Especially when the rest of the civilized galaxy was updating to more modern equipment?

"Personally, I don't understand what he sees in that kind of launcher," Golovskina continued into Cutler's thoughts. "There have been several proposals for replacements, but the Emperor continues to ignore or table them." She winced, a small wrinkling of her nose. "I wonder sometimes if he still yearns for the days of Frederick the Great, when majestic wooden wet-navy ships exchanged massive broadsides in battle."

"Those were certainly glorious days," Cutler muttered. And if that was indeed what Gustav was envisioning, he was sadly out of luck. The only way a modern ship could launch a broadside was to lower her sidewalls and keep them lowered long enough to guide the missiles all the way to their targets. Unfortunately, a missile's flight typically took several minutes, during which time the attacker's entire flank would be vulnerable to counterattack.

Twin-arm launchers were the past. Cell launchers were the present. Electromagnetic railgun launchers were the future.

And yet there sat Emperor Gustav, who thought he was Frederick the Great, firmly clinging to the past.

Cutler looked at his tablet. Gustav had been a brilliant tactician once. What had happened to him?

"I'm sure the most glorious days of the Andermani Empire are still to come," Golovskina said diplomatically. "Actually, Sir—if I may be so bold—perhaps you're right about the report. I can do that tomorrow. Perhaps this night is one for celebration and conversation."

Cutler eyed her, Gustav's powdered wigs and two-meter-tall *Totenkopf* guards suddenly forgotten. "What exactly did you have in mind, *Frau Kapitän*?" he asked carefully. Attractive she might be; but he was her superior, and there were certain proprieties and distances that had to be maintained.

"Oh, nothing untoward, Sir," she said hastily. "A few friends and I were going to meet for coffee."

"Other Navy people?"

"Yes, Sir," Golovskina said. "We discuss how things are going in our respective areas—nothing classified, of course. We also like to get into strategies and tactics, sometimes from classic eras, other times more modern ones. I know your insights and presence would be welcome."

Cutler hesitated. Going in cold to a group of people he didn't know wasn't exactly his favorite way to spend an evening.

"The man who told me about *Schreien*'s upgrades might also be there," she added. "He may have more information to offer you."

"That might be useful," Cutler agreed, frowning as a sudden thought struck him. "I thought you said you didn't have anything else to do tonight."

"I was going to cancel so that I could finish the report. But since you said I could do it tomorrow...I really think you'd find this interesting, Sir. Please come."

Cutler had to smile at her intensity. And really, why not? Getting out with a group of officers he'd never met would be helpful for broadening his contacts within the Navy.

And those contacts couldn't hurt. Especially if Uncle Gustav wasn't going to give him the respect he and his late mother had earned. "If you think I'd fit in," he said. "Yes. Let's go meet your friends."

⚒ ⚒ ⚒

He'd expected the meeting to be large and perhaps somewhat boisterous. He'd also expected it to be held at some gasthous or café.

He was wrong on both counts. The place Golovskina took him to was a private home—a very nice, comfortably large home—and aside from Golovskina and himself there were just two others present.

"This is *Konteradmiral* Heinrich Eulenberg." Golovskina made the introductions. "Currently commanding *Kolin*."

"*Herr Konteradmiral*," Cutler said, shaking hands. *Kolin* was a battlecruiser, a sister ship to Riefenstahl's *Faust*, though somewhat less well equipped.

"*Herr Flottillenadmiral*," Eulenberg greeted him in turn. Eulenberg was a good twenty T-years older than Cutler, with a balding skullcap of white hair and the wrinkled face of someone who'd started his rise through the ranks from the reactor compartment. "I understand you're the one who snatched victory from the jaws at First Tomlinson."

"Not sure it qualified as a victory," Cutler had to admit. "But I'd agree I helped make it less of a defeat."

Eulenberg grunted. "Sometimes these days that's all one can hope for."

Cutler frowned. An odd sort of comment. He opened his mouth to ask what Eulenberg meant—

"And this is *Fregattenkapitän* Li Gong-Hu," Golovskina continued, gesturing to the other man. "Currently commanding *Wilhelm*."

"*Herr Fregattenkapitän*," Cutler acknowledged, again shaking hands. Li was an unusually young man to be commanding a heavy cruiser. That, even more than his small smile and air of quiet confidence, spoke volumes about his competence.

"*Flottillenadmiral* von Tischendorf," Li greeted him in return. "Can I get you some coffee?"

"Thank you," Cutler said, glancing around the conversation room. The four of them appeared to be it. "The rest of the group couldn't make it, I gather?"

"The rest of the group wanted us to speak with you first," Eulenberg said. He gestured to one of the comfortable-looking chairs in the circle. "Please."

Cutler sat down, frowning as the others took seats facing him. "May I ask what this is about?"

"Of course," Eulenberg said. "To put it in the most direct and concise terms, we're concerned that Emperor Gustav may be going insane."

Cutler snorted. "Hardly an original thought," he said. "People have been saying that since he first started speaking German."

"And as long as he was just speaking German, wearing powdered wigs, and insisting his personal guards were over two meters tall, no one had any problem with it," Li said. "But now, his eccentricities are threatening the entire Empire."

Cutler looked at Golovskina, the second knot of the day forming in his gut. "You might have told me what this meeting was *really* about."

"It's not what you think," she insisted, her voice low and sincere. "We're just a group of officers concerned about our nation."

"You swore allegiance to the Emperor."

"We also swore allegiance to the Empire," Eulenberg reminded him. "Tell me, *Herr Flottillenadmiral*: what's your military opinion about having *Schreien* outfitted with yet another set of obsolete twin-arm launchers?"

"The Emperor is a brilliant tactician," Cutler said, forcing down his own misgivings. "Whatever his reasons, I'm sure they're good ones."

"Are you?" Eulenberg countered. "Certainly he *was* a brilliant tactician. Whether he still remains one is the question before us."

"And not just us," Golovskina said. "There are other star nations out there, nations like Angelique and Cantiz, who are watching us closely."

"As well as star-spanning corporations like Tomlinson's parent company PFT," Li added. "They'll be watching us closely, and the last thing we can afford is for one of them to perceive us as weak or disorganized."

"I doubt that's an issue," Cutler pointed out. "Not after Tomlinson."

"Maybe not after *Second* Tomlinson," Eulenberg said. "But *First* Tomlinson is another matter. The theory has always been that a sufficiently numerous swarm of small ships can overwhelm a battlecruiser or even one of our wonderfully impressive battleships. No offense to you, *Herr Flottillenadmiral*, but it seems to me that First Tomlinson effectively proved that to be the case."

Cutler ground his teeth. What was he supposed to say to that?

"And Second Tomlinson doesn't really help that perception," Li added. "There, the Emperor needed two battleships and a large percentage of the rest of the fleet to beat them down."

"He didn't exactly *need* them," Cutler argued. "And don't forget, Tomlinson also had all those little missile bases. He only took two battleships to make sure it wouldn't even be a contest."

"Yes, I'm sure that's what he was thinking," Li said. "I'm not sure that's what our enemies will take away from it."

"Let's cut to the end," Cutler said. "What exactly are you suggesting, and what are you proposing?"

The others glanced at each other. "We think it's time—past time, even—that Emperor Gustav had a full psychological examination," Eulenberg said. "To that end, we propose to ... detain him ... and require him to—"

"Detain him by force?" Cutler interrupted.

Eulenberg's lip twitched. "Others have tried petitioning, requesting, even pleading with him to undergo a proper medical exam. The Emperor has refused all such requests, citing extreme busyness."

"All the more reason for him to take the time necessary for a few tests," Golovskina added. "The stress of his position can't be good for a man of his advanced age."

"And who would perform these tests?" Cutler asked.

"Medical and psychological experts, of course," Eulenberg said. "With some of us standing by to make sure they don't simply rubberstamp the Emperor's own preconceptions about his health."

"And if they decide he's unfit to rule?"

"The Throne would pass to his son," Eulenberg said. "Though since a five-year-old is obviously unprepared to rule a multi-system empire, a regency council would have to be appointed until the boy comes of age."

"So you're talking about a coup," Cutler said flatly. He pinned Golovskina with a hard look. "And mutiny."

Golovskina squirmed under his gaze. But her voice was calm enough. "We're talking about the survival of the Andermani Empire," she corrected. "Angelique isn't just going to sit by and wait until Gustav turns his eyes toward them. Neither are Babel, Cantiz, or any of the other colony worlds out there."

"And yes, we know that Gustav has stated he has no further territorial aspirations," Eulenberg said. "Do you think any of them believe him?"

Cutler lowered his eyes, scowling at the ornately carved table in the center of the circle. This conversation, and the actions being advocated, certainly had the *appearance* of treason.

And yet . . .

Gustav Anderman, pretending he was the reincarnation of Frederick the Great. Worse, Gustav Anderman genuinely *believing* he was the reincarnation of Frederick the Great.

He was still a military genius. Li's disparagements notwithstanding, Second Tomlinson had proved that.

But even genius could start fraying around the edges. Twin-arm launchers instead of railguns. Condemning a successful tactic simply because it had been risky. And, really, the damn powdered wigs.

And if Eulenberg and the others—and Cutler himself—had noticed, the Empire's potential enemies certainly had.

"What do you want from me?" he asked.

He sensed a lowering of the tension in the room. "Nothing you should have trouble with," Eulenberg promised. "We really just want your voice added to ours afterward, calming the nation and hopefully averting panic or chaos."

"You're a hero, you know," Golovskina said, giving him a tentative smile. "The man who kept First Tomlinson from being a complete slaughter."

Cutler clenched his teeth. No, it hadn't been a *complete* slaughter. It had only taken *Bayern, Rosshach,* and *Bretagne,* plus most of their crews.

And Cutler's own mother.

"After it's over and the Emperor is undergoing his examination there are bound to be rumors and accusations," Eulenberg continued. "The more voices calmly saying there's no need to fear, the better."

"And if the tests prove the Emperor is fine?" Cutler asked.

"Then he'll be restored immediately to his position, and the nation will be stronger for it," Eulenberg promised. "Needless to say, those of us most closely involved will of course submit our resignations."

A chill ran up Cutler's back. "I see."

"Not you, of course," Li hastened to assure him. "As we said, yours would simply be one of the many voices of reason afterward. There would be no reason for you to face any adverse consequences."

"But the fact that we *are* willing to face them should be an indication of how strongly we feel about this," Eulenberg said. "The Empire is at risk, *Herr Flottillenadmiral.* How will you respond?"

Cutler lowered his eyes again to the table. It was a risk, but a minimal one.

And if Emperor Gustav really *was* unfit to lead?

"Very well," he said. "When do you propose to move?"

Once again, there was additional lowering of tension. "Eight days from now," Eulenberg said. "The Emperor is holding a dinner meeting with the captains and XOs of his capital ships. That will be our opportunity to slip our people inside the Palace. Later that night, after everyone else has left, we'll detain him and take him to a place where the experts will be called to administer the tests."

"Very well," Cutler said again. "In eight days."

"In eight days," Eulenberg confirmed. "And in nine . . . we'll know what the future of the Andermani Empire holds."

IV

"Andrew?" Marija Shenoa called across the nursery. "Time to get washed up for dinner."

There was no response, of course. Andrew Anderman, five T-years old and heir to the Andermani Empire, was building an elaborate spaceship with his lockblocks, and Andrew in the throes of creation might as well be on the other side of the Solarian League.

Which was why Marija always left herself enough leeway for three separate announcements before the actual and proper time for meals, baths, or bedtimes.

"Andrew?" she called again, getting up from the couch and crossing over for a closer look. It was certainly an elaborate ship, though nothing like any actual vessel she'd ever seen. "It's time for your bath."

"Shh," he whispered, his eyes still on his creation. "The pirates have sneaked aboard."

Marija raised her eyebrows. "Really. How many?"

"Twenty-six," he whispered back. "They came in here." He pointed to a small shape sticking out from the rear part of his ship.

"Uh-oh," Marija warned. "They're near the hyper generator. Are they trying to steal the ship?"

"Uh-huh," Andrew said. "But don't worry." He shifted his finger to a spot near one of the radiator fins. "Harold is waiting for them here."

"*Our* Harold?"

"Our Harold," Andrew confirmed. "I told him to go fight the pirates."

"Ah," Marija said. Not that Andrew could actually order his chief *Totenkopf* bodyguard to go fight bad guys somewhere else. But as long as the pirates weren't real, she supposed that Harold would agree to go fight them. "They're in for a big surprise."

"They sure are," Andrew agreed.

"But I don't think Harold would agree to go away and fight unless he knew you were keeping up your strength," Marija said. "And Annalise would be *very* upset if the pirates got here and ate the dinner she made before you got to it."

Andrew looked up, blinking. "Oh. It's dinner time?"

"Yes, indeed," Marija said. "We're eating in here today. Go wash up, and I'll set the table."

"Okay," Andrew said, frowning a little. "I'm not eating with Daddy?"

"Your father has a dinner meeting," Marija said, wincing at his obvious disappointment. She'd tried to let Gustav know how important these father-son times were to the little boy, but there were always a million voices clamoring for the Emperor's attention, and a lowly child's nurse was pretty far down on the priority list. "Go on, now. After you finish your dinner, you can play a little more, and then it'll be time for your bath."

"With swirlies *and* bubbles?"

Marija smiled. "With swirlies, bubbles, *and* a grand ocean battle if you want," she promised. "But first, dinner."

"Okay," Andrew said, scrambling to his feet. "I guess the pirates can eat now, too."

"And Harold?"

"Sure," Andrew said. "And Harold."

⌘ ⌘ ⌘

The dinner had been decent enough, as meals in the Imperial Palace tended to be. The conversation, revolving around distant star nations, corporations, and threat assessments, had been mildly enlightening.

But Eulenberg had been too tense to properly enjoy either. His people were in place, and were supposedly on the move. But until he got the message there would be no way of knowing if they were on schedule.

If they failed, of course, some of the black-clad *Totenkopfs* standing guard at various places around the palace would undoubtedly be by to inform him of that unpleasant development.

Gustav was doing his usual wrap-up when Eulenberg's uni-link gave a silent vibration. Keeping his movements slow—the Emperor wouldn't like it if he caught one of his officers taking messages while their lord and master was talking—he slipped it out onto his thigh and glanced at the display.

Monitor room secured. Guard room secured.

He slid the uni-link back into its case, taking a slow, careful breath. They'd done it. They'd taken the two places in the Palace where concerted opposition could be directed from. The plan was in motion, the objective in clear sight.

And they were committed. Right up to their necks.

The recap continued for another five minutes. But Eulenberg wasn't really listening. The possibilities—the risks—the rewards—all of it flowed past him like water swirling across a river rapids.

The departure from the Marble Hall and the Palace went at a leisurely pace. Eulenberg made sure to chat with several of his fellow officers, making sure at least one or two would remember seeing him leave with everyone else. Gradually, he fell back from the general exodus, making comments to the stragglers, until he was the last one out the massive door. He paused there, standing a couple of meters in front of the two door guards, watching the other officers stride away.

Feeling a tingling sensation between his shoulder blades. The *Totenkopfs* behind him were two of the ones his people were supposed to have replaced. If they'd failed . . .

The last of Gustav's visitors passed out of the courtyard on his way to the car park. Taking a deep breath, Eulenberg turned and started back toward the door.

The two guards made no attempt to stop him. In fact, as he approached, one of them reached to the handle and pulled the door open for him. "Good luck, Sir," the man murmured as Eulenberg went back inside.

Eulenberg nodded to himself. Yes, they would still need some luck.

But from this point on it would require mostly skill. Skill, nerve, and courage of their convictions.

Fortunately they had enough of all three. Listening to his footsteps as he strode down the empty corridors, alert for any trouble, he headed to the monitor room.

❊ ❊ ❊

"I appreciate you staying behind for a few minutes, *Herr Admiral*," the Emperor said as he walked around the desk in his study. "Please; be seated."

"Thank you, Your Excellency," Riefenstahl said politely, remaining on his feet as the Emperor settled into his ornate chair. His new title still sounded odd in his ears, the higher rank of full admiral carrying both the weight of additional authority and the sobering knowledge that he was now an unofficial part of the Emperor's inner circle. That latter role added a new level of responsibility, but also included a few extra privileges. Speaking his mind and offering advice, presumably, were among them.

Seating himself before his Emperor was not.

Riefenstahl had never been to the Emperor's private study, and he was struck by the differences between Gustav's public face and his private one. Everywhere else in the Palace—in the audience room, Marble Hall, music room, gallery, even the service corridor—the décor was full of pomp and glory and echoes of Old Earth's pre-Diaspora Prussia.

Here, though, the tone was more intimate, even reflective. There were still plenty of reminders of the time of Frederick the Great, but the historical mementos and copies were interspersed with more personal memories: relics and reminders of Gustav's days as a mercenary commander. There were pictures, too, genuine antique-looking pictures of some of his closest comrades-in-arms. Many of them had small black ribbons across their lower-right-hand corners.

The ribbon across the picture of *Großadmiral* Jennifer von Tischendorf von Tischendorf, he noted, was very new.

"You're wondering why I asked you here," Gustav said, reaching into the bottom drawer of his desk and pulling out a bottle of schnapps. As usual with Gustav, it wasn't a question, but a statement. "I wanted to discuss a possible obstacle to the appointment of *Flottillenadmiral* Wan Tun-chang as your flag captain."

Riefenstahl frowned. "I was unaware there were any problems, Your Excellency."

"There are none from your end," Gustav assured him. "It's a question of whether some of the ship's other officers may need to be replaced." He smiled thinly. "The *Flottillenadmiral* has built up a degree of mutual animosity with our impetuous *Flottillenadmiral* von Tischendorf. Von Tischendorf, fortunately or otherwise, has a certain dedicated following within the officer corps."

"Mm." Riefenstahl looked again at the picture of *Großadmiral* von Tischendorf. "Or his mother had."

"Indeed," Gustav agreed. "And her reputation and honor were well deserved."

"Of course, Your Excellency," Riefenstahl said.

"So," Gustav said, turning on his tablet and peering at it. "Let us go over some names together, men and women who might resent Wan's appointment, and discuss what we shall do about them."

❊ ❊ ❊

"*Flottillenadmiral* on the bridge!" the woman at the missile station called as Cutler maneuvered easily through the hatchway.

"*Herr Flottillenadmiral*," Puntar, the *oberleutnant* manning the OOW station greeted him, unstrapping with practiced ease and coming to a floating attention. "Your presence is an unexpected honor, Sir."

"Yes," Cutler said, glancing around at the rest of the bridge crew. Their faces were all at full parade-ground neutral, but he could tell they were all glad to see him. "I must first apologize for my neglect of my ship and her crew while I was engrossed in the research project to which I was assigned."

"We all serve at the Emperor's wish," Puntar said. "That said, Sir, I know everyone aboard *Schreien* is delighted to have you back aboard."

"As am I," Cutler said, pulling himself forward to the OOW station. "I understand the repairs have been completed?"

"Yes, Sir, as has the dorsal launcher upgrade. The ventral upgrade should be completed within the week."

"Excellent," Cutler said, carefully filtering any hint of scorn from his face and voice. "That's the reason for my visit tonight, in fact. I wanted to see first-hand how the rearming is going."

"Yes, Sir," Puntar said. "*Korvettenkapitän* Bermann anticipated your request, and said he would await you in Dorsal Missile. At your convenience, of course."

"Excellent," Cutler said again, casually looking over at the tactical. All of the ships of the Home Fleet were in their proper orbits, as designated by the standing orders.

All except one. *Konteradmiral* Eulenberg's battlecruiser, *Kolin*, was out of place, circling the planet in a much lower orbit than usual. "Is there a problem with *Kolin*?" he asked.

"No, Sir," Puntar assured him. "There are some major resupply shipments scheduled, and *Konteradmiral* Eulenberg requested a lower orbit to facilitate the transfers."

"Ah," Cutler said, an odd feeling settling into his gut. How convenient that Eulenberg's ship would be orbiting unusually close right at the time he and his colleagues were supposed to be detaining the Emperor for his mental exam. "Keep an eye on her, will you, *Oberleutnant*?"

"Of course, Sir," Puntar promised.

"And let me know immediately if anything about her changes," Cutler added, reversing direction and heading again for the bridge hatch. "In the meantime, please inform *Korvettenkapitän* Bermann that I'm on my way."

※ ※ ※

The Palace monitor room was everything Eulenberg had hoped.

"Not bad," he said, resting his hand on Li's shoulder as he gazed at the wall of displays. There were fifty of them, showing the grounds and gardens and all of the Palace's public spaces. Conspicuous by their absence, unfortunately, were views of the Emperor's private study and all the rooms in the family wing.

Still, he should have expected that. "At least we have a view of those corridors," he continued. "If Andrew or his nurse poke their noses out, we'll know it."

"Maybe," Li said sourly, swiveling around to another console and punching up a schematic. "Maybe not. Apparently, our Emperor is also an admirer of secret passages."

Eulenberg frowned, leaning closer. "What the *hell*?"

"Secret passages and rooms, Sir," Li said. "A whole network of them, running under the Palace at sub-basement depth."

"I'll be damned," Eulenberg growled. "The old man was even more paranoid than I thought. Do we know where the entrances are?"

"No, this just shows which above-ground rooms are connected to it," Li said. "Still, there can't be many places you can hide a door in something the size of his study or audience room."

"I suppose not," Eulenberg said. "No monitors down there, either, I suppose."

"Would you expect there to be?"

Eulenberg scowled. No, of course not. The first job of a secret passage, after all, was to remain secret. "No matter. If we stay on schedule, no one should have time to use any of them."

"So we continue?"

"Of course we continue," Eulenberg said gruffly. "We've come too far to back out now. All other communications have been dealt with?"

"Yes, Sir," Li said. "The diversions are up and running, and so far seem to be keeping the Hussars' attention without making them suspicious. Internal and external coms and uni-links are running the same glitches and misconnects as everything else in the city. It won't keep them busy forever, but it should give us the time we need. The entire emergency call system is disabled, of course."

"And the *Kolin*?"

"We have a solid connection to the bridge," Li confirmed.

"Good," Eulenberg said. Of course, the staged communications snafu also meant that his people in the Palace also had no way to communicate with each other except by sending messengers back and forth.

But that was all right. They'd been well trained in what needed to be done tonight. Now that they had the Palace proper, it was the *Totenkopfs* guarding the exterior who would be most inconvenienced by the communications trouble. "Very well," he said, straightening up. *In for a centicred*, the old saying whispered through his mind, *in for a cred*. "The Emperor will be in his study. His son will be in the nursery.

"Take them both."

V

There was a loud splash, a sudden geyser of water, and a war whoop. "There!" Andrew crowed, raising one of his toy boats and spinning it around his head like a captured trophy flag. "*That* to the enemies of the Empire!"

"That to the enemies of warmth and dryness," Marija warned, pointing toward the wide towel-warming rack that angled out into the room where it would be easily accessible from both the tub and the large shower stall behind it. "Just remember that if you get all your towels wet, you'll have to dry off with face tissues."

For an adult, she reflected, that would be a credible threat. For a five-year-old, it was more of an challenge. "Can I?" Andrew asked eagerly. "Really?"

"No, not really," Marija said, crossing the bathroom for a closer look at the towels. Despite the tub's sixty-centimeter-high walls, Andrew's wet-navy battle had created some collateral dampness in the top row of towels. Fortunately, the bottom two rows were still more than dry enough for their intended purpose. "But I think it's time for the battle to be over. Put your toys up, and start playing with the soap."

Andrew's eyes widened, and Marija leveled a finger. "By which I mean start washing. Starting with your toes."

His face fell, just a little. "O-*kay*," he said theatrically.

"I'll go get your pajamas," she said. "Be safe."

"I will," he promised.

He would, too, she knew as she headed back to the door leading into the playroom. Andrew had learned to swim almost before he'd learned to walk. And while the tub itself was impressively big and tall, she was always careful to never put in more than half a meter of water.

She walked out of the bathroom, shivering briefly as the cooler air hit her skin, and headed across the playroom toward the nursery suite's door. Before she fetched Andrew's pajamas she would alert Harold that the boy was nearly done with his bath, and would soon be calling for his chief bodyguard and nurse to perform one of the dramatic, two-voice readings that was the standard prelude to bedtime these days.

She shook her head, smiling at the memory of the night three months ago when Andrew had declared that instead of an ordinary bedtime story he wanted to watch one of his videos. As that had been strictly forbidden by his father, Marija and Harold had quickly improvised a dramatic reading of the evening's story. The boy had been delighted, and the pattern had continued ever since.

Of course, Harold had a tendency to roll his eyes at some of the stories. Not entirely professional, but definitely one of the best ways to get giggles out of their young charge. Marija reached the door and pulled it open.

Harold wasn't there. Neither was Karel, the other bodyguard.

For a long moment Marija just stood there, the door open a crack, staring out into the empty corridor. It was impossible. The nursery's door was never left unguarded. *Never.* If Harold and Karel had been called elsewhere, two other *Totenkopfs* should have taken their places.

A motion down the corridor caught her eye. To her relief, she saw two men in black *Totenkopf* uniforms come into view, striding purposefully toward her. She smiled and started to call to them—

The greeting died in her throat. The two men were passing one of the tapestries on the hallway walls . . . and they weren't anywhere near tall enough to be family guards. Based on how far they came up on the tapestry, both were at least fifteen centimeters shy of the two meters Emperor Gustav insisted on for his personal bodyguards.

They weren't *Totenkopfs*. But they were wearing *Totenkopf* uniforms.

And suddenly Marija understood.

Quickly, silently, she closed the door and locked it, her whole body suddenly shaking so hard she could barely fumble out her uni-link. She thumbed back the cover and keyed the emergency button.

Nothing happened.

She peered at the device, only then seeing that the display was flicking between on, off, garbled words, and static snow. Dropping it back into its case, she hurried across the room to the desk and. The internal Palace intercom system was surely working.

Only it wasn't.

For a few seconds she stood over the intercom, pushing buttons at random, panic bubbling in her throat. But it was no use. She and Andrew were alone, cut off from the rest of the universe, with two men of unknown identity and purpose coming toward them.

She looked at the door. It was locked, and it was solid, but it wouldn't stand for long against determined attackers.

But there was a secret passageway connecting the nursery to some of the other private areas of the Palace. She'd never been inside, but Harold had made sure she knew where the door was and how to open it. She and Andrew could get out that way.

Only what then? If there were men coming for Andrew, did that mean they were also coming for his father? Worse, was the Emperor already in their hands?

And even if she and the boy escaped, what then? If the attackers didn't already know about the secret passages, it wouldn't take them long to figure it out. Once they started a concerted search of the nursery, they would surely find the door.

No. If she was going to keep Andrew safe, she would need to make them all think she'd taken the boy out some other way.

And the only way to do that would be to take down the two men coming for them.

Harold was a *Totenkopf* Hussar, one of the finest warriors in the Andermani Empire. But even the best-trained soldiers knew they had limitations. Accordingly, one day Harold had sat her down for a long talk about end-game scenarios and on-the-fly battle tactics.

He'd then proceeded to show her all the spots in the nursery where he'd hidden his last-ditch weapons.

He'd spent some time over the subsequent weeks training her in their use. But right now, with her heart thudding in her throat and her hands shaking, she knew it was no time to get fancy.

There were two pepper sprays in the room, both safely higher than Andrew could reach. She got both of them, slipping one into her pocket and concealing the other in her hand. Her next job would be to get Andrew out of the tub, hide him in the secret passage—

There was a knock on the door. "Marija?" a voice called. "His Excellency's calling for his son."

Marija clenched her teeth. So that was how they were going to play it.

And now it was too late to get Andrew out of harm's way. The only way to make this work was to make them think she was completely unaware of their scheme, and taking too long to answer the door would raise suspicions she couldn't afford.

Unless they planned to simply shoot her and the boy where they stood. But in that case there was nothing she could do anyway.

Still, the fake *Totenkopf* uniforms and the polite voice surely meant they were going to keep up the charade as long as possible. Anyway, that was her only hope.

The men were standing casually outside as she opened the door, smiling encouragingly at her. *"Guten abend, fräulein,"* the one who'd called to her through the door said. "Apologies for the late hour, but His Excellency has asked to see his son before he goes to bed."

"Of course," Marija said. To her relief, the initial adrenaline surge had apparently run its course, and her voice was as calm and casual as his. "Let me get him out of the tub."

She turned and headed for the bathroom. She'd made it three steps before he caught up. "I'll come with you," he offered. "Sometimes it takes two adults to get a child out of his tub."

"Absolutely," she agreed, feeling her heart pick up its pace again. She'd counted on one of them coming with her.

It was all up to her now.

They reached the door and she opened it, taking the opportunity for a quick glance behind her. The other fake guard was standing just inside the doorway, his attention turned outward into the hallway.

Perfect. Marija stepped through the bathroom door, gesturing the guard to come in behind her.

"Who are you?" Andrew asked, peering at the newcomer over the tub edge and through a soap-bubble beard.

"He's come to take you to your father," Marija said, closing the door behind them. "I—oops."

"What?" the man asked, turning toward her.

And from a meter away, Marija blasted him squarely in the face with the pepper spray.

He tried to gasp, or maybe he tried to shout. But with his eyes instantly useless, his throat and lungs instantly on fire, he could do nothing except scrabble for the pistol strapped to his side. Marija blasted him again and again, wincing as he finally got the weapon free, wanting to dodge but afraid that if he lost sight of her he would simply turn the weapon on Andrew—

She expected an ear-shattering explosion as he fired. But the shot was utterly silent. His first round slammed into the wall beside her head, his second hit the wall a meter from her side. She fired another blast into his face, and another, and half of another, and then the spray bottle ran dry.

And then, to her relief, he crumpled to the floor, his gun skittering away across the tile, his labored breathing slowing as he lost consciousness. Marija glanced at Andrew, saw him sitting bolt upright in the tub, his face rigid, then hurried forward and picked up the gun. It was an airgun, she saw now, with far less range than a standard handgun, but delivering a silent round carrying a lethal electrical charge.

She hefted the gun, a new resolve settling into her heart. Harold hadn't given her any training in this specific weapon, but it had the trigger and safety in the usual places. That should be all she needed.

Because if the other attacker hadn't heard the brief battle . . .

Only one way to find out. Stepping to the door, Marija opened it a few centimeters. "Come quickly!" she called, putting some desperation in to her voice. "There's been an accident. Hurry!"

If she'd given him time to think, she reflected later, maybe he wouldn't have reacted so quickly and so carelessly. But she hadn't; and he did. He all but sprinted across the playroom, his own holstered gun ignored at his side. She opened the door further as he approached and started to step out of his way.

And with him half a meter away, impossible for even an amateur like her to miss, she fired twice into his chest.

His mad rush carried him on, slamming his body into the door and shoving his way through. The impact ate up the rest of his momentum, and he toppled to the floor to lie motionless beside his unconscious comrade.

Marija stepped over him, fighting back the sudden urge to vomit. She hadn't expected such a horrible mix of ozone and burned flesh. Probably she should have. Clamping her teeth together, she looked over at the tub.

Andrew was still sitting motionless in the water. But his face was no longer rigid with surprise and terror. "Are they dead?" he asked, only a small quaver in his voice.

"One is," she said. "I think the other's still alive. Come on, we have to get out of here."

He nodded, a jerky motion of his head, and climbed out of the tub. He grabbed a towel off the rack and started drying himself.

"Finish drying and then get dressed," Marija added. Gripping her gun tightly, she went back into the playroom.

The door to the corridor was still open. She hurried across to it, confirmed that the hallway outside was deserted, then again closed and locked it. The door to the hidden passageway was behind one of the bookcases at the side of the playroom, but it took her two false starts to remember how to open it.

The staircase behind the door was narrow and only dimly lit. She peered down, satisfied herself that there was no one in sight, then returned to the bathroom.

Andrew usually dawdled over his bedtime preparations. Not tonight. She went in to find him dry and back in the clothes he'd been wearing before his bath. "Good," she said. "Come, now. Quietly."

"Where are we going?" he asked.

"I don't know," Marija confessed, somewhat startled to realize that she hadn't thought that far ahead. "Your father's office, I guess."

"No," Andrew said, his face and voice solemn. "Father always told me that if something like this happened I needed to go to the safe room."

A shiver ran up Marija's back. *Father*. Not *Daddy*.

And suddenly, Andrew was no longer just a five-year-old boy. He was, indeed, the true heir to the Andermani Empire.

"Good," she said. "Do you know the way?"

"Yes," he said. He looked down at the two guards, and Marija saw his throat work. "You should probably get the other gun."

Marija winced. "Of course," she said. Bracing herself, she leaned over the dead man and slid his pistol from his holster. "Ready?"

"Yes." The boy took a deep breath. "Follow me."

❈ ❈ ❈

"All right," Gustav said, tapping his tablet to send the latest batch of names to Riefenstahl. "Which ones of *these* do you know well?"

Riefenstahl wrinkled his nose. "I don't know any of them *well*, Your Excellency," he admitted. "But I of course know them all by name, and a few by reputation. *Fregattenkapitän* Li Gong-Hu has a very good record, and *Oberleutnant* Alves served with my XO—"

"Quiet," Gustav cut him off, a suddenly intense look on his face. "Did you hear something?"

Riefenstahl frowned, playing back his memory of the past few seconds. "No, Your Excellency," he said. "What did it sound like?"

And immediately jumped as something abruptly smashed hard against the door behind him.

He was out of his chair in an instant, dropping his tablet onto Gustav's desk to free up his hands. His first reflexive thought—some kind of groundquake?—quickly vanished as a second blow came against the heavy panel.

"It sounded like that," Gustav said, his dark tone edged with scorn. "Except quieter, like the thudding sound of two of my guards dying at their posts."

Riefenstahl caught his breath. "*Mein Gott*," he murmured.

"I doubt *Gott* has anything to do with this," Gustav said. He hesitated a moment, then stood up and stepped over to one of the curio cabinets against the wall. "Listen to me carefully, *Herr Admiral*, and do exactly as I say. Do you understand? *Exactly*."

"Of course, Your Excellency," Riefenstahl said. Gustav nodded and did something to the side of the cabinet.

And to Riefenstahl's amazement, the entire cabinet swung out into the room, revealing a ladder leading downward. "Go to my son's nursery," the Emperor said. He reached to the desk, scooped up Riefenstahl's tablet and thrust it into the other's hands. "Find him, and get him to safety. Do you understand?"

"I—yes, Your Excellency," Riefenstahl said. "How do I—?"

"Down the ladder," Gustav said, pointing. "There's an intermediate level; ignore that and keep going. When you reach the lowest level head down the corridor to your left—it will twist and turn; don't let that confuse you, just keep to the right-hand wall. The third stairs you reach—a circular staircase on your left—will lead back up to his playroom. Do you need that repeated?"

"No, Your Excellency," Riefenstahl said, crossing to the door. "What about you? You're coming, too, aren't you?"

"Not yet," Gustav said. Stepping back to the desk, he took his powdered wig off the stand and set it almost delicately on his head, giving Riefenstahl a quick and malicious smile as he did so. "First, I want to know who these people are, the people behind these acts of murder and treason. Your mission right now is to find and protect Andrew. Go, and do *not* let them catch you."

"Yes, Your Excellency." Clenching his teeth, Riefenstahl stepped through the narrow opening and onto the ladder. There was a handle on the inside of the hidden door; gripping it tightly, he pulled the door closed, catching a final glimpse of his Emperor doing up the buttons on his tunic.

Just in time. He'd just heard the soft *click* of the lock when there was a final thud from the other side—

"Stand fast!" Gustav bellowed. "You will bow in the presence of your Emperor."

"Your indulgence, Your Excellency," a voice said. Even through the panel Riefenstahl could hear the sarcasm in the other's tone. "Forgive the intrusion, but you need to come with us."

"I will do no such thing," Gustav said scornfully. "Your very presence in this office uninvited is an act of treachery. *And* you've ruined my door."

"You will come with us, Your Excellency," the voice said again. "Willingly, or otherwise."

There was a short pause. Riefenstahl squeezed the ladder's side rails, visualizing guns being leveled at his Emperor . . .

"Very well," Gustav said, his voice rigid with dignity. "We will go to my audience room."

"I'm afraid that won't be possible, Your Excellency. We'll wait in the monitor room until it's time to leave the Palace—"

"We will go to my audience room!" Gustav thundered. "And we will light a fire, and we will speak as civilized gentlemen. *Then*, if *I* deem it necessary, we will leave the Palace."

"Fine," the voice said acerbically. "We'll go to your audience room. But you will answer our questions, and you will *not* make trouble. Is that clear?"

"Perfectly," Gustav said, his voice all calm again. "Lead on, *Herr Konteradmiral*, and I will follow."

Riefenstahl caught his breath. A *Konteradmiral*? But that was incredible. For someone of command rank to be involved—

Meant that this was nothing less than a full-blown mutiny.

The conversation had changed to the sound of murmured instructions and multiple footsteps. Cursing silently to himself, Riefenstahl started down the ladder. He climbed past the first level, reached the second, and turned in the direction Gustav had indicated.

The lighting down here was dim, just enough to see the walls and floor and maybe the outline of a person if there'd been anyone else down here. The passageway was every bit as twisty as the Emperor had warned, with multiple side passageways heading off God only knew where. But at least the floor was level.

The mutineers could have killed Gustav where he stood. They hadn't. That meant they still wanted or needed something from him.

Only they'd never get it. Not from Emperor Gustav Anderman. Not a chance.

Not unless they had something to use as leverage.

Cursing again, Riefenstahl picked up his pace. If the mutineers hadn't yet taken Gustav's son, that was clearly next on their list.

The Empire's—and Andrew's—only hope was for Riefenstahl to get there first.

✻ ✻ ✻

Only he didn't.

The playroom was deserted. The boy's bedroom was deserted.

But the bathroom . . .

"Damn," Riefenstahl muttered angrily, uselessly, helplessly. One of the *Totenkopf* guards sprawled on the bathroom floor was unconscious, with the telltale swelling of pepper-spray poisoning. Probably a full canister's worth, from the looks of it.

The other guard was dead, taken down by a pair of shock rounds.

Which meant it was all over. Gustav's fierce affection for his son was known throughout the Empire. If the mutineers had Andrew, Gustav would do anything they demanded rather than see the boy killed.

Riefenstahl had to do something. But what? Until he knew how they'd gained access to the Palace, contacting the monitor room or even grabbing one of the *Totenkopfs* from his post might unwittingly play into the mutineers' hands. He'd already tried unsuccessfully to use his uni-link on his way through the tunnels, and it was unlikely that the mutineers had forgotten to similarly block the Palace's own internal com system.

But he had to do *something*. And if grabbing the nearest *Totenkopf* got him summarily shot, it was a chance he would have to take. He hurried across to the playroom door—

And stopped short, staring.

The door was locked.

From the *inside*.

He stared at the lock another few seconds, trying to make sense of it all. If the mutineers had killed Andrew's guards and snatched the boy, how had they gotten out with the door locked? Did they already know about the sub-basement secret passages?

Andrew's guards fighting to the death to enable the boy to escape ran into the same problem. The only way it worked was if the mutineers had killed the guards, grabbed the boy, and left the same way Riefenstahl had arrived.

But why? Why bother with the dark, cramped environs of the passageway when the hallway outside was better lighted, more comfortable, and permitted concentration of firepower if they unexpectedly met an opponent?

Unless...

He hurried back to the bathroom, and this time took a longer look at the casualties.

Longer, ironically, being the operative word. These two men were tall, but they were at least fifteen centimeters short of the two-meter-height Gustav insisted on for his family's personal *Totenkopf* guards.

Which meant Riefenstahl had it exactly backwards. The men lying at his feet were in fact two of the mutineers. They'd been taken down by person or persons unknown, who'd followed up his or her victory by hustling Andrew to safety.

Riefenstahl stared down at the men, the rest of the pieces rapidly falling into place. The silent shock rounds, which were hardly standard Navy issue, had been brought in by the mutineers. That meant Andrew's defender hadn't used his own weapons, but had somehow managed to get his opponents' weapons and turn them against them. The very presence of silent weapons implied that the mutineers didn't have the entire Palace behind them, or at least weren't numerous enough to take down the entire *Totenkopf* contingent simultaneously.

But that didn't mean that all Riefenstahl had to do to raise the alarm was go out into the hall and start shouting. In fact, just the opposite. A small group clever enough and determined enough to have gotten this far wouldn't be easily taken. In fact, chances were good that they'd already mapped out choke points and ambush spots to take out anyone who came running to the rescue. It might save Gustav and Andrew, but it might just as easily backfire and precipitate a blood bath.

But it was even more certain that the mutiny wasn't going to be stopped by negotiation or stern language. Riefenstahl needed some weapons, and he needed them now.

He stood up and once again headed across the playroom to the door. Andrew's ill-fated attackers must first have eliminated the *Totenkopfs* who'd been standing guard outside the nursery. They must also have hidden the bodies; and given the size of their victims, they probably hadn't moved them very far.

And if Riefenstahl was *very* lucky, they wouldn't have bothered to strip the bodies of weapons before dumping them.

Riefenstahl hissed between his teeth. *Lucky.* Not really a word that applied to any part of this situation.

But this was the hand they'd been dealt, and it was up to him to see it through. Checking to make sure the hallway outside was still deserted, he slipped out of the nursery to start his hunt.

VI

Eulenberg had never been to Gustav's audience room. But after the almost homey atmosphere of the private office, the quiet grace and intimacy of the room wasn't really a surprise.

Nor, really, were the reasons the Emperor had insisted on moving the conversation here.

The audience room was smaller than the private study, for one thing. That meant a smaller number of guards could be present if they didn't want to get in each other's way. There were also two doors, one on each end, leading into the Marble Hall and the music room. Two doors meant two possible escape venues, should he be mad enough to try.

Most important, though, was the fact that the hidden floorplan had showed this was also one of the rooms connected to the Palace's secret maze of underground tunnels. Gustav probably figured this would be his best bet to try and make an escape while Eulenberg's people uselessly guarded the regular doors.

On the other hand, his study had also been on Li's map, and he hadn't tried to run from there. Maybe the doors weren't designed to be opened quickly. Maybe Gustav had decided it was beneath his dignity to run like a hare.

Maybe he'd simply forgotten the escape route was there.

He eyed the Emperor as the other paused to look around the ornate décor, the paintings, and the elaborate furnishings. Sometimes he seemed so normal, so much in command of himself and those around him. He could give orders, discuss strategy and tactics, and talk about the Empire's future.

But then there was the powdered wig and the Frederick the Great obsession. Those were the first signs of a man standing on the edge of reality, and everyone from here to the Solarian League knew it. Gustav *had* to be neutralized before he fell off completely, taking his dreams and reflexive strategic background and the whole damn Empire with him.

That neutralization would happen tonight. And whether he was counting on the audience room's visible doors or its invisible one, there would be no escape for him. Not with Eulenberg, Golovskina, and two of their soldiers ready to stop him.

"All right, we're here," Eulenberg said, letting Gustav finish his posturing and then pointing him toward one of the couches by the fireplace. "Now, Your Excellency, we need to talk—"

"Fire," Gustav said curtly.

Eulenberg tensed, reflexively glancing around for hidden gunports and *Totenkopf* guards preparing to cut him down. But nothing appeared, and nothing shot at him—

He made a face as his brain caught up with his combat reflexes. Oh—*that* kind of fire.

"We don't need a fire, Your Excellency," he said, eyeing the cold fireplace. "We need to talk—"

"You will make a fire," Gustav again cut him off. "When I met with Wenzel Anton Furst von Kaunitz-Rietbert over the Poland problem, we discussed the country's partition in front of a roaring fire. If you seek to wrest my empire from me, kindly allow me the same courtesy."

Eulenberg looked at Golovskina, raised his eyebrows. She gave a microscopic shrug and crossed the room toward the fireplace. For a moment she peered at the edges, clearly looking for the gas jet. "Where's the ignition?" she finally asked.

"The matches are on the mantel," Gustav said with clearly strained patience. "Light one and apply the flame to the kindling. Does *no* one understand true culture anymore?"

"No, but we understand stalling," Eulenberg growled. "Sit down, Your Excellency. *Now.*"

Gustav didn't move. "Fire," he said again.

Eulenberg dropped his hand to his sidearm. "I said *sit*, Your Excellency."

"It's all right," Golovskina said hastily. "I've got it."

Grinding his teeth, Eulenberg watched as she lit a long match and touched it to the bits of wood under the two big logs in the fireplace. They caught immediately, the flame spreading out and igniting the logs. Within two minutes, the fire was burning brightly.

"Now, Your Excellency—" Eulenberg began.

"Not yet," Gustav said, his full attention on the fire. "A moment to savor, if you please." He gestured toward the fire. "Do you smell it,

Konteradmiral? That's genuine North Slope cedar. See how the wood crackles and sparkles? This is truly a regal wood for a regal fireplace. Very similar to the Bavarian evergreen known as—"

"Sit *down!*" Eulenberg roared.

For a pair of heartbeats Gustav continued to gaze at the fire. Eulenberg squeezed the grip of his weapon...

"Thank you, *Konteradmiral*, but I prefer to stand," the Emperor said, turning to face his captors.

And in that moment, he was the Emperor again. Not an old man on the path to full senility, but a true leader and commander.

A shiver ran up Eulenberg's back. If the man had been like this all the time, he would have been unbeatable.

Unfortunately—or perhaps fortunately—he wasn't. The damn powdered wigs...

"I congratulate you on the efficiency of your first salvo, *Konteradmiral*," Gustav said. His eyes flicked to each of the others in turn. "I'm forced to say, though, that if this is indeed an attempted coup, you have sorely underestimated the weight of troops required."

"No one has spoken of a coup, Your Excellency," Golovskina said.

"No?" Gustav countered. "Social calls, in my experience, involve less death and destruction of doors."

"We're concerned about you, Your Excellency," Golovskina said. "Your behavior of late has been—"

She broke off at a sharp gesture from Eulenberg. "We're concerned about the Empire, Your Excellency," he said. "Accordingly, we're going to take you somewhere for a proper examination."

"Interesting," Gustav said, his voice thoughtful. "And if I refuse to cooperate?"

"I don't think it's possible to not cooperate with a brain scan," Eulenberg said with a tight smile.

"And if I refuse to cooperate?" Gustav repeated.

One of the others muttered something under his breath. "We could just shoot him," he suggested darkly.

"That would be foolish indeed," Gustav said calmly. "I've returned once from the grave. I can do so again."

"No one's going to shoot you, Your Excellency," Eulenberg assured him. Certainly not in such a public and blatant way. "As

Korvettenkapitän Golovskina said, we're merely concerned for your welfare and the safety of the Empire."

"Safety," Gustav spat. "Great nations are not built on safety, *Konteradmiral*. They are built on the willingness of their rulers and their people to do whatever is necessary, and to make whatever sacrifices are needed to defeat the foe and bring honor and glory to the realm." He leveled a finger at Eulenberg. "So tell me, *Konteradmiral*. Who are these allies who are prepared to make sacrifices for you?"

"Who my allies are is irrelevant," Eulenberg said.

Gustav snorted. "So you seek to deny them their share of the honor? Such pettiness ill becomes a true leader."

Eulenberg glanced at Golovskina, saw her same confusion at the apparent non sequitur. "What are you talking about?" he demanded. "What honor?"

"The defeat of Frederick the Great is the ultimate accomplishment, *Konteradmiral*," Gustav said loftily. "The records of this era will forever laud the names of those who took part in such a glorious achievement. I ask again: do you seek to deny them their place in history?"

He was stalling, Eulenberg knew. Stalling for time, and simultaneously trying to worm information out of him.

He felt his lip curl with fresh contempt. Fine. Let him. The operation was well on schedule, and they still had nearly ten minutes before the transports arrived to take them and their prisoner to the secluded spot where the examination was to take place.

And where, unbeknownst to most of the conspirators, Emperor Gustav Anderman and his son would be shot trying to escape.

He frowned. *And his son.* He'd been concentrating so hard on Gustav that he'd completely forgotten that Andrew and his captors should have joined them by now.

His face cleared. Of course. The others hadn't expected Gustav to insist on going to his audience room. Andrew and the others would be waiting in the monitor room, wondering in turn what had happened to Eulenberg and *his* team.

He beckoned Golovskina to him. "Go to the monitor room," he said quietly. "The others should be waiting there by now. Bring them back here."

"And the boy?" she murmured back.

"And the boy," Eulenberg confirmed. Even men as stubborn as Gustav became amazingly cooperative when there were guns pressed to their loved ones' heads.

"Yes, Sir," Golovskina said. Walking past the soldier standing guard beside the Marble Hall door, she opened it and left the room.

Eulenberg turned back to see Gustav staring hard at him. For a moment he wondered if the Emperor had overheard the conversation, then decided he didn't care. Gustav was an old man, and he was being watched by three armed men with clear lines of fire.

And really, if he genuinely *was* trying to escape when he was shot, so much the better.

"Names, *Konteradmiral*," Gustav said quietly. "Tell me their names."

Eulenberg shrugged. There was nothing else they could do until the transports arrived. He might as well show Gustav just how large and wide-ranging the conspiracy was. The sheer number might impress and demoralize the supposed universally beloved leader.

Besides, as long as Gustav thought he was putting one over on his captors, he was likely to stand quietly instead of attempting any additional ruses or heroics.

"Very well, Your Excellency," Eulenberg said. "Would you like them alphabetically, or in descending order of rank?"

Gustav inclined his head. "The latter, if you please."

Eulenberg inclined his head back. "Aside from those you see here, our numbers include *Flottillenadmiral* Cutler von Tischendorf, *Fregattenkapitän* Li Gong-Hu, *Fregattenkapitän* Xiao Chen-tzi . . ."

⁎ ⁎ ⁎

Marija had feared the safe room would already be under enemy control. To her relief, it was not only empty, but apparently even unwatched.

Still, it wasn't until she got the massive door swung shut and locked that she finally felt the tension drain out of her.

But only some of it. Andrew was safe, but the Emperor was still presumably in the building. What was she supposed to do now?

Call for help, of course. Making sure the door was sealed, squeezing Andrew's shoulder reassuringly as she passed, she hurried to a small communications desk along the side wall. The layout was unfamiliar, but the controls were clearly labeled: internal com, external com, emergency com. The coms in the nursery hadn't worked, but surely the ones in here would.

Only they didn't.

She tried each of them twice, fighting against the panic once again trying to bubble up her throat. For a moment she stared at the board, wondering what she was doing wrong.

She looked up at the ceiling, belatedly realizing why the safe room and the secret corridors they'd traveled to get here had been so dark. The only lights that were functioning were the battery-powered emergency ones. Somewhere along the line, the conspirators had cut the power to this section of the Palace.

Leaving her and the boy helpless.

Or maybe not. Lowering her eyes from the ceiling, she focused on the other side wall . . . and the subdued glint of racked shotguns, rifles, submachineguns, and handguns.

She straightened her shoulders, peripherally aware that Andrew was watching her. "Is there a place in here to lie down?" she asked him.

He pointed to a door a couple of meters past the gun rack. "The beds are in there."

"Good," Marija said. "Let's go settle you down, okay? It's just about your bedtime."

He looked up at her as if she was crazy. "I don't think I can sleep," he said.

"Maybe not, but you can at least lie down," she said. "Okay? For me?"

He managed a faint smile. It was amazing how much he looked like his father when he did that. "Okay," he said.

The room was laid out like a barracks, with twenty bunkbeds lined up neatly along the walls. Marija got Andrew settled, promised him a story if he was still awake when this was all over, and headed back to the vestibule.

The boy wasn't really safe in there, Marija knew as she gently closed the barracks door behind her. No safer than he would be out here in the vestibule with her. But at least in there, lying down, he would be out of the direct line of fire if and when the conspirators broke in.

The rifles and submachineguns were tempting. But Harold had always told her that for close-quarters work shotguns were an untrained fighter's best bet. Collecting all three of the shotguns from the rack, she carried them over to the wall facing the heavy outer door. Two handguns were next, and then the chair from the useless com board. She loaded all five weapons and set four of them neatly on the floor around her within easy reach.

Then, laying the final shotgun across her knees, she settled in to wait.

Getting past her wouldn't be very difficult, she knew. But at least it would be one more chore for them to do before they could get to the Emperor's son.

⚒ ⚒ ⚒

Riefenstahl hadn't expected the mutineers to have moved Andrew's guards very far. He certainly hadn't expected them to treat the dead with any dignity.

He was right on both counts. He found the two bodies stuffed into a service closet just around the corner from the boy's nursery.

But for all their cleverness and treachery, they hadn't been quite clever enough. Focused on getting to Andrew, they hadn't bothered to strip the two *Totenkopfs* of their weapons.

Twenty seconds later, Riefenstahl was finally armed.

Only armed for what?

Andrew was gone, presumably still free. But where would he and his nurse have gone? Riefenstahl had looked over the Palace floorplan in the days before tonight's working dinner, mainly to make sure he wouldn't embarrass himself by taking a wrong turn somewhere and getting lost. There had been no indication of emergency exits or safe rooms or anything of that sort. Nor had he seen anything like that labeled in the underground passages he'd just been in.

But surely the Emperor would have prepared for all contingencies, from revolt and mutiny to all-out revolution. Andrew had gone *somewhere*.

Riefenstahl mouthed a curse at his stupidity. *Anything like that labeled in the underground passages.* Of course nothing had been labeled. Nor would it be on any of the public floorplans or blueprints.

But *private* floorplans . . .

One of the dead *Totenkopfs* had unfortunately locked his tablet.

But the other had left his open. A few tense minutes of sorting through menus, and Riefenstahl had a full map of the underground maze.

And there, in all its glory, was a section labeled *Safe Room*.

Riefenstahl froze, half in and half out of the closet. From somewhere nearby came the sounds of soft voices and hurrying feet. He tensed, gripping his gun . . .

To his relief, the footsteps receded, running now, and faded quickly into the silence. Huffing out a silent breath, he took another look at the tablet. If he went back into the nursery, through the hidden door and down the circular staircase into the passageways . . .

He frowned at the tablet, his eyes flicking across the various rooms: *Private Office, Nursery, Private Quarters, Sitting Room, Safe Room*. Something about the locations seemed oddly familiar.

And then he got it. The Palace itself might be a copy of Frederick the Great's own official residence, but the underground rooms were laid out like an unfolded battleship deck plan. The Emperor's hidden study was where the flag bridge would be; his private quarters were a larger version of CIC; the nursery and kennels were at the forward and aft impeller rings; and the safe room was at the hyper generator.

And with *that*, the route, directions, and positioning were now obvious. Even the various twists, turns, and dead ends in the passageways fit the overall pattern. Tucking the tablet inside his tunic, he hefted his gun and headed toward the corner and the nursery beyond it—

The sound of fresh footsteps was his only warning, and it nearly came too late. He scrambled back from the corner just in time, backing up as quietly as he could. The footsteps were rapidly approaching, and with nowhere else to go he stepped into the closet with the two dead *Totenkopfs* and pulled the door closed. Shifting his gun to his left hand, he gripped the door handle with his right and braced his shoulder against the jamb. The footsteps were harder to hear in here, but he was pretty sure they were getting closer.

The tug on the door came with no warning. But it was quick and superficial, and Riefenstahl already had a death-grip on his side of the handle, and neither the handle nor the door budged. "Locked," a voice came from out in the hall.

"This one, too," another, more distant voice came. "Where the hell did they stash them?"

"Maybe they didn't," the first man said grimly. "Maybe the guards got the drop on them and already have the kid out of here."

"You'd better hope that didn't happen," the second warned. "Keep looking. If we don't find them, and fast, we're going to have to shift from extraction to siege."

"Or worse," the first man said. "You take that corridor; I'll take this one."

The footsteps moved away. Riefenstahl pressed his ear to the door, hoping to follow their progress. But the faint sounds had already faded away.

Leaving Riefenstahl in a complete and horrible limbo. Until the mutineers gave up and took their search elsewhere, he didn't dare leave his hiding place.

But without anything to cue him, he had no way of knowing when that moment happened. All he could do was make the best judgment he could, and hope to God he didn't walk straight into their arms.

And in the meantime, Andrew was out there with no one but his nurse to protect him.

Riefenstahl mouthed a curse, not daring even to give whispered vent to his frustration. His Emperor had sent him on a mission, and so far, he had completely failed.

But there was nothing he could do. It would gain the child nothing if Riefenstahl simply got himself killed.

He would have to wait. And to trust that he would be free in time to make a difference.

⌘ ⌘ ⌘

"Interesting," Gustav murmured, tapping his lip thoughtfully. "I don't believe you for a moment, of course."

"You take me for a liar?" Eulenberg asked. Not that he cared. Gustav had now burned nearly all the time he had left before the transports arrived, time he probably could have used more productively to plan an escape or something.

Still, if the Emperor preferred to stand by the fire and listen to his captor talk numbers and plans, far be it for Eulenberg to stop him.

"Of course," Gustav said. "None of those you named would dare rise up against their Emperor. I am beloved throughout my Empire—"

Behind Eulenberg, a door slammed open. Eulenberg spun around, dropping his hand to his sidearm—

"They're gone," Golovskina said, her voice tense. "Both of them. And the—"

"Who's gone?" Eulenberg demanded.

"The boy and his nurse," Golovskina said. "And Peter and Michael are dead—one shot, the other probably suffocated."

Eulenberg turned back to Gustav. The Emperor had a tight, knowing smile on his face. "What about the boy's guards?"

"Gone," Golovskina said. "I don't know where—I didn't want to take the time to search for them. But Peter and Michael were inside the nursery, so I assume they'd already eliminated the guards."

"You *assume?*" Eulenberg snapped. "Don't assume, *Korvettenkapitän.* Send someone to find out for sure."

"I did," Golovskina said stiffly. "I caught Chin and Mac and sent them back to look for the bodies. Do you want me to go help them?"

Eulenberg clenched his teeth. An extra person could make a big difference in a search.

But the transports would be here any minute, and he wanted her on the one with him and Gustav. "No, they can handle it," he told her. "Go see if the transports have arrived, then come back here."

"Yes, Sir." Once again, she slipped out of the room.

"And so your defeat begins," Gustav said softly.

Eulenberg turned back. "The unexpected occasionally happens," he said. "But it's of no concern. We have you, we have the guard room, and thanks to our diversions and uni-com tricks no one outside the Palace even suspects what's happening in here. And even if by some miracle they found out, we have the firepower to deal with them."

Gustav shook his head. "No, *Herr Konteradmiral.* Even as we speak, your plot unravels. Your allies edge toward panic; your troops are forcibly converted from traitors to corpses. But if you surrender now, I promise to be lenient."

"Your promises are no longer of any value, you old fool," Eulenberg snarled. "You will die tonight, as will your son, and the rule of New Berlin will come to one who can command respect and fear from the Empire's enemies."

Gustav sighed and shook his head. "And so it ends," he said, a twinge of sadness in his voice. "The second reign of Frederick the Great." Carefully, he took the powdered wig from his head. For a moment he gazed at it; and then, ceremoniously, he tossed it into the fire.

And with a tremendous *whoosh*, the fireplace erupted into a cloud of dense white smoke.

Reflexively, Eulenberg snatched his gun from its holster. But it was too late. The billowing cloud had already filled the room, enveloping and blinding him. He tried anyway, firing three shots at the spot where Gustav had been standing a second earlier, knowing full well that the Emperor was long gone.

A sudden wind pressed against his back, the white cloud around him swirling in reaction. One of the men had opened the door to the Marble Hall. Eulenberg stood where he was, resisting the urge to do something—*anything*—and waited as the smoke flowed out. A minute later he found himself in a room containing himself, his two men, and a nearly smothered fire.

And no Emperor Gustav.

"Where is he?" Eulenberg snarled.

"I don't know," the guard at the Marble Hall door insisted. "He didn't get out this way."

"I had this one blocked the whole time," the one at the music room door added.

Eulenberg swore again. So the Emperor had gone down his damn bolt-hole. Apparently he *was* willing to run like a hare. "Don't just stand there," he snapped. "There's a hidden door somewhere in here. Find it. Tear the room apart if you have to, but *find it*!"

For a moment he watched in silence as they hurriedly started checking the walls. The plan had been for the conspirators to present themselves as the men and women who'd saved the Andermani Empire from its leader's dangerous lunacy. Now, Gustav's vanishing act had threatened to unravel that rationale.

But that was all right. Eulenberg would have been a fool not to anticipate such a contingency and work up a response to cover it.

He grabbed one of the men as he hurried toward a different section of wall. "New plan," he said. "Go back to the monitor room. Tell Li to call *Kolin* and give the code word *Götterdämmerung*. Then bring Golovskina back here."

"Yes, Sir."

He fled from the room, and Eulenberg crossed to the likely-looking wall tapestry the other had been headed toward. Gustav was clever, all right. But he wasn't clever enough.

Because if Eulenberg and the others couldn't be the patriots who'd saved the Empire from its leader, they would just have to be the patriots who'd sadly been too late to save the Emperor from a mutiny.

VII

Cutler was in *Schreien*'s dorsal missile compartment, glowering at the new electronics for the utterly outdated twin-arm launchers, when he got the call from the bridge.

"*Oberleutnant* Puntar, Sir," the OOW identified himself. "You asked me to keep watch on *Kolin*."

"Yes, I did," Cutler confirmed. "Is she showing unusual activity?"

"Possibly, Sir," Puntar said. "She's activated her nodes. I think she may be preparing to bring up her wedge."

Across the compartment, *Korvettenkapitän* Bermann looked up. "Have you received any orders regarding an imminent departure?" he called toward the intercom.

"*We* haven't, Sir, no," Puntar said. "There's been no general warning from Astro Control to shipping, either. Though that may be waiting on whenever *Kolin* actually begins raising her wedge."

"And nothing from Command?" Bermann pressed.

"No, Sir," Puntar said. "But if the orders are only for *Kolin* there's no reason we would necessarily be copied."

Cutler and Bermann exchanged looks. No, it wasn't necessary. But it *was* usually done, especially with the relatively close-packed ships in Potsdam orbit.

Unless, of course, *Kolin*'s orders weren't coming from Command.

"Let's take a closer look," he said. "Take us down toward her orbit. Make it a slow approach—I don't want it to look obvious."

"Hard not to be obvious when your wedge is up, Sir," Bermann pointed out.

"That's why we won't be using the wedge," Cutler told him. "Reaction thrusters only. Nice and slow and casual."

He looked at the repeater tac display, at the distant ship still hugging the horizon. "And," he added, "put the ship on alert."

❊ ❊ ❊

Even in an audience room as elaborately decorated as Gustav's, there were only so many places a secret door could be hidden. Three minutes after Eulenberg's men started their hunt, they had found it.

There was probably a trick for opening it. One of Gustav's heavy trophies was equally effective.

"Quiet," Eulenberg warned, peering into the diffuse light of the curved tunnel beyond the door. The dim emergency lighting was a good sign; it meant Li's efforts to cut the power to the Palace had also hit this secret section.

Less good was the fact that the tunnel was very short, circling around the fireplace and dead-ending in a spiral staircase leading down.

A staircase leading down into unknown territory, with the pursuers open to attack the whole way. Suddenly, darkness no longer seemed like their friend.

"Sir?" the man behind him prompted.

Eulenberg took a deep breath. If Gustav thought he would hang back and let his men lead the way into danger, he didn't know him very well. "Follow me," he said over his shoulder. "Watch for movement and be cautious around corners. We're looking for a safe room, possibly labeled *Tower* or *Inner Keep* or something equally archaic."

"Yes, Sir."

"And be careful," Eulenberg added. "His Excellency may have picked himself up a weapon."

❊ ❊ ❊

Riefenstahl stood silently in the darkness with the two dead men as long as he could stand it. Then, very carefully, he turned the handle and opened the door a crack.

No one shouted triumphant discovery. Even better, no one shot at him. He eased the door open the rest of the way and cautiously looked out.

The passageway was deserted. He stepped out of the closet, eased around a corner, and headed back to Andrew's nursery.

He half expected the mutineers to have left a guard. But the playroom was deserted.

He crossed to the bathroom. Also deserted, though he noted that the two dead men had been roughly turned over, their glazed eyes now staring unseeing at the ceiling.

He had turned back, intending to cross the playroom and check out Andrew's bedroom, when he heard a sound from the other side of the door.

The mutineers had found him.

For a frozen second he stood there, wondering if he should try to find cover in the handful of seconds he had left. The tub was deep enough to hide him, but there was still half a meter of steaming water in there, and a splash would be a dead giveaway. The shower stall on the other side of the towel rack was big enough to hide him, but the only cover was the rack itself, and there weren't enough towels there to make that work.

Which left him only one option. Crouching down beside the bodies, he leveled his gun at the playroom door. If he could get in the first shot, at least he'd be able to sell his life at cost. The door swung open—

He barely managed to quash his reflexes in time. "Your Excellency!" he breathed, twitching aside his gun.

"Where is he?" Gustav demanded, his eyes flicking around the bathroom. He was still dressed in all his heavy finery, though he'd lost his powdered wig somewhere.

"I don't know, Your Excellency," Riefenstahl said. "I had to hide from the mutineers and only just arrived."

"Then we shall hope he has already reached the safe room," Gustav said, stepping back and gesturing impatiently. "Come—*come*. Do you have a second weapon?"

"I do, Your Excellency," Riefenstahl said, producing the second gun as he hurried forward.

"This was Harold's gun," Gustav said, looking hard at the monogram on the weapon's grip as he took it. There was a fire in his eyes that, perhaps paradoxically, sent a cold chill across Riefenstahl's back. "We shall pay them back in full, you and I." He crossed to the hidden door and popped the catch. "Quickly," he murmured as he swung it open and started down the stairs. "Silence from here on. We may yet be too late."

Earlier, Riefenstahl had gotten the impression that the secret passageway system was more of a maze than his brief journey had demonstrated. Now, as he followed Gustav, he saw that it was far more complicated even than he'd guessed. The Emperor zigged and zagged, passing by some side passageways and turning down others, and twice changing levels. With no obvious passage identifiers or intersection markers, Riefenstahl reflected, an average Potsdam civilian would be hopelessly lost in minutes.

But with the insight he'd pulled from the dead *Totenkopf's* tablet, Riefenstahl was able to visualize exactly where he was, and which direction he was going.

He was starting to feel both smug and hopeful when the chair was pulled straight out from under him.

It came without warning. Three meters ahead, Gustav came to a sudden halt, his gun held ready. Riefenstahl stopped, too, straining his ears and eyes, trying to figure out what had caught the Emperor's attention.

And then, he heard it. Footsteps, several sets, somewhere in the near distance.

For a long moment, Gustav stood stock-still, clearly listening, possibly mapping the intruders' movements in his mind. Then, without a word, he gestured back over his shoulder.

They were retreating.

Riefenstahl walked in front, his heart twisted with anger and frustration, until they reached an intersection wide enough for Gustav to get around him and lead the way further into the maze. The footsteps had long since faded into the background by the time the Emperor took one final turn that ended them in front of a heavy-looking door.

"The safe room?" Riefenstahl murmured hopefully. It shouldn't be; the hyper generator was in the other direction, back where they'd heard the footsteps.

Gustav didn't answer, but simply punched in a code on the door's keypad. There were half a dozen clicks as lockpins disengaged, and Gustav pulled the door open.

Riefenstahl nodded heavily to himself. Of course. The hyper generator was the safe room.

The armory was the armory.

"Here," Gustav said, pulling a submachinegun from the weapons rack and handing it to Riefenstahl. "You'll want these, too," he added, scooping up two additional forty-round magazines.

"Thank you, Your Excellency," Riefenstahl said, checking over the gun. He hadn't fired this specific model in twenty T-years, but it was similar enough to the weapons he *was* proficient with to make no difference. "And you?"

In answer, Gustav tucked Harold's sidearm into his waistband and selected another submachinegun and two extra magazines. "You'll also want these," he said, handing Riefenstahl a small box. "Ear protectors with built-in coms." His gaze darkened as he pulled out another set and slipped them into his ears. "It is likely to become very noisy."

"Yes, Your Excellency," Riefenstahl said, the weight of the weapon seeming to also bear down on his heart and soul. If the Palace's internal *Totenkopfs* had all been compromised or diverted elsewhere—and from the confidence the mutineers had shown as they moved freely through the corridors that seemed likely—then it was all down to him and Gustav. Two men, against an unknown number of enemies, with both the Empire and Andrew's life hanging in the balance.

"It's not as bad as you envision, Herr Admiral," Gustav said. "*Konteradmiral* Eulenberg is clever and determined, and has assembled a cadre of equally determined men and women. But he has both blind spots and preconceptions, and they will bring an end to him and his mutiny."

Riefenstahl nodded, a sour taste in his mouth. Eulenberg. He should have known. It was practically a joke among the senior officers how every conversation with the man seemed to end up with his concerns about the state of the Emperor and the Empire.

The general conclusion was that he simply had a one-track mind when it came to politics. Now, Riefenstahl realized, the man had been deliberately trotting out his theories in order to troll for supporters.

"So be of stout heart and good cheer," Gustav continued, gesturing him back into the passageway. "Even now we move to establish ourselves upon the high ground."

"The high ground, Your Excellency?" Riefenstahl echoed, frowning. "Where is that?"

"You shall see," Gustav said, closing the armory door behind him with a solid *thunk*. "It all rests on Andrew now."

Riefenstahl frowned. "On *Andrew*?"

"He has his instructions," Gustav said. "I have no doubt he will carry them out to the fullest."

VIII

Marija didn't realize she'd dozed off until she was startled awake by a thudding knock on the safe room door.

She jolted in her seat, coming within an ace of knocking the shotgun across her lap onto the floor. "Who is it?" she called, her heart thudding hard. *Please let it be Emperor Gustav,* she begged silently. *Please let him be all right.*

"*Konteradmiral* Heinrich Eulenberg," a voice came back through the speaker beside the door that she hadn't noticed before. "Emperor Gustav sent me to check on his son. Is the Crown Prince there?"

"Yes, he's safe," Marija said, breathing a sigh of relief. *Konteradmiral* Eulenberg—she was pretty sure she'd heard that name when Harold was talking about the evening's guest list. "Is the Emperor there with you?" she asked, standing up and reaching for the door lock.

"No, but he's safe," Eulenberg assured her. "He wants me to bring Andrew to him so that they can get out of the Palace together."

Marija froze, her hand on the lock. "Excuse me?" she called.

"I said Emperor Gustav wants me to bring Andrew and get them both out of the Palace," Eulenberg said.

Marija stared at the door, the flood of relief reversing itself. Of course the Emperor would want Andrew safely out of the Palace under these horrifying circumstances.

But Gustav himself would never run away. Never. He would stand and fight; alone if necessary, to the death if God willed it.

And he would *absolutely* not cower somewhere while he sent someone else into danger to bring his son to him.

"I see," she said, stepping back from the door and raising the shotgun to hip level. "Tell me, *Konteradmiral* Eulenberg: where exactly is this safe place where Frederick the Great cowers?"

For a long minute she thought Eulenberg had left. "I see I underestimated you," Eulenberg said, his voice now dark and menacing. "I trust you will not in turn underestimate *me*. You may think the room you're in is secure. It's not. I've sent for explosives, and when they arrive I *will* bring down this door."

"Killing us will gain you nothing," Marija said, fighting to filter the shaking from her voice. The door was thick, but she had no doubt that enough force would bring it down. "Until you have the Emperor, you haven't won."

"Oh, we'll have him," Eulenberg promised darkly. "I make you an offer, *fräulein*—what's your name again?"

"I'm a loyal subject of the Emperor's," Marija said. "That's all you need to know."

"Very well, then," Eulenberg said. "I make you an offer, Loyal Subject. Come out now—surrender the boy—and you'll both be treated well. We'll let you take him into exile, in the Solarian League or wherever you choose, where he can have a long and peaceful life. But if you stay in there—if you continue to defy the tide of history— you'll face the most severe and horrible consequences."

Marija snorted. "And why should I trust you?"

"Because I have no reason to lie," Eulenberg said. "And because you really have no other option. The Emperor is alone and on the run. Do you really think he's going to come and rescue you all by himself?"

"Yes," a young voice said firmly from Marija's side. "He will."

Marija jumped. With her attention on Eulenberg and the door between them, she hadn't even noticed that Andrew had joined her. "Andrew, shh," she hissed, putting a warning hand on his shoulder.

To her surprise, he shook his head. "My father will always come for me," he called loudly toward the speaker. "Whether he is a prisoner or free; whether he is ill or well; whether he is afar or near; it makes no difference. He will come to me, and he will rescue me. And when I am safe, all his enemies will die."

Marija stared at the boy. His face was flushed, his fingers twitching nervously at his sides. But his voice was steady, the words flowing like—

Like one of the Emperor's speeches, actually. Was this something Gustav had given Andrew to memorize for just this sort of occasion?

Was the speech a coded message?

But a message to whom? Unless the situation was even stranger

than Marija guessed, the only ones out there were the Emperor's
enemies.

"So think well about what you are doing," Andrew continued.
"There may yet be redemption for you. But if you continue, you *will*
face the wrath of His Excellency."

"Yes, we're trembling where we stand," Eulenberg said
scornfully.

But to Marija's ear, there was a new edge of thoughtfulness
beneath the contempt. As if the traitor had just had a revelation . . .

"Very well," Eulenberg continued. "I'll leave you to think it over.
But I'll be back. *And* with my explosives. So think well, and think
quickly."

Marija let the silence linger another few seconds. Then, she
stepped to the door, located the speaker control, and turned it off.
"I'm sorry, Andrew," she apologized, laying her shotgun on the chair
and crouching down to face the boy. "That wasn't something you
needed to hear."

"It's okay," Andrew said. His voice was shaking now as he allowed
his rigid control to crack. "It'll be okay."

"I know," Marija said. She pulled him to her for a long, tight hug.
"Your father or his men will get us out of this."

"I know," Andrew said, his voice muffled in her shoulder as he
clung to her.

Marija pursed her lips. "That thing you said," she said. "That . . .
speech. Were those your father's words?"

"Uh-huh," he said. "He told me I should always say that if anyone
ever threatened me."

"You did an excellent job," Marija complimented him. "I'm sure it
scared them off."

"It's not supposed to scare them off," the boy said. "It's supposed
to . . ." He paused, as if searching his memory. "It's supposed to give
them a solid data point that my father will then know that they have."

Marija frowned. "What does that mean?"

"I don't know," Andrew confessed. "But he told me to say it. So I
did."

"And I know he'll be very proud of you," Marija said. She gave him
a final squeeze and drew back. "And now, it's time for you to get back
to bed. Come on, I'll come and tuck you in."

And she did. This time, she made sure she carried the shotgun into the sleeping area with her.

⌘ ⌘ ⌘

And with that, Eulenberg thought with satisfaction, the next move was clear.

"You two stay here," he said, pointing to two of the men. "Golovskina, get back to the monitor room. Grab everyone and bring them to the nursery."

"The *nursery*?" she echoed, frowning in the darkness.

"You heard the boy," Eulenberg said. "His father will always come for him. So that's where he'll have gone."

"Only the boy isn't there," Golovskina reminded him.

"But that's where Gustav will start," Eulenberg said, glaring at her. Didn't *anyone* understand the Emperor except him? "That's where he'll have gone, so that's where he'll leave from, so that's the set of vectors we need to cover. You and the others come at it from the public side, we'll come at it from the rat-hole side, and *one* of us is bound to run into him."

"Yes, Sir," Golovskina said. She didn't sound convinced, but obediently turned and hurried down the passageway.

"And you two stay sharp," Eulenberg added to the rear guard. "If we don't catch him en route, he'll come here. Keep watch, and make sure you're far enough apart that he can't take you with a quick two-shot."

"Don't worry, Sir," one of them said. "If he comes, we'll get him."

"Good." Eulenberg gestured to the other two. "Come with me. We have a walking dead man to catch."

The maze of secret passageways was undoubtedly designed to confuse intruders. But as usual, Gustav had been too clever for his own good. The diagram Li had pulled up in the monitor room had clearly showed how the sentimental old fool had tried to relive his glory days by laying out his private lair like an unfolded battleship. Anyone who'd ever served aboard *Friedrich der Grosse* or *Liegnitz* would find the labyrinth perfectly easy to navigate.

Still, it was a longer and slower path than the outside route to the nursery via the monitor room. As a result, he was just pushing open the secret door in Andrew's playroom as Golovskina and her team came in from the hallway.

"Anything?" Eulenberg murmured, glancing over the group. Golovskina had taken him at his word, bringing everyone he'd left in the monitor room except Li himself, bringing their assault team to ten.

Which would probably be good numbers to have if Gustav had sneaked back into the secret maze and they had to hunt him down.

"Nothing about Gustav," Golovskina said. "Li says he hasn't seen any movement on the monitors."

"Because everyone's been using the rat maze," Eulenberg growled. Damn Gustav for not extending his usual paranoia to the extent of putting monitors down there. "Any word from *Kolin*?"

"*Fregattenkapitän* Xiao Chen-tzi confirms they're standing ready and requesting instructions."

Eulenberg felt his throat tighten. A single, surgical laser blast to destroy the palace—*Kolin*'s wedge going up to protect it from a knee-jerk reaction from the rest of the Home Fleet—Eulenberg's XO shooting everyone else on the bridge and then claiming he'd stumbled upon a mutiny but had arrived to late to stop it—the subsequent inquiry that would show all the deceased officers had received quiet payments from Tomlinson's former government and the PFT corporation—

An unwanted shiver ran up his back. It wasn't ideal. Far from it. But if he and the others failed to take Gustav into custody in the next few minutes, it would at least ensure that the Emperor's madness was ended. "What did you tell him?" he asked.

A muscle in Golovskina's cheek twitched. "I said that if we haven't checked in in fifteen minutes they should take the shot."

"Understood," Eulenberg said. Ten more minutes to find Gustav and Andrew, five to get themselves out of the Palace and the blast area if they didn't. "That gives us—"

He jerked his head toward the door leading to the boy's bathroom. Had that been a *splash*?

"What the *hell*?" one of Golovskina's men muttered.

"Stay close," Eulenberg murmured.

Another splash came as he crossed to the door and carefully turned the handle. Resettling his grip on his gun, he gently pushed open the door.

And found himself facing an extraordinary sight. Emperor

Gustav was sitting in the tub, apparently fully absorbed in the two toy boats he was playing with. He looked up as the door swung open—

"Ah—*Konteradmiral*," he greeted Eulenberg. "Come in, come in. Did you bring your bath toys?"

"I did not, Your Excellency," Eulenberg said, frowning as he took a couple of steps closer. The steaming water was piled high with suds that hid everything below Gustav's shoulders, but a quick look at the towel rack where the Emperor had draped his clothing showed he was indeed stark naked in there.

"Well, I'm not going to lend you any of mine," Gustav huffed, waving one of the boats for emphasis. "But we could have a water fight." He slammed the boat into the water, sending water and suds fountaining into the air. A few drops made it over the edge of the tub, joining the large puddle already there.

A puddle, Eulenberg saw now, that extended all the way to the bodies of Peter and Michael, still lying where they'd died.

Eulenberg looked back at Gustav, his stomach churning with sudden anger. For some reason the Emperor's complete indifference to the dignity of the deceased was hitting him harder than anything else that had happened tonight. "Enough of this," he bit out. "You're coming with us."

"I haven't finished my bath," Gustav protested mildly.

"You're coming with us *now*," Eulenberg snapped. Once he had the Emperor outside the safe room that damn nurse would have no choice but to open the door or let her young charge listen to his father die.

Gustav folded his arms across his chest. "Make me," he challenged.

Eulenberg swore. They didn't have time for this. "You heard your Emperor," he growled "Get him out of there."

Two of his men strode forward, holstering their guns as they did so. They passed the two bodies of their comrades—

And with a sudden windmilling of arms and legs their feet shot up from under them and they slammed onto their backs on the floor, each sending up a small fountain of water as he landed.

"Be careful," Gustav said, peering over the edge of the tub at them as they tried to scramble to their feet. "There might be soap on the floor."

"The rest of you—go get him," Golovskina ordered.

The men streamed past Eulenberg, moving carefully on the slippery tiles. Gustav looked at Eulenberg and gave him a sly, smug smile.

And abruptly, Eulenberg had had it.

Never mind that people would have questions. Never mind that there would be enquiries and suspicions. Never mind that everyone in the room would know he'd gunned down the Emperor in cold blood. Cursing viciously at the man and at the stubborn insanity that had forced him to do this, he raised his gun and pointed it at the old fool—

※ ※ ※

—and rising from concealment behind the towel rack, Riefenstahl leveled his submachinegun and opened fire.

His first burst caught Eulenberg squarely in the chest, the hail of lead collapsing him into a crumpled heap on the floor and sending a splatter of blood and flesh into the far wall. He swiveled toward the nearest of the other mutineers—

Just as a second burst of fire erupted from the submachinegun that had magically appeared from under the suds in Gustav's tub. Two men flailed and died in that blast; three more collapsed in the fire from Riefenstahl's second attack. At the door Golovskina, now dropped to one knee and holding her gun in a marksman's two-handed grip, sent a three-slug burst into the tub wall directly in front of Gustav's torso. Out of the corner of his eye, Riefenstahl saw the tub's porcelain coating disintegrate into white chips, revealing the solid core of battle steel beneath it—

And then the floodlights along the tub enclosure's back wall blazed to life, burning into the mutineers' eyes. Golovskina threw one forearm across her face as she sent one more useless burst at Gustav, and died in that same position.

Riefenstahl lost track of how many times he and Gustav fired their weapons. All he knew afterward was that all the mutineers were dead.

For another few seconds the only sound was the slight ringing in Riefenstahl's ears that the ear protectors hadn't quite compensated for. Then, slowly, he lowered the gun to rest on the top of the towel rack. "Are you all right, Your Excellency?" he asked.

"I am," Gustav said. His eyes were steady on Riefenstahl's as he rested the muzzle of his submachinegun on the rim of the tub. "Guard the door—there may be more of them."

"Yes, Your Excellency," Riefenstahl said. He stepped carefully around the bodies and blood, trying not to look at any of it. It was one thing to kill an enemy ship with a missile from half a million kilometers away. It was quite another to stare into their eyes as you ended their existence.

"Well done, *Herr Admiral*," Gustav said. "We will join my son now, and will there await the end."

Riefenstahl looked behind him. The Emperor was minimally dressed again, though it was clear from the state of his clothing that he hadn't bothered to dry off first. "I'm ready, Your Excellency."

"To the secret door, then," Gustav ordered. "And be cautious. There may still be enemies to face."

※ ※ ※

It wasn't until *Kolin* was in the final stage of her maneuver that Cutler realized just what her commander was going for.

She was lining up her laser on the capital. Probably, specifically, on the Emperor's Palace.

And suddenly the full intent of the whole awful plot unfolded into view before him.

We will simply detain him, Eulenberg had promised. *We will question him, and have psychologists examine him. If he is competent to rule, we will of course return him to the throne.*

Lies. All of it. Eulenberg wasn't planning an intervention. He was planning an assassination.

Cutler squared his shoulders. Like hell he was.

"Signal *Kolin*," he ordered. "I want to speak to whoever's in command."

"Yes, Sir." There was a moment of silence—

"This is *Fregattenkapitän* Xiao Chen-tzi," a voice came from the bridge speaker. "XO of *Kolin*."

"This is *Flottillenadmiral* Cutler von Tischendorf," Cutler said. "You seem to be turning your laser toward Potsdam. Explain."

"*Flottillenadmiral* Cutler von Tischendorf, you say?" Xiao said. "Ah."

Cutler felt Bermann's eyes on him. "That's hardly an explanation, *Fregattenkapitän* Xiao," he said stiffly.

"Do you really need one, *Flottillenadmiral*?"

"No, I suppose not," Cutler agreed, glancing at the tactical, confirming *Schreien* was in the position he'd ordered. "Let's make it formal. You will cease your current maneuvering. You will then yaw your ship so that all weapons are pointed away from the planet. You will then also shut down your nodes."

"Excuse me, *Flottillenadmiral*?" Xiao asked cautiously. "Do you not understand?"

"I understand perfectly," Cutler said. "Understand in turn that as *Kolin*'s laser is aimed at the Palace, so *Schreien*'s laser is aimed at you. You will obey my orders immediately, or I *will* open fire."

There was another silence, a longer one this time. Cutler kept his eyes on the tactical, watching the still incomplete formation of *Kolin*'s wedge and the not-quite-there positioning of the ship's forward laser. Another three degrees and he would be ready to destroy the palace. Two more degrees and Cutler would have no choice but to blow *Kolin* out of the sky. Would Xiao really insist on sacrificing his life and his ship for nothing?

"*Kolin*'s thrusters activated, Sir," Bermann reported, an odd edge to his voice. "She's yawing to portside, swinging her bow away from the planet."

"Acknowledged," Cutler said, some of his tension flowing away. Whatever was happening down there, at least the Emperor would have nothing to fear from up here.

"Her nodes are also powering down, Sir." Bermann said. He hesitated. "Sir . . . what did *Fregattenkapitän* Xiao mean by your not needing an explanation?"

"Nothing, *Korvettenkapitän*," Cutler said quietly. "Nothing at all."

✕ ✕ ✕

Riefenstahl, Gustav, Andrew, and Marija ended up spending the night in the safe room. Riefenstahl stood guard by the door most of that time, just in case.

The precaution proved unnecessary. Desperation, as every ship commander knew, was no match for skill and training. In the end, all of the traitors were dead; some in battle, others by execution at the conclusion of their trials.

All of them except one.

IX

"The Emperor," *Admiral* Riefenstahl said, his voice stiff and formal, "thought long and hard before deciding what to do with you."

Cutler stood at attention, anger and hopelessness seething together in his gut. He'd asked to speak directly to Emperor Gustav. Instead, the Emperor had sent Riefenstahl.

It wasn't fair. It wasn't right. Cutler had saved the Emperor and the Empire by forcing Xiao to stand down. He deserved better.

"The problem is that you were part of the conspiracy," Riefenstahl continued. "You met with Eulenberg and agreed to join his coup."

"That's a lie," Cutler bit out.

Riefenstahl raised his eyebrows. "It's in the testimony, *Flottillenadmiral. And* it's on Eulenberg's own recordings."

Cutler winced. He'd had no idea Eulenberg had recorded their meeting. Son of a *Hündin.* "And you know full well from that recording that I only agreed to assist in giving the Emperor a proper mental examination."

"From *that* recording, yes," Riefenstahl said. "But who knows what else was said at later meetings?"

"Nothing was said, because there *were* no other meetings."

"So you say," Riefenstahl said. "But you have no proof."

"A negative cannot be proven."

"That is indeed the dilemma you face."

Cutler ground his teeth. "I've served the Emperor all of my life," he said. "As did my mother before me. Surely that counts for something."

"It does," Riefenstahl agreed, nodding. "That's why the Emperor has graciously decided that you will be released and permitted to go into exile."

Cutler stared. *Exile?* "Meaning?"

"Meaning exactly what it says," Riefenstahl said evenly. "The Navy has a spare ship, the frigate we captured at Second Tomlinson. You'll be allowed to take that ship, along with any officers and crew you can persuade to leave the Empire with you, and seek your fortune elsewhere."

Cutler's hands curled into fists. "May I be permitted to appeal this decision to the Emperor?"

"The decision was *made* by the Emperor," Riefenstahl said. "There is no appeal."

"I would like to see him anyway."

"He does not wish to see you."

"I see," Cutler said, a bitter darkness swirling in front of his eyes. So that was to be his fate. He would be cast out, alone, far from any semblance of civilization, facing the galaxy with only a single minor warship.

It was a death sentence. Or at least, Riefenstahl probably expected it to be. Was undoubtedly counting on it, in fact.

But there was one crucial factor he hadn't taken into account. This was Cutler von Tischendorf he was dealing with . . . and the von Tischendorfs always survived.

"Very well," he said, standing up, ignoring the weight of the restraints tugging at his wrists. "I'll take the Emperor's generous offer. But understand something."

He pinned Riefenstahl with the kind of look he'd learned at an early age from his mother. "I won't be gone forever," he continued. "I *will* return. And when I do, the Emperor *will* see me. Whether he wishes to or not."

Giving Riefenstahl his best about-face, he started toward the door, his two guards falling into step beside him.

Yes, he would be back. But not as Cutler von Tischendorf. Gustav was too clever a tactician to throw him out without keeping close track of him.

And so the name *Cutler von Tischendorf* would have to die.

He smiled tightly. *Kapitän Jen*, they'd called his mother. *Jen's son*, they'd called him.

So be it.

Cutler von Tischendorf was no more. In his place was Cutler Gensonne.

Who would one day make Emperor Gustav regret what he'd done.

※ ※ ※

"He's gone?" Gustav asked.

"He is, Your Excellency," Riefenstahl confirmed. "He hit the hyper limit two hours ago."

"With a full crew?"

"More than a full crew," Riefenstahl admitted, wincing a little. "I had no idea he was held in such esteem."

"I'd warned you about that, if you recall," Gustav reminded him. "That was the reason you were in the Palace the night of the coup in the first place."

"I remember, Your Excellency," Riefenstahl said. "I just thought that everything that happened after that would have tarnished his reputation."

"Hardly," Gustav said. "With his involvement no more than verbal, and his only real action that night to stand down Xiao and *Kolin*, there was hardly anything to tarnish him with."

Riefenstahl felt his eyes widen as he suddenly understood. "That's why you sent him into exile? Because you didn't want to risk bringing him to trial?"

"You're a good officer, *Admiral* Riefenstahl," Gustav said grimly. "But you still have much to learn of politics. With his name on the traitors' record, *Flottillenadmiral* von Tischendorf could not be permitted to remain in the Navy. But a trial that ended in his acquittal would leave him here, where he could become the rallying point for future disaffection."

"And so he had to leave," Riefenstahl murmured. "I understand, Your Excellency. But under the circumstances..."

"We will watch him," Gustav assured him. "Even now we are reaching out to nearby systems with trade and diplomacy. We will watch Cutler von Tischendorf and assure ourselves that he will never be a threat to the Emperor."

Riefenstahl nodded. "Yes, Your Excellency."

"In the meantime," Gustav continued, tapping his tablet to send a file to Riefenstahl's, "a bit of information you may find enlightening."

Riefenstahl frowned down at his tablet. Beneath the *Solarian League Navy: Top Secret* heading was the title: *Localized Transient Apertures in Gravitic Sidewalls*.

He looked up at Gustav. "Is this genuine?"

"My agents assure me it is," Gustav said. "I trust you see the implications."

"Yes, Your Excellency, I do," Riefenstahl said. "If functional gun ports become a reality, all the so-called modern navies that have installed box and railgun launchers are suddenly going to be scrambling to replace them with launchers that can also fire sideways."

He smiled tightly. "The same twin-arm launchers the Andermani Navy already has."

"Indeed," Gustav said. "I'm sure you've heard the saying that it's better to be thought a fool than to open your mouth and remove all doubt." He lifted a finger in emphasis. "But better still is to be thought a fool and accept their contempt . . . and then prove them wrong."

"Yes, Your Excellency," Riefenstahl said. Gustav would certainly have the chance to prove his enemies wrong.

He could only hope Cutler von Tischendorf wouldn't do the same.

DECEPTION ON GRYPHON

Jane Lindskold

"Hey, if you kids are free tomorrow, I'd love to take you out and show you some of the outback." Gill Votano's tone was light, his expression casual, but Stephanie Harrington immediately felt uneasy. She shifted, tugging one of her brown curls. She'd been trying to grow her hair out, and found herself constantly fussing with the new length.

"Can we bring the 'cats?" she asked, gesturing to where Lionheart and Survivor were busily—and messily—devouring a Gryphon sea bass. Sea bass was one of the local species safe for both human and treecat consumption, and Eureka Base had been established on the coast of the Calypso Sea, one of Gryphon's larger seas. She and Karl had spent the last couple of hours fishing, much to the 'cats' approval.

Most of the time treecats were hard to tell apart unless you knew them well, but Survivor's cream and grey fur was still growing back from where it had been shaved around his neck, portions of his back and belly, and a patch on one side of his face. This gave him either a moth-eaten look (as Stephanie put it) or as if he was equal parts fluff and thick velvet (Karl's description). Lionheart had long ago recovered from the wounds he had received when he'd saved Stephanie from the hexapuma, but no one could miss that his right front limb had been amputated at the shoulder, as a result of his injuries.

"Absolutely!" Gill assured her. "The furballs must be tired of hanging around Eureka. There're lots of big rocks for them to bounce on where we're going. They'll love the hoodoos! It'll almost be like being back in the forests of Sphinx."

"Hoodoos?"

Karl Zivonik looked up from baiting a fishhook. Where Stephanie was small and, at sixteen, not likely to get much taller, he was a good 185 centimeters. Life on high-gravity Sphinx had packed muscle on him, which, along with his dark hair and eyes, made him an impressive figure for a young man of eighteen.

"Sorry! Geologist-speak." Gill chuckled. "Hoodoos are tall, thin rock spires. Tent rocks, fairy rocks, earth pyramids—" He shrugged. "All pretty much the same thing: a column of softer rock that supports harder stone, like a cap that protects the column from the elements. They can be pretty spectacular."

"Sounds like fun," Stephanie said, and Karl nodded.

"We'll need to check with Stephanie's folks," he said. "But I don't think they'll have a problem. After all, one of the reasons they brought us along with them to Gryphon was that everyone figured a visit would be educational. Going out into the field with a geologist surely qualifies as an educational outing."

Gill grinned widely, but something in the way he pushed his left hand through his thick blond curls reinforced Stephanie's feeling that underneath his bluff, hardy manner, he was tense. "Sure, ask the folks. Absolutely! But, listen, could you keep this little jaunt to ourselves, otherwise?"

Stephanie stiffened. "Why?"

Gill winked. "I'll tell you tomorrow. Promise."

But he never did tell them. The next morning, while Stephanie and Karl were eating breakfast, a neighbor dropped by to tell them that Gill Votano had committed suicide the night before.

⚹ ⚹ ⚹

Eureka Base was a small community where there was no keeping secrets. In this case, the bearer of bad news was Daryl Schonenbaum, an oceanographer who was working closely with Marjorie and Richard Harrington.

"Apparently, Gill shot himself sometime in the night," Daryl said, turning the heathered tweed cap he wore on land or at sea restlessly between his hands. "His lab partner, Lorra Rundle, found his body when she went by the lab to grab something before a breakfast meeting related to today's conference. Gill had left a very short note, but a holocube of his estranged wife and two young children was close at hand."

Daryl looked uncomfortable, but not particularly sad or upset. He was a relative newcomer to Eureka Base. His specialization was ocean botany, while Gill Votano's had been mineralogy, so even in the relatively small community of Eureka Base, he and Gill Votano had probably only met in passing.

The reason for Daryl's discomfort came clear with his next words. "Gill had told Lorra he planned to take Stephanie and Karl out today to see some of the more spectacular hoodoos and painted rocks. She thought..."

He paused, obviously uncertain how to continue. Marjorie Harrington came to his rescue. Like her daughter, she had curly brown hair, but her eyes were closer to hazel, rather than Stephanie's dark brown. Those Stephanie got from her father, who was darker complected than either wife or daughter, though his hair was starting to show silver.

Marjorie forced a reassuring smile. "I'm guessing that Liz Freeth thought we needed to know before Stephanie and Karl went to meet Gill and stumbled on something unpleasant. Thank you for agreeing to be the bearer of unsettling news."

Daryl's smile, bright against tanned skin, was relieved. "Liz would have come herself, but between Gill's suicide and the conference today, she doesn't know if she's coming or going."

Liz Freeth was the administrator for Eureka Base. She was a round-bodied, energetic woman who treated her various charges— highly educated scientists, almost to a one—as if they were newly hatched chicks and she the mother hen. Based on what Stephanie had seen of most research scientists (her parents excepted) she thought that was a very wise attitude indeed.

"The conference is going on as planned, then?" Richard Harrington asked.

"Since contingents are coming in from Gryphon's other research bases," Daryl said, his tone apologetic, "we did think... Of course, if the kids are too upset..."

He trailed off again.

Stephanie spoke up. "I'm okay. I mean, I'm shocked and all, but it's not as if you guys' missing the conference is going to change that."

Daryl clearly felt he'd done his part and was eager to go. "I'll just leave you people to talk. Com if you decide you can't make the conference or if you'll be late or something."

He hurried off.

Richard Harrington turned to his daughter and Karl. "That was nice of you, Stephanie, but if you want us to stay, you and Karl are our first responsibility. The terraforming discussions are important, but there's nothing time critical on the agenda. Certainly nothing so urgent that our missing some or all of today's meetings will matter."

Stephanie shook her head. "That's true, in the big picture, I mean, but not in the smaller one. You and Mom were invited here to Gryphon as Crown consultants. That's a big deal. You need to live up to the honor."

Karl cleared his throat. Although he was not the Harringtons' son, he had known them for two years now and frequently stayed at their house, since his own family home in Thunder River was inconveniently far from the SFS headquarters in Twin Forks. As a result, Marjorie and Richard treated Karl as if he was the son they longed for, but had not yet gotten around to producing.

"Yes, Karl?" Marjorie asked.

"There's another thing, too," Karl said. "We're here on Gryphon for a limited time. From what I understand, this conference was deliberately planned for the mid-point of your visit, so you'd have a chance to see something of Gryphon first, but so you could act based on what the conference came up with. If you miss the meetings, then everything will be off schedule."

Marjorie nodded. "That's true, but I agree with Richard. You two are our first responsibility."

Stephanie fought not to roll her eyes. She *was* sixteen, after all, not a little kid. Karl was a legal adult, recently promoted to assistant ranger in the Sphinxian Forest Service.

"Mom, it's not like you're leaving for days, just tied up in meetings for the rest of today. If I need you, I can reach you. Anyhow, I have Lionheart."

Richard looked at Marjorie. Unspoken was the fact that Stephanie—who had been rather hot-headed as a child—had clearly benefited from her treecat's companionship. Most people might think that was because of the great responsibility that had been thrust upon Stephanie ever since she had discovered the treecats and Lionheart had adopted her. However, the senior Harringtons were among the few people who knew the treecat's influence actually provided a moderating effect on Stephanie's temper.

No one watching Lionheart and Survivor—both currently busily involved in rolling an assortment of small items off the countertop, clearly delighted by how high they bounced in Gryphon's lower gravity (at least as compared to that of Sphinx)—would have realized how protective the fluffy, long-bodied, feline-analog creatures could be. That the protectiveness extended to helping with emotional distress, not just in case of physical threat, was definitely a selling point with Stephanie's parents.

"She *will* have Lionheart," Richard said, "and Karl, and Survivor. And we'll be within easy com contact."

Stephanie did roll her eyes then. "And Karl will have Survivor, and me, and Lionheart. Go on! If you delay much longer, I'm going to figure you're actually looking for an excuse to play hooky."

⌖ ⌖ ⌖

After Richard and Marjorie left, Stephanie looked at Karl. "I don't believe Gill's death was suicide."

"You don't?" Karl said. "Well, neither do I. You want to offer your thoughts first, or should I tell you mine?"

Stephanie took a deep breath. "You start."

Karl grinned at her. Although he was now officially an assistant ranger, while Stephanie remained a probationary ranger, Karl never treated Stephanie as anything but an equal. If Stephanie had appreciated that when she was fourteen and they'd first met, she appreciated it even more now. She'd been so worried he'd pull rank on her.

"First," Karl said, ticking the point off on one finger, "why would Gill ask us to go on a trip with him today if he was so depressed he was about to kill himself?"

Stephanie nodded. "I thought about mentioning that to Liz Freeth, but I figured her answer would be that he was trying to distract himself from whatever was bothering him. Heck, she might even say that he'd asked us to go with him as sort of surrogates for his own kids, even though they're a lot younger than us—because he was missing his family."

"Then he got overwhelmed because he was going out with us instead of them and shot himself," Karl shook his head. "I just don't see it. Remember, Gill was going to share a secret with us. I'm sure of that. I have trouble imagining that he'd kill himself without telling someone about that secret and, at least from what we were told, the note he left was too short to have passed anything on."

"Yeah," Stephanie agreed. "I know Daryl said Gill got overwhelmed, thinking about his wife and kids, but I'm not happy with that. Why would he shoot himself in the lab? Why not in his quarters?"

"Someone might hear the shot?" Karl offered, but Stephanie knew he was only playing devil's advocate. "I suppose we could find out if Gill had a recent message from home."

Stephanie rubbed the tip of her nose. "Even if we find out there was one, I'm not going to believe he killed himself."

Karl took a deep breath. "Because of how Survivor and Lionheart reacted yesterday, right?"

Stephanie nodded. "That's it. Lionheart may have looked as if he had nothing on his mind but making sure he got more than his fair share of that sea bass, but he was prickling all over with an awareness that Gill's emotions didn't match all that bluff and hearty, 'Let's go for a field trip, kids!' Thing is, Lionheart wasn't upset—not like he was by that horrible Tennessee Bolgeo. He just knew Gill's outside and inside didn't match."

"Yeah," Karl tilted his head to one side, seeking words for an experience that remained new to him. "I'm not as certain as you are about how Survivor felt, but I could tell he was reacting to Gill in a way that didn't fit the mood Gill was showing us."

"I bet," Stephanie said, voicing a point she'd often discussed with Karl—and with the other three treecat adoptees, Scott, Jessica, and Cordelia, "that treecats don't lie nearly as much as humans do."

"That's why Lionheart adopted you," Karl said, deadpan, though his dark eyes twinkled. "You don't lie either. You just don't tell the whole truth."

Stephanie gave him a haughty look. "I simply believe there are times when it's easier to beg forgiveness rather than ask permission. Which brings us to the question: Do we tell Liz what we suspect?"

Karl considered, then shook his head. "I don't think we can. Most of the points we've made could be countered pretty easily with other arguments. Even if we were at home, I'd hesitate to try and explain about the 'cats reaction—though I think I'd tell Chief Ranger Shelton. He's seen enough by now that he'd at least take it into consideration. Asking Liz Freeth—who's already upset because she's lost one of her flock, and who has to deal with a community that's in shock, *and* a bunch of people arriving for a conference—asking her to accept treecat voodoo is too much."

"Yeah," Stephanie said. "Especially since if Gill didn't commit suicide, then there's only one alternative."

Karl took a deep breath and spoke the words aloud. "He was murdered."

✖ ✖ ✖

Climbs Quickly was pleased when Death Fang's Bane and Shining Sunlight decided to go outside. There wasn't anything *wrong* with the nesting place they'd been staying in since their arrival at this new place, but outside was much more interesting. Then there was the additional pleasure of running about feeling as if he had grown invisible extra legs, jumping higher and running more swiftly. That almost made up for the lack of proper trees.

When they had first arrived, Climbs Quickly had thought this place might be a different region of the Hot Lands he had visited with Death Fang's Bane and Shining Sunlight a short time before. The extraordinary lightness was the same, though this place was not nearly as hot. That, however, could be a result of a turning of the seasons. However, the thing that made Climbs Quickly think that they had come to another place entirely was that the pattern of lights in the sky was different.

When they had been in the Hot Lands, he had noticed the difference quickly. As a scout he had learned many and varied light patterns, as well as how those patterns changed with the seasons. When he had studied the skies in the Hot Places, he'd found the patterns completely different. Here they were different again. Most telling was the moon that loomed large in the sky. It was far larger and brighter than either of the moons at home. Indeed, there was nothing like it in either the skies of home or of the Hot Place.

<*They are walking to the Bitter Waters,*> Keen Eyes sent happily. <*I wonder if we could catch one of those big swimmers like we ate yesterday ourselves, rather than having the two-legs pull them up on their lines. That would be something to brag about to Swift Striker!*>

Climbs Quickly agreed. <*I was thinking that, if we stop at one of the fishing places, maybe we should show the two-legs that we want to try using the lines ourselves. I have watched. Using a line does not seem that difficult. The two-legs just sit there with the lines in the water, and the swimmers do the work.*>

Keen Eyes bleeked laughter. <*That would leave you out, then. You and sitting still are like the sun and the moons, never in the same place at the same time!*>

They had come to where salty water splashed long fingers up through sand and gravel, bringing with it all manner of interesting things. Climbs Quickly bounded down from his perch on Death Fang's Bane's shoulder, with Keen Eyes a breath behind. Together they chased little creatures with many legs through water and foam.

Keen Eyes caught one and sat up on his haunches to study it. <*These have an entire hand more legs than the shelled-swimmers at home.*> He popped it into his mouth and crunched down. <*They taste a little sharper, but not bad. A little like the stinky cheese Healer likes.*>

Seeing Keen Eyes eat the ten-legged creature, Shining Sunlight made a mouth noise the two People knew meant he was exasperated but, since Shining Sunlight didn't react as if he thought Keen Eyes had just poisoned himself, neither paid him much attention.

<*Shining Sunlight may have a point,*> Climbs Quickly said, when Keen Eyes next caught a small fish and began examining it. <*Maybe you should not eat everything you can get your hands on. We know this isn't home. Here there is no Memory Singer to share with us what is safe to eat and what may be dangerous.*>

<*I am no new-weaned kitten,*> Keen Eyes responded with a haughty flip of his sodden tail. <*Why do you think I am examining these so carefully? I am trying to see if these are among the foods the two-legs have been serving us. Surely you remember how there was an entire bowl of those hard-shelled scuttlers the other night? They had*>

been heated in the steam-maker, but that should not change how wholesome they are.>

Climbs Quickly gave a meditative scratch to the fur along his chin. *<I wish I was sure of that. At home there are roots that are not safe to eat unless they have been heated beneath the coals of a fire. True, the raw ones will not kill you, but they will give you a mighty bellyache.>*

<My belly is fine,> Keen Eyes insisted, but he did drop the fish. *<What do you think of our two-legs' moods? They have eaten only safe food but, from their mind-glows, you would think they had eaten something that disagrees with them badly.>*

Climbs Quickly wrinkled his nose as if smelling something rotten. *<The ache started when that two-leg came calling this morning. From almost his first mouth noises, the two-legs all became quite serious. Before that, the elders had been somewhat distracted, the young pair feeling some anticipation. Whatever the visitor said shocked them all. The elders then began to worry.>*

<The young, too,> Keen Eyes added, *<but the worries had different flavors. The elders were worrying about how the shock would affect the younglings. The younglings were worrying because they were adding something they knew to something they had just learned. Beyond that, I am lost.>*

Climbs Quickly bounced back as a long finger of salty water dug the sand out from under his feet and tried to drag him under. *<Perhaps they will do something that will give us an idea what so worries them. One thing about these two. They are not among those who worry, then do not act.>*

<That is true,> Keen Eyes agreed. *<If they were, my clan would likely be dead. Let us hope that this time less-grave matters have caught their attention.>*

※ ※ ※

As they walked along the beach, Stephanie tried not to let Gill's death completely overshadow what had, to that point, been a very pleasant holiday.

Gryphon was quite different from Sphinx, the planet on which Karl had been born and on which Stephanie had lived since she was ten. For one thing, Gryphon would require quite a lot more terraforming than Sphinx. Unlike Sphinx and Manticore, the Star

Kingdom of Manticore's capital planet, Gryphon orbited Manticore-B, the second star of the Manticore Binary System, and its planetary biochemistry differed from that of its sister planets in several small but significant ways. A lot more of its flora and fauna was inedible by humans. For the most part, that just meant it was indigestible, but some of it was mildly or even fatally poisonous, and the survey teams had barely scratched the planetary surface in too many ways.

That was, in fact, the reason they were here. The Star Kingdom had finally gotten around to establishing the study bases which would map out the planetary terraforming strategy, and Marjorie Harrington was generally acknowledged as one of Manticore's top two or three plant geneticists. She was here only as a temporary consultant, but the full-time scientific staff was clearly eager for her input.

The decades-long Plague Years the Star Kingdom had just survived explained a lot of the delay in the process, but the truth was that no one had felt a great sense of urgency because Gryphon was also just less desirable planetary real estate. Its orbital radius was almost the same as that of Manticore, but Manticore-B was cooler than Manticore-A, so its average temperature was quite a bit lower than the capital planet's. It *was* warmer than that of Sphinx, whose orbit was almost twice as far from Manticore-A, but it also had the greatest axial tilt of any of the Star Kingdom's three habitable planets. Coupled with its limited hydrosphere—barely half its surface was covered in water—that produced a dry "continental" climate with extreme seasonal changes between its icy winters and summers that were scorching hot, relatively speaking.

Where Sphinx was a heavy-grav planet, with a gravity of 1.35, Gryphon's gravity was, at 1.05 G, just slightly over Terran normal. Where Sphinx was heavily forested, Gryphon's extreme weather patterns were not conducive to large stands of timber. And whereas Gryphon's seas were scattered and shallow, Sphinx's oceans were broad, deep, and cold, like the Tannerman Ocean. The Tannerman bordered the Harrington Claim, but Stephanie was a hang glider, not a sailor. She and Lionheart had spent at least some time on the Harrington freehold's beaches, but Sphinxian oceans were colder than most humans would choose to swim in. Karl, on the other hand, had never lived near anything larger than a lake, and Survivor's clan had come from high in the mountains. Although both had seen large bodies of open water, neither had ever lived close to an ocean, so Eureka Base's shoreline was a source of fascination for humans and treecats alike.

"We're lucky," Stephanie said, watching as Lionheart and Survivor darted in and out of the surf zone chasing the tiny deca-crabs and foam-fish revealed by the rising and falling waves, "that treecat fur does a pretty good job shedding water. Even so, I wonder if we should try to rig some sort of swimsuit for them, to keep all that fluff from getting coated with salt water."

"Maybe after we figure out how to prove Gill Votano was murdered," Karl said, a faint note of reproof in his voice. "Even if you can treat the whole thing as an intellectual puzzle, I don't think I can. I just might be the closest thing to a duly constituted law officer here on Eureka Base."

Stephanie understood. Forest rangers were classified as law officers—a necessity especially on Sphinx and Gryphon where there was lots of land and relatively few people. Among the courses she and Karl had taken a few months ago on Manticore as part of a special accelerated training program for Forestry Service personnel had been one on forensics and criminology.

"You may well be," she said. "Liz probably has some judicial powers to let her mediate disputes, but I doubt there's a full-time law officer assigned to Eureka Base. There would be too little to keep one busy."

"Even the medical doctor is part-time," Karl added. "Most of the time, Jorge Prakel is as involved in research as the rest of them. He doctors when needed."

"You know," Stephanie mused. "I bet Liz called Jorge in to act as medical examiner. I wish we could have seen the body." She stopped, thinking about what it would be like to see the corpse of someone who, only a few hours before, had been enthusiastically suggesting they take a field trip. "Let me rephrase that . . . I wish we could've seen the evidence. We might've noticed something Dr. Prakel would have missed."

"Too late for that," Karl said. "I'm sure the body's been moved, probably to one of the cold storage lockers they use for larger specimens. They might've taken some photos, just because, but asking if we could see them would seem ghoulish."

"I agree," Stephanie said. "Anyhow, whether or not you're senior law officer here isn't the reason we need to look into this. If murder has been committed, then it's our moral responsibility, not just your job, to do something. Right? Maybe we can find something that'll convince Liz to open up the case."

Stephanie halted in mid-step, not even noticing when a wave reached up a long tendril and soaked her foot.

"Steph?"

"I just realized, there's another reason we can't tell anyone. Until we know who the murderer is, we're risking telling the wrong person."

Karl swallowed hard. Clearly, like Stephanie herself, he'd been thinking of Liz Freeth as an ally, but what if she was somehow involved? Maybe that was why Gill Votano had wanted to confide in someone from outside Gryphon's tightly intertwined community.

"You've got a very good point, there, Steph. Okay. Where to start? There's the classic triad: means, opportunity, and motive. Means won't take us anywhere. Gill was shot, apparently with his own gun."

Stephanie took up the next element. "Opportunity isn't going to take us anywhere, either, but for the opposite reason—there're just too many possibilities. Practically anyone could've gone to meet Gill in his lab and not been seen, especially at that hour. When the weather is good—like it is now—everyone who can is working outside during the day. That means they're sleeping really soundly at night."

Karl scooped up a flat, rounded stone and skipped it across the waves. "Yeah. There's plenty of time when the weather turns nasty to do analysis and other sorts of indoor work. If Gill's lab partner hadn't gone by the lab when she did, his body might not have been found until we started asking why Gill hadn't shown up for our field trip."

"And we'd have waited to ask," Stephanie added, picking up a stone and topping Karl's skip by one, "since he asked us to keep quiet about it. Say, do you think Gill's lab partner might have killed him? I remember from criminology that it's always important to suspect the person who finds the body, because that's the one person who has an ironclad alibi for why he or she left evidence at the crime scene."

"We certainly won't discount her," Karl said. "However, Lorra Rundle had a very good reason for going by the lab before breakfast.

She's participating in that big conference your folks are attending today. She went by to pick up some samples she wanted to have with her."

"I don't want it to be Lorra," Stephanie admitted. "She's Liz's partner. The two of them have gone out of their way to make us welcome."

"I know," Karl said, "but we can't let who we do and don't like color our investigation. We can't even let who the 'cats do and don't like influence us too much. They might not like someone for an entirely unconnected reason."

"Yeah," Stephanie agreed. "Not everyone here is exactly thrilled about my parents being invited to consult on how Gryphon's native plant and animal life might be modified to better suit human nutritional needs."

She looked disgusted and Karl knuckled her gently on the skull. "Well, it's not all that hard to understand, really, is it? I mean, for some of them, calling your folks in was like saying their own scientific teams are incompetent."

"That's blackhole thinking," Stephanie said. "My folks are talking as much about how some of their attempts have failed as about their successes. But so many humans are blackholes . . ."

Karl interrupted her. "Can we take the rant as written? I know your low opinion of the majority of the human race. Here's an idea I want to run by you. Because Gill wanted to take us out in the field with him, I'm guessing that his secret is going to be related to something he would have shown us."

"Why not to something else?" Stephanie shot back. "Maybe he'd discovered Lorra was fooling around with Ingo and wanted us to be the ones to tell Liz, because we don't live here full time." She knew she was being contrary, but she resented, just a little, how focused Karl was being.

She shuddered. Wasn't Karl at all nervous? Didn't he remember how horrible it had been back on Manticore when those hired thugs had tried to kidnap Lionheart? Stephanie hadn't been in the least scared at the time—adrenaline had kept her focused, but she still woke from nightmares of how it had felt to have someone's kneecap crack under the force of her kick. Sometimes the face of the thug attacking her had been that of Tennessee Bolgeo, who just might have killed her, for no better reason than greed. Other times the face wasn't human at all, but was dominated by the snarling fangs of the hexapuma who'd nearly killed both her and Lionheart years before.

Stephanie shivered again and wished, almost, that Lionheart would come and wrap his tail around her and bleek reassurance. *But Lionheart's tail is currently very soggy. Anyhow, Steph, haven't you felt lately that Lionheart thinks you need to deal with these things? Comfort isn't at all a good thing if it keeps you from coping with your fears.*

But if Lionheart was making Stephanie tough it out, Karl hadn't been as focused on the problem as Stephanie had thought. "Chilled, Steph?" he asked, wrapping an arm around her shoulder. "It's not cold compared to Sphinx, but it's not exactly hot. Those ocean breezes can be brisk."

"I'm okay," Stephanie said, enjoying the snuggle, then determinedly ducking free. "I got distracted. When you think about it, the killer has got to be someone who knew Gill well. I mean, Gill was shot at close range. That's creepy."

"Remember what we learned in criminology," Karl said. "Murder victims usually know their killers. Once we figure out what Gill's secret might have been, we should keep that in mind when narrowing the field."

"Go back to what you were saying about why Gill's secret is probably related to something he would have shown us." Stephanie thought she knew—she was far from dumb; in fact, she knew that by objective measures, she was brilliant. But she wanted to see how Karl's thoughts matched up with her own.

"Sure," Karl said, "but make me feel better and put on my jacket over yours. I've got a sweatshirt on underneath."

"Fine," she said, gratefully slipping into the roomy softness. "Now, talk."

"Mostly, it's how he said he'd tell us tomorrow," Karl admitted, "but also I think it was his insistence on taking us out with him. He'd chatted with us before, even showed us some holo images, but this field trip was new. I think he wanted us to see something, so we could—I don't know—testify? Images are so easily falsified. He might have wanted human witnesses unassociated with the local community. Those aren't easy to come by."

"You have a point," Stephanie agreed, "a good one. I wonder how we figure out where he'd have taken us?"

Karl considered. "We might be able pull something off the nav comp of the vehicles he most typically used. There's a general vehicle pool, but people tend to be assigned the same vehicles."

Stephanie's brown eyes flashed with excitement. "I remember Liz telling us that doing that made it easier for her to know who to blame for damage. Good thinking. Let's leave a message for my folks that we're going to take a drive to clear our heads, then go do some snooping."

※ ※ ※

At that hour, the vehicle bay was pretty much deserted; the crews who were going out into the field for the day had already left, and the people who had flown in for the conference had settled in various meeting rooms. A tech greeted them cheerily from under a battered-looking air truck where he was tinkering with something.

"You know where everything is?" he called.

"Sure, Kwei," Stephanie called back. "We're just going to take a drive."

"Okay. Your parents' assigned air car's in stall forty. You have the keys?"

Stephanie fished the fob out of her pocket and waved it at him.

"Works," he said. "Sign yourselves out on the terminal, would you? I've just about tracked where the break in this line is and I don't want to lose my place."

"No problem," Karl said, tapping his uni-link. After they'd signed out their car, Karl and Stephanie took advantage of the connection and downloaded whatever they could find regarding Gill Votano's recent activity.

"Gill hadn't registered a flight plan yet," Karl reported as they walked deeper into the garage, "but it looks as if he usually used Air Van 37. It's listed as still in its slot. Let's see what it can tell us."

Thirty-seven was in its assigned place. The rather battered-looking van had clearly been used hard, judging from the scratches and scrapes. Of course, it was a work vehicle, not someone's personal air car. It was bound to pick up dings and scratches out in the field, but one long scrape down its right side was deeper than any of the others. Its passenger area was unlocked, but the cargo bay, which held a variety of gear ranging from mundanities like shovels and picks, to some sleek devices that would have seemed perfectly at home on the bridge of a starship, was locked tight.

"Forgiveness not permission," Stephanie said, leaning into the cab. "I'm going to have that put on my coat of arms when I'm knighted."

Karl snorted, not deigning to reply to such a silly comment. Instead, he hooked his uni-link so he could download information from the van's nav comp. "You could be doing something useful, like making sure Kwei isn't wondering why we're over here. Or go fill the water bottles or fetch us lemonade, like a good little girl."

"Lionheart and Survivor are playing lava tag by jumping between the roofs of the vehicles," Stephanie retorted. "If Daryl isn't noticing that, he's not noticing us. You know the 'cats'll sense anyone new coming in long before we do. And our car is good to go. We can grab lemonade from the house on our way out. I'm going to stay close and make sure you don't screw something up."

Karl raised dark eyebrows in an "as if" expression, but his gaze was focused on the readout on his uni-link. He frowned, then made a startled exclamation.

"What!" Stephanie hissed, hand reaching automatically for the sidearm she wasn't wearing.

Karl grinned at her. "Nothing! Wanted to make you jump. Download's done. Let's get the 'cats out of here before someone complains about scratches on their paint."

"Pig," Stephanie said. "Just for that, I'm driving."

"No problem," Karl said. "After all, you had a great teacher. Me!"

Stephanie laughed. "I walked right into that one."

✖ ✖ ✖

When Stephanie pulled the air car to a stop in front of the Harrington's borrowed house, Karl looked up from his uni-link. "Hey, I wasn't serious about the lemonade. The water bottles are full. Let's go. I've found some interesting stuff."

Stephanie rubbed her chin. "I'm not stopping for lemonade. Well, not only lemonade. If we were at home and going into the bush, we'd be armed. Just because we're on another planet, I don't think we should be less careful."

Karl opened his mouth as if he'd been about to remind her that Gryphon didn't have the plethora of megafauna that blessed Sphinx, then he stopped, shut his mouth and nodded. "Yeah. Given what we're tracking, that's a good idea."

A few minutes later, they left the house, burdened not only with lemonade but with a sizeable picnic—and with handguns concealed beneath light jackets. They'd also taken time to put on their SFS ranger utility belts. Both were equipped with useful items like lights, vibro-knives, canteens, and compasses. Since Karl was an official assistant ranger, his belt included some more expensive items that Stephanie's lacked.

Returning to the air car, they found Erina Wether—affectionately known to all of Eureka Base as "Stormy Wether"—sitting on the curb, looking up at the car's roof.

Stormy was a grandmotherly older woman whose silvery hair was cut in a close cap that darkened to grey where it brushed the mid-point of her ears. Her slender brows were also dark, accenting lines that could be stern, but were more often cheerful. At this moment, her expression was quizzical as she leaned back, head tilted, looking to where Survivor and Lionheart were staring down at her from the car's roof.

Stormy waved and got to her feet as Stephanie and Karl approached. "When I saw the 'car, I thought Richard and Marjorie might be between sessions. I have some climate figures they asked me to put together for them."

"Sorry, Stormy," Stephanie said. "When I texted Mom earlier, she said they were going straight from the morning sessions to a lunch meeting, then on a lab tour before the afternoon sessions, then from there to a consultation over dinner. They invited us to join them for lunch, but..."

Stephanie trailed off, not wanting to be rude. Stormy's eyes twinkled and she laughed.

"...But a meal where every bite you eat is assessed for its nutritional value, possible ease of being genetically adapted, and a dozen other related items isn't very appetizing," Stormy finished for her. She gestured to the basket Karl held. "So you're going on a picnic?"

"We wanted to get out for a bit," Karl said. "We checked the weather for the next few hours. Looks as if it's safe enough to go for a flight. Any updates?"

Stormy shook her head. "Summer on Gryphon can be so nice that it fools you into thinking you're on Manticore, at least if you're near one of the seas. Still, it's never good to get careless. Thermal build-up can create unpredictable winds, and winds..."

She raised and lowered her shoulders in an elaborate shrug, more eloquent than any words. "Remember to keep an eye on the tides, too! They shift rapidly here. What was apparently solid ground can be underwater while you're napping on your beach towel."

Stephanie nodded. Egg, Gryphon's single moon, was quite a bit larger than Old Earth's Luna. In fact, it very nearly classified as a twin planet, and its sheer size meant Gryphon's shallow seas experienced very powerful tides.

"We'll be careful," she promised. The 'cats had flowed down into the air car's back seat and had each claimed a window. Their impatience to be moving was palpable.

Stormy smiled. "Have a nice picnic. If you haven't seen them already, the rock lilies up near Sunset Bluffs are lovely..."

With a wave, she went trotting off down the street.

"People here are so nice," Karl said wistfully.

"I know," Stephanie said, getting in on the driver's side, "but like you reminded me not too long ago, one of them's a cold-hearted killer."

⌘ ⌘ ⌘

<*That two-leg female,*> Keen Eyes said slowly, <*the taste of her mind-glow is off. You have more experience than I do. What is it?*>

Climbs Quickly considered. <*On the outside, she is full of smiles and laughter, but her insides are as grey and roiling as storm clouds.*>

Keen Eyes scratched at his belly with his left hand-foot. <*I wonder if whatever has Death Fang's Bane and Shining Sunlight so unsettled has unsettled her as well? Elders will dampen their mind glows lest they upset the kittens. This two-leg female has a grey pelt. Doesn't that usually indicate age?*>

<*It can,*> Climbs Quickly agreed. <*Though often they stain them dark, as if they would hide how many rings their tails bear. But, yes, you are right. This two-leg is an elder. Likely she seeks not to upset the younglings.*>

<*I wonder what happened?*> Keen Eyes said. <*I wish our two-legs could mind-speak like People, not rely on those confusing mouth noises.*>

Climbs Quickly bleeked laughter and moved to where he could better see out the clear side of the flying thing as Death Fang's Bane made it rise and speed away from the two-legs' settlement.

<Take it from me. This is not the last time you will wish that!>

※ ※ ※

Stephanie drove the air car low, staying close to the sea until they were out of direct line of sight from Eureka Base. Even when she turned inland, seeking one of the passes through the Shenin Mountains, she kept low. If anyone was watching them—and although she had no reason to think this was the case, why take risks?—they might wonder why Karl and Stephanie had chosen to picnic in the arid outback when there was so much delightful coastline to explore.

"It's not as if the vehicle can't be tracked," she commented, "but why make it easy for anyone to start wondering?"

Karl nodded. "When we're clear of the pass, let's set down so I can show you the map I've put together on my uni-link."

"Why not use the 'car's HUD?" Stephanie asked, then answered her own question, "Because, you don't want me distracted. Fair enough. 'Calm' conditions on Gryphon can still be gusty. According to the maps, there's a perfect spot about five minutes ahead. It even has a small spring. We can break out some of the lunch stuff while we're at it. Lionheart has been poking the back of my neck for the last half-hour. I think he smells the celery."

While they were noshing on slabs of dense bread topped with soft cheese, sweet-tart sting-fruit, and bullet-shaped "nuts" that tasted like pecans, but were actually the dried fruit of a Gryphon kelp, Karl pulled up a tri-d schematic on his uni-link.

"Back when Gill was showing us holos of some of the more fantastically shaped rock formations he'd seen the in outback," Karl said, "I asked for copies of some of the cooler ones. They're tagged with information regarding the location where they were taken. I cross-referenced that with the locations Gill mentioned in his published reports. They're all from basically the same region."

"But?" Stephanie bounced. "Give!"

"But when I triaged the information we downloaded regarding where Gill had been taking Air Van 37 so that it would omit Gill's usual work area, I came up with a substantial number of trips to a completely different section. I then ran that back against any mention at all in his reports—even minor ones, like a site visit. Guess what?"

"There's no mention of his doing any official work there."

"Super Genius Stephanie lives up to her reputation yet again," Karl said, dodging her punch and reaching for a sting-fruit. "Interested in taking a look at what's in that area?"

"Absolutely," Stephanie said, downing the last of her bread and cheese in a manner that would have made her mother wince. "Give me the coordinates."

Their destination proved to be a wide valley sharply cut from various colors of rock, as if Nature had spilled her paint box over a sculpture garden. Starkly beautiful reddish-orange sandstone predominated, but there was plenty of dark grey, muted green, honey yellow, and shimmering white. There were slender columns, massive arches, and pylons pierced with irregular windows. Hulking mesas towered like giant's furniture, dominating their surroundings.

"I bet anything that this is where Gill was going to take us," Stephanie said, her voice reverent. "Remember what he said about lots of big rocks for the 'cats to bounce on, almost like a forest? Check out over there."

Karl looked along the line of her pointing finger toward an assortment of striated columns. "I think you're right. Those are Gill's 'hoodoos,' for sure. Shall we go take a closer look?"

Stephanie maneuvered the air car with care. "This would be an interesting place to hang glide. The wind moving through the rocks creates really erratic air currents. The thermals are unpredictable, too. That 'forest' would make an interesting obstacle course."

"Maybe someday," Karl said, glancing between his uni-link and their surroundings. "Veer a little to the left and set us down in the shadow of that hoodoo that looks like a robed monk. That's about as close as I can get to where Gill went."

"You found it in one," Stephanie said, as she parked. "See that mark on the rock? Looks like a pretty good match for that deep scrape on Old 37, doesn't it? I'd say he parked here, more than once, probably."

"Shall we get out and scout around?" Karl suggested.

The way he was undoing his seatbelt and opening the door on his side of the air car made clear the suggestion was rhetorical. Stephanie locked the car's starter and followed suit. A moment later, she felt the solid thump at her back that meant Lionheart had assumed his customary perch with his hand-feet resting on her shoulder, and his true-feet resting on the brace built into the back of her jacket. This left his true-hand free for action—or for patting his human on the top of her head, which is what he did.

Survivor was riding Karl. The treecats were always careful in an unfamiliar area. Gryphon, with its lack of trees, was stranger than most places they'd been. Although the treecats had superlatively hard claws and very sharp fangs, their basic tactic involved getting above any problem, then dropping down where the pointy bits would do the most good. On heavily forested Sphinx, this was so easy as to be automatic, but Gryphon was becoming a study in caution.

"What are we looking for?" Stephanie wondered aloud.

"No idea," Karl admitted. "If we'd had time, I'd have dug through any news feed related to Gryphon to see if there was anything significant, like a lost experimental satellite or missing person. If we don't find anything in, say, an hour, we can go back to the car, finish the lemonade and cookies, and see what we can find in the news archives."

"Deal," Stephanie said. "Do we stay together or spread out?"

"Spread out," Karl said. "We've both got our links. Remember, Gryphon might not have hexapumas and peak bears, but it does have rock leopards and a whole variety of little nasties with big poisons."

Stephanie lifted one foot to show that she had—as Karl knew perfectly well—exchanged her sodden walking shoes for heavy boots during their stop at the house. She took a pair of light but strong gloves from her pocket and slid them on for protection in case she had to grab a sharp bit of rock.

"Should we try to lock the 'cats in the car?" she said, knowing that was perfectly impossible unless the treecats cooperated.

"Give them the choice," Karl said, "but I have the distinct impression that Survivor wants to go exploring."

※ ※ ※

<*If I was not seeing this with my own eyes,*> Climbs Quickly exclaimed, <*I would not believe a land could look like this!*>

Keen Eyes, beating his tail back and forth so vigorously that

Shining Sunlight reached back and held it still, percolated with excitement. *<I know! Look at those rocks! They* are *rocks, are they not? They smell of stone and dust, so they must be, but what amazing shapes! Do you think the winds cut them?>*

<Wind or water,> Climbs Quickly speculated. *<This area is dry now, but maybe there is a wet season or a snow season. We are like kittens born in summer who cannot believe that snow is real, even though they see it in the Memory Singer's images. A hand or so of days is not enough to know a place.>*

<I wonder what makes the rocks such colors?> Keen Eyes marveled. *<Those reds are as the sky at sunset. The yellow makes the foliage of golden leaf dim and fragile by comparison.>*

<And no leaves I know have such amazing stripes,> Climbs Quickly agreed. *<That rock trunk over there is banded like the tail of an elder of impossible age—if an elder's tail rings could be red and orange and pink and yellow. Even though we bring the memories home with us, the People will wonder if we somehow mistook dreams for reality.>*

<Seeing is not *enough,>* Keen Eyes stated, leaping down from his perch on Shining Sunlight. *<A scout must touch and smell, hear— even taste.>*

<Do not eat anything!> Climbs Quickly warned, wondering at his friend's fascination for learning through putting everything in his mouth.

<I am not an idiot kitten,> Keen Eyes replied, exasperated. *<I know that the littler the biter, the more likely a hidden sting. How else can they keep from getting eaten? But sometimes one can tell what a rock is made of by a little lick—whether there is salt or chalk, iron or copper. That is all I meant.>*

Climbs Quickly could taste the sincerity in Keen Eyes' mind-glow and was reassured. He did his best to reassure Death Fang's Bane that while he and Keen Eyes did indeed want to explore, they would take care and not go too far. He could not be sure she understood, but— perhaps because her own mind-glow was bright with curiosity—she did not fuss.

Although the two-legs were obviously delighted with their surroundings—pausing to exclaim over an enormous rock formation where a large rock seemed to balance on a narrow trunk or where a flat wall was pierced by holes, as the two-legs pierced the walls of their nests—they were also clearly scouting. They studied the ground, looking for tracks, examining any place where the rocks split into crannies, pockets, or narrow passages.

Keen Eyes, veering off to look at a cluster of scrubby plants with fat, spongy leaves, called to Climbs Quickly. *<Here and there, I catch a bit of what smells like two-leg scent. It is several days old, but strong here, where the plants give it something to cling to.>*

<I have caught such a time or two myself,> Climbs Quickly agreed. *<I admit, I did not consider that it might be important. Now that I think on it, perhaps our two-legs are seeking traces of another of their kind.>*

<I wonder if someone is lost?> Keen Eyes said. *<That would explain the concern we have tasted.>*

<The two-legs did not send out scouts,> Climbs Quickly replied, *<but perhaps the missing one is only late, not gone long enough to risk shaming him or her by sending out searchers. Humans do have pride in that manner. I am sure of it.>*

<I think we should help search, then,> Keen Eyes stated, his mind-glow warm with happiness that he might be able to relieve their friends of anxiety. *<We will be better at this than they are.>*

Climbs Quickly bleeked agreement. The scent they traced was faint, for the wind-scoured stone did not hold scent. After a time, Climbs Quickly caught a stronger patch, and his excitement brought Keen Eyes to join him.

<Found something?>

<Sniff for yourself.>

Keen Eyes did. *<Two-leg scent. Let me think . . . This is the Worried Male, isn't it? The one who was hiding something when he spoke with Death Fang's Bane and Shining Sunlight last night.>*

<That is who I smelled, too,> Climbs Quickly agreed. *<He must have been working here recently, but there is no sign of what he was doing, no digging or cutting.>*

<Maybe he was using one of those tools the two-legs have, like the image-maker or the voice-carrier,> Keen Eyes suggested. Then he lived up to his name, seeing something Climbs Quickly had missed. *<Look! He* was *digging, but he was careful to hide the signs of his working.>*

Impulsively, Keen Eyes bounded forward, trying to fit his claws around the edge of a concealing slab of stone to pull it free. Climbs Quickly joined him but, although they pulled together, the stone slab remained firmly in place.

<*Let us get Death Fang's Bane and Shining Sunlight,*> Climbs Quickly said. <*Even if they cannot lift it, they could use one of their make-it-lighter things to move it easily.*>

<*Good thought,*> Keen Eyes agreed.

※ ※ ※

When Lionheart came racing up, his leaf-green eyes wide with excitement, Stephanie didn't need a shared language to know he'd found something he wanted to show her. Nor was she surprised when her uni-link chimed a moment later and Karl's voice said, "Steph, you okay?"

"I'm fine," she replied, laughing. "Let me guess. Survivor just charged up to you, and wants to show you something."

"That's it. Since I don't think you've suddenly become clairvoyant, I'm guessing that Lionheart did the same."

"And now that we're reassured neither of us are injured or something," Stephanie said, "shall we find out what they think is so important?"

"Meet you wherever," Karl agreed.

Stephanie thought Lionheart was excited rather than frightened but, nonetheless, she gave a quick check where her handgun nestled in its shoulder holster, making sure the deadly thing was ready. During an emergency was *not* the time to find out you'd left your gun in the air car or forgotten to reload. Stephanie never did either of these things, but double-checking was one reason why she didn't.

The place to which Lionheart guided her proved to be a massive, elegantly striped red and gold sandstone mesa that dominated the surrounding area. The base of the mesa was deep in pale gold sand, muffling footsteps and making walking difficult. When Karl and Survivor joined them, the two pairs met up near where the striped overhang had sluffed off several slabs of stone, which now lay piled like irregularly shaped pillows against the base of the mesa.

"Pretty," Karl said, and might have said more, but Survivor and Lionheart had rushed, twin flows of cream and grey against the golden sand, to tug at one of the stone slabs.

"Right!" Stephanie said, pushing her way in. "If you want us to take a look, you're going to have to move over."

"Stephanie," Karl reminded. "Spiders, snakes, scorpions, and other nasty things not necessarily beginning with 's,' remember?"

Stephanie held up a gloved hand. "I'm guessing the 'cats wouldn't let me get close if they smelled something nasty but, you're right. This isn't Sphinx. They might not *know* what's nasty. I promise not to stick my hand in anywhere—even if I could, which I can't. There isn't any obvious crack or crevice here, but I think I see why the 'cats are so worked up. It's hard to see unless you're right on top of it, but this rock shows scraping marks, like it's been moved."

"Recently," Karl agreed, kneeling down next to her to take a closer look. "Definitely not when it dropped off the main rock face. Do you think we can move the slab?"

Stephanie gave an experimental tug. "Possibly with both of us, but let's use counter-grav. If this is part of Gill's secret, that's what he would have had to do. He couldn't have possibly moved it by himself."

Karl unbuckled his SFS-issue utility belt. It incorporated a personal counter-gravity unit which was useful only too often on high-gravity Sphinx, and it was specifically designed to adhere to heavy objects that needed moving.

Inspecting the slight wear marks on the various pieces of stone, they estimated the best place to anchor the unit, then both stepped back while Karl operated the unit remotely. When no drowsy desert-dweller surged forth to protest this invasion of its space, Stephanie went forward to help guide the stone slab to one side and lean it against the cliff face.

"A cave!" she exclaimed, once she had a clear look. "Or a big crevice, at least. I think we could both get in there." She removed a small light unit from her belt and flicked it on, shining it up and down the sides of the crevice so they could get a better look. The crevice was high enough that she could walk in without ducking and even tall Karl would only need to bend a little.

"Check ahead," Karl suggested, "and see if it opens out."

Stephanie nodded, then glanced over at Lionheart. The treecat was sniffing at the edges of the crevice, his long whiskers curling forward. Interested, then, but not apprehensive. When Stephanie began to edge her way in, Lionheart immediately joined her, taking point. Knowing that treecats saw very well in low light, Stephanie kept her beam close, making sure she didn't trip over something hidden in the thick sand.

"Oh! Here's something interesting," she called back to Karl. "No footprints for the first ten meters or so, but now I'm seeing some. The sand is soft, so the prints don't have much shape, but they're about the right size to be Gill's."

"Only him?" Karl asked, his voice echoing slightly against the enclosing wall.

"I think so," Stephanie said. She stopped and used her uni-link to take some pictures, then continued forward, avoiding the prints when she could.

Now that they were certain the crevice went somewhere, Karl came after, inspecting the walls and floor with his light. The treecats climbed along the walls themselves, where rough surfaces provided ample purchase for powerful treecat muscles and sharp claws.

"Another thing," Karl commented. "This crevice is natural, but it's been expanded here and there, so someone human-sized could get through. The upper walls are pretty rough, but you can see where the lower areas were cut."

"More and more interesting," Stephanie said.

They had advanced a hundred and seventy meters or so from the entrance when Stephanie felt the air move and freshen. "There's a slight draft," she said. "We're probably coming to an opening. I see light ahead."

A dozen or so strides later, Stephanie found herself in an open area formed where the striped sandstone met another type of rock. This second rock was a pale moss-green, with a smooth, glossy surface and veined with something almost black. Where the light hit it, the green rock shimmered from tiny flecks of mica caught in its matrix. High above, through a narrow slot, Stephanie could glimpse the sky but, otherwise, the rock walls closed in, pinching at the ends to form an eye-shaped canyon about twenty meters wide and three times that long. No plants grew here, nor did any of Gryphon's insect or lizard analogs scamper for a hiding place, giving Stephanie the sense that she'd entered a sanctuary dedicated to some strange desert religion.

Turning slowly to inspect her surroundings, Stephanie speculated aloud. "Sandstone's pretty soft—as rock goes. This green rock looks igneous, not sedimentary, though. It's much harder, anyway. I'm guessing that, over time, wind and water action eroded the sandstone, creating this pocket. From above, it must be nearly invisible, unless someone came right to the edge and looked down. Even then, they'd mostly see shadows."

"I see your geology units weren't wasted," Karl teased. "Y'know, even with counter-grav, it would be a pain getting any equipment down here through that slot—not to mention pretty hard to hide what you were doing or that you'd left an air car up there. Let's look around and see if we can find what brought Gill here."

"I don't think we need to do much searching," Stephanie said, pointing with her light to where Lionheart and Survivor were bouncing up and down in front of a segment of the green rock. "Our scouts have already found it."

Beneath the pleased gazes of two pairs of leaf-green eyes, the humans inspected an area where the moss green rock had been carefully cut away to reveal a vein of a dark blue, slightly crystallized mineral.

Karl grunted in satisfaction. "Looks as if someone other than wind and water were excavating here. So, Miss Geology, do you recognize this mineral?"

"Other than that it isn't any of the common ones we learned about in our geology unit," Stephanie replied, "I don't. You?"

Karl shook his head, angling his uni-link to take some pictures. "Still, I'm willing to bet that if an expert like Gill Votano was interested in whatever it is, it's probably something rare."

"Rare enough to get him killed?" Stephanie asked, but that wasn't really a question. Gill had been hiding something. Secrets, even those kept for the best reasons, could be deadly, something she knew all too well.

Karl straightened. "We'll take a sample, then go back and check these images against one of the larger databases. Once we know what this mineral is, we'll have a better idea of its value. After that, we should have what we need to convince Liz to take a second look at Gill's 'suicide.'"

⌘ ⌘ ⌘

The two People could taste the satisfaction pouring off their two-legs like water during ice melt time. They reveled in it as they led the way back through the tunnel in the striped red rock, already anticipating clusterstalk and sweet, cold water.

<We helped them,> Keen Eyes commented with a satisfied flick of his tail.

<We certainly did,> Climbs Quickly agreed. <Death Fang's Bane and Shining Sunlight are very good scouts for two-legs, especially Shining Sunlight, but this barren land is as new to them as it is to us. I am astonished how a place without many growing things can hide so much. Even though the two-legs set their flying thing down near that big, striped rock, they would certainly have missed the hole, covered as it was.>

<I wonder why Worried Male went to so much trouble to hide a section of rock?> Keen Eyes asked. <Even though the area the tunnel led into was sheltered, I cannot believe he meant to nest there.>

<What two-legs value still mystifies me,> Climbs Quickly admitted. <But that second piece of rock, the one Shining Sunlight was so careful to cut a piece from, that was crucial.>

<Maybe . . . > Keen Eyes stopped in mid-thought and mid-motion, poised as if he'd become part of the stone wall. <I taste a two-leg's mind-glow. Distant but familiar . . . >

Climbs Quickly suspected, although he would never rub his friend's nose in it, that he was better at tasting the varied elements of mind-glows. <It is the female who was watching us before we left the central nesting place. She is very worried and maybe angry. I cannot tell what troubles her, though.>

<Could it be because our two-legs have seemingly vanished? They are younglings among their kind.>

<I am not certain,> Climbs Quickly said. <This tastes more like worry for self than worry for another. And it does not taste like the anger an adult feels at a wayward kitten, either. I know Death Fang's Bane does not wish me to attack two-legs unless they attack first. Sometimes though . . . A warning bite, not piercing the skin. How could that hurt?>

Keen Eyes' mind-glow made quite clear that *he* knew why it could hurt, but he understood his friend's frustration. Not long ago, in the Hot Lands, Climbs Quickly, Death Fang's Bane, and Shining Sunlight had fought off some two-legs who had intended to capture Climbs Quickly. This was not the first time Climbs Quickly had been forced to deal with two-legs whose outer smiles hid far darker natures within.

<We will warn our two-legs,> Keen Eyes said, and leapt down to press his true-hands against Death Fang's Bane's leg. They had used such gestures before to slow the younglings when there was something dangerous near, so Death Fang's Bane stopped immediately. Shining Sunlight would have crashed into her if he had not sensed Keen Eyes' changed mood.

Climbs Quickly, for his part, leapt to Death Fang's Bane's shoulder. Patting her cheek so she would look at him, he slowly moved his head from side to side in the motion that meant "No" among the two-legs. Then softly, not as threat, but as emphasis, he hissed.

⚹ ⚹ ⚹

"Something's wrong up ahead," Stephanie said softly.

Karl's reply was to nod, reach for his handgun, then stop. "We can't shoot here. Remember those slabs under the cliff? We might trigger another rockslide."

"But do we just march into the hexapuma's den?" Stephanie asked. "I suppose we could retreat, climb up to the slot in the rock back in the canyon."

Karl shook his head, not so much in negation as in concern. "If they know about this crevice—which was so carefully hidden—then they know about that one. I'd have it covered."

"I wish the 'cats could tell us who's out there," Stephanie fretted. "But, even if they could, that wouldn't help much. Hate to do it, but we'd better com for help."

She activated her uni-link, touched the emergency override that would reach both her parents. The override was restricted for really, really bad emergencies—"Like drowning" her dad had said.

We're not drowning, but if there's a murderer out there, I think this qualifies. If it's a false alarm, I'll apologize later.

Stephanie counted seconds, betting that either her mom or dad would pick up in less than five seconds. Five stretched to ten. Stephanie examined the uni-link more closely.

"The signal isn't going out!" she said, the softness of her voice not concealing her shock.

Karl didn't ask dumb questions, only tabbed his own link. "Mine either. Either this rock is blocking the signal or—more likely—whoever is out there brought a high-powered jammer."

Stephanie nodded and let her wrist drop to her side. The jamming confirmed that whoever was out there was not a friend.

"We've estimated that treecats can sense to about two hundred meters in areas without a lot of conflicting signals," Karl continued. "Shame we don't have low-light gear with us. It would make getting closer undetected easier."

Stephanie forced a grin, dipped a hand into an inner pocket, and passed Karl a set of lightweight goggles, chuckling deep in her throat at the soft sound of surprise he made. "Well, we were going after a geologist's trail," she said, "and geologists study rocks, and rocks are often best studied underground. These aren't military grade, but they're pretty good. Mom and Dad brought them for late night botanizing and animal spotting."

"Forgiveness not permission, again," Karl said, gently cuffing her curls. "Good thinking, Steph."

Together they moved forward, keeping to the edges of the tunnel. The 'cats dropped down to ride on their human's shoulders, tense and alert. The low light gear made possible a stealthy approach, but Stephanie knew that eventually one or more of them would be visible from the crevice's mouth. Stephanie was framing her argument why she should be the one to rush out first when she heard a hiss, joined quickly by another, then another. Something cool flavored the air with a not unpleasant tang.

She barely had time to think "Gas!" before her head was swimming, and she stumbled. Behind her, Karl coughed. Stephanie thumbed at her uni-link, hoping it would not be completely useless.

She fell, Climbs Quickly falling with her, thrust out her hands to cushion the fall, met golden sand, then darkness.

❋ ❋ ❋

The inside of Climbs Quickly's head felt like raw egg. His eyes burned with dryness, as if he had not blinked for far too long. His guts felt tied in knots. His ears would not twitch, and his tail hung like a rope behind him. Seeking the brightness that was Death Fang's Bane, he found it curiously muted, as if she slept without dreams, without even a sleeper's awareness of her body. Her breathing was shallow and uneven.

Questing out, Climbs Quickly found the equally muted mind glows of Keen Eyes and Shining Sunlight. Another mind glow, this one crisp and unimpaired, warbled a song of dark triumph from a short distance away. Warned by that heartless glee, Climbs Quickly stopped trying to move, concentrating instead on his vision. People had two sets of eyelids. Although the outermost of his remained partly open, the other had protected his eyes from damage. Concentrating with all his might, Climbs Quickly sought to move only the inner lids in a slow blink to clear his clouded vision.

The effort seemed to help his other senses as well. His nose told him that he was in the back portion of the flying thing that they had ridden in earlier. Tantalizingly, he could even catch the faint scent of clusterstalk, though his tormented belly warned him against trying to eat. His nose also told him who the clear mind-glow belonged to: the silver-pelted female two-legs he now tagged as Poisoner.

Having ascertained where he was and that there was little useful he could do, Climbs Quickly concentrated on getting control of his body. Knowing that the two-legs needed to give at least some attention to guiding the flying things, he risked wriggling each of his fingers and toes, starting with his true-feet and moving forward to his remaining true-hand. Next, he slowly worked each joint of his tail. He was considering whether he should try to move his legs when he became aware that Keen Eyes' mind-glow had brightened.

Shaping images with great care, Climbs Quickly shared what he had learned with his friend. Perhaps because he had slept somewhat longer, Keen Eyes grasped the situation well.

<I cannot move with any speed,> Keen Eyes complained. <And my mouth is dry as dust. Even if we attacked Poisoner, we could not operate the flying thing. What should we do?>

<Poisoner is taking us somewhere in particular,> Climbs Quickly replied. <If we have misread her and she takes us safely to Healer and Plant Minder, then all is well and good. However, if she means harm— as we both suspect she does—then she will need to set the flying thing down before she acts. We will bide our time until then.>

How much time passed before Poisoner brought the flying thing to rest, Climbs Quickly could not judge. Strength returned to him in increments, but even small exertions caused his mind to swim and his vision to dance. Nonetheless, when he heard Poisoner's footsteps crisp and purposeful against gravel, he readied himself to fight if he felt harm coming to Death Fang's Bane or Shining Sunlight.

Although Poisoner's mood grew, if anything, darker and more twisty, she moved with care, even gentleness, as she began to take items out of the flying thing. First came a thick blanket that the two-legs sat on when eating outside. This she spread on an area where the gravel gave way to sand. Next came the basket holding the remnants of the earlier meal. Then she lifted out Keen Eyes, who disciplined himself to limp stillness with admirable courage. He was set near one edge of the blanket. Shining Sunlight was moved next, this time with the help of a making-lighter thing. He was positioned on the blanket, then Keen Eyes was moved, as if he cuddled up to him in sleep.

As Climbs Quickly himself and then Death Fang's Bane were moved into a similar pose, Climbs Quickly began to understand what Poisoner intended. Dying as a result of attack was something the two-legs would investigate, but death as a result of accident—perhaps from bad food or an attack by some of the little biters of which this sandy land had so many . . . Would the two-legs look for another cause?

When Poisoner finished her work, she brought out a container about the size of the food basket, and shook the contents into the rocks a short distance from the blanket. She looked down at the apparently sleeping foursome and made a series of mouth noises, then turned away and tapped the wrist thing that seemed to control so many of the two-legs' marvels. A short time later, another flying thing swooped down to land beside the one in which they had arrived. There was no one in the second one, and Poisoner climbed inside. Then it rose into the air and lifted beyond Climbs Quickly's vision.

<*I am watching,*> Keen Eyes said, sensing Climbs Quickly's puzzlement. <*She is leaving . . . Now the size of a rock-squirrel, now of a beetle, now a dot. Gone. Can you stand?*>

Climbs Quickly tried and was pleased to find his careful exercising of his limbs had done a great deal of good. He was unsteady, but could stand and even walk, although there was a wobble to his gait. Death Fang's Bane and Shining Sunlight continued unmoving, but he tasted how the emptiness of their sleep had begun to invite dreams.

<*We must guard those two,*> he said to Keen Eyes. <*They are not*

going to wake for some time and when they do, they will be weak as newborn kittens. Somehow, I do not think Poisoner brought us to this place so we could admire the flowers or the rich red of this rock.>

Mind-glow alive with agreement, Keen Eyes wobbled over to the basket that held food. *<There is water here and clusterstalk, both. We will get stronger faster if we refresh ourselves.>*

Climbs Quickly consulted his stomach and found that it agreed with Keen Eyes' assessment. *<Bring the food. I want to keep watch— especially near where Poisoner shook out that box. I wonder what seeds she may have planted?>*

Keeping careful watch, they consumed not only the water and clusterstalk, but also a large portion of some sort of meat. Yet neither was so distracted that they missed motion among the flower-shadowed rocks. A horrid creeping thing about as long as one of Climbs Quickly's own limbs emerged, moving sinuously through the sand. It had three limbs in front, like elongated, jointless fingers that dragged a thicker, wriggling after part.

<Not good!> Keen Eyes stiffened, arching his back and hissing. *<We were warned to avoid those when we first arrived!>*

<Doubtless,> Climbs Quickly replied with a dry bleek of laughter, *<they feared you would try to eat one.>*

He cast about, looking for a way to stop the creeping horror without touching it directly. It was difficult to attack something if you did not know what parts were dangerous. Keen Eyes shared Climbs Quickly's concern. Grabbing the narrow container which had held water, he lifted it up and drove it down onto the creeping thing's purple hide. Had the surface been honest rock or packed dirt, the creature would have been squashed, but it merely sank more deeply into the sand and began to wriggle itself free.

Climbs Quickly dug through the gravel until he found a sharp-edged stone. Gripping this in his more powerful hand-feet, he brought it down hard on the thing, where the three "fingers" joined the larger hind part. The purple stuff proved to be a hard outer shell, while the interior of the thing was like tough leather, but Climbs Quickly managed to half-cut, half-tear the thing into parts. Like the most persistent—and most stupid—of the biters at home, the monstrosity continued to move for a time before dying. Inspection revealed that its underside held not only tiny whiskers that served it as legs, but a series of lipless mouths that oozed a milky liquid only slightly lighter than its shell. The mouths on what Climbs Quickly found himself thinking of as the "arm" were larger, ringed with jagged serrations that surely served at least as well as teeth.

<Nasty!> Keen Eyes said. <I somehow doubt that is the last of them. Could we get the two-legs safely into their flying thing? They're vulnerable here on the ground, especially with their naked skin.>

<Even if we both dragged,> Climbs Quickly said, <I do not think we could move Death Fang's Bane—much less Shining Sunlight. Everything may be lighter here, but I think our two-legs would still be beyond us. We will need to defend them until whatever Poisoner gave them wears off.>

<Now that we know the creeping biters keep their mouths below,> Keen Eyes said, <fighting them will be easier. Still, I do not think we should touch them. There are both plants and animals that wear poison on their skins.>

<This place has plenty of rocks,> Climbs Quickly replied with a grand gesture. <Help yourself.>

At first the creeping biters came in ones, then ones and twos. These the pair handled easily. Unlike two-legs, they did not need to look around for each to know where the other stood. They *knew*, even as they knew when one set of eyes spotted a newly emerging threat. As long as the creeping biters came in small groups, Climbs Quickly and Keen Eyes worked as a team, one pinning the creeping biter, the other cutting it into parts, preferably where the three fingers met the "arm."

Too soon, though, whether angered by the smell of their dying kindred or driven by some other impulse, the creeping biters surged from their rocky shelter in larger groups. The People's fur gave them some protection, for the creeping biters did not seem to understand that thick fur was not the same as skin and wore themselves out streaking the People with sticky goo. This was fine until a creeping biter, whether by luck or design, squeezed a long rope of purple goo where Keen Eyes' fur was still thin.

He wailed in pain, shrieking as it ate into his skin. Climbs Quickly caught an echo of his friend's agony, as did Shining Sunlight. Shining Sunlight was wrenched from the torpor that had claimed him. Like some sort of warrior tree come to sudden life, the towering two-legs lurched to his feet. Enraged, he grabbed the monstrosity off Keen Eyes and flung it away. Then, analyzing the situation with admirable swiftness, he reached for his thunder barker and smashed the approaching wave of creeping biters with well-aimed shots.

Death Fang's Bane rolled to her knees, then staggered over to the flying thing. Not for nothing was she the daughter of the one the People revered as Healer. She tore through the box of healing supplies, seizing first water to wash away the slime, then a spray that numbed the pain between one screech and another.

Roiling away from the sound—or perhaps the vibration—of the thunder barker, the remaining creeping biters fled for the shelter of the rocks, leaving behind them a sandy stretch smeared with purple goo.

Climbs Quickly continued to keep watch, even as Death Fang's Bane cleaned the worst of the burning guck from his coat. Still shivering from little jolts of pain, Keen Eyes watched the other flank.

<The creeping biter hit a place where I had gotten scratched and the skin was raw,> he explained apologetically. <It felt like mingled salt and bitter fruit juice.>

Death Fang's Bane and Shining Sunlight—both still far from steady on their feet—bundled the blanket and the rest of their gear into the flying thing, giving each item many careful shakes first. Then they called for the two People to join them.

How Death Fang's Bane brought them safely back would forever be a mystery to Climbs Quickly, for as soon as all were inside and the flying thing in the air, he and Keen Eyes collapsed in a fatigue nearly as deep as death.

❌ ❌ ❌

"We have evidence," Stephanie announced as soon as Richard and Marjorie Harrington returned from their final meeting of the day, "that Gill Votano was murdered and by whom. Can you help us?"

"You're kidding!" Richard exclaimed, then looked at them and shook his head. "You're not." He dropped his data case and other gear onto the nearest table. "Give us a quick briefing."

"First," Karl said, "can you call Liz Freeth here? We don't want to waste time repeating ourselves. Tell her you're worried because we haven't come in yet. That's important. We don't want it known we're back."

Once upon a time, the senior Harringtons might have argued or asked for details but, in the last few years, they'd learned to trust Stephanie and Karl's judgement. Liz Freeth wasn't thrilled to be called out this late, nonetheless, true to her "mother hen" nature, she arrived, clucking with concern.

She was astonished to see the "missing" pair seated side by side on the sofa. "What?"

"We have something tough to tell you," Karl said. "Let me check something with you. Who's the senior law enforcement officer on Gryphon?"

"We don't have one," Liz said. "When there's trouble one of the on-planet administrators can't handle, we restrain the troublemakers, com Manticore, and someone is sent out."

"That means I'm the senior officer," Karl said. "In my role as such, I would ask you to please do two things. One, can you make sure Erina Wether doesn't leave Eureka Base?"

Liz blinked, but she hadn't managed to excel in her job without having a certain amount of flexibility. "I don't have police officers or anything like that to call on, but I can com Lorra and ask her to keep an eye on Stormy's house—if she's there."

Stephanie smiled tightly. "She is. We have the 'cats keeping watch. They're good guards, but they couldn't stop Stormy if she got in a vehicle."

Liz shook her head and commed her partner. "Now, tell me what this is about."

Karl grinned. "Listening to that was the second thing I was going to ask you to do. Tea? Cocoa? Coffee? Sit down. It's a long story."

They started at the beginning. Fatigue dropped off the older Harringtons as they listened, helped by the refreshments Stephanie handed around. Liz accepted tea, but she was so focused that it grew cold in her hands.

"As soon as I realized we were being gassed," Stephanie concluded, "I set my uni-link on both audio and visual record. I have the whole file saved, but here's a short montage of the key bits that Karl put together on the way home, after we'd both taken a stimshot from the medkit in the air car. We left the car, by the way, hidden on the outskirts, then came in on foot."

"Stormy Wether," Marjorie breathed in disbelief. "But she's so nice!"

Karl shook his head. "Not so nice. Look here, right before she leaves us."

The holo-image wasn't great, but there was no doubt who was speaking. "I wish I could've worked it so I could make it look as if you'd snacked on something poisonous. That would be more certain. Still, the billipedes should provide a more convincing accident. I'll think of you when I'm living in style somewhere far, far away from here."

"But why?" Liz said. "I don't doubt you, but why?"

Stephanie keyed up the holos they'd taken of Gill's hidden excavation. Karl presented the mineral sample. "It's about this rock. Do you have any idea what it is?"

"None," Liz said, "but Lorra should be able to tell us. First, though, Karl, you and I need to arrest Stormy and get her safely locked down. I think we should take Jorge Prakel into custody as well."

"Why?" Karl asked, as he rose to his feet, checking his belt for restraints and that his gun was in place.

"Because Stormy and Jorge have an 'understanding.' I suspect he provided the knock-out gas and maybe even served as back up. For all I know, he overlooked a few things about Gill Votano's wounds in his medical examiner's report, too." She smiled thinly. "I do watch over my flock, I do. I dearly failed one here, but thanks to you, justice will be done."

※ ※ ※

Jorge Prakel broke as soon as Liz and Karl showed up at his residence and confronted him. In return for a recommendation of leniency, he admitted to helping Stormy by providing the knock-out gas, acting as back-up guard, and overlooking anything that would get in the way of Gill Votano's death being accepted as suicide. He claimed that he'd had no idea that Stormy intended to kill Karl and Stephanie. The gas had actually been set in place for Gill, but when Stormy had realized that Gill meant to confide in the off-worlders, she'd upped her timetable regarding him.

"And for all we know," Richard Harrington said judiciously the next evening, when the Harrington party dined with Liz and Lorra at their comfortable house, "Jorge was telling the truth. The knockout gas was effective but unlikely to cause any problems other than a walloping hangover. He couldn't have known that the treecats metabolize differently and would come around more quickly."

Left unsaid was, *And how smart they are.* Suspicions of treecat intelligence would remain a jealously guarded secret as long as the treecats' legal status remained a matter of debate.

Liz nodded. "Stormy is still refusing to give a statement but, from Gill's papers and Lorra's analysis, we can piece together what must have happened. Lorra, tell them what you found out."

Lorra Rundle didn't seem to share anything with her partner other than the first letter of their names. Where Liz was short, fair, and round-figured. Lorra was tall, dark, and lean, with some of the manic energy of a ferret.

"Warshawskium," Lorra said, tossing the sample back and forth between her hands. "That's what. It's a rare earth, very valuable. It's used in every gravitic engineering application. It can be produced artificially, but the process is complicated and expensive. It's a lot cheaper and more efficient to extract the naturally occurring rare earth from the host mineral. Most people wouldn't recognize it, but Stormy was a rock hound, always talking about how someday she'd strike it rich. Thing is, while skoldian may contain warshawskium, it doesn't always. I'm guessing Stormy asked Gill to test it for her. Then she told him to keep quiet, because she was going to make them both very rich."

"That particular parcel of land," Liz put in, "is the property of an absentee landlord who, like most of those who own land on Gryphon, would be just as happy to sell it off. I've found a few preliminary queries in Stormy's files. My guess is that Stormy planned to buy the land, then resell it—after revealing the value of the minerals and jacking up the price accordingly."

"I wonder what happened with Gill?" Karl said. "Did she just not want to cut him in?"

"Either that or he started feeling guilty about stealing from the landowner. He had a conscience. That's one reason his wife left him. He wasn't ambitious enough to bend his reports to make himself look better."

"Poor guy," Stephanie sighed. "At least his kids won't be saddled with the guilt that he killed himself over them. That's something."

"That's a lot," Liz said. "You two have done very well. A murderer is no longer free. You may have even saved Jorge's life, too. Stormy has demonstrated a definite desire to leave no witnesses. Jorge might have been the next person to have an 'accident,' although, I suspect, not here on Gryphon."

"This certainly has been an educational trip," Marjorie added with a laugh. "Karl's proven himself as a reliable law officer, and one probationary ranger will surely have positive notes added to her record."

"It's been educational in lots of ways," Stephanie agreed somberly. "But even though Karl and I did our part, we're not the heroes of the day. That award goes to Lionheart and Survivor. Not only did they find the hidden crevice, but if they hadn't saved us, none of this would have come out and you'd be planning a couple of funerals, not dreaming of promotions."

The six humans raised their glasses to two treecats who paused in their systematic shredding of celery and sea bass to blink two pairs of leaf-green eyes.

"Bleek!" the 'cats acknowledged in unison. "Bleek! Bleek! Bleek!"

THE SILESIAN COMMAND

Jan Kotouč

Evelyn Chandler did a last quick check on her new uniform before proceeding to the pinnace hatch. The uniform which no longer included a white beret. In the past, Chandler might have looked at it with apprehension; indeed there were times when she had dreaded the time when she would no longer be in charge of her own ship. Now, it was simply one more reality she had accepted.

The flight engineer gave the thumbs-up to indicate safe seal and opened the hatch. Eve stepped out and floated down the connecting tube. Captain Angelique Strauss, the other passenger aboard pinnace *Juliet Papa One*, was just two meters behind her.

A line on the deck indicated where the gravity field started again and also marked the official beginning of the boat bay of Her Majesty's Ship *Nicator*. The boat bay was huge compared to the one Chandler and Strauss had just left behind them, and despite the fact that this was a pre-pod design, it also reminded Chandler of her old superdreadnought command, which she had held only three months ago.

She caught the grab bar and swung across the interface into *Nicator*'s internal gravity, and the bosun's electronic pipes whistled sharply and the side party came to attention.

"Cruiser Squadron Fifty arriving," the boat bay officer announced as Chandler's foot touched the deck.

"Permission to come aboard, Lieutenant?"

"Permission granted, Ma'am."

"*Juggernaut* arriving" was the next call as Captain Strauss stepped into the boat bay as well.

Eve exchanged salutes with the BBOD, and then the young lieutenant stepped aside and made room for the short dark woman in the white beret. Chandler herself was rather small, but this woman couldn't be taller than one hundred and fifty centimeters. Twenty less than Chandler herself.

"Welcome aboard, Commodore," she said. "And welcome to Silesia. I'm Captain Beáta Robinson. Admiral Sarnow sends his compliments and he is expecting you in the briefing room."

"Thank you, Captain Robinson." Eve shook her hand, then indicated Strauss, who was the tallest and also thinnest of the three of them. "This is Captain Angelique Strauss, my flag captain."

Robinson and Strauss exchanged handshakes, and then Captain Robinson's gaze shifted back to Eve. "If you'd follow me, Ma'am. Captain."

The lift car trip was long, and Robinson tried to make small talk, but Chandler wasn't in a talkative mood. Strauss however substituted nicely, and the other two women began to discuss the uneventfulness of the voyage to Silesia and then moved on to the issue of the events of the last few months. Eve listened, but she seldom volunteered any information. After all, why say anything? It had all been said before. After five years of armistice, the Star Kingdom of Manticore was once again at war against the Republic of Haven. As if that wasn't enough, Manticore and the Andermani Empire had formed an alliance and carved Silesia in half. Combine that with the fall of the High Ridge government, the withdrawal of Erewhon from the Alliance, and the disastrous destruction of the Grendelsbane shipyards and it could be called a very interesting few months. In the Chinese sense of the word.

The sudden eruption of hostilities was also the reason one Captain Eve Chandler found herself promoted to commodore, given command of a heavy cruiser squadron, and expedited to Silesia, all in the space of a few weeks.

The lift car came to a stop and Robinson led them down the last few corridors before to the flag briefing room. The Marine sentry announced them, and Eve and the two captains entered.

"Commodore Chandler and Captain Strauss of *Juggernaut*, Admiral," Robinson said.

Admiral of the Red Sir Mark Sarnow sat at the far end of the table. There were two other officers present. One was a captain of the list with the braided aiguilette of a staff officer, but the other was a captain (JG) who was neither a staff officer nor wore the white beret of a starship commander. He looked a little out of place, but Chandler focused on Sarnow, who smiled slightly as she entered, then stood up and walked towards the newcomers.

"Commodore Chandler, welcome to Silesia! And it's good to see you again!"

"Thank you, Sir. It's good to see you again, too," Eve said and meant it. Sarnow had reminded her of the simpler times, before... Well, of happier times. "This is Captain Strauss, my flag captain."

Another round of introductions.

"You didn't bring your chief of staff with you?" Sarnow asked then.

"I don't *have* a chief of staff at the moment. I'm afraid my squadron got its orders to sail at extremely short notice. I had a chief of staff, but he took personal leave two days before we departed— family issues—and BuPers didn't have time to find me a replacement. So now Captain Strauss shares a piece of that responsibility along with my operations officer and my flag lieutenant."

"No surprise. Last time I checked, you commanded *Queen Samantha* in Home Fleet."

"You're right, Sir. I commanded *Samantha* up until a few weeks ago. Then one day I got rushed to the Fifth Space Lord's office with the explanation that I was being promoted to commodore, given a cruiser squadron, and spacing out to Silesia ASAP."

Sarnow chuckled. "I know the feeling well. That's how I got the Silesian command, except that I was ushered directly to the Queen." He noticed the puzzled look on the other officers in the room. "Commodore Chandler and I served together on *Nike* at Hancock. She was Duchess Harrington's tac officer."

"Ah," Robinson said, and a new look of appreciation came to her face. Duchess Harrington had attained almost legendary status and many of her former subordinates had risen high in their own careers.

"You were also bumped to exec after Hancock, am I right?" Sarnow continued.

"Yes, Sir. I was *Nike*'s executive officer during refit and then during the campaign at Santander and Nightingale under Captain Van Wyhe."

Sarnow's smiled disappeared. "I also heard about your daughter, Eve. You have my condolences."

Chandler's face lost all emotion. "Thank you, Sir."

Strauss knew the story. The others apparently didn't, but decided not to ask. Sarnow indicated the other two officers in the briefing room. The staff officer was a broad-shouldered man with dark hair and a double chin.

"This is Captain Avery Talisien, my chief of staff. And this is Captain Lucius Hagen of the . . . BuShips, Office of Maintenance."

That made Eve pause while she shook hands. Hagen was a thin man with fair hair and totally forgettable features. He noticed Eve's pause and a mischievous grin appeared on his face. A grin not even Sarnow's trademarked fierce grins could match.

But why would an engineer be included in this meeting?

"Sit down, Commodore, Captain. Sit down," said Sarnow as he returned to his own chair. "I'm afraid you won't be here long, Commodore Chandler. Normally, I would love to give you a few days to get your bearings and to invite all your captains to dine with me, but unfortunately, I need to send you to your patrol area as soon as possible. What do you know about the current situation here in Silesia?"

"I got a full briefing with Admirals Caparelli and Givens before I was sent here, Sir," Eve said neutrally, after everyone sat down. "I know some of the older units of Task Force 34 stayed when Duchess Harrington returned to Manticore. I know your order of battle."

"Yes, yes." Sarnow smiled. "Including this squadron and my own flagship. They are also due to rotate back to Manticore in a few months, but I need them here. By the way, the CO of this squadron is Rear Admiral Webster, another old hand from the *Nike*."

Eve smiled. Those really were simpler times in many ways. Samuel Webster had been Sarnow's comm officer back then. At that time, he'd been junior to her but she had long since stopped caring about such things.

"I guess you also realize that our forces are stretched extremely thin," Sarnow continued. "It's nice to have battle squadrons, but what I need are destroyers, light cruisers," he nodded to Strauss, "and heavy cruisers. You're only the second cruiser squadron to arrive here, Commodore. The goal of my station, and of the Admiralty as well, I might add, is to have at least one RMN unit in every system in our half of Silesia. But while that may be the goal to which we aspire, so far our forces are stretched too thin. And we still need to decommission the entire Silesian Confederacy Navy. That's the important step for securing this whole area. The first step, I'd say. To ensure the ships don't fall into the wrong hands."

Eve nodded. Piracy was always a problem in Silesia, and the recent annexation by Manticore and the Andermani Empire had not so far done much to ease the problem. It would happen in time, but for now, Silesia was a hotbed for every type of problem. Eve had read the briefs about the new "liberation fronts" and "freedom alliances" that had spawned all over Silesia. Various planetary governors and naval officers had decided they had nothing to lose and started to wage their own little wars against Manticore; independence movements that had been long dormant saw the change coming and figured they could use the confusion to take a piece of some planet for themselves. Eve was prepared to admit that at least some of them genuinely believed Manticore was the "evil invader coming to destroy their way of life." But most of them were just corrupt bureaucrats and officers who knew Manticore was endangering their profitable status quo and were trying to fight it any way they could. And of course, many SCN captains might decide to start freelancing and become pirates themselves. Eve had been deployed to Silesia several times during her early career and knew that at least some of the SCN officers had indulged in a little piracy on the side even then, and the current circumstances could only make that even more tempting. That was why securing all the SCN fleet bases and shipyards was the top priority.

"We've lost some ships already," Sarnow said, as if reading Eve's thoughts. "Some Silesian skippers in Posnan decided to ignore the orders of their governors and went freelance. We managed to destroy them, but not without losing two cruisers and a destroyer first. That's why I've assigned an entire battlecruiser squadron to Posnan and plan to take my battle squadrons on a show-the-flag trip around Silesia. I intend to visit every sector capital and get to know the situation personally. But in the meantime, I have smaller units like yours to help me put out all the fires. Your squadron's going to the Terrance Sector, Commodore. You'll be our senior officer there for the time being."

Eve nodded. During the entire voyage from Manticore to Silesia via Gregor, she'd wondered where she would be assigned. Now at least that guessing game was over.

The admiral continued. "Terrance is one sector where we plan to decommission SCN units. Specifically, in the Caroline System. I've spoken with several of my economic advisors and we've decided that if we decommission most of the ships in a few selected systems, we can provide local jobs. Which surely won't hurt our prestige." Sarnow smiled faintly. "You do know what my position here is, Commodore, right?"

"Er, I know you are the commander of the RMN forces in Silesia, Sir," Eve said.

"Yes and no. I have the command, but I was nominated as governor-general by the Queen as well as the CO of the newly formed Ninth Fleet, and my job is likely to become less that of a naval officer and more that of a governor soon. So I have to focus on things like economic growth in the various Silesian systems, and figuring out where we'll decommission SCN units is a good first step. In the Terrance Sector, it will be the Caroline System. We need to decommission the ships in orbit, then several local and Manticoran companies are interested in breaking them up for parts before they go to the smelters for reclamation."

"Will the Silesian ships' crews go there voluntarily, Sir?" Strauss asked.

"You have to remember that Manticore and Andermani didn't conquer the Silesian Confederacy," Sarnow replied. "We struck a deal with the Confederacy government. The SCN's ships received legal orders from their government to report to the Caroline System. Having said that, with an organization as corrupt as the Silesian Confederacy Navy—and the Confederacy itself—many of their ships' officers have decided to run for it and became pirates, freelancers, or mercenaries, or have joined revolutionary groups."

"What do these groups want to achieve?" asked Eve.

Sarnow opened his mouth, but Captain Hagen was faster.

"The usual: liberty, equality, fraternity. The happy mix."

If Sarnow was annoyed at being interrupted by an engineer, he didn't show it. He simply continued.

"We've sometimes put an officer and a small cadre aboard an SCN vessel to make sure it will arrive where it's supposed to, but that can be dangerous. If the crew decides to go rogue, there's nothing our people can do to stop them, unless we put a platoon of Marines aboard with them. Which we've sometimes tried, as well."

"I understand, Admiral."

"Yes, such jobs aren't usually very popular with the poor guys and gals who get volunteered for them," Hagen snorted.

This time Sarnow did throw a warning glance at the engineer before continuing.

"And the Terrance System—in the Terrance Sector—is where I need to send you now, Commodore Chandler. So far I have only three warships there for the whole sector: *Wolfhound*, *Testudo* and *Claymore*. A destroyer, a light cruiser and one of those old *Broadsword*-class Marine transport cruisers, respectively. Additionally, there's one repair ship and one ammunition ship and several dispatch boats. I also have a two-ship battlecruiser division under Captain Ellis on its way to the Chalice Cluster—which nominally belongs to Terrance as well. Remember Chalice, Commodore? It seems some people actually remember Warnecke's rule and wanted a second shot at independence. Nothing widespread or serious, but I've decided to send Ellis's division there to show the flag. Either way, you'll be senior officer in Terrance for the time being. Your main goal would be to oversee the decommissioning."

"I understand, Sir," Eve said.

"I hate to send you away so soon after your arrival, Commodore," Sarnow continued. "But I have a dozen fires in Silesia to put out and your squadron is the only screening element I have available for that sector. We need to secure and decommission all the SCN units ASAP."

"I understand completely, Sir," Eve repeated. She might not have been in command of a force that was stretched as thin as Sarnow's was, but she could certainly imagine it.

"That's where I come in," Hagen said. "I hope you won't mind if I enjoy the hospitality of your flagship during our trip to Terrance, Commodore." Hagen flashed another of his mischievous grins. What was this guy grinning at?

"Captain Hagen is in charge of decommissioning the Silesian units," Sarnow explained.

"Ah, I see. We'll be glad to have you aboard, Captain."

Hagen flashed another of those grins.

"Thank you, Commodore." He looked at Strauss. "I won't bother you aboard your ship, Captain Strauss. I'll have only a small staff. For the decommissioning itself, I will require the help of your ships' crews, though, Commodore. BuShips has promised me a bigger unit of trained people. Unfortunately, they seem to be in the same place as Admiral Sarnow's reinforcements."

"And that's where?"

Another grin. "Not here."

Sarnow cleared his throat. "There's still a lot to be done, Commodore. I'd like your ships to be on their way within twelve hours. I know that there's a supply ship in Terrance, but if you have any pressing logistical needs, please bring them to my logistics officer."

"I will, Sir, but I don't believe we'll have any."

"Good. Then I would ask your intelligence officer to confer with mine so they can get on the same page. Once you arrive at Terrance, you'll pay a courtesy call to the local governor, who's been very cooperative so far. And make sure any SCN units there are sent to Caroline for decommissioning. However, due to the instability of the situation, I don't want your ships to wander alone. You can split your squadron into divisions of two but not into individual units. Those are my standing orders. Is that understood?"

"Yes, Sir."

"All right, I believe I've addressed the main points." Sarnow looked at his chief of staff, who nodded. "Now if you'll follow me to the CIC, my operations officer can show you my force deployments in more detail."

⌘ ⌘ ⌘

"So our first goal is to proceed to Terrance to pay a visit to the governor and other dignitaries. Then to assist in decommissioning the Silesian naval units." Eve Chandler nodded towards Hagen, whom she had invited to this briefing with her staff while Cruiser Squadron Fifty accelerated towards the Silesia System hyper limit, less than twenty-eight hours after they'd made their translation into the system. "Beyond that, the deployment orders are up to our discretion, and I'll be the senior officer in the sector for the time being."

"Yes, the burden of responsibility," Hagen mumbled.

Strauss shot a glance at him. The engineer produced yet another of those mischievous grins.

Eve decided not to react, although some other staff members looked irritated.

"What is going to be the squadron's disposition?" asked Lieutenant Commander Norman Bettany, Baron Black Oak. Chandler's ops officer was the most nobly born of her officers. It was also unusual for someone so young to inherit a noble title, as Bettany was only thirty-two T-years old. But his mother, Baroness Black Oak, had commanded an SD(P) division that was destroyed at Grendelsbane during the Havenite attack when hostilities were resumed.

We've all suffered losses.

Eve replied to his question. "I'm getting to that. The admiral's standing orders are for our ships to travel at least in pairs. For the immediate future, I'll keep the squadron concentrated into two divisions." Nods. Heavy cruiser squadrons of eight units were typically split into two divisions. "What I'm thinking is that we'll proceed directly to Terrance with the first division and send Captain Pankowski's second division directly to Caroline to help with the decommissioning." She looked at Hagen. "How many SCN ships are there already?"

"About a dozen," he said lazily. "I'd have to check my memo."

"Then check it, please!" Eve managed not to growl. Hagen seemed to be one of the brand of engineers who were...not really thrilled about military discipline and all that. She remembered a deputy commanding officer of the *Vulcan* who been like that, as well. Never held starship command, never seen action, but was a miracle worker and good at organizing things.

Of course, Eve wasn't sure that Hagen was good at organizing anything or if he had some other redeeming characteristics.

Now the junior captain looked at his memo. "According to my information—which is three weeks old—there are currently sixteen ships in Caroline. Four *Silesia*-class battlecruisers, six *Jarmon*-class heavy cruisers, two *Wroclaw*-class light cruisers, four *Joachim*-something-I-don't-know-how-to-read-class destroyers. And only one of our warships there, *Claymore.*"

"I thought the standing orders were for warships to travel in pairs," Black Oak objected.

Hagen produced another grin. "I guess *Claymore* didn't get the memo. No, those were originally escorted there from the Silesia System by two divisions of our battlecruisers, but then one division had to go back to Silesia and the other proceeded to Chalice. Admiral Sarnow put prize crews on most of those ships in Silesia, so we had nothing to worry about with them. *Claymore* is now keeping an eye on things in Caroline."

"And are the prize crews and *Claymore's* crew already working on those Silesian ships?" Strauss asked.

"Yes, Captain, what they can do. Mostly they help ferry spacers to Mariposa, that's the planet in the Caroline System. We'd need more people for the decommissioning itself. Has any one of you ever been involved in decommissioning?"

"I was once in a team preparing for the decommissioning of a flight of twenty old *Falcon*-class destroyers," Eve said. "That's about it."

"All right," Hagen continued, mostly for the sake of the others. "I'll require a team of spacers from each of your vessels to assist with that. We don't have the manpower to move so many ships to Manticoran shipyards to be disposed of, which is why we'll be doing it locally. We'll need a large local workforce to cut the ships apart, but before we let the civilians poke into them, we'll need to make sure they're permanently shut down. That will consist firstly of removing ordnance, perishables, fuel and computer cores. Then we'll move on to removing the fusion plants. Luckily for us lazy engineers, all SCN ships, including their battlecruisers, have fusion reactors that can be ejected. Finally, we'll open all airlock hatches and release the atmosphere."

"And that situation," said Eve, "is why I'm sending Pankowski directly to Caroline. The ships' crews can immediately assist with the decommissioning." She looked again at Hagen. "While I'm thinking of it, maybe you'd like to go with them, as well?"

Hagen shook his head. "Thank you, Commodore, but with your permission, I'd like to continue with you to Terrance. I have a few contacts there I need to make first, so I'd like to go with you."

Another grin.

Black Oak cleared his throat. "Ma'am, can I make a suggestion? For the decommissioning, we'd need larger crews, so I'd suggest sending our older *Star Knights* to Caroline while we retain our *Saganamis* for patrol duties. We'd have to break established divisions but..." He shrugged and Eve decided he had a point. It wasn't as if the divisions had been given much time to train together properly, anyway, and mixing it up might work.

Cruiser Squadron Fifty had been patched together really quickly, out of whatever units were available, after the resumption of hostilities. *Juggernaut*, Eve's flagship, was the only *Saganami-B*-class ship. *Taylor*, *Borelli* and *Locatelli* were *Saganami-A*s and *Fearless*, *Druid*, *Star Warrior* and *Apprentice* were older *Star Knights*. They had much larger crews—and much larger Marine complements— which would undoubtedly prove handy in Silesia in a host of ways. And Black Oak was right that sending the *Star Knights* to Caroline would provide more warm bodies for the tedious task of decommissioning.

"Good idea, Commander," she said. "Put the new unit composition in writing. I'll discuss it with Captain Pankowski. And we may just have enough time to do some squadron exercises before we split to our different destinations." She smiled and remembered a phrase of her old teacher in simpler times. "Let's be about it."

❋ ❋ ❋

"Admiral, Mr. Marius is here."

Marcus Bartoli finished pouring his wine and smiled.

"Let him in."

The hatch to his main dining room opened and Captain Christian Venner—Bartoli's flag captain—escorted Marius and his bodyguard Sheila Lubke into the room.

"Ah, Adrian, welcome back aboard the *Scimitar*!" Bartoli rose and walked around the table. Before he shook Marius's hand, he bowed slightly and kissed Lubke's. She was one of those bodyguards who looked like a decorative companion or a professional escort, and she wore a long blue dress made of the best Hume silk. Bartoli knew that this kind of camouflage could be successful even in this modern day and age. In Haven, society was slightly more conservative and egalitarian. No one would ever dream of greeting a woman by kissing her hand. But both women like the one Lubke pretended to be and manners like hand-kissing were common in some parts of Silesia, and Bartoli enjoyed playing the role he was expected to play. Of course, he knew Lubke had one loaded pulser in her handbag and another strapped to her thigh. He'd also made sure that Marius knew *he* knew and that he'd let her come armed into his presence. After all, Marius would have to be royally stupid to try to assassinate Bartoli aboard his flagship. Not to mention that Bartoli was fairly certain that Marius was quite happy with the partnership they shared.

"Ma'am," Bartoli said, once he let go of Lubke's hand. Then he turned to Marius and their hands finally clasped. "I heard your mission was successful."

"Indeed it was," Marius grinned. As the former senior administrator in the Terrance Sector, he managed to get access to a great deal of information. And he knew many Silesian senior officers.

Officers like those of the SCN battlecruiser *Autonomy*, who had decided—or had been persuaded—to volunteer their freelance services to Bartoli rather than turn their ship over to be scrapped and lose their extra income. If Bartoli understood correctly, *Autonomy*'s crew had been one of the few Silly BCs that operated independently under the old government . . . and whose captain had managed to make some private deals with various pirates on the side.

"It's four battlecruisers, six heavy cruisers, two light cruisers and five destroyers. All of them are going to be in Caroline by next week."

Bartoli beamed. "Excellent! So, please, sit down!"

Both his guests and Captain Venner took their seats at the richly decorated table in a compartment that was equally richly decorated. Originally it had served as a flag deck gym, but Bartoli had refurnished it and now it was a luxurious dining suite. The deck was covered with what looked like old wooden parquet flooring and ancient-looking paintings—the best-looking replica of some ancient oil on canvas—hung on the walls. It didn't follow any particular style.

Bartoli didn't know much about ancient interior decorating styles, but he liked it. Especially since his former colleagues in State Security would consider it "elitist," "bourgeois," "decadent," and worst of all: "something Legislaturists would do; not something the warriors of the people should do." There were many reasons why Bartoli had entered StateSec years ago. The desire to "fight for the people" was not one of them.

After his guests were seated, Bartoli selected a bottle of wine and personally poured a glass for each of them. That was another piece of theatrics he enjoyed. Everyone would expect someone in his position to have an army of stewards, and he liked to do these things himself to throw everyone off balance. And if StateSec had taught him anything, it was to function without a steward.

Marius wasn't a fanatic, and neither was Lubke. Like Bartoli, they wanted to take the biggest bite possible from the carcass that now was Silesia. For many senior bureaucrats like Marius, the sudden imposition of Manticoran and Andermani rule meant they'd suddenly been cut off from their source of extra income. Bartoli, on the other hand, saw it as an opportunity. That's why he decided to take *Scimitar* to Silesia. The full implementation of the new order would take decades, and change of regime always created opportunities.

He raised a glass. "So, here's to our mission, ladies and gentlemen."

❈ ❈ ❈

The invitation called for mess dress uniforms, to the great dismay of everyone in CruDiv 50.1. But protocol had to be followed, so Evelyn Chandler, her staff officers, the captains of her ships and a few others had to don their "monkey suits."

So now, Eve stood on the giant, luxurious open balcony in Governor's Palace on Terrance. The palace was on the edge of the mountain ridge overlooking the capital city of Barnaros on one side and the Pinaros Mountains on the other. The panorama was spectacular and Eve enjoyed the view of the beautiful mountain massif that almost allowed her to forget that there was a city of five million on the other side of the palace.

There were about two hundred people on the balcony. Governor Braun had decided to throw a party in honor of the Manticoran people "finally stabilizing Silesia." Eve didn't doubt that Magdalene

Braun was as corrupt as they came, but she seemed to realize that the old ways were over and that she needed to support Manticore and hope for the best.

From what Captain Blackridge, the CO of *Testudo*, told Eve, this was one of several parties, formal dinners and receptions the governor had organized since they'd been here.

Eve's squadron had arrived two days ago and things seemed at least a little less hectic here than in the Silesia System. Blackridge, along with Commander Kozlov from *Wolfhound*, had explained the situation to Eve and discussed possible patrol areas for her squadron. The repair ship *Anders* was also in orbit, and Eve had given permission for her to repair the Number Two Gravitic Sensor Array aboard *Locatelli* before continuing to the Caroline System. That was why Captain Donner wasn't at this party; she was overseeing the repairs to her ship.

So Evelyn Chandler was walking around, sipping her wine, mingling and making small talk. She had just tactfully disengaged from a conversation with a planetary agriculture minister who was telling her passionately how interested he was in the way farmers grew crops on Manticore, especially how they grew neocorn. Eve had had to bitterly disappoint him by telling him that she had no idea how Manticoran farmers grew neocorn.

After the minister left, she spotted Captain Lucius Hagen coming more or less toward her. He was laughing and several people in the vicinity turned their heads towards him.

"Are you enjoying yourself, Captain Hagen?" she asked politely when he was within earshot.

He chuckled. "No!"

"Why not?" she asked.

"Huh, what?" Hagen finally looked directly at her. Eve could guess from the smell coming off him that he found something considerably stronger than the local wine to drink. Terrance was famous for its brandy.

"I asked if you are enjoying yourself and you said no. Don't you like this party?"

"Oh, enjoying myself! Yes, Ma'am. I'm enjoying this party a great deal. I thought you asked if I'm *behaving* myself." He laughed again. People were starting to turn heads towards them.

Eve couldn't believe this. For a few seconds she couldn't comprehend this man, a Queen's officer, behaving like that at the party like this.

Dignitaries, politicians, everyone was looking at him.

She took a step closer and fixed her eyes on him. "Pull yourself together, Captain Hagen!"

He laughed again. "Ma'am, I'm as together as I can be!"

The smell of brandy was strong enough to make her slightly drunk.

She grabbed his arm, then scanned her surroundings. She noticed Captain Veronika Salasek, the CO of *Juggernaut*'s Marine detachment. Next to her was one of *Juggernaut*'s midshipmen, who Captain Strauss had brought with her to learn the social skills required from any Queen's officer.

Social skills indeed.

Both were already looking at Eve and Hagen and when the Commodore nodded, the Marine stepped towards her with the middy in tow.

"Major Salasek, take Captain Hagen back to the spaceport and hand him over to the shore patrol and Marines. I want him back aboard the flagship and under quarters arrest until I say otherwise. I'll have words with him later." She turned her gaze to the midshipman and ignored Hagen's mumbled protests and laughs.

"Midshipman Hansen, I'm making you responsible for escorting Captain Hagen back to his cabin aboard the flagship. You are under *my* orders and you are going to ignore any attempts he may try at ordering you to do anything. Is that clear?"

"Yes, Ma'am!" the youngling said.

"Get him out of here!"

The guests at the party watched as Salasek and Hansen hauled the engineer away. Some politely turned away; no one dared to comment on it.

Eve tried to calm down and threw a reassuring smile at the minister who was standing nearby. He smiled knowingly back.

Who was this Hagen? Was he stupid or suicidal? This could very well cost him his career. Eve didn't mind officers letting off a little steam. She had done that herself on more than one occasion before... before she lost Diana.

She put that thought quickly aside. Hagen was behaving like he didn't have a worry in the world.

"I hope the Silesians don't consider this guy a typical Manticoran officer," she murmured to herself.

"Pardon, Ma'am?"

She cursed herself. She didn't realize she'd said that so loudly. But when she turned, she saw only Commander Black Oak; thankfully no Silesian was within earshot.

"Commander Black Oak, I just said that I hope people won't think Hagen is a typical Manticoran."

"I still can't get used to that name. I still don't feel like a baron. But you're right. He is strange. And frankly, I don't understand his behavior."

Eve wondered about the advisability of discussing a senior officer with another who was his junior, but given the situation, it didn't matter much. Hagen wasn't Bettany's—Black Oak's—direct superior and he wasn't even a line officer. He was a yard dog and a pretty low breed at that.

"Like the fact that he is behaving like a disgrace to the uniform? I've had to straighten up some officer who got a little out of line on shore leave, but never a JG captain. How can he get this drunk?"

"No, Ma'am. I meant something else. Did you know that one of my uncles is an actor?"

Eve blinked at the sudden change of topic. "No, I didn't know that."

Black Oak smiled. "It's not something you'd expect from nobility, right? Well, Uncle Theodore is rather far removed from our title, but I know him well. He's a stage actor and works in the Royal Theater in Landing."

"I see. And why are you telling me this?"

"Because I wanted you to know that I'm rather close to actors and acting, Ma'am. And because of that, I can tell the difference between someone being drunk and someone *pretending* to be drunk."

Eve's eyes widened. "You are saying Hagen isn't really drunk?"

"Yes, Ma'am. He's sober. He put on a good show, but you could see it in his eyes. They were still sharp and looking exactly where they wanted to. They were the eyes of someone who knew exactly where he was and why."

"But why would he run around a party like this pretending to be drunk? Why did he let himself be dragged away?"

"I wish I knew, Ma'am."

※ ※ ※

Hagen welcomed her with a smile and all-too sober expression when a Marine escorted Eve to his cabin aboard *Juggernaut*.

"Hello, Ma'am. It's kind of you to visit."

Eve wanted to say something but stopped herself. She turned to the Marine.

"Leave us, Private."

"But, Ma'am . . ."

"I said leave us."

The Marine didn't argue anymore. He gave Hagen a stern look and then left the cabin and closed the hatch behind him.

"Captain Hagen, you'd better explain yourself."

"Since you sent the Marine away, maybe you have some idea, Ma'am?"

Another mischievous grin.

Eve's eyes turned cold. "My idea is that I can send you back to Manticore on the next dispatch boat with an efficiency report that's going to *guarantee* that you'll never ever wear this uniform again, Captain Hagen. And if you have something to say which would change my mind, you say it now. For one thing: Why pretend you were drunk when you weren't?"

Hagen nodded. "I'm sorry I didn't tell you sooner. But I needed your reaction to be genuine."

"You *what*?"

"I work for the Office of Naval Intelligence. You could say I'm the chief spook for the Manticoran Sector here in Silesia."

Eve stared at him for several seconds, then just nodded slowly. Somewhere inside, she had suspected. Or more precisely, she'd suspected that Hagen was not just an engineer. She just hadn't known what Hagen really was. Black Oak had probably guessed more; that's why he didn't trust him.

And now the question was if anyone could trust him.

"You can verify my story in the last download you received from *Nicator* before leaving Silesia for Terrance. There's a coded file named Report on the Export Values of Terrance Agricultural

Products—strange how the best way to hide important documents is to give them a totally uninteresting title. You can open it using your flag officer command code. There you'll find my name and confirmation of my position from Admiral Givens."

Eve was still frowning. "I thought Sarnow's intelligence officer was in charge of this kind of work in Silesia."

"Captain Scott is a great guy, but his job is to analyze all the information that comes to him. My job is to travel around, make contacts, reestablish old contacts and be the point man for any intelligence operation in the field. Admiral Givens decided someone like me is necessary here after she discovered how her predecessor underestimated—and screwed up—the intelligence operations in Silesia . . . and everywhere else, for that matter. So, I use my job of decommissioning SCN units as an excuse to travel around Silesia. I'm naturally the pain in the posterior that makes lots of smartass remarks, so no one takes me very seriously."

"Yes, you certainly excel at the last thing. But why did you need to pretend to be drunk?"

"So I could be seen like that in public—somebody who may have a little drinking problem who embarrassed himself so badly he had to be hauled away. Next time I'm on the surface, I'm the vulnerable link. Someone who's made a mistake and whose career hangs in the balance. I know there are some people on the governor's staff who would approach me. Who want someone on the inside on the Manticoran staff. They are going to court me and make me their snitch."

"And who might want to do that? And why?"

"Admiral Sarnow got an intel report that some forces are not keen on our plan to decommission the SCN ships. And want to do something about that."

"You mean on the governor's staff?"

"On the staff, some separatists, or even the crews of those ships themselves who might want to try some piracy instead of turning their ships to scrap. Since I'm the engineer in charge of decommissioning, I'm the natural target for their interests."

"So your plan was to make yourself an embarrassment and then wait and see who comes to you?"

"Essentially."

Eve sighed. "And those are the admiral's orders?"

"Yes, but the method is mine. No one suspects a loud total jerk of being a spy."

Eve studied him for a moment. "The problem is that you've dug too deep a hole for yourself, you know. I can't just let this slide. But there is a solution."

"Yes?"

"You stay a few more days under quarters arrest, then you get to the planet. I'll let the crew know that I dropped a hammer on you. Or let them assume it, to be exact. Then you'll behave at all the staff meetings, to reinforce the fact that I'm giving you one last chance. I understand you are a spook, but I can't have you embarrassing the whole squadron. Is that clear?"

Mischievous grin. "I believe I can work with that, Ma'am."

⌘ ⌘ ⌘

"What the hell is going on?" asked Captain Oleg Pankowski, as he stormed onto the bridge of HMS *Fearless*.

Alarms were still ringing through the hull and he made his way to the master plot.

"Two bogeys, Skipper," the exec said. "The impeller signature is huge."

Pankowski saw it. It was decelerating directly toward the system's sole habitable planet, where his division was supposed to start decommissioning the Silesian warships in orbit.

Pankowski's four-ship division had arrived in the system barely thirty hours ago. They had decelerated to the same destination for Pankowski's first courtesy meeting with Captain Johnson from HMS *Claymore*, whose people had already started working on two of the Silesian vessels. Pankowski's officers were now putting together a plan to send teams from each of the four *Star Knight*-class ships to the Silesian vessels to start work on the decommissioning before the repair ship *Anders* arrived, along with Captain Hagen. Pankowski was actually looking forward to the job.

But now they had a bigger problem.

"One of the contacts is definitely in the superdreadnought range, Skipper," the tac officer said.

"Is it ours or someone else's?" asked Pankowski. But he'd been briefed on deployment patterns, the same as Commodore Chandler. No Manticoran superdreadnought was supposed to travel here. "And what's a single superdreadnought doing out here?"

Ships of the wall didn't operate solo, or with one smaller ship; they operated in entire divisions and squadrons. And if this was a raid, no sane Navy would have used superdreadnoughts in the first place. Hitting a system like Caroline with SDs would be an extreme case of overkill.

Unfortunately, their mysterious visitor didn't seem to mind that it was overkill.

"It could be a CLAC," his exec suggested. "Havenite CLACs are the same size as SDs . . . so are the Graysons for that matter."

"Maybe," Pankowski agreed. "What about the other ship?"

"CIC believes it to be battlecruiser-range."

"When will they reach us?"

"Present course and acceleration, in three hours twenty minutes," the tac officer said.

Pankowski watched the approaching icon. It would have been better if it was a CLAC. Against a bunch of LACs, his five cruisers would have at least some chance. The same chance as against a battlecruiser.

He was proud of his ship and he had a thing for the *Star Knight* class. His first assignment after his snotty cruise had been aboard *Star Knight* herself, a year before she was destroyed in the first days of the war. But four *Star Knights* and one *Broadsword*-class cruiser were no match for any ship of the wall.

※ ※ ※

"We seem to be too late," Captain Venner said testily, as Bartoli studied the master plot.

Scimitar, accompanied by the Silesian battlecruiser *Autonomy*, was decelerating towards the depot.

The depot with four extra Manty ships.

"The intel said there would be one vessel as escort," said Bartoli. "The intel could have been wrong, but I think they've arrived recently."

"And what if they didn't?"

"If all the Silesian ships have full Manty decommissioning crews aboard, there's nothing we can do, and we'll retreat. Win some, lose some. But I don't think this changes anything just yet." He kept looking at the master plot. "Send a signal to our people in the system."

※ ※ ※

Pankowski watched the master plot and the icon coming towards them.

"It's confirmed, Sir!" said the tac officer. "The battlecruiser is a *Silesia* class. The SD is definitely a Peep ship, though. CIC is ninety percent certain it's a *DuQuesne* class."

"Pre-pod design," said the exec. "At least that's something."

"Not that it's going to help us much," said Pankowski. It was clear to him what had to be done.

He loved his ship. He knew that when *Star Knight* was the newest class of heavy cruisers, it had been the plum assignment for any young captain. Duchess Harrington had engaged a Peep battlecruiser—and won—with this very ship!

Pankowski knew these ships could do lots of things. But he wasn't crazy. It would be something else if his ships had pods, but they didn't even have that.

"We have to retreat," he heard himself saying.

"Sir, our people are still on those SCN ships," the exec said.

Pankowski closed his eyes. Most of the ships had a small, Silesian station keeping crew numbers of a few dozen people at most. But two of them, a destroyer and a heavy cruiser, had a big team from *Claymore* working there.

"Signal the work crews to evacuate immediately back to *Claymore*." He turned to the astrogator. "Debra, do we have enough time to evacuate our people and avoid action?"

"Yes, Skipper," the astrogator said. "Assuming the whole evacuation won't take more than an hour, at least."

"But we can't pull out the Silesian station keeping crews, too," the exec pointed out. "They can evacuate in lifeboats, but the window's too tight to ferry them all aboard here."

"Tell them to evacuate and set course to pick our people up," Pankowski said.

"Skipper," said the comm officer. "The Silesian crews aren't responding to our hails."

Pankowski turned to the comm station. "None of them?"

"Correction, all but two aren't responding."

⌘ ⌘ ⌘

"We got the message, Sir," Bartoli's comm officer said. "Lots of comm traffic in the clear, but our signal is amongst it."

Bartoli smiled as his two ships accelerated towards the Manties and their Silesian prizes. "Very well, let me speak."

"Yes, Sir. Live mike."

❋❋❋

"Attention all Manticoran units in the Caroline System, this is Admiral Sterling of the Republic of Haven's ship *Soult*. We are liberating this system for the people of the Silesian Confederacy. You have no way of winning an engagement with us. Withdraw and we guarantee we won't pursue you. To the Silesian vessels and crews: do not resist, we are on your side and we are here to help you maintain your independence against Manticore and the Andermani Empire."

Pankowski exchanged looks with his exec.

What the hell?

"What's the ETA on our returning crews?" he asked.

"The last shuttle is docking with *Claymore* right now, Skipper."

"Good. And the Silesian ships?"

"Two have evacuated, the rest are not responding."

Pankowski tried to think. He was responsible for the stationkeeping crews, but at least they could safely evac those ships. Hopefully the Havenites wouldn't have any reason to blow up decommissioned ships and, whatever else had happened since the Theisman coup, the Havenites seemed to avoid atrocities. For a moment, Pankowski thought the Havenites might want to board those vessels, but that didn't seem plausible. Why would they bother? Anything the SCN had was hopelessly obsolete even by the standards of the pre-war People's Navy. Now that the Peeps had SD(P)s and CLACs themselves, they wouldn't care for any Silly ship.

But they could blow them out of space just for good measure.

"Order the Silesian crews to evacuate the ships and make for Mariposa." Mariposa was the sole habitable world in the Caroline System. "If the Peeps overtake them, they're ordered to surrender."

No one protested, but that didn't stop Pankowski feeling like a traitor. He was responsible for those ships.

"Set a course towards the hyper limit and to give a wide berth to the Peep superdreadnought. Then contact *Claymore*. I want to speak with Captain Johnson."

"What are your plans, Sir?" the exec asked.

"I'm going to keep the division in system to keep an eye on the Havenites. And I'm going to send *Claymore* to Terrance for help."

As his division raced towards the hyper limit, he found out to his astonishment that the superdreadnought had started to send small craft towards the SCN vessels.

Oh my God, they are boarding the decommissioned vessels.

His decommissioning crews had slagged the engineering net's computers aboard the heavy cruiser and the destroyer upon which they'd been working. Repairing that would require complete replacement, which no one would be doing anytime soon. But the rest of the ships had little more than caretaking crews that probably couldn't even sabotage the ships in any meaningful way before they were boarded. And why had they stopped communicating?

As he sent *Claymore* out of the system to raise the alarm, all he could do was keep his four heavy cruisers on station and watch helplessly.

And try to come up with some semi-sane reason a Havenite superdreadnought with a Silesian battlecruiser would come and try to *steal* the Silesian fleet.

⁂

There were better days and there were worse days.

Eve Chandler had never been much for comfort and, as a naval officer, she had gotten used to the spartan accommodation a Queen's ship offered. However, she couldn't help but notice that, despite the smaller complement and high degree of automation, the flag quarters aboard *Juggernaut* were considerably smaller than the captain's quarters aboard *Queen Samantha*, her last command. That was to be expected, as a *Saganami-B*-class heavy cruiser was almost twenty times smaller than a *Medusa*-class superdreadnought. She didn't mind too much, but as Diana used to say, "one gets used to the better things fast."

The thought of Diana hurt her, another stab of pain that she was now only too used to. Chief Steward Mandalo stopped pouring her coffee when he noticed her expression. She made a *don't worry* gesture and he continued. Mandalo had been with Chandler for a short time; her previous steward Chief O'Keefe, who'd been with her ever since she'd made captain of the list, had retired from the Navy just a few months before the resumption of hostilities. Mandalo was a capable steward, but he was still learning the quirks of his new charge.

"Thank you, Denver," she said to him, and tasted the coffee. One thing Denver Mandalo was not good at was making a proper cup of coffee. That was mostly her fault, since she'd grown accustomed to Army coffee, which—as everyone agreed—was something totally different from what spacers and Marines drank. Some said that most of the Army coffee ingredients weren't even in the Periodic Table. Chandler's ex-husband Mike was an Army reservist and he had introduced her to it. And Diana had loved it as well. Maybe that had influenced her decision to go into the Army.

Another stab of pain.

Chandler shrugged and tried to work on the regular paperwork as Mandalo left. Irrationally, she felt guilty, as well. She was supposed to get over it! So many people had lost their loved ones in the war. Her own ops officer had! Why was she like this even years afterward?

She remembered how hollow and broken Honor Harrington had looked when she reported back aboard *Nike* after Paul Tankersley's death. How deep in grief she'd been. But that was only for a short time. Then the despair made way for purpose. Honor had first shot and killed Pavel Young, then basically helped build the modern Grayson Space Navy from the ground up. Eve Chandler had had to go on compassionate leave with half-pay for how long? Two T-years? More? Even now she didn't remember how she survived those first days.

Her therapist had explained to her that each human reacts differently, that it wasn't a competition. She had to face her own griefs. She knew all that, but it had still helped to hear it from somebody else, and the therapist might have been the sole reason she was still alive. She'd also come to realize that the pain would never go away, she'd only get used to it. And in time, she'd started to manage to function. Her therapist had suggested she get back to work and so she had. During the ceasefire and the Janacek downsizing, there hadn't been that many billets, but her former CO from the *Nike*, Cindy Van Wyhe, now a rear admiral, understood her situation and got her the command of an SD(P) in the Home Fleet. While the Janacek-appointed Home Fleet CO had let the general readiness of the fleet slack, that hadn't been true of HMS *Queen*

Samantha or her squadron, and Eve had always loved the drills, the day-to-day work. She'd thought she'd get back on the horse.

And she had. To a point. But the job she loved and that she did well, had become ... distant. Like she was dealing with every routine and every problem through a thick pane of glass. Like she was separated from it. Like there was just a huge momentum propelling her forward.

For some reason, the feeling had gotten worse once she got to Silesia. Maybe because life aboard a superdreadnought in Home Fleet was a comfortable routine. Here she had a command of eight ships and was responsible for their deployment across the whole sector. She knew she'd do her job well, and she trusted her own abilities, but the feeling of detachment grew even stronger.

And every once in a while, a dangerous thought crept in.

What if I can't do it any longer, whatever I tell myself?

She kept on reading reports and managed to stay focused on them. Captain Donner had finally gotten the sensor array for *Locatelli* replaced and certified. They'd received a dispatch saying that the ammunition ship *Katla* was en route.

A buzz announced that she had a visitor.

"Commander Black Oak to see the Commodore," the Marine sentry announced.

"Send him in."

The youthful operations officer entered, and Eve wondered if he was struggling with the same demons as her.

It's not a competition, a voice that sounded like her therapist's whispered in her mind.

"Ma'am, I have the squadron deployment plan you requested."

Eve nodded and invited him to take a seat. "All right, let's do it. Do you want some refreshment?"

"Yes, thank you, Ma'am. If Denver can produce a cup of coffee that isn't the awful Army stuff, I'd happily accept a cup." He smiled and Eve found herself chuckling. It was as if her old personality always tried to pop out when she wasn't looking. Her old cocky self.

Black Oak pulled out his minicomp. "Basically, *Juggernaut* and *Locatelli* would travel to Caroline on schedule. *Taylor* and *Borelli* would take the southern route towards Frieda, their first stop would be Margot and then..."

Twenty minutes later, she got a priority message from the duty comm officer that *Claymore* had translated out of hyper and Black Oak's carefully planned deployments would come to naught.

⚮ ⚮ ⚮

"A superdreadnought!" Captain Strauss exclaimed. "A fucking Peep superdreadnought!"

"Is it one of the ships Duchess Harrington fought at Marsh this January?" Black Oak asked.

Captain Johnson of *Claymore*, who'd come aboard *Juggernaut* to present his report personally, shrugged. "There's no way to establish that one way or the other. But it was definitely a pre-pod design. And they're accompanied by the Silly battlecruiser."

Eve's staff had assembled in the flag briefing room along with Captain Johnson and even Captain Hagen, who had managed to behave himself since her talk with him and whom she invited to this meeting.

Now the commodore sat and watched as her command responsibilities became much more complicated.

"The Havenites who attacked our base at Marsh in January had both pod and pre-pod designs," Lieutenant Basil Sit, Eve's staff intelligence officer, said.

"And don't forget that they'll probably still be in transit home to Haven after Duchess Harrington licked them," said Lieutenant Angela Garba, staff astrogator. "It's a long way, especially if they have damaged ships, since they can't use the Gregor or Basilisk Terminus."

Angelique Strauss looked like a confused hexapuma. "I agree that once hostilities resumed, commerce raiding makes sense, especially since our forces in Silesia are stretched so thin. But it seems too soon."

Eve looked at Johnson. "You've had the longest time to think about that, Captain. What do you think?"

The CO of *Claymore* shrugged. "I think this ship must have come out of the Havenite fleet while it was retreating. If I'd been the CO of that fleet, I'd definitely see the appeal of leaving some ships behind to attack our supply lines."

"Yes, but why a superdreadnought?" Strauss asked. "That's what seems crazy to me. Commerce raiding is part of every war, but why not leave a squadron of battlecruisers for that? Who'd send a lone superdreadnought?"

"A moron?" Black Oak asked and then shrugged. "Sorry, but I remember the saying that while we shouldn't underestimate our enemies, it can be even more dangerous to overestimate them. It's possible the Peep CO thought a superdreadnought would be useful. Or several of them. We've encountered only one so far, but that doesn't mean there aren't any others."

"I'd point out that ONI has confirmed that the Havenite fleet that attacked Marsh was commanded by Lester Tourville," Sit pointed out. "I'd happily acknowledge that the man is an asshole, but he is not stupid." He blushed a little. "Pardon my language."

"I'm sure the good Commodore has heard the word before," Captain Hagen mused.

"Why are you even here again?" asked Strauss, but Eve raised her hand. She'd have to tell the crew eventually, but that'd be for another day.

"To the point raised by Basil and Norman," she said, nodding towards Sit and Black Oak and ignoring Hagen, "I'd point out that even the best of strategists can simply do a really stupid thing. As you probably know, I took part in the Sixth Fleet's offensive towards Trevor's Star, I was at Santander, Nightingale, Seabring . . . Earl White Haven and Admiral Kuzak are two of the best tacticians and strategists the Royal Navy has and even they made mistakes." She should know; she'd commanded the *Oracle* as part of the screen at Seabring. White Haven had massively miscalculated there, and it had cost Eve a fifth of her crew. "Maybe Tourville saw something we didn't or had a plan we don't understand." She shook her head. "But we should focus on the problem at hand, people. We have an enemy ship of the wall in our territory. And the fact is that it could destroy the infrastructure of every world in the sector before we get reinforcements strong enough to stop it."

"True, although it'd need ammunition," said Strauss, who had calmed down. She didn't even spare a glance at Hagen. "Of course, the Havenites could have detached a supply ship to support her."

"There's another thing that concerns me," Eve said. "Apparently it was sending boarding parties to the decommissioned Silesian ships. Why?" She glanced at Johnson. "Again, you've had some time to think about it, Captain. What do you think?"

"I think they may want to give those ships to some anti-

Manticoran faction or liberation groups. Donating some of their own vessels to them like they did at Masada might have been better, since they'd be more modern and more dangerous, but using SCN ships makes sense if it was something the retreating Havenite CO—Tourville—conceived on the fly. If nothing else, their new owners would be more familiar with their systems and capabilities. Spares and ammunition would probably be easier to come by, as well."

"And then it would make sense to use an old pre-pod SD," Black Oak interjected. "At least some sense. They have very large complements so they can afford to detach lots of personnel as prize crews."

Eve nodded. It was time for her to make some decisions.

She knew what she wanted to do and what she ought to do.

She still seemed detached from it all.

Looking at the problem through thick glass.

"All right, people. First, we need to send reinforcement requests to Silesia but, more immediately, we need to call in Captain Ellis's battlecruisers. We have one dispatch boat. I plan to send her on the longer leg to Silesia and detach Commander Kozlov's *Wolfhound* to Jarmon, where Captain Ellis should be by now. If she finds them there, they'd proceed over here."

"And do you plan to go to Caroline immediately?" Strauss asked.

"No."

Eve could tell they weren't particularly happy about that. "We'll wait for *Katla*. She should arrive any day now, and she has pods in her cargo holds. I know the *Star Knights* don't have the fire control to handle many pods, but our *Saganami As* and *Bs* have, and so does *Testudo*."

"But there's a danger that the Peep will leave in the meantime, along with all the Silesian ships," Black Oak observed. Some members of the staff used the term Havenite rather than Peep, to acknowledge the change of regime in Haven. But for Black Oak, they were always going to be Peeps. It was the current regime that had killed his mother.

"You're right, Norman," Eve said. "But some of those vessels were so far decommissioned it'll take time to get them moving again." She looked at Hagen. "Captain Hagen, how fast do you estimate the ships can be recommissioned? Is it even possible?"

"Of course it's possible," Hagen said. "Especially since we haven't started to work properly on most of the ships yet. And ... well, it doesn't matter. They can get the ships underway and out of the system. Especially since the vessels still have their fusion cores aboard. But it's not going to be that quick a process."

"Either way," Eve said, "we need to prepare to move on a moment's notice. Cancel all leave and bring our impellers to standby. I have a few orders to write."

❋ ❋ ❋

Eve had just sent the dispatch boat and *Wolfhound* on their way and was in a meeting with Angelique Strauss over coffee—both the Army and the Navy versions—when the Marine sentry announced Lucius Hagen.

"Commodore, may I have a moment?"

"Captain Hagen, we're really busy," Strauss half snapped. The engineer had worn out his welcome as far as she was concerned.

"I know, believe me. Do I look like someone who would just bother you if it wasn't important?"

"Yes!"

"Anyway, I'm sorry to disturb you both," said Hagen with an expression that said that he really wasn't. "I just need to ask you for a ride. I need to get down to the planet surface."

"What?" Eve put her coffee back on the table. "Captain Hagen, you'll need to accompany us and ascertain the condition of those Silesian ships if we find them in time."

Another mischievous grin. "Don't worry, I plan to accompany you, but I need to get to the planet now."

Eve frowned. Apparently this was the spook part of his persona.

The persona Strauss didn't know yet. As became painfully clear when the flag captain almost thundered: "You do recall that I've cancelled all leave and all our shuttles and pinnaces are now ferrying crews *back* to their ships. And we need you here."

Strauss saw Eve's expression and stopped. Then she looked again at Hagen. "Unless you are not really an engineer."

"Oh, I am an engineer. It's just not all I do. I work for the Office of Naval Intelligence."

Strauss looked at Eve, and she nodded. "It's true. I learned that after his ... outburst at the reception on Terrance."

"My drunken outburst bore fruit," Hagen said. "I've made some contacts and as you remember, I told you about some forces that would like to get their hands on some Silesian Navy hardware. But I didn't know they'd have a Havenite superdreadnought."

Strauss was still gaping. "But why the charade?"

"If I look like a pain in the posterior, nobody takes me seriously."

Eve chuckled. "Yes, you certainly excel at that. All right, so why do you need to get down to the planet?"

"Because I've made some contacts there and . . ." He looked at Strauss. "I originally wanted to tell you in private, but I can use the good captain's opinion as well."

"What is it?"

"I'm going to meet a Havenite official."

"You're what?" Strauss shouted.

"See? That's the perspective I was talking about." He turned back to Eve. "Yes, before the resumption of hostilities and the annexation, Haven had a trade consulate here. And as is usual, half of the people on the trade consulate were spies." Another grin. "Amateur! An engineer is much better cover than a trade attaché."

"Captain Hagen . . . !"

"My point is that these people are now waiting for a lift home. Their trade mission was officially closed here, and they need to go back to Haven, but it takes time. Anyway, when we visited the governor's palace, and when I pretended to be drunk, you remember? I know I didn't fool the good Commander Black Oak— must be his noble genes—but I may have fooled you. Anyway, I went into the city to establish some contacts. One of those contacts apparently got in touch with the local Havenite consulate and one of their liaisons, a gentleman named Preston, has contacted me."

"And he wants to meet you?" Eve asked.

"No, he told me the short version, that the superdreadnought in Caroline is a renegade warship and not part of the Republic of Haven Navy."

"That's rubbish," Strauss said.

"Maybe. Maybe not. Anyway, he'd like to meet me." He looked at Eve. "And you too, Commodore. Apparently, he wants someone of sufficiently high rank to convince them he is telling the truth."

✶✶✶

"Absolutely not, Ma'am!"

Eve Chandler remembered the days aboard *Nike* when Honor Harrington returned broken with cold grief from Grayson, accompanied by the Grayson armsmen who guarded her overzealously.

At this moment, Captain Veronika Salasek, the CO of *Juggernaut*'s Marine detachment, was willing to give the Graysons a run for their money.

"I need to do it, Major," Eve said to the Marine, using the traditional courtesy promotion, so there would be only one "Captain" aboard the ship. It was interesting that it was used only with Marines; other naval officers of the rank of captain were simply addressed by their rank *and* name, like Captain Hagen.

"No, Ma'am, you don't," Salasek said. "You're a flag officer and you're all too likely a prospect of assassination. Remember the Peeps have always loved their assassinations."

Eve realized the prospect of potential assassination—and of being the victim of one—didn't bother her in the least. And it wasn't because of any bravery on her part, it was . . .

She pushed the thought aside.

"There's a source of information about our current mission and I need to meet him," she said again.

Salasek was not impressed. "Seriously, Ma'am, what if you get killed?"

More calmness. Eve looked at Angelique Strauss who was standing behind her commodore, apparently in agreement with her senior Marine.

"In that case, the mission will continue in Captain Strauss's capable hands."

"This is no joke, Ma'am!"

"I know it's not, and I've made up my mind." Eve said. "I'm going down to the planet. Unless you two," she glanced at Strauss and back at Salasek, "want to tie me up in my quarters?"

Something in Salasek's expression suggested that thought had occurred to her. She took a deep breath. "All right, Ma'am, but I'm going with you, along with a squad of my Marines. And that's not negotiable."

Eve sighed. "All right, just stay out of sight."

"Oh, believe me, I'll deploy my people around so that they stay out of your sight and out of sight of every Havenite assassin that might be lurking there somewhere."

Eve was wondering if she needed another Army coffee or some booze. Things were happening really fast.

Salasek left and Strauss cleared her throat.

"Commodore..."

"Please, Angelique, I'm going down."

"I know...I wish I could talk you out of it, but I know I can't. I know you well enough for that. But I wanted to suggest you should take someone else with you."

"Thank you for the offer, Angelique, but I need you here. Not to mention that I meant what I said to Salasek. You're the most senior captain in the squadron, and you take over if anything happens to me."

"I know. I'm not recommending myself. You should contact *Locatelli* and tell Captain Donner you need one member of her crew. A plotting specialist first class named Leo Statman."

This was now beyond ridiculous. "A who?"

"Spacer First Class Leo Statman, a plotting specialist, Ma'am. He's been adopted by a treecat."

Eve opened her mouth and then closed it again. A treecat. She hadn't even known there were any treecats in her squadron. The only treecat she'd ever served with was, of course, Nimitz when she was aboard *Nike*. She'd never doubted the 'cat's intelligence or his telepathic abilities. She even knew that they'd mastered sign language since then.

And that they could tell if somebody was lying.

"I see," she said. "I'd best contact Captain Donner then."

Juggernaut's pinnace arrived safely at the Barnaros spaceport on Terrance and Eve disembarked, accompanied by ten Marines and Lucius Hagen.

On the ground, she learned that the pinnace from *Locatelli* had already arrived. Captain Donner had accompanied her spacer herself.

"Commodore Chandler!"

"Captain, I didn't expect you here."

Donner glanced at Hagen. "Well, let's just say I didn't want to send my spacer alone . . . especially if ONI is involved."

"Believe me, Captain, we're mostly harmless." Characteristic grin.

Donner was not amused and nudged the youthful spacer. "Here's the one you wanted."

The spacer was on the smallish side. Smaller even than Eve. He was a boy who probably wasn't much over twenty, although it was hard to tell with prolong. His fair complexion and scared eyes made him look even more like a kid. He wore the blue stripe of the astrogation department and had spacer first class insignia. But his most distinctive feature was the cream-colored treecat on his left shoulder.

"Spacer Statman?"

"Y-yes, Ma'am! Leo Statman, Spacer First Class!"

"Keep calm, Mr. Statman. And what is your companion's name?"

"Tebo."

"Tebo?"

"Yes, Ma'am . . . like . . . ahem . . . like the magical tiger from the HD show *Lost Mountain*."

Eve suppressed a smile. "I see. Do you know what you two are supposed to do?"

"Well, Ma'am, the Skipper—I mean Captain Donner—explained it to me sort of, Ma'am, but . . ."

"It's simple. We need to know if the Havenite contact is lying. You'll stand behind me, pretending to make notes like a yeoman would. Then Tebo will verify if what the Havenite said is true. Can you do that?"

"Well . . . I'll do my best, Ma'am."

"Just stand behind me and don't draw attention to yourself. Can you do that?"

"I really don't know, Ma'am! I'm no spy or diplomat! I just signed up so I'd have money for college."

He looked like he would soon explode from pure nervousness. Eve remembered how Duchess Harrington told her treecats were supposed to make their adopted persons more composed and calmer. If that was true, she didn't want to know how Statman had behaved *before* the 'cat adopted him.

"Don't be afraid. It's not that difficult. You'll just sit and Tebo will do most of the work anyway." Eve smiled at the treecat who bleeked happily.

"Y-yes, Ma'am."

Eve turned back to Hagen and Salasek. "I guess it's time we paid your contact a visit, Captain Hagen."

⚒ ⚒ ⚒

It was late afternoon on the planet and Ragusa Park was almost empty. There were some animals in the river which looked like Old Earth coypu. Eve didn't know enough about that to determine if they were real Old Earth rodents the colonists had introduced here or just something very similar looking.

But she did notice a man standing on the edge of the river and feeding the little animals, which surrounded him since he was giving them food.

She wondered if the old-regime Dolists worked in the same way.

The man turned toward them as Eve, Hagen and Statman—and Tebo—approached him. Captain Salasek had deployed her Marines. No one knew how exactly it worked now with the jurisdiction of the Marines and the local police, but luckily *Juggernaut* had a competent JAG officer who'd almost certainly figured it out.

And if not, well, Eve had bigger problems on her plate.

She focused on the man and there was something in his stance and posture that made her wonder if he was military. He had brown eyes that seemed too big for his small head, which was shaped like a ball mainly due to his very short hair. He was taller than Eve, and those large eyes quickly measured her and Statman—and Tebo—before turning towards Hagen.

"I was wondering if you'd come." They turned to Eve again. "Commodore Chandler. Pleasure to meet you. I'm Rear Admiral Jeremiah Preston."

"You're the Havenite contact?"

"Yes. I wanted to talk to you personally, to tell you what's going on. And I've studied a file on you."

Eve didn't know if she should be pleased to know the Havenites had a file on her.

Preston offered her a sad smile. "Yes, yes. We have a file on you. In fact, we stood against each other once in a battle. I was in command of *Mustafa* at Seabring in 1911."

Eve's eyes widened. That was the intel failure she'd mentioned before at the briefing. Her own ship, *Oracle*, had suffered heavy damage and she'd had to limp back to Manticore for repairs that took over three months.

Maybe it was some sort of maneuver from this man. Maybe that's what Hagen thought, when he spoke a bit abruptly.

"You can exchange happy war stories later. But I believe you wanted to speak with the Commodore for a different reason. So speak. And I hate to tell you the unhappy news but, since you've identified yourself as an officer, you could technically be arrested. But I'm sure the Commodore will be kind if you just say what you came here to say."

Preston chuckled. "I'm no longer an officer. After Seabring, someone in Haven considered me politically unreliable, so they sent me here on a trade mission. At least they didn't shoot me. But yes, I want to tell you about the ship that pushed your forces out of Caroline."

"That would be welcome," Eve said. "And how did you learn about that?"

"We have our sources."

Eve nodded.

"For our part, we're still wondering what you're going to tell us and if your story isn't just an elaborate ruse to give us false information." She smiled bleakly. "And given your government's recent sneak attack and your doctoring of the diplomatic correspondence, we are hesitant to trust you."

"We *didn't* falsify the correspondence, but I know there is no point arguing about that now. And I believe I know enough about the Manticoran star system's fauna to guess the reason you brought your spacer over there." Preston smiled and looked sideways at Statman and Tebo. The young spacer blushed while the treecat simply stared at the Havenite intently. "So shall we get down to it?"

"You wanted to speak to us, so speak," Eve said, refusing to be taken aback by the fact that Preston had guessed what Statman was there for and what treecats could do.

"As you wish." Preston took a deep breath. "The superdreadnought that attacked you doesn't belong to the Republic of Haven Navy. It's a renegade ship commanded by a man named Marcus Bartoli. He used to be a captain in the State Security Fleet Forces. About two years ago, when we were about rounding up the last remnants of the SS loyalists, he was in charge of holding the New Rodrigo shipyards against our forces. Seven superdreadnoughts and numerous smaller vessels were docked there, and Bartoli didn't have any staff to crew those ships. Just as our strike force was arriving in the system, Bartoli sent a proclamation that he and all his men and women 'are children of the revolution and will never let any of the traitors lay one finger on a shipyard that belongs to the people.' He then blew the shipyards up and all the ships with it. We assumed he went with it too. He even became a sort of martyr for the various former State Security groups in exile. Those who call themselves the People's Navy in Exile and similar names."

Eve spared one look at Tebo and the treecat nodded slowly.

Preston continued. "A few months ago, we got reports about a superdreadnought operating outside of Silesia and so I investigated. It turned out to be our old friend Bartoli, who never really exploded with the shipyards. He packed his bag and ran and took one of the superdreadnoughts along with him, as well as several service ships and smaller vessels. It's ironic. He's regarded as a martyr by many of the ex-SS goons, but he's really just an opportunist."

"And your fleet that attacked us at Marsh didn't encounter him?" Eve asked.

"No, that wasn't its job and even I wasn't aware of its plans and goal."

Tebo nodded.

"I won't disclose any operational details and, in my position, I don't know all that many. But we had some ships here before, tracking him, and we found one system where he does business, a system called Quatre Bras, to the galactic east of Silesia. But then the relationships between our nations . . . got worse and we had to focus on different problems. But we do know that, apart from his superdreadnought and a few support ships, he employed several former SCN officer and pirates."

Another slight nod from Tebo.

"And why do you think he attacked Caroline now?"

"I believe he wants a bigger fleet—and it's easier to get spares for cruisers and battlecruisers than for a *DuQuesne*-class superdreadnought. I understand he has already procured one Silesian battlecruiser. But for him, a ship of the wall is a matter of prestige. While many local star nations have cruisers and destroyers, *no one* has ships of the wall."

Eve looked at him. "And why are you telling us? From your perspective, he's helping Haven now, no?"

Preston shrugged. "Believe me or not," he winked at Tebo, "I love the new regime, no matter what happened between our star nations. And I don't want people to think Bartoli's actions are sanctioned by us. *And* I think the galaxy would be better off with one less warlord like him."

Tebo nodded again.

"And I want a piece of him, yes, even indirectly. Of him and all the SS bastards." He produced a small data chip. "Here's all the information I have. His base is in the Quatre Bras System. From what we know..."

※ ※ ※

"He said *what*?"

Despite being Baron Black Oak, Lieutenant Commander Norman Bettany sometimes had a tendency to forget protocol.

Not that anyone could blame him in this case, as Eve Chandler met with her staff in *Juggernaut's* briefing room.

"I'm sorry, Ma'am," Black Oak quickly added. "What I meant to say..."

"I understand, Norman, believe me," Eve said with a smile. "I can understand that. And to answer your question, yes, Admiral Preston said that Marcus Bartoli wants to steal as many SCN units as he can before retreating from Silesia and founding his own empire somewhere to the galactic east of here. The Quatre Bras System is most likely going to be one such subsidiary. Preston thinks that Bartoli plans to subjugate one or more star systems in the area; some through bribes, some through a show of force, some through straight-out conquest. The first time the Havenites got wind of it was when a Havenite trader spotted his superdreadnought in Quatre Bras and reported it back home. They also have a few reports spotting Bartoli in several other places. Bartoli apparently flies in with his superdreadnought—originally it was named *Soult*, now he calls it the *Scimitar*—to demonstrate his power and invites the local government representatives to discuss alliances. To be honest, I don't know enough about the local political systems to know what kind of response he's likely to get, and our shipboard archives are very incomplete in this area. But it's safe to say that Bartoli wants some of those systems east of Silesia. One way or another."

"But . . . but that's crazy, Ma'am," Black Oak said. "He must know he can never get away with this!"

"Can't he?" Captain Strauss asked quietly.

"Well . . . of course he can't!" Black Oak was taken aback. "Once we know about him, we'll shut him down!"

"Will we?" This time it was Eve who asked that question. "Think about it, people. From his point of view—Manticore and Haven are fighting for their lives. Haven can't spare a force to send after him this far out. We may be almost next door to him, but we have our work cut out for us. Hell, half of the political commentators at home are saying Manticore's bitten off more than it can chew with Silesia, and that's not counting the Talbott Cluster. He knows that it may very well take a decade—or more—before we have Silesia in such order that we can feel really secure here. He undoubtedly plans to shift the blame to Haven, that's why he claimed to be a Havenite admiral. And even if shifting the blame doesn't work, he doesn't know we know about Quatre Bras. From his perspective, he has a pretty good chance of becoming a king or some sort of ruler in his own little empire."

"I still don't believe he'll pull it off," Black Oak protested stubbornly.

"You don't? Ask Gustav Anderman. In two hundred years, Bartoli might seen by historians the same way we regard Anderman now. And Anderman certainly 'pulled it off.'"

"Christ," Lieutenant Sit murmured. "And here I was, thinking Silesia was crazy enough without mad StateSec officers turned renegades turned empire builders."

"I'll be the skeptical one, but can we trust this Preston in the first place?" Lieutenant Garba asked. "Granted, we talked with him with a treecat present and granted, he gave us some files but still. I find it hard to believe."

"Well, the treecat confirmed Preston was telling the truth," Eve said.

"Yes, Ma'am, I know." The astrogator nodded. "But while I may not know much about treecats, they can't be omnipotent lie detectors. People can train themselves to resist all kinds of interrogation techniques, so why not to resist a treecat? Especially since the Peeps seem to have a fairly good idea of how treecats work ever since they captured Duchess Harrington. For that matter, the 'cat can only tell if Preston *believes* he's telling the truth. They could have planted him with false information."

"I think you're reaching, Angela," Sit told her.

"I may be. But I am not prepared to just take Preston at his word. With or without the treecat."

"We're not taking him at his word," Eve said. "Lieutenant Sit," she nodded to her intelligence officer, "and his people will go through all the information in detail. In the meantime, we'll proceed to Caroline once the squadron assembles here. If the Havenite ship is still there, and if we have the tactical advantage, we'll engage her. If she's not there, we'll go to Quatre Bras. As for Preston telling the truth or not, well, I don't believe anyone would try this as some sort of complicated ruse. What would they gain by that? Taking us to Quatre Bras on a wild goose chase? What difference would that make to them? We still plan to go to Caroline first, so it's not like they're diverting us from that system."

No one said anything, and then Black Oak cleared his throat again.

"I understand that, Ma'am. I just . . . It's hard to trust the Peeps. Especially after they falsified the pre-war correspondence and attacked us . . . But you're also right, that . . . well, I can't imagine this giving them any advantage. Falsifying the correspondence and the sneak attack clearly *did* give them an advantage. This? Not so much."

"Exactly." Eve took a small breath and looked over her officers. "We'll definitely have to send another message to Admiral Sarnow. And in the meantime, we're waiting for *Katla* and hopefully also our battlecruisers."

✖ ✖ ✖

Recommissioning vessels was a slow process, but not that complicated, given that the Silesian watch keeping crews hadn't done any permanent damage to the ships.

The destroyer and heavy cruisers whose engineering systems the Manties had wrecked were inoperable, but the rest were serviceable and now in the process of being restored.

Four *Silesia*-class battlecruisers, five *Jarmon*-class heavy cruisers, two *Wroclaw*-class light cruisers, three *Joachim Cheslav*-class destroyers were in condition good enough to repair. Especially the battlecruisers were going to be a huge prize.

Marcus Bartoli was happy as he observed the work from *Scimitar*'s flag bridge.

His flagship was placed to cover a least-time approach to the planet, but it was also close enough to the hyper limit for a quick withdrawal, in case the Manties came calling with a much heavier force than expected. The battlecruiser *Autonomy*, supplied by Marius, had been stationed in planetary orbit to keep an eye on the Silesian ships.

Two battlecruisers had already departed from the system, as well as three heavy cruisers and all the destroyers. *Scimitar* had escorted each batch of ships to the hyper limit to make sure the Manties wouldn't try anything.

The four Manty heavy cruisers watching the system worried some of his people, but Bartoli wasn't concerned. After all he was part naval officer and part member of the secret police and there were some rules that were valid in both institutions. If you know who your spy is, you don't remove them, because then you risk a new spy arriving whom you know nothing about. You let them be and they'd lead you to all their friends.

But soon Bartoli would leave the system with *Scimitar*, *Autonomy* and all their prizes.

The current standoff had lasted for seventeen days, now, and Bartoli knew that the voyage time from Terrance to Caroline was much shorter than that. So the Manties had to be assembling reinforcements before going against him with confidence of someone who *knows* (or at least thinks) they can take on a superdreadnought.

And on the seventeenth day, the Manties arrived.

"Talk to me!" he told his ops officer.

"CIC thinks the huge ship is one of their *Volcano*-class ammunition ships, the other big contact is probably some sort of repair or service ship," the officer said. "These two aren't accelerating towards us. The rest are warships, and the two biggest of them are definitely battlecruisers."

Only two battlecruisers. Bartoli watched. The four Manty cruisers observing the system were now moving to rendezvous with the main Manty force.

Which meant they weren't confident in their advantage. But on the other hand, they could be carrying pods.

Bartoli knew how effectively Manties could use pods even before they started building the hollow-hulled ships of the wall full of pods. They'd used pods effectively even at Hancock at the very beginning of the war.

He checked his plot. He knew the Manties could see his own superdreadnought so close to the hyper limit on the opposite side of the ecliptic. And they would soon realize they had no chance of catching *Scimitar*, so they'd proceed to the *Autonomy* and remaining ships with Bartoli's crews aboard. And they wouldn't be able to do anything against the Manties. Even if they didn't have pods—which they damned well would have, with the ammunition ship along— two Manty battlecruisers against one Silesian wouldn't even be comparable.

Bartoli had managed to get what he could from Caroline. But his time had run out, and he would have to cut his losses.

"I think it's time we implement Silent Stalker," he ordered.

Captain Venner looked at him from the screen that connected Bartoli to the main bridge. "Are you sure, Sir?"

Bartoli nodded. "Yes."

"What about our people on those ships?" Venner asked quietly and Bartoli shook his head. They both knew what had to be done. In New Rodrigo, they'd blown up a whole shipyard to cover their escape.

The crews aboard the ships here in Caroline didn't know that, but they knew they were playing a dangerous game.

※ ※ ※

Eve Chandler was also thinking about how she'd used pods to destroy lots of Havenite battlecruisers and even some dreadnoughts at Hancock. As the tactical officer of the squadron flagship, most of the nuts and bolts had been her job. But now, it was more complicated as her reinforced task group had joined with *Fearless*,

Druid, Star Warrior and *Apprentice* and they were slowly decelerating toward the depot.

Wolfhound had returned in time with the two battlecruisers of Captain Ellis's division, *Royalist* and *Xerxes*. Luckily they had only been wrapping things up in Chalice and Eve's orders hadn't really destabilized the situation elsewhere. What was better, *Wolfhound* had also found the light cruiser *Aspis*, a sister ship of *Testudo* in the system on an unscheduled visit. That was great, because newer vessels like the two *Avalon*-class light cruisers or her own flagship could handle many more pods thanks to their increased fire control.

So that was their plan. The task group was accelerating towards the Havenite superdreadnought—named *Scimitar*, according to Preston. The ammunition ship *Katla* had given pods to every vessel, and they'd all been slowly moving towards the system primary. A ragtag group of eight heavy cruisers, one Marine support cruiser, two *Reliant*-class battlecruisers, two light cruisers and one destroyer.

All fourteen of them massed barely more than half as much as their massive opponent, and not one of them could match her firepower or the thickness of her massive defenses. But simple size wasn't everything.

Of course, Ghost Rider reported that the superdreadnought was already almost at the hyper limit. That geometry meant they were unlikely to catch the SD if she decided to run, and Captain Pankowski had already reported that several of the Silesian ships had left the system before Eve's arrival, but the enemy battlecruiser and remaining SCN ships were too far in-system to escape.

Everything still seemed too distant to Eve. She was still watching it through that pane of glass. She hoped the battlecruiser crew wouldn't be stupid and would surrender before she had to kill them.

But everything was distant.

Something was off.

"They must have expected us," she said. "They're waiting at the edge of the system."

"In their place, I'd have done the same," Strauss said. She was standing with Eve, along with Black Oak and Hagen. The flag captain would go to the command deck soon, but they still had time and she was still a member of Eve's staff, and not everything could be discussed through visual pickup.

Like this strange feeling Eve had.

"Am I missing something?" she asked quietly.

"I don't know, Ma'am," Strauss said. "We can't catch the Havenite; he was ready for us. But why hasn't he translated out already? Maybe he's just a cool customer. On the other hand, he has time and he can wait and see what's going to happen."

Hagen started whistling something on the flag bridge.

Which was even more annoying than his usual manners.

"What are you whistling?" Strauss asked.

"You don't know? It's an ideal melody for long deep space travels. It's called *The Blue Danube*. I'm surprised you don't know it, Captain. After all, your name is Strauss."

"Tell me, does being so obnoxious come naturally to you, or is it part of your image or cover as a spook?"

"Well, I'd say half and half. On the other hand, I'd be lying if I said I didn't enjoy it as well. I always strive to be annoying in new and original ways."

"Yes, and you're succeeding," Strauss said, but she also smiled. Given the danger that was coming at them, it was actually refreshing to be irritated by the simply obnoxious Captain Hagen.

※ ※ ※

Bartoli watched the Manty task force closing in. *Autonomy*'s impellers had been on standby when the Manties arrive, and the battlecruiser was already racing towards the hyper limit on the far side of the system, but it wouldn't escape the Manties.

Neither would the remaining Silly ships with Bartoli's crews aboard. Crews that knew about his base at Quatre Bras.

Only *Scimitar* would escape. She'd already crossed the hyper limit, which had taken her directly toward the enemy, but unlike *Autonomy*, she would disappear into hyper well before the Manties could range on her. Which left only one thing to do.

He entered a combination on his keyboard and the *Scimitar* sent a signal.

One hundred and fifty-two seconds later, the light-speed command reached its destination and *Autonomy* and the remaining SCN vessels exploded. The nukes he had installed aboard each of those ships did the job.

No prisoners the Manties could interrogate.

Bartoli didn't like doing it. He'd once worked for StateSec and he knew how to be ruthless, but he wasn't malicious. He didn't enjoy it, and he knew that good people were hard to come by. More to the point, if his long-term plans were to work, he needed a cadre of loyal people. Of course, he still had lots of SS fanatics under his command who were almost eager to sacrifice themselves. Some had blown up on those ships, some remained on *Scimitar*. Unfortunately, he also needed people who *weren't* fanatics, and by and large, he preferred *living* loyal people who weren't fanatics.

But sometimes he had to be ruthless.

Like at New Rodrigo.

※ ※ ※

The flag bridge was very silent.

The sensors had noted the explosion of the parked decommissioned ships and of the enemy battlecruiser.

And now the Havenite superdreadnought's icon vanished from the plot, as well, as she translated into hyper.

Eve watched it all helplessly.

Could she have prevented this? Come up with better strategy? Could she really not be as focused and involved as before? Before...?

Was she just an automaton, performing a set function? It had worked in Home Fleet in *de facto* peacetime, but not here in Silesia!

"Lay in a zero-zero course for the depot," she heard herself saying on autopilot. Other standard orders followed.

"Look for survivors from those ships. Then contact Mariposa. I'll have to speak to the local authorities, hear it from their perspective and tell them what happened."

"And then, Ma'am?" Black Oak asked.

She said nothing. They should go to Quatre Bras. Immediately. In Bartoli's wake. But he could have many other SCN ships or maybe even ex-Havenite vessels. What she had here was ample to bring down one superdreadnought—if she used pods. But there was a limit to the number of pods she could tow, which imposed a limit on her maximum throw weight. If she had to face *Scimitar* when the SD was backed by many escorts and other ships, to help blunt her salvos...

But Bartoli could disappear. For six months. For a year. And then attack something else. Somewhere else.

Maybe someone with more vision should take over.

Someone who wasn't totally detached from everything.

How she envied Honor Harrington. She could always go on, finish the job. Do what was needed.

Evelyn Chandler had thought she could too. But she couldn't.

"I'll inform you later," she said finally. "Stand down from battle stations and bring the whole task group to condition two. Instruct Captain Johnson to take charge of the search and rescue; his ship is best suited for it."

She left the flag bridge as soon as possible.

⌘ ⌘ ⌘

Chief Mandalo had prepared a cup of Army coffee for her along with some refreshments, but she didn't want either. She just... wanted to be alone.

She had been in her quarters for barely thirty minutes when the Marine sentry announced Captain Hagen.

Her jaw tightened. The last thing she needed just now was the spook and his utterly annoying personality, and she hovered on the brink of telling the sentry just that. But she couldn't, of course.

"Enter," she said, instead.

He came in.

"Yes? What is it, Captain?"

"I'm sorry to disturb you, Commodore. Just wanted to point out that there were no survivors on those decommissioned ships, no one to interrogate."

"I see." The pane of glass was still standing. "You're about to suggest we go to Quatre Bras?"

"Yes, the sooner the better."

"I'm not sure we can accomplish anything without reinforcements."

"Bartoli is still there, I'm sure you line officers can figure out something." This time he grinned.

"I'm not sure I can, Captain. Maybe we've run out of tricks."

"We? Or you?"

Eve frowned. "Captain Hagen, I'm sure you need to be elsewhere."

He didn't take the hint. Or more precisely, he did, and just decided to ignore it.

He stopped smiling.

"So, Commodore, how exactly did your daughter die?"

Eve's head snapped towards him.

"I beg your pardon?"

"I asked how did your daughter die, Ma'am. I understand I may be opening old wounds, but since we have so many fresh wounds, maybe we should open some of the old ones as well. Create a good mix. And since we aren't going to pursue Bartoli, we don't have much else to do except talk. Frankly, you look like you need to get that off your chest. You've been behaving like a tightly sealed pressure cooker ever since I met you. So I thought it might not hurt to talk about it. You certainly don't talk about it to anyone else. But naturally, if you choose to answer 'none of your frigging business, asshole,' then I completely understand."

Eve fought the urge to punch him.

This was really over the line. How dared this bastard ask about Diana in this way? Bringing back all those memories at a time like—

The mental pane of glass shattered.

"She was just twenty," she heard herself say hoarsely. "She was in the Royal Manticoran Army, a private in the 198th Shadow Vale Regiment. I never forced her to join the Navy or any other branch but one day, in the last year of high school, she just decided to go. I was in deep space, fighting the Peeps, when I got the message. I remember how proud I was of her. The Royal Army expanded exponentially in wartime, you remember? She got through boot camp and other training and then she was shipped to one of the Peep star systems we'd conquered, Samson, two weeks before her twentieth birthday. She was there barely twenty-four days when she was killed along with eight other soldiers by a State Security suicide bomber with a small vest pocket explosive." She looked at the ONI agent. "Just like that. He was just walking along their patrol. She was just twenty!"

"I thought the SS didn't have enough fanatics to do something like that. It's more fitting for a place like Masada."

"That's true. Diana was just lucky to get killed by 'one of the few.'"

Hagen was silent.

"We were having a party on the *Athena* for the exec's birthday when I found out," Eve continued, still not believing she was telling this to Hagen, of all people. "The com officer took me aside and told me. I remember that I didn't say anything. I just went to the forward observation lounge, and I just stood there. For hours. I don't know. Looking at the stars. I asked to be relieved there and then and my request was granted. I still missed the memorial service. And then... commiserating with my ex-husband, family reunions... it all seems like a dream. Afterward, I thought I should just dig back into the job, but even that didn't work, I just couldn't. I couldn't."

A lone tear appeared on her cheek.

"I got compassionate leave of absence and went home. I just... couldn't do anything. People around me were angry about the ceasefire, about Janacek. I got condolences from Duchess Harrington, Mike Henke, Cindy Van Wyhe, all my other colleagues and friends. But I couldn't do anything. Couldn't get back to work, do something, anything. They all suffered losses and could go on, were examples to others. I was just... broken. I just couldn't. I've been like that for almost two years. Doing nothing. And when I got back to space and got a new command... it just was so different. Like it was all far away. Distant. I think of it as being behind a pane of glass. And I've lost something. My therapist would probably tell me there's no shame it that. But Bartoli slipped away because of me."

"No, he didn't," Hagen told her. "There was no way you could have caught him before he hypered out. Or done anything to save the ships he blew up. No one could have."

"But if I'd waited to deploy Pankowski until *Katla* came up, sent him with pods in the first place, Bartoli could never have—"

"And you couldn't do *that*, either," Hagen pointed out. "Your orders were to deploy him as soon as possible, not wait weeks until *Katla* turned up."

"But—"

"If this was a case of failure, I think it was a *collective* one," Hagen said firmly. Then he looked at her, and for once there was no sign of his smartass personality in his expression.

"Commodore," he said almost gently, "for what it's worth, I'm sorry, Ma'am. I didn't mean..."

Eve smiled weakly. Her brain was looking at all the shattered pieces of the mental glass. "You did mean to. You did."

Hagen shrugged. "One advantage of being obnoxious is that I don't have to worry about other people's delicate feelings. Sometimes I have to poke the hornet's nest."

Eve shook her head. "So, what now?"

"I think you compare yourself too much to other people, struggle with accepting grief, and blame yourself for everything. There are no standard responses to losing a child or how long it should take to get back to your life and work, if you ever manage it at all."

"Yes, my therapist told me all that."

"Or course she did; she's no doubt a smart woman. But she's also not here. We are, and we have a StateSec warlord to catch."

Eve looked at him. "Just like that? I have valid reasons to wait, you know."

"Of course I know, Ma'am, but we both know that there's also the fear that you've screwed up, you're not up to it anymore, and that you can't do it. And we both know that's bullshit, Ma'am."

Eve stared at him. "You do realize that you're not supposed to talk to your superior officers like that?"

"Feel free to arrest me and demote me. But please don't let my fate stop you from going to kick Bartoli's ass. And unless I'm mistaken, you have a score to settle with the StateSec people, no?"

"You think you can motivate me with a vision of revenge?"

"You'd be surprised how well that works. As an ONI agent I can tell you that the best spies are those who are out for revenge. Idealists are unreliable, and those who do it for money can be bought by someone with bigger wallet. But revenge, oh my, that's a great motivator."

⌘ ⌘ ⌘

She let Hagen go. She still wanted to be alone. After he left, she was at first angry at the bastard. And he hadn't really told her anything she didn't know before.

But while she was alone, finally eating the food her steward prepared and drinking coffee, she found herself thinking about Bartoli and the whole situation.

Thinking . . . and being involved.

For the first time in . . . she didn't even know.

And then she decided.

The flag bridge was rather quiet when Eve appeared.

"Set course to Quatre Bras, Ms. Garba," she said to the staff astrogator. "The task group will depart as soon as we finish going over the wreckage."

The crew snapped to action.

Eve Chandler wasn't sure she wasn't reacting anymore, but she intended to find out.

※ ※ ※

"The yard master says that the first Silesian ships can be ready within a few weeks," Captain Venner stated, once he'd been ushered into Bartoli's private cabin aboard *Scimitar*. "Per your instructions, I have them working on the battlecruisers first."

Bartoli nodded. His richly decorated dining table supported an equally rich dinner. Venner knew his admiral's routines and knew that Bartoli had to enjoy dinner even now. Or maybe especially now. He knew that Bartoli wasn't just having dinner because he was hungry or because he wanted to show off. It was a psychological game. He'd contacted Prime Minister Montero and Prince Tannah while he was eating to make the slight suggestion that he wasn't worried all that much about the recent unpleasantness and that he was feeling confident.

Venner had been invited to dinner, but excused himself, preferring to oversee the yard workers as well as the return of the prize crews back aboard *Scimitar* from the captured vessels docked at the Harlequin Station, the main shipyard and port in orbit around Navarra, which itself was the sole inhabited planet in the Quatre Bras System.

Venner was happy it had all worked out. He hadn't wanted to encounter the Manties, and he was delighted they hadn't had to fight their way out of Caroline. However, they might still need to—

A sharp buzz sounded from Bartoli's desk and he reached for the intercom button.

"Yes?"

"Bridge, Lieutenant Daumier, Sir. We've just picked up a hyper footprint. A big one, coming in on a bearing for a least-time course from Caroline."

Bartoli and Venner exchanged glances and Venner felt as if his bones were suddenly made of ice.

"The Manties," Bartoli said, and Venner nodded.

"How could they have found us?" Venner asked.

Bartoli's expression mirrored the surprise of his flag captain. He didn't expect this. Not so soon. "Give me details!"

"It's hard to tell at this distance, but the impeller signatures are almost identical to the ones at Caroline."

Bartoli had already known that had to be the case. But how could they have found him? So soon!

He'd known that someone would spot him here eventually, but he'd hoped that by the time that happened it would be a done deal.

"Thank you, Lieutenant. Don't do anything yet. We'll see what the Manties—if it is the Manties—do first, and we have plenty of time to go to battle stations later."

"I understand, Sir!" Daumier was a fanatic. He still hated the Manticorans as symbol of everything that was bad in the universe. That would prove useful.

He turned to Venner. "I think I should contact Prime Minister Entebe."

※ ※ ※

"There she is, right in orbit around Navarra," Black Oak said, as the imagery came back from the heavily stealthed Ghost Rider drone, and Eve nodded. During the voyage from Caroline, she had managed to eliminate some more of her inner doubts and sense of detachment. And she'd even shared a dinner with Black Oak, during which they discussed their personal losses openly and painfully.

She wasn't "okay" in any sense of the word now, but she was focused and ready for what was coming.

The superdreadnought was in front of them and her task group was steadily accelerating toward the ship. During the last nine days, they'd planned all kinds of contingencies, but the question was still about blunt force.

She'd halted her squadron just short of the hyper limit, ready to pounce whatever direction *Scimitar* might choose to run, and she'd distributed pods to all ships as before, but she still had a significantly small force. With pods, they could almost certainly destroy the monster before it escaped, but if it came into energy range, they'd be dead, too.

Plus there was this question of other Silesian ships.

"Any news of the SCN units?"

"Inconclusive so far, Ma'am," Black Oak said. "The local space station in Navarra orbit has a great number of ships docked, and quite a few of them seem to be current or ex-ECN units. But so far we don't have clear enough emission signatures to say positively that any of them came from Caroline."

"Understood. But we need that nailed down ASAP, Norman."

"Yes, Ma'am. CIC is working on it."

The question would also be how spaceworthy the ships were and if they might pose a threat. Eve doubted that, but she also knew that other SCN units had defected to Bartoli and could be somewhere in the system.

"Commodore, we are picking up a transmission. It's from Navarra," Lieutenant Lindstrom said. "The header says it's from the office of the Prime Minister."

Eve nodded. During the voyage here, she and her staff had tried to learn as much as they could about Navarra. Not that there was much *to* learn. The Manticoran databases were rather sketchy and, as far as Eve knew, no Manticoran shipping charter had ever traded in the Quatre Bras system. Haven had had an occasional freelance trader visit the place; that was how Haven had learned about Bartoli in the first place.

Quatre Bras was a G1 star, with a twenty-two light-minute hyper limit, and Navarra was a relatively insignificant world. It had very few export values for a distant star nation like Manticore or Haven, or even Silesia, but it often traded with some of its non-Silesian neighbors. That was most likely why they had such a big shipyard, and maybe why the local rulers had made a deal with Bartoli. They might have a shipyard, but their own "navy" consisted of only about a dozen LACs for system defense and one obsolete *Durandal*-class destroyer, which the Navarrans had purchased from Haven some forty years ago.

Politically, Navarra was basically an autocracy with a ruling prince who appointed his own government. It had a parliament with elected officials, but the prince chose who to appoint as his prime minister.

And it seemed as if the current prime minister was calling. Which made a certain sense. There'd been just about enough time for their standard identification to reach the planet and the Prime Minister to react.

"Put it through."

A small, balding man appeared on the display by Eve's leg.

"Good afternoon. I am Prime Minister Dorsan Entebe, head of His Grace Prince Tannah's government. I'm speaking to the approaching vessels. Please identify yourselves or you will be treated as hostile by the Navarran Navy."

"Prime Minister Entebe, this is Commodore Evelyn Chandler of the Royal Manticoran Navy. We are chasing a pirate and terrorist out of Silesia. His name is Marcus Bartoli and he possesses a Havenite *DuQuesne*-class superdreadnought. The same ship which is currently in orbit around Navarra."

After the inevitable light-speed lag, Entebe answered.

"Commodore Chandler, I'm aware of the superdreadnought *Soult*'s condition and of the fact that she has been in battle recently. As far as I know, she is a legitimate Havenite warship, not a pirate. According to the Deneb Accords, we are permitting her crew to conduct basic repairs to make her spaceworthy, but not to improve her fighting capability. However, since Navarra is neutral in your current war between Manticore and Haven, we have to impose the law of neutrality also defined by the Deneb Accords. *Soult* is in a neutral system and belligerent warships are forbidden to wage war in neutral territory. Also, when leaving the system, belligerent ships have to abide by the twenty-four-hour rule. I believe, Commodore Chandler, that you will abide by the Deneb Accords, since both Manticore and Haven are signatories."

Eve stopped herself from opening her mouth. The Deneb Accords included several centuries' worth of naval codes, rules of war and regulations on the treatment of POWs. But this particular part seldom came up in modern warfare. *Technically*, belligerent warships could approach no closer than twelve light-minutes to a neutral system's hyper limit without that star system government's permission. That was a rule that was most often ignored, however, especially by star nations with powerful fleets, and when it happened that belligerent warships entered a neutral star system, usually the combat erupted well outside the orbit of any inhabited planet. In fact, more often than not, any fighting was over before the neutrals ever realized there *was* any fighting. Eve didn't remember any instance during the First Havenite War when this stipulation of the Deneb Accords had even come up.

The rule against fighting in neutral harbors was older than space travel, but it was usually very difficult to enforce.

As it would likely be now.

"Prime Minister Entebe, I'm well aware of the Deneb Accords," she said and noticed Hagen winking at her. "However, since we have irrefutable evidence that the superdreadnought *Scimitar*—or *Soult* as you've come to know her—and Marcus Bartoli have committed numerous acts of piracy, we ask you to allow us to engage his vessel."

Another wait for an answer and Eve looked up at Hagen.

"That was smart of them, coming up with Deneb Accords," the ONI agent said. "It never even occurred to me. I just wonder how they think they'll be able to enforce it."

"And she damned well hasn't suffered battle damage!" Strauss muttered.

"No, but I can see why Entebe is claiming she has," Eve said dryly. Strauss looked at her, and she shrugged. "As long as she's 'repairing damage' within the stipulations of the Accords, we can't demand that Navarra order her to leave 'neutral space.' So if they want to buy a lot of extra time..."

"Bastards," Strauss growled, and Eve surprised herself with a chuckle. She started to reply, but before she could—

"Commodore Chandler," Entebe said, "I cannot confirm or disprove that RHNS *Scimitar* is a pirate ship when all evidence suggests that it is a legitimate combatant. As such, my government needs to err on the side of caution. As long as *Scimitar* is inside the Quatre Bras territorial limit—which, I remind you, begins twenty-four limits from the system primary, in our case—she is in neutral space and has a right to be protected." Entebe's mouth corners twitched slightly and Eve had the feeling that the Navarran was about to play his trump card.

"As it happens, I have here Mr. Alanis Fasman, a Special Envoy of the Solarian League Foreign Office, who is on Navarra on an official visit, and he confirms my view of the situation. Mr. Fasman?"

A new face appeared on the screen. This was a younger and taller man with long dark hair, smiling at the pickup. "Good afternoon, Commodore Chandler. Mr. Prime Minister Entebe is entirely correct. According to the Deneb Accords, RHNS *Soult* is protected in neutral territory. That is the stand of the Solarian League. If the Star Kingdom of Manticore were to violate that convention, I can assure you that the Solarian repercussions towards your Star Kingdom would be severe. Also keep in mind that while your own ships may currently be outside the Quatre Bras hyper limit, you are already well within its *territorial* limit. As such, they are also subject to the twenty-four-hour rule and will be prohibited from leaving the area earlier than twenty-four hours after the departure of the Havenite vessel."

✖ ✖ ✖

"Well, we can safely say we never saw *that* coming," Hagen said twenty minutes later as they sat in the briefing room.

"The Solarian League was the last thing I expected here," Strauss said with a sigh. "Do you think this Fasman is what he says he is?"

"A Solly official?" Hagen shrugged. "I'll bet he has the credentials to prove it. But then, the Solarian League has so many secretaries, undersecretaries, liaisons and special envoys that the question really is, how important he actually is? My guess is not that much. No Solly bureaucrat with good connections or with power would voluntarily travel here to the ass-end of nowhere. Begging the Commodore's pardon, Ma'am." He produced a mischievous grin. "My other guess would be that he's in Bartoli's pocket and he has him exactly for something like this; to protect him with words like 'the Solarian League doesn't want you to do this and if you do, there will be repercussions.'"

"Well, it worked," Eve said grumpily. Her task group continued to hold station outside the system hyper limit. "Even if we ultimately ignore his threat, they knew this would stall us. Especially since Bartoli knows or thinks that our ships aren't enough to make the issue certain. We can still lose, so he gambled that we would wait for reinforcements. Maybe he assumes that his will arrive sooner."

"Fasman is likely someone in a position to persuade his superiors to acknowledge Bartoli's new little empire as an independent state," Hagen said. "Because his superiors generally won't care one way or another. But I don't think he expected to come face-to-face with us directly."

"Do you think he'll manage to make any kind of repercussions for Manticore if we just go ahead and attack?" Black Oak asked.

"No one knows," Hagen replied. "I guess that he might, or he might just count on his belief that we won't risk it."

"Maybe we should talk to Mr. Fasman," Eve said. This was purely outside her area of expertise and maybe more in Hagen's league, but it was enough. "I think I should visit Mr. Fasman and Prime Minister Entebe on Navarra."

"Ma'am, are you—" Strauss started and then cut herself off.

Eve smiled. "Am I out of my mind? I don't think so. I think that we need more information from the surface. So while the task group should stay outside the limit, I can pay an official visit to the Prime Minister."

Strauss sighed. "I guess I won't dissuade you, right?"

Eve grinned. It seemed more natural to her than it had in years. "Not really."

"At least this time you won't tell me the mission would continue in my capable hands." She was right. While she was the most senior captain in their cruiser squadron, they'd added more ships to their task group, so Strauss was now junior to Captain Ellis of the *Royalist* and Captain Phelps of the *Xerxes*.

"No, I won't," Eve agreed. "And I'm just going to talk to the Prime Minister and to Mr. Fasman. I'll have just a small group of aides with me." She smiled. "I'm thinking Captain Hagen, Commander Black Oak and Spacer First Class Leo Statman."

✳ ✳ ✳

"Your Excellency, Commodore Evelyn Chandler, Captain Lucius Hagen and Lieutenant Commander Norman Bettany, Baron Black Oak, of the Royal Manticoran Navy," the aide made the introductions— including Black Oak's noble rank—without mistakes. Apparently, people were used to noble titles here. She also specifically didn't introduce Leo Statman, as someone too junior, basically on the level of servant. Also, no mention was made of the treecat on Statman's shoulder.

Prime Minister Entebe rose, but did not walk around his elaborate desk or offer his hand. He smiled and bowed his head slightly. "Welcome, Commodore Chandler, Captain Hagen, Commander Black Oak. Please be seated." He nodded to a tall man standing by the Prime Minister's office room window. "I have asked Mr. Fasman to join us here to provide the Solarian League's view on the matter."

"A pleasure to meet you all," Fasman said, with a huge smile, as he took a seat in one of the luxurious armchairs with which the office was furnished.

"A pleasure to meet you Mr. Prime Minister, Mr. Fasman," Eve said with a false sincerity that should have made even Hagen proud.

"I assume you wish to discuss the various implications of the Deneb Accords," Entebe suggested. "I understand you claim that

Admiral Bartoli and the crew of his flagship, the *Soult*, aren't Havenites but in fact pirates and terrorists. Unfortunately, since we have no direct evidence on the matter, my government—held with executive powers after the passing of Prince Tannah—has to err on the side of caution. I discussed the situation with Mr. Fasman and he concurs that the precedents set by the Solarian League would agree with me. As long as Admiral Bartoli is in neutral space, no actions may be legally taken against him or his ship."

"Oh, we understand that completely, Mr. Prime Minister," Eve said with another smile that almost turned into one of Hagen's mischievous grins. "We don't intend to violate the Deneb Accords, but I'm sure you understand our need to contain this pirate." She chose that word on purpose as if she was sharing some private joke with Prime Minister Entebe. "On the other hand, I must ask; do you plan to intern the *Scimitar—Soult*—here for the duration of the war, as is also stipulated by the Deneb Accords?"

Entebe's smile disappeared, and even Fasman was taken aback. "I beg your pardon?"

"Article Eighty-Five, Section Seven of the Deneb Accords states that a neutral power has the authority to intern a belligerent warship in their territory. Especially if the warship in question has finished all of her repairs and is only using the neutral territory as a hiding place."

Entebe may have been taken aback but, as a career politician, he quickly recovered and smiled. "It may come to that, Commodore. However, as you probably know, we are in no position to force such a huge warship to stay here."

Eve smiled. "Oh, we understand that. Unfortunately, we also can't let it leave without our knowledge, so I'm afraid we'd need to stay."

The Prime Minister frowned. "Stay?"

"Yes, of course we'll keep safely outside of your hyper limit, but we'll need to stay; so will our reinforcements."

"Excuse me, but you mean the *territorial* limit, don't you?" Fasman said a bit sharply.

"No, Mr. Fasman, I mean the *hyper* limit. We will initiate no combat within the hyper limit *or* within Quatre Bras territorial limits unless *Scimitar* approaches within six light-minutes of our own vessels. Should that happen, we will be free to engage under Article Eighty-Five, Section Eight, Clause Three, which permits a belligerent power to assume hostile intent even in neutral space if approached by a warship of another belligerent." Eve smiled. "I invite you to examine Solarian League-vs.-Allenton System, where that principle was upheld by a Solarian admiralty court."

"And if the superdreadnought *doesn't* approach within six light-minutes?" Entebe asked sharply.

"Why, in that case, we would be unable to engage, of course. However," Eve's smile turned sharklike, "my ships are outside the limit. I assure you that we can micro jump into a position which will force her to approach us that closely if she wants to cross that limit in order to translate out."

"But you can't *do* that!"

"I'm afraid we can, Mr. Prime Minister." She looked back at Fasman. "Do you think the Solarian League will view this as an aggression, Mr. Fasman?"

The diplomat looked unhappy, and shrugged. "I'm afraid it will."

Behind her, Tebo made the almost inaudible sound they had agreed on.

He's lying.

"The Solarian League supports the neutrality of this world," Fasman said. "As you know, the Solarian League has always striven to provide a channel for communication and diplomatic negotiation during the war between Manticore and Haven and this is a situation in which interstellar law must be followed. I'm afraid the Solarian government may view this as *force majeure* and react appropriately."

Another *he-is-lying* sound.

"Well, I'm afraid I have my orders," Eve said. "And since reinforcements are coming here anyway, I'm afraid we'll have to stay put. It's completely possible that Admiral Sarnow, my commander, will decide I was in the wrong, but we can wait until after his battle squadron arrives."

Entebe froze. "What do you mean, battle squadron?"

"As in six superdreadnoughts, at least. I sent the admiral only a very preliminary dispatch, in which I emphasized that I had no information on the actual force we might encounter." She shrugged. "I can't be *certain* he'll bring the entire Capital Squadron, but I'm confident he'll bring most of it, under the circumstances."

"Not to mention that, apart from Mr. Bartoli's ship, we're also looking for some stolen Silesian Navy vessels," Hagen added with a mischievous grin. "And I'm afraid that several obviously Silesian ships are docked at your Harlequin Station."

Entebe took a deep breath. "In that, you are mistaken. Yes, we have Silesian ships docked there, but we purchased those from the Confederacy."

He's lying, Tebo bleeked behind her, not that she needed him for this.

"I understand," she said. "We would like to inspect the station, of course, and compare it with our notes on the ships in question. They still have their active IFFs, after all."

Fasman cleared his throat: "I'm afraid the Solarian League would see this a clear violation and respond forcefully."

He's lying.

Eve smiled. "I understand. Well, we all have our orders. And mine mean I have to keep my forces here until my superiors arrive. You understand, I'm sure."

⚒ ⚒ ⚒

Marcus Bartoli stopped the replay of the HD camera in the Prime Minister's office.

He'd hoped Fasman would be more useful, but unfortunately, that hadn't happened. Not when that Commodore brought a fucking treecat to the meeting. Bartoli had heard legends about those beasts, and he'd been at Barnett when they brought in Harrington as a prisoner with her treecat. He'd never known if she believed the stories about them being intelligent mindreaders but he knew Chandler wouldn't have brought it to the meeting if she didn't expect to gain something from it.

So the Manty task group did not plan to leave. And they were expecting reinforcements. Bartoli technically also had reinforcements he could call on, but they weren't really reliable. And he wouldn't be able to use the ships docked at Harlequin Station for several weeks. Not to mention the Manties would blow them apart if they tried.

No. He was in a corner. He'd hoped his involvement with Entebe and Fasman would stay secret for some more months for him to consolidate power. He'd helped Entebe . . . retire Prince Tannah, the local monarch. The general assembly of the planet—basically a bunch of oligarchs—were to assemble next month and vote for

Bartoli as the new ruler. His superdreadnought was a pretty strong argument in favor. And Navarrans generally understood the advantages he would bring them with his ship. Not to mention that they were loyal to their monarch but didn't really care who he was.

Unfortunately, now the Manties had endangered Bartoli's scheme. He'd have to do something drastic. The Manties so far had only two battlecruisers. Maybe a frontal assault would simply solve things. Not likely, but Bartoli planned for everything.

He pushed the button on his intercom. "Captain Venner to my office, please." When his flag captain arrived, Bartoli looked at him. "I think we need to implement the Second Death scenario."

⚹ ⚹ ⚹

"Ma'am, you're pretty good at bluffing," Black Oak said then they were on their way back toward *Juggernaut*.

"Nonsense," Eve said. "I suck at bluffing. I learned that years ago during the regular wardroom poker games aboard *Nike*. No, I simply needed to gauge how far they're willing to go." She nodded towards Spacer Statman and Tebo. "And to figure out how sure they are of their position."

"Yes, Ma'am," Statman said and blushed. "If . . . if I may, what happens now?"

"Now we wait, exactly as we said we would. But I doubt that Mr. Bartoli will want to wait here for a squadron of superdreadnoughts."

⚹ ⚹ ⚹

"She's coming out, Sir!" Black Oak said from his station. "Her wedge is up and she is starting to accelerate!"

Eve was immediately behind him. "Course?"

"Looks like they're coming straight at us, Ma'am." He shook his head. "My guess is they want to force a battle."

Eve nodded. "Bring the Task Group to Battle Stations. Ms. Garba, please set a course for intercept of the *Scimitar*."

"Course is already set, Sir," the staff astrogator said.

Eve was now back in her command chair and punched in a code for the *Juggernaut*'s bridge that connected her directly to Strauss.

"Captain here."

"Angelique, it seems they want to force a fight with us. With the pods from *Katla*, we can kill *Scimitar* long before she can get into range of her missiles, let alone the energy range."

"I know, Ma'am." Eve hadn't used *Juggernaut*'s captain as her sounding board very often, but she was trying to get back to her old habits. "Bartoli may not know we have pods. Or he has something up his sleeve anyway."

"He may, but I can't imagine what. A *DuQuesne* doesn't mount the tubes for multi-drive missiles, so she can't match our range with shipboard missiles. And he doesn't have pods of his own." Eve thought about it. "That we know of. I don't want to overanalyze this, but I won't risk our task group. We'll fire the moment he's in range."

"Understood, Ma'am."

"I just hope we won't have to," Eve said. Hagen had talked about her taking revenge against State Security people. She still didn't know what she thought about it. These people were from the same cloth as those who'd killed Diana. But she wouldn't just slaughter them.

Bartoli can't be stupid, he knows he can't just shoot his way out. He has to.

Or is it that he just doesn't care?

She shook her head.

"Com, hail the approaching superdreadnought. Order them to strike their wedge and surrender."

"Yes, Ma'am."

As the superdreadnought kept closing, Eve realized she felt more alive than she had for months. It might have been strange, considering they could be dead in a few hours, but she felt the cold anticipation mixed with an eagerness she hadn't felt in a long time.

* * *

Bartoli sat tapping on the armrest of his chair, watching the plot as *Scimitar* continued her unwavering approach to the Manticoran formation.

He said nothing. Nothing remained to be said.

Not long now.

* * *

"We'll be in range in one minute, Commodore," Black Oak said.

Eve nodded. The glass pane had long been shattered. She saw Diana's face, now, somewhere in the back of her mind as she watched the approaching superdreadnought. She wasn't detached. Not anymore. She was involved. *Very* involved. And she felt a sort of savage hunger.

She shouldn't. She was about to massacre thousands of human beings. But, in the past few years, she hadn't behaved in the way she should have.

And Hagen was right. There was no formula on how she should behave or not behave.

She'd given them a chance to surrender. They'd ignored all her hails.

"Open fire," she ordered.

❊ ❊ ❊

The Manticoran pods, supplied by the ammunition ship *Katla* and controlled by Eve's squadron, had been loaded with laserheads designed to kill capital ships. And they all had just one target.

For a long moment, Eve wondered if Bartoli had some ace up his sleeve, if *Scimitar did* have pods. But nothing happened.

The lasers bit into the massive ship. *Scimitar* was built to withstand great deal of punishment, but a "great deal" wasn't enough.

The superdreadnought exploded.

"It's confirmed, Ma'am!" said Black Oak. "She's gone! The superdreadnought is gone!"

The flag bridge started cheering. Officers tried to calm people down, but not too hard. *Scimitar* was the only functioning enemy ship in the system and they knew it and were prepared to allow a small breach of discipline as long as their Commodore would allow it.

Eve was just staring at the master plot, again at the place where the icon was.

"You did it, Ma'am" said Hagen with a mischievous grin. "You did it!"

Eve was looking at the plot.

Yes. She'd done it.

But she was still looking at the plot. The elation wasn't there. She didn't cheer all those deaths. Neither did she feel satisfaction.

She only saw Diana.

And, as the crew was cheering around her, she realized something else.

She was back. Not a grieving soul, not an avenging angel, not an automaton.

Just . . . herself.

❊ ❊ ❊

"Excuse me, Commodore."

Evelyn Chandler raised her head as Captain Hagen came to the flag bridge.

She hadn't seen him much in the eight days since the destruction of *Scimitar*. He'd been making some contacts on the planetary surface, as she understood it, but she and the rest of her people had been just a bit busy in orbit around it.

One day after the battle, the Marines from *Claymore* and *Star Warrior* had boarded Harlequin Station and secured the stolen Silesian ships. For a few hours, she'd thought they might meet actual armed resistance, but the fight had gone out of Bartoli's remaining followers with his death, and apparently the Navarrans weren't stupid enough to piss off a Manticoran task group which had just killed an SD in its space. The tense blockade had continued, but the Navarran Prime Minister had suddenly become much friendlier. Mr. Fasman had made a token protest on behalf of the League, but the captured Silesian ships were pretty strong evidence of Navarra's involvement and this definitely wasn't the hill Fasman wanted to die on.

He'd actually left the system two days ago.

Now Eve looked at Hagen.

"Yes, Captain Hagen? What can I do for you?"

"Can I speak to you? In private."

Eve frowned. "Eh, sure."

Eve climbed out of her bridge chair and led the way into the flag briefing room. Once they were alone, it was Hagen's turn to frown.

"You know I've been spending time down on the planet, Ma'am?" he said, and Eve nodded.

"I assumed it had something to do with your 'spook' duties," she said, and it was his turn to nod.

"It did," he agreed. "I had a strange feeling I needed to confirm."

"What kind of feeling?" Eve asked.

"I've been thinking about Bartoli's tactics as he tried to leave the system. And I think it was pretty stupid of him."

"I agree, but he probably wasn't the type of person who'd surrender."

"No, Ma'am, he wasn't. What he was, was a pretty ruthless SOB. He blew the New Rodrigo shipyards to cover his tracks *and* then did the same thing in Caroline, when he didn't want to risk his ships to fall into our hands. Or his people."

"I know."

"So, going on a suicide charge doesn't seem to be his style."

"Maybe he ran out of options?" Eve suggested.

"Maybe. But as I said, I went to the planet. Went to the dinner the very nervous planetary rulers prepared for us."

"I know," Eve said. She hadn't gone, but she'd sent Captain Ellis as her most senior subordinate to serve as her deputy where the defeated oligarchs of Navarra wanted to appease the Manticorans.

The spook continued. "And—I'm sorry to admit—I did the 'drunken officer routine' again. With Captain Ellis's consent this time. Anyway, afterwards, one of the oligarchs—who wanted to make Manticore happy no doubt, gave me some information. I don't have any evidence to support it, of course. But he did give me some coordinates."

Hagen pulled a small piece of archaic paper from his pocket. "And I believe you might want to find a group of Marines who could undertake an . . . let's call it 'unscheduled maneuver' on these coordinates, Commodore."

✾ ✾ ✾

On the seashore of one of Navarra's southern continents, there was a luxurious villa two hundred kilometers from the nearest urban center. For more than a year, it had belonged to a Mr. Olaf Falkberget, who actually never visited the place but paid a staff of maids and servants to keep the villa in shape.

Mr. Falkberget had appeared only a few days ago, to the staff's considerable surprise. He'd brought a few friends with him and informed the staff that they were all going to live there for the foreseeable future.

Now, Marcus Bartoli—Mr. Falkberget—was walking in his garden and humming softly. The sadness over the loss of the *Scimitar*—and over the fact that he himself had been forced to send the code which blew the fusion bottle—was still there, but he was a realist enough to know that it had always been a possibility. That was why he and Christian Venner had developed the "Second Death" plan. That was why they'd had so many ex-SS fanatics on board. People willing to die for you—or at least risk almost certain death for you and for the cause—were always useful. There were enough of them to staff the *Scimitar* while the rest of the crew had disappeared into the planet's population and awaited contact from Bartoli. Some of them might decide that living on Navarra was more comfortable than working for him, but he was used to that. That was part of the game.

What all of them needed now was to disappear for a while. Silesia would remain a hotbed of chaos and corruption for years to come before the Manties could put it into at least some semblance of order. They wouldn't care about the area here, outside of Silesia.

Bartoli could wait. Yes, he'd lost his superdreadnought and with it his most powerful negotiating tool, but he was smart. He would find other means of achieving his plans. He still had some former SCN ships in other systems, and he still had Adrian Marius and other allies. He had lots of money in various bank accounts across the Solarian League and elsewhere. He was sure the Solarian Office of Frontier Security would love to have a partner like him in the area. So, most likely, would Mesa—even though Bartoli didn't like them—and he might even get in touch with other ex-SS units in exile like that idiot Luff.

The possibilities were endless, and the sky was the limit, as they said, and with that . . .

A sudden high-pitched sound appeared somewhere above him. Bartoli's head snapped up and he saw a blur streaking across the horizon. It must have been a pinnace or . . .

Then he noticed small dots in the sky left by whatever it was that had just overflown the garden. They were directly above the villa and—

Oh my God, those are antigravs. This is a drop!

His training took over and he ran to the villa. Ran past the computer panel in the main hall from which he and Venner observed the battle eight days ago. Next to the computer was a closet with a pair of loaded pulsers. If he could . . .

He heard shouts and screams from the outside, probably from some of his servants.

The roof came down as several figures in battle armor fell straight through it. Bartoli ducked as pieces of building blocks fell into the house. Clouds of dust made it almost impossible to see. He noticed shapes, raised his hand with the pulser . . .

A massive hand snapped his arm and he screamed with pain as he dropped the pulser. That same hand in power armor grabbed him by his shirt with all the subtlety of an Old Earth bull in a china shop.

The shock forced all thought of resistance out of Bartoli and the armored figure threw him over its shoulder and carried him away. He was disoriented, shocked, and could hear only his own breathing and the screams of the servants as they ran away. Then the armored figure took him back to the garden, where a pinnace was landing on the grass. He noticed another armored figure dragging Christian Venner out of the building. They'd taken the other senior officers who'd lived here with him. But they were letting the servants go.

Suddenly, they were aboard the pinnace and the armored figure dropped him on the deck. He noticed standard issue Manty Navy boots in front of him. No power armor. He raised his head weakly and saw before him a man in RMN uniform with a mischievous grin.

"Captain—or Admiral if you prefer—Marcus Bartoli, you are under arrest."

※ ※ ※

Eighteen days after the battle, an entire battle squadron arrived in the Quatre Bras System, called in by the dispatch boat send from Terrance. It had gone first to Caroline and then to Quatre Bras, on the trail of Eve's task group.

Eve Chandler found herself once again in a conference room aboard Mark Sarnow's flagship.

"I think this is not how you imagined your first few months in Silesia, is it, Commodore?" the Admiral said with one of his fierce grins.

Totally different from those crazy grins of Hagen's.

"No, Sir Mark. It isn't," she replied. "Especially after I had to kill so many people. After Bartoli sent *Scimitar* out to die."

Sarnow nodded. She'd transmitted him her entire report as his squadron was decelerating towards Navarra. So he knew about the arrest of Bartoli who was now being interrogated—again—in *Nicator*'s brig by Sarnow's intelligence officer and Captain Hagen.

He also knew that the escaping superdreadnought had been destroyed with no survivors, even if there'd been only a skeleton crew aboard.

"Her crew may have been StateSec fanatics, but that doesn't make me feel any better about killing people he *knew* couldn't fight back when he sent them," Eve added, and she meant it, yet her regret was an emotion—a feeling—she recognized. She grieved for those deaths but it was an involved grief, something she knew. Something she could work with.

The pane of glass was gone, and it hurt, but she would no longer feel detached. She would live.

"A superdreadnought," Sarnow said. "With a Havenite warlord. As if we don't have enough problems in Silesia."

"It's not over yet, Sir Mark. Bartoli had an ally in Silesia, Adrian Marius. He also controls some ex-SCN ships and we haven't apprehended him yet. Bartoli was only too happy to tell us all he knows about him—and we had a spacer with a treecat confirm his response, but this Marius no doubt went into hiding."

Sarnow smiled at the mention of treecats and then nodded. "Yes, but you deprived them of a superdreadnought and of their most important base in the region. Don't sell your achievements short, Eve, just because there's still work to be done."

"I understand, Sir Mark. I know. We've all done it. My people. But Bartoli killed a lot of people—got *us* to kill a lot of people—first." She shook her head. "The price was high."

"I know. It always is. We've both known that ever since Hancock, right?" He smiled a bit sadly, and she nodded. Despite the astronomical difference between their ranks, she and Sarnow had both gotten their first taste of a real battle at Hancock.

"Now then, I'm already scheduled for some meetings with the local government, and I'm sure there's some peace treaty they'll be only too happy to sign. After that, I want you to accompany my flagship back to Silesia. We'll escort the retrieved SCN ships back to Caroline, where there should be more of our ships waiting."

Eve nodded. "I understand, Sir Mark."

"Good. Then I hope you and your staff officers and captains will join me aboard the *Nicator* for dinner. I recall that I've owed it to you since your arrival in Silesia." He grinned. "And perhaps I should invite Captain Hagen as well."

※ ※ ※

"CruRon Fifty arriving!"

As Evelyn Chandler stepped into HMS *Juggernaut*'s boat bay and heard the Bosun's pipes, she smiled.

Then she greeted Captain Strauss and Commander Black Oak and her smile grew.

She was back.

In more than one sense.

IF WISHES WERE SPACE CUTTERS

Joelle Presby

Planet Grayson,
1922 PD.

Noah Bedlam slid into an empty office in the Burdette Steading church offices. The nameplate over the door read "Deacon Roundhouse," but on the piece of tape crossed over the name someone had scrawled "vacant." A single desk held a console, and when Noah powered it on, he found it accepted a guest login. Good. He got up, shut the door, and turned the lock. The Church of Humanity Unchained was the most reliable place for him to get a secure network connection that he didn't have to spend austins to use. But the cost of accessing the free service came in interruptions, veiled criticism of his irregular prayer meeting attendance, and inquiries into how long it had been since his last confession.

The bank screen he needed opened immediately to his palmprint. He considered the line of numbers, automatically converting everything from austins and cents to the more important units of Monthly Rent (m) and Cups Instant Noodle (n). As any social services regular could tell you, a thousand cups of noodles equaled one month rent at a dirty unfurnished efficiency apartment where the landlord would look the other way about housing two or three people in a place zoned for single occupancy. Of course he'd rather be housed for only the price of his dignity through one of the charity programs, but if you lost your eligibility for those, you couldn't sleep on the street in any city within Burdette Steading—not even the ones with one of the new Skydomes of Grayson Downs—without getting locked up.

Bank of Burdette
Accounts with Head of Household *Bedlam, N* access
B. Jezzy: 35(n)
B. Mary: 0(n) – Account closed
B. Grace: 0(n) – Account closed.
L. Lillian: 2(m) 308(n)
[GSN Credit Union] B-L. Cecelie: 4(m) 32(n) – Transfers blocked.
B-L. Lucy: 0(n) – Account closed.
B-L. Evelyn: 12(n)
Primary: B. Noah: 0(n) – Overdrafts for B. Jezzy in last six months: three. Overdrafts for L. Lillian in last six months: one. Overdrafts for B. Grace: four.

"Oh shit, oh shit, oh shit." Noah sent an urgent message off to Aunt Lillian. "Aunty L, please go buy something fast! We are about to lose benefit status if anyone notices!!!"

He hurried to check the official records, ready to send another message to Aunt Lillian if they'd already been dumped from the program. He found the household of "Bedlam, N" listed on the Burdette Social Support Services site, and, he breathed relief, the green letters "assistance eligibility approved" still floated next to his official photo.

The system used the picture of him from three T-years ago at a too-thin fourteen with a busted lip and two black eyes. He looked away from it, and the screen auto-scrolled to the legal dependents section to show Lucy Bedlam-Lecroix heavily makeup caked and smirking at the police cameraman. Mary Bedlam was just as thickly made-up but her mascara was running, and Noah could tell the processing officer must have given her a handkerchief and chance to clean up a little before snapping the photo in front of the black height lines on the wall. "Presumed Deceased—Blackbird Residency" was bolded beneath both their names. "Suspected of prostitution, no convictions." was on there too, but at least it wasn't highlighted anymore. Jezzy Bedlam, Lillian Lecroix, and Grace Bedlam all appeared in respectable dresses with their official photos clearly taken from the local parish registry of members. Ensign Claire Bedlam-Lecroix, Grayson Space Navy, had two photos: one in her Sunday-go-to-meeting demure best, giving the camera a dead-eyed glare, and a second in her full-skirted dress uniform with a trace of a smile curving her mouth as if she'd had to be reminded a few times that one wasn't supposed to be grinning while posing for a Grayson Space Navy official photo.

"Damn, Claire, I'm so glad you got out," he said to the screen. "Just please don't die out there."

"Language!" A soprano voice snapped from the hallway, and she slapped an open palm on the door of the office. "I told you before, Deacon! We don't tolerate your profanity down here in Burdette Steading. I talked to Elder Larson's fourth wife myself about your foul dock-worker mouth, and I'll tell her again, I will!" The woman's hand hit the door three more times in emphasis, and Noah gave a silent prayer of thanks to the Tester that he'd locked the door. A shame some deacon was getting the blame for his words, but he didn't want to be lectured like a little boy.

He checked the room's one window. This ground floor office in the large parish support building across the street from the temple proper faced into a small garden populated, at the moment, only with statues of the martyrs of First Landing. He could get the window open if he had to, but the bushes just beneath looked sharply thorned for all that they were blooming with brilliant tiny red flowers.

The hammering on the door started up again, and Noah started working on the window. "I'm back, Deacon Roundhouse," the woman's voice took on a hiss of growing anger. "The Elder wasn't in, but if you don't answer me this instant, I'm going directly over the Steadholder's Ladies Tea to have a chat with the First Wife about whether or not you should be allowed to keep your lay ministry position. The Tester alone knows why you've..." Fuck it. He couldn't let some man lose his job.

Noah swung the door open. A shocked woman perhaps two decades older than his mother stood in the hallway with her hand still lifted to bang on the door. He ducked his head and tried to give his heavily muscled shoulders an apologetic hunch. "Ma'am," he told her neatly polished leather shoes, "I'm very sorry. I should have realized the doors were thin and . . ."

"Well, you most certainly should have realized," the woman said, only partially mollified. "But, my, you are, hmmm." Her knobby hand reached out and lifted his right hand to check for rings. Her tone changed. "I know some ladies you should meet, young man."

"I don't think so." Noah looked at her.

She batted her eyelashes. Old enough to be his grandmother but she still fluttered them. "Nonsense," she said. "All the young men think they want to try being single for a while, but every youngster should start to seriously court his first wife while he's just starting out. We might not have quite the night life of the dome cities in Mayhew Steading, but we've got better church socials right here in Burdette City than anywhere on the whole of planet Grayson or in orbit either." She gave him an up and down look that wasn't as discreet as Noah'd expected in a church office hallway, and added, "I should think you'd have quite the pick of the young girls too."

"Ma'am," Noah said, blushing, "that's really not the best idea."

The soft breeze of an airlock door cycling around the bend of the hall and the click of heels warned that other parishioners were coming. His own mother, Jezzy Bedlam, walked around the corner of the church hallway escorted by another older woman in a somber gray dress. Mom Jezzy's eyes widened at the sight of him and she gave a very quick headshake.

"Oh, Mrs. Wilson, there you are!" the other older woman said. "This is Miss Jezzy, the example who is coming to talk to our prayer circle tomorrow to thank us for the parish's generous contributions to the Social Support Services baskets."

Mom Jezzy looked at Noah and looked away. She was signaling something, but he wasn't quite sure what. "Mom?" he said.

Mrs. Wilson narrowed her eyes and looked back and forth between Noah and Mom Jezzy. Disgust filled her face and she stiffened her spine, turning to the other woman. "I think not, Mrs. Carlson. We agreed we'd be showing the prayer circle an example of the deserving poor."

Mrs. Carlson blinked. "I still say that's not the best term to use in front of the recipients. But did he say, 'Mom'?"

Mom Jezzy said, "I told Mrs. Carlson already that I had a young son."

"And she has two daughters and a niece who died on Blackbird. They were, what did you say, working in one of the Uriel orbit sewing factories customizing skinsuits for our Navy men?"

Noah blinked. Skinsuit fabric couldn't be sewn. Claire hadn't told a ton of stories about life in the Grayson Space Navy, but he was sure of that much. What had Mom Jezzy been saying?

"Not hardly." Mrs. Wilson looked down her nose at Mom Jezzy. She looped her arm through Mrs. Carlson's. "The Elder can deal with these two when he returns. We're going to be late to the Steadholder's Ladies Tea."

"Oh, I'd love to go to that. I've never had an invitation, you know. But I was going to buy Miss Jezzy a lunch, something with vegetables but not too extravagant," Mrs. Carlson said. She allowed herself to be walked further down the hall, no longer even looking at Mom Jezzy whose hand she'd let go of when Mrs. Wilson took her arm.

"Let me save you from that," Mrs. Wilson said, not bothering to lower her voice as she walked away towing the other woman. "That woman's son is hardly better than a whoremonger. I'm sure you've heard about the Bedlam-Lecroix family?"

"No, she's not that one, there are lots of Jezzies . . ." Mrs. Carlson's voice trailed back. "Miss Jezzy isn't Jezzy Bedlam, the mother of Noah Bedlam . . ." Her voice hitched. "Oh dear. What will I tell the prayer circle?"

"We'll just do a Blackbird remembrance planning session," Mrs. Wilson said. "We need some special flowers for the narthex what with Protector Benjamin's upcoming visit to honor our dead . . ." Their voices finally trailed out of hearing range as one of the airlocks cycled the women into another section of the building.

At least they hadn't said anything about trying to get the family blocked from receiving charity support. Maybe they'd forget about them in the excitement of seeing Steadholder Burdette, Lord Nathan Fitzclarence, and however many of his wives were in good enough health to attend. The high aristocrat's second wife was rumored to be an inpatient at the Dr. Allison Harrington Clinic. Lord Nathan already had two boys, but perhaps he wanted three.

"I'm sorry," Noah said. "I should have called you 'Mom Jezzy,' not just 'Mom.' It just slipped out. I know you don't like people to be reminded that I've only got one mom. I'd not mean to be rude."

Her face was crinkling up in a mixture of distress and an attempt to pretend nothing was wrong, so Noah knew he had definitely not apologized for the right thing, but he wasn't quite sure how he'd messed it up. Mom Jezzy crushed him into a hug. He couldn't see her eyes, which he was sure would be filling up with tears. She'd hate to be seen crying in public, and other people could walk through at any moment. He could, at least, help distract her. Tell her about the money problems? No. He wanted her to laugh, not to be further stressed out. If it came to it, they could fit all their belongings in a couple of trash bags again and find another temporary place. The Barbara Bancroft Society had some hostels for the "down on their luck" to stay in for two weeks at a time. The hostels didn't compare resident lists, so he and Mom Jezzy might be able to go from one to another hopping around Burdette's cities if they could manage the travel costs and the places weren't full. But first he needed a thing to say to his mom. His mouth jumped on that last thing Mrs. Wilson and Mrs. Carlson had been talking about.

"Yeah, uh, Mom Jezzy, what's this about the Lord Protector visiting Burdette? Are all the high and mighty steadholders pretending to like each other now that we're at war? Didn't Lord Fitzclarence give a speech comparing the Mayhew Fleet Expansion Bill to giving cosmetics to a supermodel and insist there were initiatives on the surface of the planet that'd see more benefit from the funds?"

She gave a muffled laugh in his shoulder. "Of course my boy knows all about the Steadholder's speeches! Did our Steadholder, Lord Nathan, really say all that?" She pulled back and looked at him without a trace of tears.

"Well, it was before Blackbird," Noah admitted. Everyone knew about this stuff, he was pretty sure. Did Mom Jezzy really not know it? Or was she pretending for his benefit? "The full confidence vote immediately afterwards all but begged the Lord Protector to go annihilate someone." Tester's mercy, this wasn't a humorous topic. He'd not found the best thing to talk about, but at least Mom Jezzy wasn't crying.

"Burdette had the third highest number of space workers lost of all the steadings, Mrs. Carlson said." Mom Jezzy shook her head. "I had no idea of the numbers of our steaders working up there. All the way out in Uriel's orbit and a lot of them were men! So many families with their father only visiting home on weekends. She was quite appalled and wants the rebuild to only employ unmarried men, as if there are anywhere near enough of those." Mom Jezzy's mouth twitched. "Mrs. Carlson opposes women's employment most fervently, but in the same breath, she said she's going to pay me to clean her house next week to get ready for a visit from her two mothers-in-law. They're the sister wives of her husband's deceased mother, and quite particular about the dusting. Mrs. Carlson was worried, and I assured her that I can scrub very well. It might turn into a regular thing monthly, maybe. Oh. Well, I had the job, I suppose." She rolled her eyes. "I'll get something else lined up."

"We'll be fine," Noah assured her with a façade of confidence that he doubted she believed.

"Of course we will," she said. "We're a good family." She tilted her head at the empty office. "Was there a console in there? I wanted to check the times for the ladies' prayer meetings at Chapel Yanakov. There might be a lunch one."

"Yep." Noah held the door for his mom. He was pretty sure nobody in the Grayson system besides his mom would characterize the Bedlam-Lecroixs as a good family.

She whistled a little tune and gathered the needed details quickly. She rambled a bit about how Aunt Lillian had been doing lately and a few guesses about Claire's doings.

"Wait," Noah said. "Is Claire actually answering your messages? I haven't heard from her since that mess with Deacon Randall trying to get her to resign her commission."

Mom Jezzy waved a dismissive hand. "You know how our Claire-Claire is. She'll get over her mad eventually, and she could just be too busy to answer. I get the news from the GNS *Ephraim*'s Wardroom Wives' Club, you know. Since Claire's not married, Commander Greentree's second wife Elsabeta put your Aunt Lillian on the distribution list. The ships are doing a bunch of extra patrols and a lot of the ships, not just the *Ephraim*, are really busy, Mrs. Greentree says. And speaking of bad families, you remember that Rustin nonsense?"

"Those letters from Claire's roommate that her little sister put on the *Tester's Blessings on the GSN* message board for everybody to laugh at?" Of course he remembered. It had been a rare time that a Bedlam relation got a little bit of positive fame.

"I doubt that little Rustin girl Suleia meant to have it all go the way it did," Mom Jezzy said with more compassion than Noah was entirely sure was deserved. He did remember those letters and how they'd clearly been intended to be private before the little sister had retyped them to share them with the planet in exchange for a bit of reflective fame. "But it seems Commander Greentree was pretty offended on Ensign Rustin's behalf. And that Suleia is writing letters again, this time about her own doings. Elsabeta got them from her husband and shared them with the wives' club. Elsabeta said Ensign Rustin had to be talked into the sharing, but the ships are pretty bored doing non-stop patrol duties so a bit of entirely unclassified gossip to chatter about during the off hours seems to be good for morale." She showed him.

Posted to the shared GNS Ephraim Wardroom Board
Tagged Subject #SiblingPayback
Captain, XO, Bosses, & the Rest of You Guys:

It's payback time. Remember how my little sister posted all my letters home on a public forum a while back? Well, she's been accepted to a prestigious cross-steading internship program and has been sending me her journal entries about it. She doesn't seem to realize what she's done yet, but Oh Glory Be is she going to regret sending me these. Just wait until you see what she's written on day three.

I present—for your amusement, the amusement of your friends on other ships, the amusement of complete strangers you meet on shore leave, and for the entertainment pleasure of the known universe—my sister Suleia Rustin's private journals.

Vengeance belongs to the Tester alone, but who are mere siblings to stand in the way of righteous payback?

Very Respectfully,

ENS Cecelie Rustin

GSN Officer By the Grace of God & Tool of the
Tester's Vengeance against Younger Sister Suleia Rustin

※ ※ ※

Addendum 1: Please stop asking ENS Lecroix to tell on Suleia to the Lady Steadholder. I know Suleia. Let my sister dig herself a proper hole. There will be plenty of time for us to make it worse for her later. Trust me.

Addendum 2: These are all the entries I have from Suleia. I'll update you when I know something. And I still don't think it's time to "help" further. I blacked out the names she used in her letters. Suleia is not the most unbiased of observers, and I prefer to let others out themselves if they so choose.

⚝ ⚝ ⚝

"Mom Jezzy," Noah said. "Just how bad is this going to get?"
"Don't worry," she said. "Our family isn't mentioned after that."
Noah read on, not sure if he should be relieved or not.

⚝ ⚝ ⚝

Posted to the shared GNS Ephraim Wardroom Board
Tagged Subject #SiblingPayback
Wardroom—

This is the final draft of Suleia's thank you letter for her internship admission. Yes, I have a copy. Who do you think Suleia begged editing and revision help from as she crafted it? I'm including it in the file primarily for context. You can see that *I* set her up for success. This first letter sounds totally fine without even a hint of her natural snot-nosed self. I warned her that she'd have to pretend to be a much, much more polite version of herself. I give all credit to Suleia herself for the rest of this; she did it entirely on her own.

Though, of course, I have assisted in promulgating her mistakes. What else are sisters for?

V/R,

ENS Rustin

P.S. Sis, when one day you see this, you're welcome.

⚝ ⚝ ⚝

#Suleia'sLetters1 #SiblingPayback
June 3rd, 1922 PD
Madame Lady Steadholder, Mrs. Theresa Burdette:

I would just like to take this opportunity to thank you so very much for selecting me as one of your interns for this summer steading exchange program. I look forward to learning more about Burdette Steading and especially learning from your poverty outreach initiatives. As I'm sure you know from my application, I had never been out of my own steading before this opportunity. My sister, Ensign Cecelie Rustin, has been loads of places, and she inspires me every day. I assure you, I will work tirelessly for you this summer and will absolutely help make a difference.

> Gratefully Yours,
> Suleia Rustin

❋ ❋ ❋

#Suleia'sLetters2 #SiblingPayback
June 4th, 1922 PD
Dear Diary,

Today was the first day of my internship. I met L—— and M—— my fellow interns. Very nice young ladies. I'm sure they'll say the same about me. I can't wait to begin working with the Lady Steadholder.

[Entry ends. Zero views.]

❋ ❋ ❋

#Suleia'sLetters3 #SiblingPayback
June 5th, 1922 PD
Dear Diary,

I metadata tagged paperwork all day today. Have not yet met with Lady Steadholder. I can't wait to get started on the internship.

[Entry ends. Zero views.]

❋ ❋ ❋

#Suleia'sLetters4 #SiblingPayback
June 6th, 1922 PD
Dear Diary,

Mrs. R—— continues to assign busy work while the Lady Steadholder is otherwise occupied. I've taken the initiative to identify more useful work.

[Entry ends. Zero views.]

❋ ❋ ❋

#Suleia'sLetters5 #SiblingPayback
June 7th, 1922 PD

Dear Diary,

I'm sure the Lady Steadholder understands that while Mrs. R—— means well, it is not a good use of three very knowledgeable interns' time to spend all day sorting tax records and correlating with levels of food bank use. I'm sure Mrs. R—— has many other things she does quite well and this is merely a case of her not having a task aligned with her natural abilities.

[Entry ends. Zero views.]

※ ※ ※

#Suleia'sLetters6 #SiblingPayback
June 8th, 1922 PD

Is anyone even reading this?

[Entry ends. Zero views.] <–See that Cecelie?

Nobody is reading these. —Suleia

※ ※ ※

#Suleia'sLetters7 #SiblingPayback
June 9th, 1922 PD

Mrs. R—— insists on an entry. Here is an entry.

[Entry ends. Zero views.]

※ ※ ※

#Suleia'sLetters8 #SiblingPayback
June 10th, 1922 PD

Dear Diary,

Now Mrs. R—— commented that the character count on our diaries seemed shorter than usual. She mentioned that she doesn't have the access code to read them. But she encouraged us to write more. Fine. I'll draft my letter here. I didn't want to have to do this, but Mrs. R—— is not getting better. If anything, she's become downright snippy.

※ ※ ※

Dear Madam Lady Steadholder, Mrs. Theresa Burdette:

I do, of course, absolutely understand you must have a very busy schedule. But I am here. I can do all kinds of things. If you need your office dusted while you brainstorm solutions for social problems in the steading, I'm here. Just for example, of course, but I could do that. I'm a great brainstormer, and I could take care of whatever little office things you need done while you think. I'd sit in the background while you work things out and take down the notes with, of course, additional ideas and corrections for anything that might have been inadvertently forgotten.

Oh, but you do need to know: Mrs. R—— is completely incompetent. She is utterly inept at managing interns. I'm quite sure she misunderstood her tasking and there's just been an administrative oversight. Please don't feel bad. It's only a week lost. In a large household these things can happen. I'm great at fixing these sorts of things.

Once I'm in your office, I'll make sure to do some reassignments, so this kind of thing doesn't happen again.

With Greatest Respect,
<thumbprint signed>
Suleia Rustin,
Intern to Madame the Lady Steadholder
Theresa Burdette
[Entry ends. Zero views.]

⚹ ⚹ ⚹

#Suleia'sLetters9 #SiblingPayback
June 11th, 1922 PD
Dear Diary,

Mrs. R—— is pleased with the increased diary use. I almost feel sorry for her. Except that she made me redo the *entire* steading's food bank data verification process by myself. L—— and M—— were sent off to coordinate the flower deliveries for the Steadholder's Lady Wives' Economic Growth Gala. [Cecelie: This is the thing everyone calls the Steadholder's Ladies Tea. Apparently it has an official title related to its yearly theme.]

I did not talk back. I merely pointed out that she was wasting our time and should focus on what she was good at instead. Some people should never be given management roles.

[Entry ends. Zero views.]

⚹ ⚹ ⚹

#Suleia'sLetters10 #SiblingPayback
June 12th, 1922 PD

Dear Diary,

I cracked the authorized readers list on this Inter-Steading Diary file today. It wasn't set up. Not surprising. Mrs. R—— probably doesn't know how. Anyway, no one's ever going to see this but me.

So: hi, me.

This is now my personal log. I've got to write something to keep Mrs. R—— happy. I might as well make it useful to me instead of just pasting in gibberish, which believe me, I've seriously considered doing.

Someday when I'm running a family of my own, I'll need to have records like this to know what *not* to do.

[Entry ends. Zero views.]

⁜ ⁜ ⁜

#Suleia'sLetters11 #SiblingPayback
June 12th, 1922 PD
Dear Diary,

Yes, I'm making a second entry in one day. Good things have happened and I want to make a record while everything is fresh.

Finally! Something useful. Burdette Steading is underwriting one of the station rebuilds. They bought the orbit rights and are going to set up a whole space-based manufactory. The underprivileged have the option of accepting some of their sustenance assistance in the form of ownership shares. L——'s idea, unfortunately. Not mine. But Mrs. R—— did repeat it to the Lady Steadholder, and she brought it to the Steadholder Himself who asked for a full proposal! He modified it somewhat and, I think, made it entirely useless. But arrgh, no one is listening to me here.

Mrs. R—— and the other girls didn't notice my work because the Steadholder undid it all. His sharp note about "not starving the children for the sins of the grandparents" rather stung, but they didn't understand it at all. Not having seen the original submission, they just took it for an adamant agreement. Idiots.

Useful idiots, apparently, but still idiots. I miss my sisters. They would never have let a file go through without a copy back and reading it themselves just before sending. But then, they did grow up with me, so perhaps they've got that "experience" everyone keeps ranting on about.

L— and M— are going door to door visiting eligible households and talking them into signing up for the program. Of course they are getting lots of takers. Something like 80%. Mrs. R— is all excited for them. It's disgusting. Of course people are signing up. The Steadholder took all the teeth out. (He had this lengthy thing about there being an urgent need for training up more space workers after so many skilled technicians were killed in the attack...the future of the steading's economic prowess in its people, etcetera, etcetera.) They don't have to give up *any* of their assistance provisions they just have to opt-in and send a family member to apply to do some of the work. Paid work which they are probably not even remotely qualified for, so they probably won't even get selected to do anything.

Losers annoy me. But at least the research stuff is getting slightly more interesting. And Mrs. R— is threatening to ship me off to the station. As if that would be a bad thing.

[Entry ends. Zero views.]

※ ※ ※

#Suleia'sLetters12 #SiblingPayback
June 13th, 1922 PD
Dear Diary,

Ha! Going to the station in a couple days. Advance party no less! And Madame Lady Steadholder Theresa *HERSELF* is going to be coming up later. I'll finally get to meet her, and she'll see all my work setting up for the visit. No more Mrs. R— for an entire week, and possibly no more Mrs. R— for the rest of the internship!

[Entry ends. Zero views.]

※ ※ ※

#Suleia'sLetters13 #SiblingPayback
June 14th, 1922 PD
Dear Diary,

My first letter has been unanswered for a solid seven days now. I went ahead and checked the internal mail system. I used Mrs. R——'s login. I didn't crack it. I'm not stupid. And it was sent. It just wasn't read.

Mrs. R—— leaves herself logged in all the time and doesn't think to lock access screens or thumbprint protect any of the household files. Sloppy, sloppy. But it lets me know what is going on.

※ ※ ※

Drafting my next letter here:

Lady Steadholder—

I know you'll probably never read this, but Mrs. R—— is flat crazy. That long talk followed by that letter she wanted me to sign about "improving" my performance is completely absurd. You know that. Or you would know that if you'd had the time to run these internships yourself or attend to reading these "internship experience documentation diaries for young ladies' self-improvement."

But you aren't reading this and needs must.

I am *not* going to complete this internship without a letter of recommendation to take with me. There's no point in wasting a summer like that. I could have gone to Manticore B. I turned down a slot there with another internship.

Okay, truth be told, I couldn't go to Manticore B. That one was an unpaid internship without any travel expenses. This one isn't paid either, but at least room, board, and travel are covered. I don't know who can afford to both forgo a summer job and pay out of pocket for fancy hotels and such. Rich people, I guess.

That's what I really don't get about your poverty study programs. You intentionally set this thing up to attract the middle people. L—— pretends like she comes from money, but she doesn't. No one with much money pays anywhere near the attention to brands she does. The logos are all too big on her luggage and clothes. M——, I might believe. But she outed herself in the first week when she admitted to having never been out of her own steading and working in her uncle's shop most of her life. M——'s solidly middle. There's no other possibility.

Signed . . . Ug.

※ ※ ※

Okay, not sending that. There's no point. She isn't opening messages from people not on her screened contact list. I might be able to get myself added to her contact list using Mrs. R——'s login, but that would be noticed immediately and not in a good way. If I'd seen R—— stealing the silver it might be worth it. As is, she's wasting something with more value than silver, but they are unlikely to immediately see that. Simply not worth it. Quite a shame. But that's the nature of being young. No one recognizes your expertise when it doesn't come with years of experience to back it.

Remember that, Future Me.

Now drafting the next letter here. Might as well get a fat character count reported to Mrs. R——.

Cecelie,

I need your help campaigning with the Moms to fund an internship to Manticore next year. Look at my diary files for this one. You simply must help me make sure this doesn't happen again.

—Suleia

P.S. You aren't still mad about that letters thing, are you?

[Entry ends. Zero views.]

Grayson Navy Mail System
Personal Message for Suleia Rustin
June 15th, 1922 PD
Dear Suleia,

You will never again have a Burdette Steading Internship, I promise.

Yours,
Cecelie

✖ ✖ ✖

"No kidding she's not getting another internship," Noah said. "Mom! This kid is going to get lynched!"

Mom Jezzy giggled. "You are such a sweet boy. Remember: she's a little girl. Probably only about seventeen. They'll all forgive her."

I'm seventeen, Noah thought. He wasn't sure that Suleia would actually be okay.

"Look, look!" Mom Jezzy said. She opened another set of letters. "There's another update."

⚹ ⚹ ⚹

Sent via Grayson Navy Mail
Personal Message for ENS Rustin
June 15th, 1922 PD
Cecelie—

I'm so glad you are over your little tiff. Here's the next batch of my journal entries.
  —Suleia

⚹ ⚹ ⚹

Posted to GNS Ephraim Wardroom Board
#Suleia'sLetters13 #SiblingPayback

With regards, another excerpt from my dear sister Suleia's latest. I do believe it speaks for itself. V/R ENS Rustin

⚹ ⚹ ⚹

#Suleia'sLetters14 #SiblingPayback
Dear Diary

Working on my remediation already. Mrs. R—— said my efforts were showing a "positive trend." I apologized even. That was a tough bit of acting, but I think I pulled it off. Said I was sorry. Very carefully did not say for what. Said I'd do my best to improve our relationship and that I hoped she'd give me another chance. The woman got all choked up and hugged me.

M—— and L—— didn't buy it, but they'll keep their lips shut if they know what's good for them. ***

*** *I cut the listing of mild indiscretions my dear Suleia intends to hold over her fellow interns' heads. She plans to wait until after the station trip to send the next update. V/R, ENS Rustin*

⚹ ⚹ ⚹

"Well?" Mom Jezzy said.

"Tester bless their hearts," Noah said.

"Ain't that the truth," Mom Jezzy agreed. "It's like I always say: 'More money, more problems.'"

I wouldn't mind having a few more problems, Noah thought, *at least not if they came with more money.*

※ ※ ※

A great many people who had more money and thought they had more problems were assembled for the Steadholder's Ladies Tea. En masse, they looked like someone had animated a florist's shop full of exotic blooms and thrown them together with no regard for clashing colors or aesthetic sensibilities. The only unifying theme of the party was expense.

Off to one corner in an alcove, a tired middle-aged man was realizing that the full regalia of a lay minister of the Church of Humanity Unchained itched a lot. But Deacon Roundhouse didn't pull on the too-tight collar, or pick at the overdone embroidery, or complain about any of it. His beloved first and only wife, Nadia Roundhouse, was having a hell of a day, because her boss was having an even worse one.

"Thirty thousand austins is what this dress cost," Lady Theresa Burdette whispered at her assistant Nadia, "and it doesn't even have sleeves. I just wanted an extra ten thousand in the budget to add to the salary of the construction crew chief, but Nathan said, 'no.' Now the man I needed has gone off and accepted a position working for the Manties. I can't get my project a decent shot without more capable people to run it, Nadia."

"Yes, Lady Burdette." Nadia said, "I could arrange to sell some of last season's dresses, if you'd like."

"Nathan forbade me to increase the senior supervisor's salary range. It has to do with an agreement he and Mueller have been pushing with the other steadholders to combat rising wages in the face of the skilled labor shortages. I told him that my project would make more skilled labor. And then he said he was done arguing with me and walked out."

"Yes, Lady Burdette," Nadia said again. "Couple in the red and fuchsia headed this way. Mr. Ron Wilson of Aquaculture Delish and first wife Mindy, donated a half million. You've not met the second woman in gray. She is not one of his other wives."

Deacon Roundhouse had met both of the women before, but not the man. He wasn't sure if he'd be recognized in his finery.

A bright, if false, smile lit Lady Theresa's face as she turned. A picture of elegant femininity, the youthful aristocrat could have made a garbage bag look good. In the tasteful silver gown and elegantly tailored, gorgeously embroidered indigo over-tunic, she radiated wealth and sophistication. "Ron and Mindy!" she said. "So pleased you could make it."

"Lady Theresa, always a delight," the gentleman in red said. "Please give my best to your husband."

"Of course," the third wife of Lord Nathan Fitzclarence, Steadholder Burdette, said. "He was right over there in the central pavilion last I saw." She waved her hand towards a knot of men in the center of the gala.

"Oh, of course. I think, yes, I do see him." Mr. Wilson nodded to himself. "If you'll excuse me, ladies," he said, and he left without waiting for another word from Lady Theresa or either of his female companions.

Lady Theresa's smile didn't flicker.

"Lady Theresa," Mrs. Wilson in the fuchsia dress said, "Ronnie and I were so pleased to get your invitation to this tea, so very pleased. And I love what you're doing to get the poor of this steading off their behinds and doing some good for a change. We just love it, don't we, Mrs. Carlson?"

The other woman in the gray dress flushed. "Um, not how I'd say that, your, um, ladyship." She'd been loaded down with a lot of pearls, but unless Deacon Roundhouse missed his guess, the jewelry was borrowed. He also suspected Mrs. Carlson's gown had not cost thirty thousand austins or even much over three thousand austins, and it mattered to her.

"Oh!" Mindy Wilson said, "I forgot, you've not met before." Deacon Roundhouse was pretty sure Mrs. Wilson had forgotten nothing and was enjoying extending her opportunity to chatter with the Steadholder's wife while other members of the crowd cast covert looks in their direction and waited for an opportunity to approach the third lady wife of Steadholder Burdette. "Lady Theresa, please allow me to introduce my dear friend and co-chair for the Burdette Cathedral's Parish Poor Initiative, Mrs. Lily Carlson."

"A pleasure to meet any of your friends, Mindy," Lady Theresa said. "What does your husband do, Lily?"

"She's a widow," Mrs. Wilson interrupted.

"He ran an engineering consulting firm supporting the client businesses operating around Uriel and had offices near Blackbird. He hasn't been recovered," Mrs. Carlson corrected. "They found his business partner, or well, a piece of him. My fellow wives are waiting until, well, until."

Lady Theresa abandoned all normal proprieties and hugged Lily Carlson tightly. "I'm so sorry for your loss, so sorry," she murmured in the woman's ear.

"Oh, well," Mrs. Carlson blinked back tears. "It's not like I lost a child. I met a woman today who lost three: two daughters and a niece. She was poor and they're tougher, you know, don't feel things like we do, but still. I can't imagine."

Lady Theresa's mouth returned to a fixed brittle smile. "I'm sure I don't know what anyone else feels, not precisely, anyway. But the Tester calls on all of us to soften our hearts and return to follow more closely in His ways, isn't that right, Deacon?" she said.

Deacon Roundhouse made a small bow and stepped out of Nadia's shadow to support Lady Theresa. He'd been wrong. Both Mrs. Wilson and Mrs. Carlson recognized him from the stiffening of their postures.

"Sounds about right to me, Lady Theresa," he said. "But I'm new to ministry, as Mrs. Wilson and Mrs. Carlson know, and I haven't studied the Holy Writ enough to speak with authority off the cuff like this."

"At least you have cuffs," Lady Theresa said.

Mrs. Wilson's lips pinched, but she kept her tongue between her teeth. It was Mrs. Carlson who spoke up. "I've been grieving, and I don't have the right words to say a lot of the time. I wrote a letter a few days ago to the Elder . . ."

"Signed my letter you mean," said Mrs. Wilson under her breath.

"And well, now I'm thinking I was too harsh, and it wasn't my place. If you wish it, Lady Theresa, I'll be writing another to retract my words."

Mrs. Wilson rocked back in place, and Roundhouse thought he saw Mrs. Carlson's elbow jab the other woman.

"I, also, of course, would sign that," Mrs. Wilson said through gritted teeth. "I'm understanding a lot more now."

Lady Theresa inclined her head. "I hope you enjoy the party," she said in dismissal. The women dipped into deeper curtsies than Roundhouse had expected their aged knees to manage, and they turned away with a murmur of similar good wishes for Lady Theresa.

The lady lifted her eyebrows at Nadia slightly in inquiry.

"My husband was asked to step away from his position at the Cathedral following a letter of complaint from the ladies' auxiliary," Nadia explained.

The eyebrows went all the way up.

Nadia surveyed the crowd. "We're being given a little space," she said. "No one approaching just yet. Mindy Wilson and Lily Carlson are telling everyone about their chat with you. Lily turned away, can't read her lips. Mindy Wilson is saying you're a lovely person and you're a bit naïve but have a true heart for the people."

"Fine, fine. Just warn me if you can make out if either of them says something about stopping their donations or tells someone else not to contribute." She directed her quiet attention at Deacon Roundhouse and asked barely audibly, "What did you do? Tell them they're all dogs?"

He managed not to snort. "No, Lady. I was, um, overheard to use foul language, and I think they might not have minded that, but I'm told my demeanor is unfriendly."

"What does that even mean? Joseph Larson comes for coffee with Nathan twice a week, and I don't think I've seen him smile in a year. And the Sacristy made him the Steading's Elder," she whispered back.

"My husband's first and only homily was on the assigned text about the rich man and the poor man trying to reach the kingdom of heaven." Nadia said, "It wasn't his fault."

"That would do it," Lady Theresa said dryly.

"It doesn't matter," Deacon Roundhouse said. "The Sacristy will find someplace else to put me. Maybe in the Chaplain Service or something."

Nadia pressed her lips together. He could tell she didn't like the idea. They'd worked apart for most of their marriage and made it work. But the chaplain corps deployed with the Grayson Space Navy. In a time of war, deployments were long, and some ships never came back.

"In truth, Lady," Roundhouse said, "I think Elder Larson is

hoping I'll quit the ministry and go back to space work as a construction supervisor again."

"Incoming," Nadia said. "Your three project interns. I'll redirect them."

"Please do," Lady Theresa said. While Nadia stepped away, she turned urgently to him. "Deacon, I desperately need a skilled construction supervisor. Do you think you can go back up there? I know it isn't fair to ask it . . ."

Roundhouse felt all the saliva in his mouth dry up.

Lady Theresa looked down. "Please forget I said anything. For Nadia's sake, I'll see to it that you're given another position. Something right here in the city."

He looked from the lady to his wife a dozen steps away speaking with three bright faced young girls and back at the lady. He thought her ladyship's project was daft. But it meant a lot to the lady, and his wife adored the young aristocrat. And he'd been in charge of not fully planned out projects before. He'd always made them into something that worked.

"I'll do it," he said. "But tell Elder Larson you want me assigned as your project chaplain. That way you don't have to pay me." He glanced over at the men surrounding Lord Nathan. "But perhaps don't advertise that detail. You can redistribute the supervisor's salary to plus up some of the other key positions you still need to fill."

A genuine smile quirked at the edges of Lady Theresa's lips. "I do believe I will abide by your guidance, Deacon Roundhouse."

Nadia hurried back to her position at the lady's side as another group of attendees approached to pay their respects.

✷ ✷ ✷

Noah made it home without trouble. The long walk from the center of the city to their assigned apartment wasn't something he should do regularly if he wanted the soles of his shoes to last through to St. Austin's Mass when the well-off usually made more donations and Mom Jezzy could probably find him a replacement pair.

But Aunt Lillian had completely emptied her account without answering his message, so he wasn't sure if she'd bought something that could be turned back into austins later or not. She wasn't legally in the steading where she was working right now, and if she ran into hard times, available support services would be limited to a lift back to the closest Burdette city. Noah wanted to reserve a little bit to get her reunited with them if she needed it.

Mom Jezzy had boarded a tram at the university stop, where rides were free, and headed over to Chapel Yanakov, where she'd be getting a lunch. His stomach grumbled, but he resolved not to open any of their food. Not when Mom Jezzy would be bringing home a plate of something in a few hours.

A figure stood at the entrance of their apartment, and Noah's heart rose into his mouth. Had some authority come to evict them in person? He quickened his steps and tried to think of a believable argument if an official had noticed the account totals and seen Aunt Lillian's speedy emptying of her balance.

He got closer and slowed. The figure was female. Burdette Steading had no female police officers, so that was not an official with eviction orders. And he could tell she was young, from the way she stood in a somewhat uncertain pose, fingers tugging on a long blonde braid and then tucking it behind her back to lean on the door buzzer, and then fidgeting again with the braid while she waited. The door buzzer had never worked. In fact, Noah couldn't remember living in any charity housing where noncritical engineer devices like doorbells reliably worked.

She turned around at his approach and made a tiny startled jump. "Oh!" she said.

Shit. She was gorgeous too: curvy, with a lot of boob, and a very cute face. Her mouth opened in the beginning of a gasp and then transitioned into an eager smile as she looked him up and down and then, yep, her eyelashes fluttered. Not good.

She was looking at him with a lingering appreciation. He'd learned to read those signs.

She gave a breathless little sound that she had to repeat before he realized it was, "Hi?" Oh no, she'd not spent enough time around younger men. She didn't know how to pretend disinterest, and she was about to let herself get infatuated with a very ineligible young man. He had to start a fight or something.

She had some sort of large nametag pinned to the lapel of the walking jacket she wore over her blouse. It read, "Hi! I'm Suleia Rustin. Ask me about the new Burdette Steading Assistance Programs."

"Are there a lot of Rustins? Do you run into other Suleia's from time to time?" Noah asked.

"What?" She blinked at him. "Um, no sir. Or, I wouldn't know. I'm not from Burdette Steading originally." She straightened. "I'm an intern to Madame Lady Theresa Burdette for the season."

He was supposed to answer with his name and his occupation. Noah kept his mouth shut, trying to figure out what she was doing at the exterior airlock entry to the apartment he shared with Mom Jezzy.

In this last year, he'd shot up four inches, packed on muscle at the community gym, and gotten a few day labor jobs. The muscle gain had been intentional. It was the only way he could think of to make other non-rich folks treat his mom right. It had worked to let him avoid fistfights here in the not always safe charity housing. The female interest had not been something he'd planned for. He still had indifferent brown hair, poor man's skin, and a nose that overfilled his face, but women seemed to forgive boring faces when they came attached to strong bodies.

He found his own complete lack of prospects less forgivable.

Miss Suleia Rustin tossed her head in irritation at his failure to reply. Some tendrils of hair escaped her braid. That riot of blonde hair was destined by the Tester to clog air filters and entrance men. She'd also been given a full mouth that she now pinched as if that might let her look aloof or at least surly. She achieved endearing instead.

Oh well, at least she wasn't acting on the edge of infatuation anymore.

"Why are you here?" Noah said.

"I'm signing up all the indigents for a work program," Miss Rustin said. "I'm sure that those with records and so forth will get bumped off the rolls properly enough, but for now, we've got to get the forms out to everyone."

Those with criminal records would include him, of course. He'd become Head of Household at twelve to let the family stop being in the system as Wards of the Steading, as they'd been since his uncle had died when he was seven. But he'd become fully adult under Grayson law at fourteen T-years. Mom Jezzy, Aunt Lillian, Mary, Lucy, and Grace had all worked extra hours cleaning homes and selling sandwiches on street corners for half a year to buy him a hover bike he hadn't understood how to fly.

He still remembered the bleak horror of the accident that followed. There had been fish swimming all around and more water than he'd ever imagined. The expensive bike was a total ruin, not that he'd cared about that at first. His entire focus had been on coughing up that unbreathable water. If the aquafarm supervisor hadn't hauled him out of the tank, he'd have died.

The particular tank he'd crashed in was only four feet deep, but in the shock of the moment, with bruises everywhere and water over his head, it hadn't occurred to him to stand up.

There had been a Steadholder's boy he'd heard about in school. It wasn't the heir, just a younger cousin. The aristocrat kid had done some elaborate prank involving the fish. Everyone had been laughing and talking about it between classes. Noah had wanted—something— he couldn't quite remember now, but it had involved respect. He had hoped to earn a fraction of the admiration they'd showered on that wealthy scion.

He'd gotten a beating from the fish farm supervisor who'd saved his life, lectures from everyone else, and a court record to further constrict his already limited life options. It had been one hell of a fourteenth birthday.

"Miss Rustin," he said, "no one here needs your forms."

He could already see how it would go. If he filled that thing out, he'd get far enough through in-processing to get all the current benefits suspended, then someone—maybe even Miss Suleia Rustin—would pull up his record, and he'd be dropped from the program without even a trash bag to hold his belongings.

"They absolutely do!" Rustin said. "I'll just step inside and leave it in the airlock for them. The other two girls are not going back to Mrs. Roundhouse with more signups than me," she added cryptically.

She got the door open and stepped inside. Noah sighed and followed.

The young woman backed into the wall of the airlock interior. Burdette Steading had strict civil engineering codes, so the space was several feet across to allow all the occupants of the connected housing unit plus a few guests the ability to shelter-in-place inside in the event of an environmental breach. Ideally the attached housing would maintain atmospheric integrity during such a disaster, but making the airlock larger let the builder meet code without providing each apartment with its own emergency shelter. "This is wastefully spacious," Miss Rustin said. "I need to tell the Lady Steadholder the poor housing is too big. Why are you following me?"

"I live here," Noah said. He entered just enough to let the door close behind him and picked the opposite side of the airlock space to wait for the interior door to open. He did his best not to loom. Poor or not, he was a properly brought up Grayson. And men who were real men did not do or say things that might scare a young woman out and about on her own.

"You do not!" Miss Rustin said. "This domicile is assigned to the Bedlam-Lecroix household. It's a condensed family way smaller than steading average. Two senior sisters: Lillian and Jezzy, one widowed and the second with no spouse on record, probably a case of benefits fraud from a generation or so ago. But both had several children. Poor people for you." She paused in her recitation to bat the interior door open button. "A single—obviously spoiled—male offspring and three of the female offspring d—" Something in his expression warned her. "Are you Noah Bedlam?"

"Yes," he said. Benefits fraud. That was a new one. Usually he had people assume his mom had engaged in prostitution. That was an easier assumption for people to make about what life in Burdette Steading might be like for an underclass worker than to ask themselves whether it was always safe for a young woman to clean a stranger's home. Benefits fraud. Yes! He could imagine a young Mom Jezzy as a rakish female Robin Hood sneakily collecting assistance checks to feed her children while his father was, what, in another steading arranging the setup for an interplanetary jewel heist that would allow him to retire from crime and raise his family to a level of wealth that they'd never even know what instant noodles were? Yeah.

"Um, fine," Miss Rustin said. The interior door still didn't open. "We'll just step inside so you can sign these on a table or built-in counter or whatever you have." She bashed the open button harder and the cover fell off.

"Air quality alert. Particulates inside above recommended levels," a soft machine voice announced. "Interior door sealed."

Miss Rustin gave him a look of complete disgust. "You don't change your air filters, do you?"

He had, in fact, never changed an air filter. Usually they lived in transition housing and had to move on to the next place every two weeks. Somebody changed the filters between occupants, maybe. This new place was a Lady Theresa initiative: a five-year residency arrangement that was supposed to let people take on longer term apprenticing positions instead of only daywork. A social services support box arrived every month. Mom Jezzy had said there was no food in it, so he hadn't opened one himself.

"You think it's women's work, I suppose." Miss Rustin put her nose in the air. "Men," she intoned with disgust. "I bet that GSN cousin of yours the files referenced used to do all the home engineering maintenance or one of your sis— Never mind." She closed her mouth over what she was about to say and pulled off a wall panel to get at a diagnostic console for the interior apartment's ventilation system. Noah hadn't known that was there, but it wouldn't have mattered if he had. Tiny little screws held a cover over the controls.

Miss Rustin produced a tool kit from her purse and accessed it in moments. "Yup," she said. "No maintenance done during any of the two and a half months this place has been assigned to the Bedlam-Lecroix household. Before that, when the Reeds had it, they were a little spotty about it, but they at least never missed more than one month in a row on any filter. And! They always changed that critical filter right next to the airlock entrance where most of the surface contaminants collect." Rustin gave him a pointed glare. "You do know that if you ever get infants or a pregnant woman in here, you immediately put in a request to double your filter deliveries, right? Those companies that say their filters are baby-grade are all scams. The thicker filters don't work any better than the usual ones because contaminants will slip around the edges of the filter at a higher rate once they're even a little bit dirt-coated. For infants in the house, you need to double your change rate. There's no other way around it without a complete tear-out and replace of the installed resident air filtration system."

Noah blinked. He wasn't going to have infants growing up in poverty assistance housing if he could help it.

"I might as well be talking to a wall," Miss Rustin grumbled. She reaffixed the cover over the buttons and put her kit back in her purse. "Here, I can just hold the forms against this spot where the airlock door juts out a bit, and you sign where I point, got it?"

"No," Noah said.

Miss Rustin huffed in irritation. "You can always quit later. Please?"

"Get out," Noah said. He pressed the exterior airlock door, gently in the upper left corner to avoid breaking off its button cover, and that side opened for him.

"But, I—" Rustin blushed furiously, clutched her purse to her belly and stepped through the airlock door. Outside, she turned back to face him and hissed, "Wastrel lay-about men like you are everything that's wrong with Grayson!"

Noah rocked back as the airlock door closed. He didn't think he'd ever been called a man by a pretty unmarried Grayson woman before.

Noah tried to hate Miss Rustin for the rude and thoughtless comments. But he was tired, so very tired. She was gone. It was time to stop indulging in maybes and might-have-beens. He tried to enter the apartment. The door didn't open.

"Air quality alert. Particulates inside above recommended levels," a soft machine voice announced again. This time it added: "Diagnostic review of air filter system in progress."

Miss Rustin had done something to the air quality settings, and he didn't have a tool of his own to change it back.

Noah popped off the wall panel next to the open button and crossed the wires needed to get the door open. He got into the apartment. The interior panel blinked and stopped the diagnostic.

I got what I wanted. Noah found himself laughing.

Noah could really have used a job, if his record wouldn't exclude him from even trying. Especially now that his sisters and cousins were gone, he didn't need to stay here. There were really nice support programs that predated Lady Theresa's for older women without any younger family. His mom would be better off without him. Aunt Lillian still, technically, had Claire, which made her ineligible for those programs, but Aunt Lillian's little illegal restaurant cart business might be enough for her to get by for a while.

He pushed those bleak thoughts out of his mind and tried to focus on the present. There were air filters somewhere in this place that were supposed to be changed at least monthly. And Miss Rustin thought girl kids had been doing it for him his whole life. How hard could it be?

The panel at the front of the apartment proved to have a new resident "Welcome to Your New Home" instructional video.

He struggled through the machinery checks for the home airlock and air filtration systems. Before his uncle died, he thought, his cousins and sisters used to do the housing maintenance. He still wasn't sure he understood it right.

Mom Jezzy had said she was doing it here, but he suspected Miss Rustin was right. These filters were filthy. He knew Mom Jezzy would get flustered if he asked her when she'd changed them last. She'd grown up in transitional housing with no dad around ever. She talked a lot about how wonderful it was when Lillian had married Joe and the little while when Joe was making enough that he let her and the kids move in with them. Noah bet she'd never changed any home filters. She might not know how. So he did it himself.

He found the social services box from last month in the kitchen cupboard under the food pantry bag of boxed meals only recently expired. The standard package of household filters was there— unopened. That meant the filter change for the air handling in the main entry airlock wasn't the only routine maintenance chore that hadn't been done.

He worked fast, changing all the household filters before Mom Jezzy got home from the prayer meeting. Mom Jezzy liked to pretend their lives were more rich-people-normal than they really could be. He knew she hated to see him doing anything close to women's work. But if she couldn't be counted on to do it herself, it had to be okay for him to do it. But Noah could at least give her the gift of doing it on the sly, so she wouldn't have to admit to herself that he was doing it.

He was washing the grit off his hands in the sink when the airlock door whooshed open to admit Mom Jezzy. She gave him a big hug and proudly produced a mouthwatering carton of barbeque complete with a slab of cornbread and a mess of mixed greens and bacon. As he ate, she proudly produced her other finds.

One of the ladies at Chapel Yanakov had allowed her free access to their charity thrift closet. Mom Jezzy had made herself into a masterful supplicant. She had a knack for finding every support service in Benedict City, and—when he wasn't present—she had no trouble convincing people that she was a member of the deserving poor who should be given the best of whatever handout was available this month.

Noah was never as successful. Not a surprise, when he hadn't wanted to grovel and be as appreciative as people like Miss Rustin always seemed to think people like him were supposed to be.

The good poor—the deserving poor—those were the titles Mom Jezzy had worked her rear end off to get affixed to their family for her entire life. Everything he did always seemed to make it harder for her.

Noah wanted to throw open both sides of the airlock, never mind the risk of letting in contaminants from Burdette City proper and yell back at the long gone Miss Rustin: "I am not everything wrong with Grayson! People like you are the ones who embody everything that's wrong with Grayson! I'm just a guy trying to . . ." But that last bit was the problem. *Trying to what?* He'd turned seventeen. He'd been legally a man by Grayson law for a while now, and he still didn't know what he was trying to do. Sure, he had a list as long as his arm of what he wanted, but he had no way of getting any of it.

Mom Jezzy noticed his distraction enough to break his train of thought with a forced cheerfully running commentary on the best of her finds.

"Look at this jacket I got for you! Almost the right size even. I'll fix it right up with a little tailoring and won't the girls be all over you!"

"That'll be great, Mom Jezzy." That was a lie. He would rather drown himself than get another dependent right now, but Mom Jezzy would get all teary-eyed and go buy him something they couldn't afford if he said so. She should be allowed to live in false hope. Noah could give his mom that much.

The parents of all the potential brides who might consider him knew he had no prospects, and a like-new jacket expertly tailored by Mom Jezzy wasn't going to change that. "Thanks, Mom Jezzy." He gave her a hug, and she squeezed him right back. These lies were important to her.

Then she pulled out the flimsy, and Noah's mouth fell open.

Mom Jezzy had met Miss Rustin on the street and obtained the form. Miss Rustin had filled out an application in his name. Mom Jezzy had signed it for him, since she was sure he wouldn't mind. "And that sweet girl didn't mind either," Mom Jezzy said. Miss Rustin had submitted it right there in the street.

"Mom," he said forgetting the "Jezzy" again in his distress, "you'll lose this apartment."

"What? Why?" she said.

"They'll suspend our benefits if I have a job. Then they'll run the background check which I'll fail. I'll be fired."

Mom Jezzy went very still.

"It's okay. It's okay," Noah assured her. "I'll go right down there as soon as the offices are open tomorrow morning and tell them Miss Rustin lied to you and the forms were submitted in error. We'll get through this. And if we have to, there are some spots available over in the Barbara Bancroft hostel on the east side."

"But I read the whole paper," Mom Jezzy said. "It says benefits status won't be changed by participation during the first year of the program."

"What?" Noah stared at the paper as Mom Jezzy turned the flimsy to point out each of the sections that repeated that. Mom Jezzy produced another chit bearing the address near the shuttle port and a range of times when new applicants could check in.

He was going to have to see Rustin again, and she was going to think she'd outmaneuvered him. There were some details about an initial training event. Lunch to be included. Breakfast available for those who could arrive early . . . Noah's eyes widened at the description of the program itself.

"You don't have to do it, Noah," Mom Jezzy said. "It's fine. You don't have to."

They wanted to use him as an orbital worker.

Mom Jezzy was looking at him with that quiver at the corners of her mouth, and he knew she was worried about him. He'd go. "Mom, it's fine." He gave her an easy smile as if he weren't at all worried about going to the wreckage of Blackbird Station.

"Just promise me you'll stay on top of the filters while I'm away," he said.

She wrinkled her nose at him as if that were a ridiculous thing for him to say. "I always do. Such a thoughtful young man." She patted him on the arm. She hummed all afternoon while she packed his bags.

There were shuttles going up all the time and pay would start as soon as he got on one. He could call Chapel Yanakov from the shuttle port and get someone to come visit Mom Jezzy and check on the filters while he was away. She'd be furious, but it'd keep her from getting sick.

It wasn't every day you could infuriate a pretty girl and your own mother by trying to do the right thing.

❋ ❋ ❋

"Learn their names, goddamnit, learn their names!" Deacon Roundhouse pulled on his already sparse hair and glared at the photos of the three young men he'd confused with each other during his self-inflicted memory drill.

He was alone in one of the many small offices in the shuttle port that Burdette Steading authorities made available. The lay minister of the Church of Humanity Unchained hadn't noticed his own blasphemy. The rough habits learned in his first career came back to the surface whenever he was under stress.

Deacon Roundhouse flicked again through screen after screen of orbital workers murmuring names as he went. Three hours ago, his mutterings had been much less blasphemous. Impure language wasn't a sin he'd ever been particularly adept at avoiding. Frustrated, and in the privacy of this borrowed space, he plowed through the work again. A new dozen faces had been added to the list in the last hour and someone named Suleia had taken a group photo "for efficiency" instead of individual pictures. That might've been fine, but someone else had made up the identity badges assigning the names wrong. So now he had to unlearn seven names and wonder how many others crammed into his mind were actually wrong.

Elder Larson expected him to be praying before starting up to orbit.

His mental health counselor expected him to be meditating and perhaps composing a resignation letter. The counselor thought it was too soon for someone like him to go back to working around the remains of Blackbird.

Elder Larson's latest missive had actually suggested he could go ahead and resign with a whole lot of extra words circling around the idea that the Church wasn't meant to be a rebound career. This despite the fact that the same man had publicly and loudly welcomed Roundhouse into lay ministry within a week of the Blackbird attack and mentioned him by name in several homilies as an example to all steaders of how they should respond to adversity by holding more tightly to the faith. Roundhouse agreed. He just didn't see that ministry politics within the Church of Humanity Unchained was necessarily in line with true faithfulness.

Neither the elder nor the therapist really understood Deacon Roundhouse, but his wife Nadia did. He was going to leave the familiar and safe habitats on Grayson's planetary surface and move to the new station being built in orbit of the gas giant Uriel right in the midst of the Blackbird wreckage, because it was the right thing to do. There were kids who needed him. He and Nadia hadn't been blessed with their own progeny, but the Tester had provided them with hundreds of young people in need. Few would ever rise as high as Lady Theresa, but few would want to if they truly understood her life. In Burdette, a steadholder's wife almost never left her elegantly padded cage.

The fear knotting Roundhouse's gut came from self-doubt. What if he'd lost his touch? What if he couldn't teach safety and engineering principles fast enough for the hodgepodge group being thrown out to him? His therapist kept poking at his feelings around the horrific attack and all the people in his old crews and their support techs who'd died. He didn't blame himself for those. No crew chief controlled whether or not a foreign military would execute a sneak attack on his build site. He blamed himself for that one found dead with his skinsuit helmet not sealed on properly or those three dead in the life pod with the pinhole leak and the patch kit floating inside unopened.

Roundhouse closed his stinging eyes. He needed a break. He opened his packed lunch. Sweet Nadia had had one of her interns drop it by earlier with apologies about the mix-up on the photos. He removed a note from under the container of chopped vegetables which he didn't intend to eat and above the container with pie that he would be eating. It read very simply, "Thank you for helping me support Lady Theresa. I know this is hard. I know you aren't going to stop now no matter how nervous I get about it. Thank you again. All my love, Nadia."

"Oh fuck, Nadie-girl, it'll work out. Don't sweat about me." Roundhouse shook his head at the note, and reaching for the pie, he finally realized he'd been using language inappropriate for a lay minister again. He gave an irritated grunt and ate sweet cherry goodness.

He browsed some files about the new Burdette Station. Ron Wilson and several other men Roundhouse recognized were on the board of directors. The initial construction had been successfully pressurized out in Uriel orbit by a picked build crew who were leaving immediately for another urgent (Roundhouse interpreted that as more lucrative) project. Gravitics was online. No creaky spin gravity with all that Coriolis effect to deal with, then. Life support, backup life support, and tertiary life support were online, along with about quadruple the usual number of built-in life pod chambers. The amount of filter maintenance they'd need for all those vent systems would be enormous. But it was an easy task to hand out to newbie spacers. That amount of life support was overkill right now, with all the GSN ships running patrols around the whole star system and paying particular attention to the rebuilding efforts Burdette and many other steadholders were working on around Uriel. But, Roundhouse supposed, Lady Theresa had needed to include so much in order to solicit large donations from the wealthier steaders and large participation from the poorer steaders.

The materials needed to build out the rest of the station were in short supply, but the new station's setup involved a plan to do some reclamation of space debris. It was partially to clear their orbit around Uriel and partially as natural Grayson frugalness. Why buy and move building materials to the new station when they could reuse some of what was already there?

He finished his pie and returned to studying the prospective crew roster. These were poor steaders, most not only with no space work experience, but also with no travel outside of their own steading, let alone into orbit or out to another planet in the system.

All he had to do right now was finish learning their names. Never again was he going to be asked to identify a body and not be able to say which name went with that half face.

※ ※ ※

Outer space was even bigger than Noah had thought it was.

It had been sobering enough to look out the viewport and see Grayson, shining in Yeltsin's Star's reflected light, with his own eyes. Like every child of Grayson he'd seen enough orbital imagery of his home world to be bored to tears, but it was very different, somehow, to see it with his own two eyes. To know that *he* was up among the planetary orbital traffic, not stuck down in one of those sealed habitats so far below him.

Then there'd been the trip to Uriel orbit. At closest approach, they were almost forty light-minutes apart. Given the current geometry, the actual range was almost a full light-hour, so the flight had taken close to eleven hours, even at three hundred gravities of acceleration. It was a good thing the seats were so comfortable, and the food service had been an eye-opener. He'd heard some of the supervisor types complaining about its quality, but it had been hot and there'd been almost enough of it!

And now, as they decelerated at last, the brilliant red gas giant of Uriel, streaked in bright yellows and blues, loomed in the same viewport, and Noah's mouth tightened as the shattered rubble of ruined station bits glimmered against that bloody planetary backdrop. Even Yeltsin's sunlight was dim so far from the system primary, but the wreckage glimmered like lonely tears under its distant kiss.

And then, the rubble dimmed. Not all at once. It was as if a moving wall had blocked the sunlight, sweeping in across his field of view. The line of darkness embraced the wreckage, sweeping smoothly across the lonely fragments.

"That shadow," the pilot said, "was courtesy of our boys in blue, the Grayson Space Navy. That's from the CLAC *Covington*. She's part of the security patrols. She's headed back out for the Uriel Hyper limit, and she's passing outside us at the moment, where her impeller wedge can cut the light. She's a light attack craft carrier and shares the name with the old *Austin Grayson*-class cruiser *Covington* museum ship which orbits Grayson. You really ought to visit when you next get home."

As Noah watched, the edge of the ship's impeller shadow moved on, clearing the shuttle to once again reveal more and more debris, scattered like a child's abandoned rock collection and festooned with the cobwebs of even smaller bits caught up in the mass attraction of the larger pieces.

He closed his eyes against the painful beauty of it, not wanting to catch sight of any more twisted metal that might hold the remains of his cousin Lucy or sisters Mary and Grace.

The pilot's voice came over the speakers again. "Check those itty-bitty cutters out, boys. Genuine old-time Grayson technology right there."

"What's he even talking about?" Noah couldn't see any vehicles at all in the midst of the debris.

A blonde-haired fellow traveler turned from her prime viewing position right next to the viewport to stare directly at Noah. "Oh, hi," Miss Rustin said. "Ha! I knew you'd show up if someone pushed you properly."

"Not now, miss," a middle-aged man said. He wore a clerical collar underneath his skinsuit. "The pilot can see things with his sensors that the mere human eyes the Tester gave us can't make out. In answer to your question, Lady Theresa received a donation of several dozen durable old commercial cutters to support our new Burdette Station. My name's Deacon Roundhouse, but don't let the church title fool you. I've been a space work supervisor for over twenty years and a journeyman technician before that. At this time in the shift cycle, there'd be only a couple of 'em out and about, but we might be using 'em for a lot more later. They might be old, but they're still in service because they work. And you'll see plenty more of them once we get Burdette Station going."

He made it off the transport shuttle without catching Miss Rustin's notice again.

Thank the Tester, Noah and the other volunteers were put to work immediately after docking. Mom Jezzy would have been appalled at all the women's work he was doing. To start, he did nothing but filter changes. The expert-space-worker-turned-deacon taught classes every afternoon between lunch and second shift. With no more senior clergy about, everyone tried to call him "elder," but he insisted on "Deacon" Roundhouse.

Morning devotions with Roundhouse included a loss of atmosphere emergency response litany: suit, visor, gloves, assist. It was weird, but not that weird. The jailhouse chaplain who'd presided over prayer services before each community service shift at the Burdette recycling plant had been drunk most of the time. The not-so-standard clergy and lay ministers in the Church of Humanity Unchained had to be given positions somewhere.

If you paid attention and passed his practical exams, Roundhouse promised there would be more interesting work assignments like spacesuit maintenance, salvage, cutter piloting, and station construction.

They had a supply hangar full of older style bulky suits of the kind a non-spacer might use. They were in a range of sizes, not individually fitted like proper skinsuits, but at least they were better than the one-size-fits-all kind of emergency suits Roundhouse called "gumbies." Cutters and other little space vessels flitting about carrying passengers usually carried those. Of course a skinsuit was more comfortable, but they were also a lot more expensive. And Noah laughed when he learned part of spacesuit maintenance involved changing filters in the air regulator system.

Some of the supervisors talked about expanding this Burdette public works space station into a cutter taxi depot after the Lady Steadholder got bored with it. A standard cutter could shuttle people or gear around from one side of a large station to another or between stations. They were nowhere near as fast as one of the more modern, impeller-drive shuttles, but that kind of speed was more than anyone needed for short-haul, local work. If the projected restorations of the hulks around Uriel and her moon were funded to replace Blackbird Station, they'd need the services of a lot of cutters, and that meant there'd be a need for a good cutter depot. Noah kept his ears open and listened in on the supervisors as often as he could.

For now, Mom Jezzy was living well. On his third call to the women at Chapel Yanakov, he'd managed to convince a kind widow to drive his mom home from prayer circle, personally check the filters, and call him back after. He'd installed about half of the filters backwards, but she'd fixed them, and was deeply amused that a son had tried to put in filters at all. Mom Jezzy had been patted on the back for having raised a compassionate young man who even did filters. His stipend was generous, and no one had stopped the social services delivery even though his total balances were too high now.

Noah had been able to transfer some extra cash back to Aunt Lillian. She and her youngest daughter, Evelyn, ran an unlicensed side business, not a restaurant exactly, but a food cart to sell hot lunches in an industrial area of Mueller. Aunt Lillian had wondered if maybe Mom Jezzy might sew some insulated carry pouches for those who wanted to buy evening meals to take home? Noah sent Evelyn a note and asked her to figure out what it'd take to get the food cart to pass an inspection by the Mueller health code, and he promised to send more money to pay for fees.

He'd tried to send a few austins to his cousin Claire as a repayment of sorts, but it hadn't been accepted.

The station supervisors complained about missing amenities and talked among themselves of positions elsewhere. But it wasn't missing anything. The life support system had multiple backups, and there were life pods all over! The air smelled fresh in a way Noah hadn't realized was possible for filtered air. Airlocks between sections cycled open and shut without even one overridden alarm. No wonder Mary and Lucy had liked station life.

"We should at least have a club here," a supervisor handing out the day's assignments said to the man next to him, who was checking off which workers had shown up for the shift.

Noah looked at his work list: filters and . . . more filters.

"Some place to relax, yeah," the man with the list said. "Didn't old Blackbird used to have one with, ah, dancers?" He lifted his eyebrows to indicate that he meant more than dance had gone on.

"The Lady Steadholder made arrangements for beer to be available in the dining hall for those who want it while off shift," Miss Rustin said.

Both supervisors started at her young female voice.

"I suppose I could ask her about having a dance troupe visit." She tilted her head to the side. "Did they really have a ballet hall on Blackbird before? I know it was big, and there were more businesses in the greater distributed space infrastructure than just the shipbuilding ones, but I'd not heard about dancers."

"Um, no, miss," the second supervisor said.

"I should ask Deacon Roundhouse," Rustin said. "He worked on Blackbird before."

"Don't bother the deacon with that. He's much too busy." The first supervisor tried to hand her a list of filter cleaning assignments.

Rustin didn't take it. She folded her arms. "But the Lady Steadholder only hired supervisors who agreed to support the project for a full year. Do I need to tell her you are planning to quit early?"

"Just keeping ourselves aware of the options, miss," the first supervisor said. "There are other people in line behind you."

Miss Rustin gave both older men a regal nod.

Noah left to go change his first filter, and she followed him like an unwelcome shadow.

"Lady Theresa should fire them both," she told him. "There's not going to be any strip clubs on one of *her* stations. And they really ought to know better than to be talking like that in front of the unmarried poor ladies. It could give them ideas."

Give who ideas? Noah chose not to tell her that the female workers around her already knew all about strip clubs. Those sorts of establishments were relatively uncommon on the planet, but where they did exist, it was the poorer people who were recruited to work in them.

Noah had managed to avoid seeing Miss Rustin at the check-in desk at the shuttle port but that didn't mean he'd escaped her "I told you so" or any other comments since. Rustin was everywhere underfoot at the station. The deacon made her scrub floors and change filters whenever he saw her, and she was annoyingly good at both. But she wasn't used to dirt. She flinched at the small bits of muck the filters managed to collect between cleanings.

"What are you doing this shift?" Rustin peered at his list and made a tsking noise at seeing nothing but filter changes. "The station was supposed to have more crew by now," she said. "Some more people should come in a few weeks, but the Lady Steadholder insists they be volunteers."

"Will she pay us more?" Noah asked.

Rustin sniffed. "It's not the pay. People want to commute back home each night. If she'd just decided to establish the station in Grayson orbit, they could do that."

Noah unscrewed a wall panel and switched a filter out. "If she'd done that we'd have no work to do that other more experienced people aren't already doing. With the station in Uriel orbit, it can provide services to whatever gets rebuilt out here where Blackbird used to be."

Rustin made a harrumph noise that Noah was pretty sure wouldn't be considered ladylike by her moms.

Eventually servo mechs would do a lot of the work the volunteers were currently learning, the deacon had explained during one morning devotional session. The topic of loving your neighbor had somehow segued into airlock safety during a loss of station atmosphere and the goals for the project as a whole. By the time programmed remotes were doing the basic station maintenance, the work crew would be trained up for more advanced tasks, he'd said. Rustin had demanded to know why the machines weren't already doing it, and the deacon had laughed at her.

Noah had expected the answer to be that it was made-up work left undone to give charity cases something to do. But Deacon Roundhouse said not. In a new build or a newly overhauled station, humans had to doublecheck that the machines were really doing everything that needed doing. Machines only followed their programming. It depended on people noticing the points where the programming fell short.

Miss Rustin continued to trail after Noah. Deacon Roundhouse had promised him a spacesuit fitting after he completed this shift's worth of filter change-and-inspect procedures. And then he'd get more training in the careful out-hull maintenance work that required one.

Noah crawled halfway into a ventilation shaft to replace a filter his long arms could barely reach. He pulled himself back out, panting from the effort of squeezing into a long narrow space not sized for nonrobotic maintenance.

"I'm not available, just so you know," Rustin said.

"What?" Noah examined the thickly dirt-crusted filter. He brushed the muck off the bottom corner where the date of install was supposed to be printed by a maintenance bot. It was blank. That made it an original preconstruction phase filter. Noah made a note to let the deacon know that this one had been missed in the cleaning bots' schedule.

"Just the way you've been looking at me," Miss Rustin explained. "Seemed like maybe you thought I was going to be super interested and stuff."

"Okay," he said. Noah considered explaining how he was absolutely not interested in gaining a dependent. Quite the opposite since the dependents he'd had from birth seemed to flee. Or die.

He hunched down to repeat the process for another hard to reach filter.

Even if he'd had to marry someone, Rustin looked like she had expensive tastes. He couldn't afford moderate tastes, let alone expensive ones.

"Good. Glad we got that out of the way. Some guys get all fussy and angry about it." She paused and gave him that slow inspection he'd come to hate. Other women were more discreet. And it felt more annoying when it was side to side instead of up and down. He slid the rest of the way back into the hall with the old filter in his outstretched hand.

This filter was nearly clean with a bot-install date of just a week ago. Good. He wouldn't have to come back and contort himself again next week. It was already in the programmed servicing schedule.

"I think I like you after all," Miss Rustin continued, while not, he noticed, actually doing any of her filter checks. He supposed she didn't care about skinsuits. Perhaps she had three of them at home and knew all about them. "We'll have to be friends," she said. "It might be nice to have some guy friends. I hear the Manticorans do that all the time. Girls friends with guys and not even because they're considering dating when the guy's ready to add another wife."

"They do?" He kicked himself. Questions were not the right way to handle this. Consistent disinterest was key. Anything else and the girl's reports to her father and mothers would include angry tears and a claim that he'd been leading her on.

"Yes. They do. You wouldn't believe the things my sister's told me about how people do things in other star systems. Or maybe you would. You talk much with that GSN cousin?"

Noah considered lying. "Some," he said reluctantly. How much had they put in his file? Maybe she'd take the hint from his monosyllabic response and not pursue the subject?

She didn't. Women so very rarely did.

"Oh, good. Then you understand. Well, at least to some extent. Your cousin is enlisted, I'd guess. My sister, Cecelie, is a GSN officer. She writes me all the time. The moms were worried at first that she'd be bringing all these officers home, and that all of us Rustins would end up GSN widows, but that was just the moms being silly. Cecelie hardly gets any leave time at all, what with the war and all. So she doesn't bring anybody by to visit."

The GSN had a very nice pension benefit. Mom Jezzy had been

very excited about it for a while. He'd been especially terrified after Blackbird that something would happen to his cousin. He'd had confused half dreams, half nightmares where they suddenly had a lot of money, but it was because the GNS *Ephraim* had been destroyed. And Ensign Claire Bedlam-Lecroix was dead. Since the money he'd get as next of kin would be so nice, Mom Jezzy had talked about it way too much. He'd gone to the church about his fears. And instead of praying for Noah and Mom Jezzy, Deacon Randall had tried to get Claire's officer commission revoked.

Noah tried a grunt. Sometimes grunts worked to get Mom Jezzy to change subjects or find a different audience. Unfortunately Miss Rustin took it as active listening.

"Officer suitors." Rustin waved a hand at the bulkhead as though farewelling a dream. "It never happened. Turns out almost every officer in the GSN is married already. Except the girls of course." She stopped to give him a glare as if she expected a mean reply and she was giving him the chance to blurt it out before she hit him with one of the used filters.

Noah wasn't stupid. He didn't say a thing. A silent nod was all she was getting out of him.

She nodded right back. What they'd just agreed on, he had no idea.

"You see then. A Rustin girl might be second wife, but not a third or fourth. So of course those men are right out. If a guy were tragically widowed, I suppose I could imagine it, but even so, there'd be all that extra emotional baggage, and it'd be so hard to retrain the household properly."

Noah nodded again, even though he had no clue what might make a household improperly trained. He rather suspected that everything about his own family would be untrained to Miss Rustin's eye and resolved not to share a single bit of his own background.

⚹ ⚹ ⚹

"You two." Noah jerked at the sharp call. "Stop lollygagging and get over here." A new black-shirted supervisor snapped his fingers. "Miss Rustin, you and Mr. Bedlam join that line over there."

Noah hurried to the appropriate group on one side of the large cargo bay. Suleia Rustin trailed along behind him.

He had to skirt the side of the bay. The half dozen cutters

normally parked docked to its transfer tubes were absent, and a mound higher than his head filled the center of the space.

The large bulkhead display screen showed a video feed of the other cutter bay. Its cutters were headed out, as well. A few of the skin-suited crew members moved with the easy confidence of long experience as they swung themselves across the station's gravity interface to swim the boarding tubes, but a lot of them had the clumsiness of trainees.

A supervisor pointed out a collection of bins and called out salvage sorting directions in a carrying voice. Rustin sniffed. "Looks like the worst organized craft room I've ever seen."

It reminded Noah of Burdette Steading's trash and recycling central holding room from past community service experience. "Not really," he said.

"Noah and Suleia. Stop the chatter," the supervisor bellowed. "Get at least two bins filled with properly sorted materials by lunch bell, if you please. The rest of you, head to hangar bay two for suit fittings. Those who paid attention to me will be able to sort in the cutters, so we won't end up with piles in both bays."

Rustin looked at the pile and the few workers pulling out bits to place into floating bins. "You aren't going to finish by lunch," she said.

Noah selected a bin at random and pulled it with him to the edge of the mound. An assessor tool hung by a cord from the side of the bin. His bin said, "nickel-based alloys." He'd been able to hear enough of the instructions that he figured out how to turn the assessor tool on and held lumps of salvage up to it until he got a green light. That lump went into the bin.

"This is such a waste of time," Rustin said.

Noah sifted through the top layer until he couldn't find anything else that had enough nickel in it to get a green light. A couple lumps seemed likely but the tool only flickered when he held them up to it. He left them for someone with more metals knowledge and went back for the molycirc bin.

Deacon Roundhouse made his way into their bay and wandered the room, going from worker to worker. When he reached the two of them, Rustin raised her eyebrows at him and smiled. "Good afternoon, Deacon."

"Afternoon, Mr. Bedlam, Miss Rustin. You see our project

received authorization to spend more time on reclamation. Good progress there, Mr. Bedlam," Deacon Roundhouse said.

"The Protector did sign off on the Sacristy's petition!" Rustin said. She grinned from ear-to-ear and danced on her toes in self-congratulation. "I told Mrs. R. that we'd get the most money out of this project if we could get the Church to fund it. Oh, yeah! I was right. Again."

A scowl flickered across the deacon's face and for a moment Noah thought the man was considering punching her.

Right after Blackbird was attacked, people had donated a lot of austins to survivors' funds and funeral relief drives. He'd made a contribution himself with a few spare austins.

"We will not be taking Sacristy funding," Deacon Roundhouse said. "We do not profiteer off the dead."

Rustin opened her mouth again, and Noah stepped on her foot, hard. Thank the Tester, she shut up.

"But . . ." Noah scrambled for some words to distract the man from Rustin. "You will bless them, right? Just in case?" The half-formed idea left him scanning the pile in front of them for limb fragments and bones. It had been more than three months since the attack and search crews had been over every bit of debris twice at a least. There'd be no more miracle rescues. No one could have survived this long since the attacks, but remains could still be intermixed and crushed in the debris.

The deacon allowed himself to be diverted. "I've been on most of the cutter rides headed to new claims, and I'll continue that. I've prayed over all of them. Funerals have already been held by most families, but some of our reclamations have turned up remains. The Church has the list of the missing. They do the contacts. Sometimes the families have bodies shipped home. Other times they want a space burial.

"So, yes, I'm praying for them. I ask that you do too. These aren't . . . Well, you know how all this debris got out there. It does all need to be cleared out and either placed in a controlled orbit or shifted into Uriel's gravity well. It's for the protection of our new builds up here, that we need to move it. But it's all a graveyard in a sense. Treat it with dignity, but make the place useful again. Any spacer would want that."

The deacon nodded to himself and moved on to talking about

more commonplace things. He talked about the cutter assignments, and the process by which they would be determining who was ready to do reclamation work, and suit fittings, and the classes for those working towards various space work certifications. Several others came by and needed specific instruction on how to assess certain system repairs they were working on.

Miss Rustin looked bored and didn't pay attention.

Finally, the deacon got back around to them.

Noah was patted on the back for his completed filter checks. Rustin was sent away to complete a few filter changes herself. Her comments about being here as an observer and not an employee were ignored, as usual.

"Does the Tester send us just to watch or to also act?" seemed to be a usefully sharp line from the deacon, which seemed to get through to her. Though her interest in a recommendation letter from the deacon on Sacristy letterhead might have been more inspirational. She did go.

After several hours of his working with the pile, Rustin returned and started talking again.

"I've been thinking about what you said, Mr. Bedlam."

Noah just kept working. He hadn't said a thing.

"You've got a point." Miss Rustin fished out a particularly well-preserved bit of molycirc and, after verifying its quality, placed it in the high grade stack. She had an eye for finding the very best stuff. "I can't just go up and propose to a Manticoran. They're odd like that and wouldn't mind, but it sets the wrong precedent. I don't want to always have to make all the decisions, you know? I need a guy who'll take a few good hints and run with it. Somebody smart."

He held his head very still as he worked. He wanted to avoid an accidental nod or headshake that she might take as an answer.

Deacon Roundhouse rescued him, sending Rustin off to go pick up a pallet of assessor kits just shipped in. The better tools should help them shift the pile more quickly.

"You doing okay, Mr. Bedlam?" Deacon Roundhouse asked.

"Yes, sir." It was nice of the minister to care, but Noah had learned the hard way that advice was worth exactly what he paid for it. He did not want another Deacon Randall experience. Rustin was an easy trouble, so he didn't complain.

They both watched Rustin's progress across the floor, and the deacon snorted to cover a laugh when she stopped halfway to the pickup point to engage in some kind of argument with one of the other workers.

"She'll be gone in a few weeks, and I appreciate your willingness to work with her. She's offended most of the others."

"Miss Rustin does report to the Lady Steadholder," Noah said. It felt strange to caution an older man, but the deacon did need to know the dangers. The tone of irritation the supervisors took with her made perfect sense considering her practice of assuming authority she didn't have, but still. Now that he took a moment to think about the bigger picture, he thought Miss Rustin might cause the whole project significant damage if she made a negative report. Losing a few key people without timely replacements could scuttle even a standard project. This effort, well, they needed every one of the few experienced spacers they had.

"She's an intern. She's got no authority and no access to Lady Theresa. Quite the opposite." Deacon Roundhouse shook his head. "The Lady Steadholder had some initial concern that Miss Suleia Rustin might get herself killed through overconfident ineptitude." Roundhouse tilted his head and shared a grin with Noah. "She actually said that, 'overconfident ineptitude.' I had to look it up after. Means 'being a dumbshit.' The young woman's troublesome, I'll give 'em that. Miss Rustin's not a dumbshit though. Helps that I got the Lady Steadholder to give out an annoyance bonus to all my supervisors if we could get her to do any real work. Miss Rustin put grit in the wrong gears at the steadholder's office, that's for sure. At first hearing about the girl, I felt sorry for her, but having met her..." The deacon shrugged. "I think she earned it."

"But she is starting to do some work." Noah pointed out.

"Yep." The deacon acknowledged. "And she's not always wrong." The woman Miss Rustin had been arguing with set down her bundle and stomped off. Rustin leaned over the load and removed a few large pieces of salvage from the top. She put her shoulder against the side of the largest mass and rolled it over. It was a battered grav lifter. Rustin turned it on. She piled the other pieces on top. The machine lifted off the floor and drove itself the rest of the way with Rustin walking behind it.

"Huh," Noah said.

The new mass assessors made the sorting go faster. They'd have finished by lunch if the cutters hadn't continued bringing in new finds.

⌘ ⌘ ⌘

Lunch was steak and as many roasted root vegetables as a man could eat. Noah was in heaven.

Miss Rustin took the smallest possible portion of beef and used the ladle to pick out only the best-looking vegetable bits in the medley. The woman with the grav lift problem sat across from them and nagged until Rustin cleaned her plate.

"It's not Montana beef," was all she had to say when asked what she had against the meat. And, after a pause, she added, "I suppose the mess hall only has a soup kitchen budget and is doing the best they can.

"Oh!" She brightened. "Of course, it isn't like a soup kitchen. It *is* a soup kitchen! They have to skip the salads and skimp on food quality or you lot would think this was an okay way to live and stay with this program indefinitely. They are encouraging everyone to move on."

Noah suppressed his groan. "It doesn't work that way," he said. The woman across the table rolled her eyes and left. Her tray was empty anyway. She seemed to have enjoyed the food, if not the company.

"Why not?" Miss Rustin looked genuinely puzzled.

"Because it doesn't, that's why." He took his own empty tray to the washer and went back to work. Tomorrow he had been promised a cutter run.

⌘ ⌘ ⌘

Miss Rustin, after a few hours doing who knew what, joined him to help sort salvage again. The lunchtime argument and the deacon's news of Rustin's powerlessness broke some dam of silence inside him. When she made a comment about poor families simply lacking proper household management, he let her have it.

"Miss Rustin." He glared at her. "You have a stupid life-is-easy perspective. That's not how my Test has been. I can't just run away and make the rest of the family figure out their way without me. That's what my cousin did. Sure, she doesn't see it that way, but it's reality as far as I'm concerned. She got out, but it sure didn't help the rest of us."

"Oh, you've got brothers then?" Miss Rustin persisted in taking the wrong information from his rant. "You're lucky. My family has just sisters so far. The youngest of the moms has been going to this great clinic though. She's expecting twin boys. It's going to be a miracle for the whole family if she can actually bring them to term. Dr. Allison Harrington has changed everything, you know?"

Of course he knew of Dr. Allison's miracles. That wasn't the point. "No. I don't know." His fingers were leaving dents in the softer salvage pieces. He reached for something tougher. "Fine, yeah, Dr. Allison is a saint. There's going to be a lot of boys born who would never have survived before. Kids twenty years younger than us will have just as many boys as girls in their classes and in a couple generations maybe most people will have just one mom instead of three. But that doesn't fix anything now! It used to be that I had my mom, an aunt, three cousins, and two sisters. And every one of them is a girl. A lot fewer now, but that's not the point. The last other male relative we had was my uncle who died when I was seven. You know what that means? Huh? Do you?"

This time Miss Rustin was the soft-spoken one. "No."

"It means I've never been in charge of a darn thing and I probably never will be. Sure, they used to bring me stuff to sign and I could ruin things for any of them with a word to the wrong authority, but nobody has a big plan figuring out what's best for each of them and how the whole family should work together. I used to have the cousins and sisters all coming to me for loans and food and clothes and, and everything. And I could only give it to one as long as I took it from another. We always ran out too soon.

"All those accounts, technically/officially/legally/whatever, they belong to me. My own account is primary and has to be the overdraft protection for everyone else's. Pretty soon everyone figured out that if they want something, they should buy it immediately on a payday and pull whatever there was in my account down to zero."

"You let them do that to you?" Miss Rustin stared at him. "My dad would take my access card away if I ever overspent my allowance."

"It's never an ice cream cone." Noah glared at her. "It's a birthday cake. Or it's a taxi ride when the cleaning job took too long and the last tram is gone. Or it's getting grandma's pendant back from the pawnbroker, because this time he's really going to sell it to someone if we don't redeem it right now." He chunked a piece of low-grade platinum into the appropriate bin. It made a satisfyingly loud clunk as it hit.

"But at least you don't have to pay any taxes," Rustin said.

"I'm a Burdette steader." Noah scoffed. "Everyone pays taxes, and they're due quarterly. To manage that, I had to buy things. Big things. Things someone would pay money for at a pawnshop. I used to go buy things as soon as Mary and Lucy's pay came in since they made the most after Claire, and I was never quite sure what Claire might need to get. Official uniforms are really costly sometimes. But whatever. So each quarter when the taxes were due, I could go pawn the things so we could pay our share. Now, of course, I wish I hadn't. All I had to do was miss a tax payment, and the steading would have taken head of household away from me and made us Wards of the Steading again. Mary and Lucy wouldn't have been professional dancers anymore. And. They'd. Be. Alive."

"They performed at one of those clubs then?" Rustin said.

"Yes."

"So impressive," Rustin said.

Noah snorted. "You're going to have to work harder than that to make it hurt. I got my family killed and the best anyone can do is call me a pimp."

"I meant they were impressive, not you. Though I suppose your insistence on facing their Tests for them instead of your own Test is kind of impressively idiotic. No training. Almost no money. But they find a way to get themselves out of their home steading and off the planet. The work was probably bad, but they might've saved enough to do something else in just a few years." Rustin rolled her eyes. "Who could possibly be so dumb as to think you were a pimp? Everyone could see you couldn't even make them stick to a budget, but people somehow think you can control their employment choices from the other side of the Yeltsin System? People are idiots."

Noah swallowed hard.

※ ※ ※

The next morning Noah wore a fitted size 10 spacesuit. Not quite a skinsuit—which were individually made and fitted—it was still a very good suit, and the sizing was almost right if a tad bit too tight in the arms and shoulders. It moved smoothly and easily. His fingers had only the lightest skimming material over them. He felt great and didn't even mind the appreciative hoots the older female workers made on his way to the cutter.

"Why does he get one that actually looks comfortable?" Miss Rustin was there, outfitted in one of the one-size-fits-nobody gumbies.

Noah shot the deacon a silent appeal. *Please don't let her come with us.*

"He did all his filter checks. You were at least twenty short." The deacon waved them both into the cutter. "Since you're only here to observe, you could stay behind. But then I wouldn't be able to tell you about those engineering student exchange programs in the Manticore System you wanted to know about."

Noah wondered just how large that annoyance bonus was. He certainly wasn't going to be seeing any of it. Though if he were really lucky, the project would succeed and there might be a permanent place for him here.

Miss Rustin claimed the copilot's seat next to Deacon Roundhouse, and Noah was forced to strap into one of the jump seats affixed to the side of the cutter's main bay. It folded out but faced forward to support against the g-forces when the little reaction-thrust craft accelerated. They seldom exceeded a single gravity—cutters were designed for strictly short-haul work—but in theory, they could go as high as six. There was nothing much to see from the bay, of course, but he'd get other chances to watch cutter piloting after Rustin was gone. With a few minutes free, he logged into his accounts from the wall terminal and checked on how Mom Jezzy was doing. He had to pull off his gloves to get the ID palm print to read right.

A note from the woman at Chapel Yanakov confirmed that she'd brought over some tea and helped Mom Jezzy get building maintenance to fix a problem with an air handler. The monthly support services box had arrived with four #2 sized filters instead of the two #4 sized filters needed for the kitchen.

A second note from the parish prayer circle leader at Burdette Cathedral let him know that Mom Jezzy had been regular in her attendance and seemed well. He sent a response asking as politely as he could about helping Mom Jezzy exchange the apartment's air filters for the right ones. Dear Tester, he wished he could hire someone to just buy the right things and put them in for Mom Jezzy.

A check on the bank accounts showed a small total, but positive balances in each. As the employee himself, this time he'd been able to have taxes withheld from his stipend. He felt a rare moment of appreciation for Miss Rustin. She'd been the one to mention that withholding was possible. Given the lack of pawnshops in orbit, it was pleasant to be able to manage money like a rich person for once.

He looked up as the deacon cycled through the internal airlock between the main bay and the cockpit.

"We're at the site," he said. "I'm going to visually inspect the claim. Cutter Control messaged about some debris field collisions making a mess of things farther around Uriel, but they've got no warnings near us. And I did a scan with . . . ah, never mind, it'll be easier to just show you after I get back in. I'm going to pray over the site and do some hands-on inspecting."

He pushed off from the bulkhead, hands automatically checking that his tool attachments were secured, as he sailed across the bay toward the port side airlock with the easy grace of the experienced spacer he was. He braked to a stop and lowered his helmet visor.

"Comms check," his voice said in Noah's earphones.

Noah nodded, then blushed as he realized the deacon couldn't possibly see that with his own helmet in the way.

"Comms check," he repeated belatedly, and heard something like a chuckle.

"Good," was all the deacon actually said, though. "Don't know how good reception's going to be with all the junk outside, so we're patched through the cutter's comms. That should keep us linked no matter what. Wait in here for a minute, though. I parked us a little close since you're both new to space walks, but I'll still probably need to realign us."

"Of course, Deacon," Noah said.

Roundhouse entered the lock. It closed behind him, and another note popped into Noah's queue as he was about to log back out. It was a Grayson Navy Mail System message from Ensign Claire

Bedlam-Lecroix, his cousin. He hadn't expected ever to hear from her again. He read through the lengthy file and whistled. Suleia Rustin had written her sister about a boy she'd met.

He tried to hide the blush.

Claire said that Cecelie said that Suleia said that she liked him, but he didn't like her, so it was all hopeless. Unless Cecelie had some recommendations? And Cecelie Rustin, definitely still mad, had asked Claire Bedlam-Lecroix what to suggest to her little sister, since Cecelie liked Claire and didn't want to inflict Suleia on one of her friend's relatives without first giving him an out.

"Please make Ensign Cecelie Rustin stop posting," he wrote back immediately. He should probably say more, but he couldn't think right now.

In her message Claire had already promised not to let Cecelie post anything that named him. Noah smiled. His cousin would never let Miss Rustin's sister do anything to hurt the Bedlam-Lecroix family's chances. Claire hadn't abandoned him after all. He lifted his helmet visor to rub at his eyes.

Noah logged off and changed the display preferences to show the debris field they were salvaging. The heat view showed space trash reflecting distant sunlight and the cutter's own emissions. They fluoresced like bright pearls on midnight silk. A nice big lump of mixed metals reflected back a clear sensor return. Deacon Roundhouse in his skinsuit shot a tether out to it, tugged on it, and drifted out to the find with more tethers trailing behind him.

※ ※ ※

Deacon Roundhouse sang a hymn to himself at full volume as he spacewalked out to the very nice-looking two-hundred-plus-cubic-meter find. There was no requirement to perform a spacewalk prior to opening up the back of the cutter and dragging in the salvage finds, but he'd wanted to pray over them. He used to use drinking songs to keep a mental count of how long a spacewalk was lasting and to keep from gibbering in terror at the sheer vastness of empty space swallowing him up, but hymns seemed more appropriate just now. They worked just as well for timing things, too. And the Church of Humanity Unchained had a lot of really good ones.

His feet reached the solid center of the find and latched on just as

he reached, "Our sword and shield victorious!" He unhooked
assessor tools from his skinsuit belt with each hand and started the
close scan.

The piece was very dense. It was looking very good. They could
probably use the cutter in its pickup truck mode. He'd open both
sides of the rear external airlock into the main space and shove the
whole find inside. Noah could help him, and he could leave Rustin
in the pilot compartment on the far side of the interior airlock to
keep her more fragile gumby suit safe until they closed back up and
repressurized everything.

Most thousand-year-old space debris in the Grayson System
consisted of particulates and dust and semi-solid lumps held together
by physics. But the recent Blackbird's debris included purified metals,
reinforced station structural members, and bits and pieces of all the
things people who love to tinker bring to a space station. This one
was mostly high-grade battlesteel.

Roundhouse imagined that it might be a warehoused piece of
ship's hull plating that had escaped a direct hit only to be battered by
other debris. He poked a finger into a long gouge dug into the side.
Something even tougher—or traveling at a *very* high velocity—had
hit this.

He forgot to start the next line of his hymn as he got to thinking
about the velocity necessary to inflict that gouge . . . and the hull
plating that had been in warehouses on this side of the Blackbird
construction yard before the strike. Those particular warehouses had
been mostly empty and in preps for a shipment coming in. All he
could remember was that one load of hull plating that had failed
inspection. It had been cut to commercial-grade thickness instead
of military-grade thickness, but it had had a stealth coating already
applied. And the stealth coating had passed testing just fine, which
meant . . .

Oh, shit.

He had to get back to Cutter 19!

Deacon Roundhouse turned and reached quickly for a tether. He'd
detected no dense particulate debris on a collision course for the
small vessel during the scans he'd performed before shutting down
his radar to avoid microwaving himself when he went EVA. But if
his gut was right—

Now Deacon Roundhouse was praying not over the debris, but over Cutter 19. If he didn't get back aboard in time—

He didn't see the thirty-eight separate, stealth-coated hull plate slivers that hit the other side of his find and stopped. He did see the eleven bits, none of them thicker than a seventeen-year-old's little finger, that missed the mass of near impregnable battlesteel, hit the cutter, and kept right on going.

"Noah!" he shouted over his com. "Suleia!"

Only silence answered, and his jaw clenched.

His tripled tether lines led back to the cutter. One of the three had been sheared off. Roundhouse left it trailing and yanked hard on the other two to send himself sailing back towards his two kids, terrified that he hadn't trained them anywhere near enough for this.

※ ※ ※

Noah heard a sound like a dozen pistols. The lights flicked off. Emergency lanterns flicked on. An alarm screamed. But a sudden ache stabbed his ears with distracting urgency. A rushing wind through the cutter bay muffled all other sound, but he thought Miss Rustin might be screaming over the intercom.

"Deacon! Deacon Roundhouse!" he shouted into his suit com, but there was no response, and when he turned to the screen to see what Deacon Roundhouse might be signaling him to do, it was blank. A scattering of fingernail-sized holes on the far side of the console matched the hole pattern on the opposite wall of the cutter.

"Low pressure alarm! That's the low-pressure alarm! I don't remember this one!" he heard over the internal com. "There was a memory trick. But I don't—I can't—Deacon . . ." Rustin's fading yells snapped Noah into motion.

He didn't remember low pressure either, but he knew that if it got low enough, it turned into decompression. And that one every soul on Burdette Station knew: *Suit, Visor, Gloves, Assist.* He remembered.

Spacesuit—already on. He had, well, he didn't remember exactly, but there were seconds, and a not very huge number of them before he had to get to the Assist part. In a space this small, he might have wasted half of that time already. He knew that because the deacon had taught him and was always talking about how fast the air would leave and how . . .

Suit, Visor, Gloves, Assist. Suit, Visor, Gloves, Assist.

He slammed down his visor, felt it seal and at once everything was better. The cacophony was muffled, the circulators in the suit kicked on, and his ears felt better. His gloves trailed from their tethers at his wrists. He pulled them on, and the smart fabric of the spacesuit wrists connected.

Assist.

The cockpit airlock cycled open. Thank the Tester! That meant she must be—

No wait, she *wasn't* okay. Rustin spilled out helmetless. She drifted untethered, with both hands clasped tight against her left leg.

He was out of memorized responses. He didn't know why the power was down. He didn't know if the deacon was alive or dead. He didn't know what to do about the spheres of rich dark red dribbling out from between Miss Rustin's clenched fingers and drifting away on the now persistent breeze as she stared in wide-eyed pale-faced fascination. Her helmet wasn't on. The tether to hold it to her suit trailed empty behind her.

He unbuckled from the cutter wall, looped the belt end around one hand, and grabbed her trailing ankle.

They hung together in the middle of the cutter bay for a moment while he tried to yell, "Helmet!" at her with no response.

He keyed his suit's external speaker and meaning to say something clear and helpful, instead gibbered, "Head, helmet, air, air, breathe now?"

One of her hands flew up and touched her face and blood globules trailing the hand caught in her haloed hair. Her eyes widened as if she'd only just realized that the reason she was suffocating was because she'd lost her helmet.

She turned a panicked head back and forth with enough confusion that Noah was certain she had no idea where her helmet had been even before the cutter was hit.

He pulled them both down to the cutter wall with his belt and clipped her into the chair by the now useless console. The emergency kit built into the wall opened easily under his gloved fingers, and praying, he uncoiled the wall-mounted oxygen hood and pulled it over her head.

"Deep breaths," he said through his suit speakers.

She batted at his hands, and Noah couldn't see her eyes through the mass of hair. The ambient pressure telltale inside his own helmet visor blinked from amber to solid red. Cabin pressure was near vacuum. She couldn't hear him. He took Rustin's free hand and cupped it around the mouthpiece inside the hood. Her hand squeezed tight on it and the other hand flew up from her wounded leg to push back hair and get the mask fitted over her mouth and the ends of the hood sealed with the top of her spacesuit.

Noah grabbed a suit patch from the emergency kit and slapped it over the puncture in her suit. Blood stopped dribbling into the cabin, but the wound underneath was untreated. A skinsuit would've known she was injured and adjusted compression. But a gumby had none of that smart tech. Noah grabbed a longer length of suit repair tape and wrapped it tightly around her whole calf squeezing the bulky suit fabric. He hoped it would be enough.

But he needed to see how badly the cutter was damaged and figure out if Deacon Roundhouse was hurt, and he couldn't stay here to do any of it.

Rustin, holding her oxygen hose firmly to her face, gave him a determined nod. Noah smiled back. She understood. She'd be okay with just the hood and the cutter's emergency oxygen for a while, even if that meant she couldn't move around until help arrived. In the meantime—

He kicked off the wall and glided to the front bulkhead and the cockpit airlock. He looked though it and winced. He counted four through-and-through punctures he could see, and there might well be more he couldn't. One had hit the main multi-function display almost dead center, another punched straight through the communications section, and Rustin's helmet floated against the cockpit canopy, holed through on both sides. He left it.

The solid salvage mass remained in matched orbit in the center of the clear armorplast viewing screen. But the deacon was missing and the next nearest cutter on a salvage run was over a quarter rotation around Uriel, and Burdette Station was still farther off. The Yeltsin System suddenly felt bigger than it ever had before.

A tether line still hung, attached to the salvage, but Deacon Roundhouse wasn't on it, and Noah's imagination supplied him a too vivid picture of what the debris that had sliced holes through

Cutter 19 could have done to the deacon's skinsuited body. If he could get sensors up, maybe he could trace where the corpse was.

Noah crawled into the pilot's chair and looked over the cutter's status boards. The main multifunction display was shot, but the smaller one in front of the copilot's chair looked like it might be functional. He punched the button to toggle between displays, grateful he'd seen the deacon do that, and the secondary display came alive with alphanumeric codes.

He didn't have a clue what all too many of them meant, but he started puzzling out the ones he could. They were running on stored energy only, he discovered. The cutter's fusion reactor had auto-shutdown. The solar converters woven into the cutter's hull remained functional, but out this far from Yeltsin's Star, those dribbles of energy wouldn't be enough to even sustain life support after the stored power ran empty. He pushed away his fears and kept looking.

He checked the radiation screens: they were still up. He let out a relieved breath. The salvage onload had had a planned work break in two hours because the find was on course to pass through one of Uriel's radiation belts not long after that. Deacon Roundhouse had been going to use the break to give them both a cutter systems overview and then they'd get back to salvaging after the radiation levels dropped back down.

Indicators for the cutter's thrusters were dead. The debris field might have cut through too much of their machinery or maybe it had severed the wrong indicator line. He remembered from newscasts about the Manticore-Haven war that if a strike on a warship got past sidewalls and shielding and reached the powerplants, that were basically gravitically contained fusion explosions already, they detonated.

But these old-style cutters didn't have those kind of powerplants. Roundhouse had said they needed less power and were designed with the understanding that their operators might be, ah, less expert than the crew of a full-sized starship. When an old reliable electromagnetic fusor of the type Cutter 19 mounted got unstable, it just quenched itself and waited to be told to restart.

Noah looked longingly at the restart button, but he didn't actually know how to pilot a cutter or know if they had the energy for more than one restart. A lot of angry red errors, cautions and warnings filled the powerplant's part of his readouts. He reached for the communications headset instead.

The comms display had a lot of buttons he didn't understand. He was pretty sure that didn't really matter, though, given the hole punched clear through it and the fact that every one of its LEDs was blank. He tried anyway, though, and pressed the button for something titled "suit comms." He called the deacon, but there was no response. He tried "standard channel" in an attempt to reach Burdette Station. Same. He tried "emergency channel" and called out by name a few of the other recovery boats he knew were out.

No sounds came back over the headset, but he couldn't be sure that meant his signals were—or weren't—actually going out. He hadn't had classes in any communication systems yet.

Of all the solid red and amber lights glowing on the console, one light blinked yellow on the secondary multi-function display: restart autopilot.

That might clear some of the errors. Or maybe *all* the systems would go offline and never start up again.

Noah closed his eyes, held his breath, and tapped the touchscreen icon.

Nothing blew up, so he opened his eyes again and exhaled explosively. The light was still blinking, but now it was green and the words "SYSTEMS CHECK IN PROGRESS. AUTOPILOT RESTART IN 3 MINUTES" glowed below it.

There was nothing else he could do while he waited, so he went back to check on Rustin.

"We're okay?" she asked as soon as he appeared in the cutter bay. She'd found the internal circuit radio in the emergency kit and the speakers inside his suit transmitted her voice without even a crackle of interference. She'd tied her hair back with suit tape and resealed her hood. That hair was going to be very short if they lived through this. "I didn't want to bother you while you were checking things out in the cockpit, but tell me, really, are we okay?"

"We're okay," he said automatically, and realizing it was a lie, he added something true: "There's a lot of damage up there, but the autopilot is rebooting."

"Oh, thank the Tester, and they'll come looking for us?"

"Should." *Except the deacon told them we'd be out of communications while dragging the salvage in and expected it to take at least a few hours.*

"Didn't Deacon Roundhouse tell Cutter Control that it'd be tough to fit hourly comms checks in while dragging in salvage and besides that Uriel would block direct transmissions and the replacement commsat relays aren't working real well for cutter-grade whisker net comms? And then the Cutter Control guy just said, 'Okay, but yell if you need anything,' and the deacon said, 'Yup, sure will'?"

Damn it. Rustin never seemed to forget anything. "Well, yeah. But they should notice when we don't come back. I mean of course they'll look for us."

"Noah," Rustin said, "where is Deacon Roundhouse?"

The deck was very interesting.

The console next to Rustin restarted. The system reset hadn't killed them both. Noah breathed out a sigh of relief.

Rustin spun around and typed furiously on the console to see the cockpit displays. You couldn't fly the cutter from here without codes neither of them had, but you could see all the consoles and read the alarms. Rustin tried to patch through to the comm system anyway.

"Deacon, Deacon Roundhouse?" she called into her headset.

"Um, I'm sorry. I think, the debris, I think he's dead," Noah said. "And I couldn't get any of the cutter's comm equipment to work."

Rustin paled, but she kept trying. It didn't work for her either. Then she looked at the wall and turned a switch.

"Bedlam! Noah Bedlam!" The deacon's voice roared in Noah's earphones with a rasp that sounded like he'd been bellowing the entire time since the debris strike, and Noah's eyes went huge. He looked at Rustin, and she pointed at the bulkhead mounted speaker. For a moment, he felt only fresh confusion, but then he understood. The deacon must have jacked physically into the airlock communications panel. He probably *had* been shouting at them over the cutters intercom all along, but with no air, they hadn't been able to hear him until Rustin switched the intercom to their suit channels!

"Yes, sir?" Rustin said. "Are you okay?"

A long, relieved breath whispered over the channel. "Oh, thank the Tester. Yes, I'm fine. The lights went out on the cutter, and after I found the entry and exit holes on the outer hull I thought I'd lost you two. The exterior access airlock won't cycle me in. It's got a false no-pressure alarm for the cutter bay."

"Um, it's not a false alarm, Deacon," Noah said.

"Oh," Deacon Roundhouse's voice lost some of its cheer. "Okay, I'll just pry a cover off over here and see if I can figure out how to manually override this thing."

Noah swallowed and told the deacon which wires needed to be crossed if it was the same as a planet-side household airlock.

The deacon grunted acknowledgement and cycled in. He launched straight across the cutter with practiced ease and scanned through the cutter's system errors on Suleia's console before heading just as quickly to the cockpit. Noah followed him and was surprised when the old space worker paused on his way through to the cockpit to drag him in and wave Rustin a cheery parting salute.

"Holding up all right, Mr. Bedlam?" Deacon Roundhouse said as they entered the cockpit.

"Uh, yes, Deacon," he said. "But Miss Rustin's injured and the cutter is broken." Noah gulped and delivered the bad news. "The comm system is down and we can't move. I'm glad you aren't already dead, but I think we're all going to die."

The deacon shook his head and smiled. "We all die, but not today."

At least some of the LEDS which had been crimson before were only yellow now, Noah noticed as the deacon floated to the copilot's chair. He swung into it with practiced ease, settled himself in front of the multifunction display, and called up each of the cutter's system analysis reports in turn. At the drive system screen, he started chuckling.

"Look at this." He pointed at the detailed readout for the fusion drive. "That's not inoperable. It's just broken."

"You can fix it?" Noah asked.

The deacon shook his head. "I can't fix it without a bunch of spare parts we don't have, and I'd much rather have a proper engineer do that work. I'm a tech. But!" He held up a triumphant finger. "I can use it. The lights might dim a bit," he added as a caution and began typing commands into the screen.

"We're in a busy star system less than a million miles away from a half dozen stations, including our home base. And we have almost an entire T-day of life support, if you count our suits, which I do. If we were all unconscious or you hadn't pushed the reset button to override the error that had the cutter trying to repressurize, then we could easily have died. But we won't now."

"The cutter was trying to repressurize?" Noah said.

The deacon gave him a sideways look. "Ah. Well. Next time I'll include more on cutter casualty responses in the early training sessions. But what matters right now is that you got the fusion drive back up. We can wait things out for a bit while I think of something. Hmm, maybe thrusters..."

He jabbed a few buttons and made an unhappy growl at the controls. He changed the screen over to the comms system and it filled up with red and yellow casualty lights. Deacon Roundhouse grunted displeasure.

"Deacon?" Rustin called over the internal speaker. "May I ask a question?"

Besides that one? Noah didn't say it.

"At least she's asking," Deacon said softly, and then: "Go ahead, Miss Rustin."

"Can we restore power to the thrusters? The control screen says they aren't damaged." Her voice went up with suppressed anxiety. "I thought maybe I should ask before pushing the button. It's got a big flashing thing that says, 'Restore thruster power? Y/N' here on the cutter systems control panel."

"You'd need a control override code to have systems control access from a remote console," Noah said, baffled.

"Oh, did you need that?" Miss Rustin asked. "It's Mrs. R's birthday. That's the default for all of the codes on Burdette Station."

"Tester save us," Deacon Roundhouse muttered.

"Oh, um, sorry," Rustin said. "Sorry to bother you. Of course, you knew the code."

"Touch nothing," Roundhouse said. "Noah: main bay. We'll be right there." Roundhouse hurried him through to the cargo section and shifted Rustin out of the seat.

With a shaking finger, Deacon Roundhouse pressed the button to restore power to the cutter's thrusters. A flurry of reports scrolled down the screen, and they were all green.

Noah and Rustin exchanged hopeful glances.

"Not always wrong," Deacon Roundhouse said, grinning. "The control lines from the cockpit console must've been one of the parts of this old rig that got shredded by the collision. Thank the Tester for the engineers who build rigs like this with backups to the backups. Strap in kids, I'm driving us home."

※ ※ ※

A few hours later back at Burdette Station, Suleia Rustin listened without speaking while Noah told her about how many people had been reading her letters. Noah waited for an outburst or maybe some angry tears, but Rustin didn't even blush.

"I'll write her another letter," she said and then she leaned in and whispered conspiratorially, "Deacon Roundhouse agreed to give me a recommendation on Sacristy letterhead. A good one that he'll let me read before he sends. And he said it'll say good things about being calm under pressure. He says he's going to tell them that I have a tendency towards being a dumbshit too but he intends to phrase it as 'willingness to speak uncomfortable truths.'" She shook her head. "That almost sounds like a good attribute. Makes me think that as long as I keep my eyes open to sometimes being wrong about stuff, then maybe, at least some of the time, I could figure out fixes for stuff that nobody else seems willing to admit is a problem."

Noah laughed. It was good to be alive, but his problems weren't over. "Think he'd write me a recommendation letter? Think that'd make any difference for a guy with a criminal record?"

Rustin rolled her eyes. "That thing on the very day that you turned fourteen? You weren't born until almost midnight. I checked the records. It should've been a juvie offense. I got Mrs. R. to write a letter to a judge friend of the Lady Steadholder's weeks ago. It'll probably be expunged from your record in a month or two whenever the system gets it processed. And it's not like it matters anyway. Deacon Roundhouse has you on the list for cutter pilot training."

"Suleia," Noah said, "you are everything that's right with Grayson."

She laughed. "No one thinks that, not even me anymore."

※ ※ ※

Grayson Navy Mail System
Personal Message for Ensign Cecelie Rustin
June 25th, 1922 PD

Hey Sis,

You know that guy I met? The pretty impressive one you'd love? I think he's not into me. But you aren't getting an introduction either. I'm onto you.

  —Suleia

June 25th, 1922 PD

Dear Madam Lady Steadholder, Mrs. Theresa Burdette:

I want to thank you again for this internship. It's been significantly more exciting than I'd expected. Mrs. Nadia Roundhouse has taught me quite a bit, and I am fortunate to have been granted the opportunity to learn from her and from her husband, Deacon Roundhouse.

Oh, and I did want to make a few last suggestions. About the rent assisted apartments in Benedict City, are you aware of the filter issues? Perhaps we could talk when I get back.

  With Greatest Respect,

  <thumbprint signed>

  Suleia Rustin,

  Burdette Assistance Program Intern

[Entry ends. Three views: NRoundhouse, LadyTBurdette, SteadholderBurdette.]

❈ ❈ ❈

Noah entered Deacon Roundhouse's office later. "You wanted to see me, Deacon?"

"Yeah, Mr. Bedlam. I've got a cutter pilot training program and a space station engineering maintenance program starting up. I'm thinking you should do the cutter pilot one. Just sign at the bottom of these forms here."

"Um, thank you, Deacon, but before I sign, I need to study up on the details of the two programs," Noah said.

"Taking control of your own future," Deacon Roundhouse said, and he smiled. "Good man."

FIRST VICTORY

David Weber

Shadow Tree Tower,
City of Grendel,
Planet Beowulf,
Beowulf System,
March 1846 PD.

"Mother, I don't think this is a discussion you want to have."

"Really?" Jennifer Feliciana Benton-Ramirez y Chou's tone was less than encouraging as she looked over her shoulder at her son.

"Really." Captain Jacques Benton-Ramirez y Chou nodded. "I love you, and I love Allison, and I really don't see this having a good outcome."

"I'm her mother," Jennifer pointed out. She turned to face him and crossed her arms, which was not, he thought, a promising change in posture. "This is the sort of conversation mothers and daughters are supposed to have."

"Oh?" Jacques' expression was skeptical. "And how well would *you* have reacted if Grandmother had decided to have the same conversation with you?"

"Your grandmother would never have *needed* to have this conversation with me."

Jacques began a quick response, then paused. That might, he

acknowledged, actually be true. In fact, he was sure his mother and grandmother would have been on the same page for this topic. Well, half of it, anyway. But...

"You may be right about that," he acknowledged. "But you and Alley aren't going to see eye-to-eye on this one. You and I both know that. And that was true long before Alfred ever appeared on the horizon."

"I have absolutely nothing against Lieutenant Harrington," Jennifer said a bit sharply. "In fact, I will be eternally grateful to him, and you know it! And I totally understand why she chose to move in with him afterward. But that doesn't mean I think it's remotely wise of her to be... tying herself down to just one man when she's still so young. She can't possibly know her own heart—know she's not going to bitterly regret an obviously impulsive decision in the fullness of time. And, grateful to Lieutenant Harrington as I am, and as courageous and decisive as he may be in combat, he isn't—and never will be—her equal as a physician. Nor is the Star Kingdom the place where her gifts can serve the most people! I refuse to stand by while her infatuation with him makes her throw away her entire life on a backwoods planet where winter lasts over a T-year and the snow is three meters deep! No, and despite what he did for her, he has no business enticing her into creeping off into obscurity that way so he can lock her into an exclusive relationship! She's not some... some *trophy* for him to drag home and hang on his wall!"

"Mother—!"

Jacques stepped down—hard—on a solar flare of anger that would have been counterproductive, at the very least.

It wasn't easy.

If there was a gene for stubbornness, his mother had inherited it from both her parents. Unfortunately, she seemed unable to recognize that... or the fact that she'd passed that same stubbornness along to her own offspring.

Especially to her daughter.

The occasional fireworks between those two personalities had been lively since the day Allison learned to talk. Over the past few years, they'd become downright spectacular, and he couldn't understand how his mother had let things get to this point. Whatever else she might be, Jennifer was almost frighteningly intelligent, and she loved both her children dearly. So why couldn't she see what she was doing to her relationship with her daughter? She'd been unhappy with his own decision to go into the Biological Survey Corps instead of medicine, but she'd accepted the inevitable with remarkably good grace in his case. Their family's generations-long commitment to the fight against genetic slavery had probably had something to do with that, but how could she not realize that Allison's determination to live her life on her own terms was at least as strong as his had ever been? Or not realize how disastrously any effort to browbeat Alley into submission had to fail?

And then there was Alfred. How could his mother not see how any attempt to force Allison to choose between family and Alfred Harrington had to end? Where it damned well *should* end? If there was a single man in the explored galaxy worthy of *his* sister, it was Alfred, and whatever his mother might think, Alfred would never see Allison as a "trophy"!

"Mother," he said after a moment, gathering up his uniform cap, "everyone makes mistakes. If you push this, it'll be one of the worst of your life. Yes, I care very deeply about Alfred, and that may color my own thinking. But the one thing Alley *isn't* is 'infatuated' with Alfred Harrington, and there's no way in hell he—or anyone else in the universe—could *force* her into a monogamous relationship. Trust me on this. And having said that, any decision she makes about where she goes in her life is up to her. You taught her that. Of course, at the time, you assumed she'd be smart enough to make the same decisions you would. But she's not going to do that, and I'm afraid you'll just have to live with who she grew up to be, however deeply you may disagree with the choices she makes. If you can't see that, this isn't going to end well."

Jennifer glared at him. The dark brown, almond eyes she shared with both her children were agates, and her lips were a thin, unyielding line.

"I love you," he said as he turned toward the door. "I love you both. So, please, listen to me."

"I'll take it under advisement," she told him in a liquid-helium voice.

He started to say something more, then shook his head and stepped through the opening door.

❇ ❇ ❇

"So, Mom. To what do I owe the honor?"

Allison Carmena Inéz Elena Regina Benton-Ramirez y Chou was as slender and petite—and beautiful—as her mother. In fact, they looked far more like sisters than mother and daughter. Jennifer had been one of the galaxy's very first prolong recipients when she was less than thirty, and prolong was more efficient with some genotypes than with others. She looked like a pre-prolong college sophomore, not a woman who'd just turned sixty, and Allison—who'd received the *second*-generation anti-aging protocols and shared the same genetic makeup—was only twenty-nine herself. She looked considerably younger, and at the moment, there was an undeniably flinty cast to the eyes she also shared with her mother.

"What do you mean?" Jennifer asked mildly.

"I mean you obviously have something on your mind. You usually do, when you suggest I 'drop by for a cup of coffee.'" Allison picked up the cup in question, sipped, then set it down again very precisely. "I mean that from the tone of your 'invitation,' this is a command performance. And I also mean"—those dark, dark eyes bored suddenly into her mother across the breakfast nook table—"that I don't think we're likely to agree about the reason you wanted to talk to me. On the other hand, I know you'll insist on talking about it, anyway. So, all things considered, I suppose we should get to it."

Jennifer's expression tightened. She knew that tone. In her more fair-minded moments, she admitted it had sprung from her own lips on more than one occasion, and her conversation with Jacques flickered through the back of her brain. For a moment, she hesitated. But this was too important. She couldn't let Allison make the mistake she knew she was about to make. She just couldn't, and she was running out of time.

"All right," she said. "Yes, I do have something to discuss with you. And I'm afraid you're right that we aren't in agreement about it. But it's still something you need to hear, Sweetheart."

"I suspect your definition of 'need' and mine aren't identical," Allison replied. "In fact, I'm sure they're not." Her nostrils flared. "I know you're doing this—or you *think* you are—only because of how much you love me, but I really wish you could just let this one go. Please, Mom. I'm old enough to know what I'm doing with my own life."

"Alley, you may well be the most brilliant young woman I know, and I say that advisedly," Jennifer said. "With all due modesty, I'm no dummy myself, and I think I've been a damned good doctor. But the truth? The truth is that you're a hell of a lot smarter than *I* am. And you have an absolutely God-given gift where the practice of medicine is concerned. You're not just a brilliant, compassionate physician or clinician. You have the touch, the gift, that will make you, in time, one of the top two or three genetic surgeons on Beowulf—one of the top half-dozen in the entire galaxy! You have a responsibility to the medical profession and all the countless patients waiting for you to change their lives for the better. Someone with your gifts, your abilities, and your awareness of your own heritage *has* to realize all of that!"

"No," Allison said softly. "I don't. Or not the way you want me to, anyway."

Their eyes locked across the table, and silence hovered for a long, still moment. Then Allison inhaled deeply.

"Mom, I don't think you realize how little interest I have in the 'family legacy.' God knows it's not because I haven't *told* you, but I think you genuinely can't understand how anyone in my position could want to be anything other than a leading member of the Beowulf medical establishment. I don't think you even begin to understand how close I came to not going into medicine at all, or to choosing maternal-fetal over genetics, expressly because I don't want to be another notch on the Benton-Ramirez y Chou gunbelt."

Jennifer sat back, hands clenched in her lap, and Allison shook her head.

"I need to be *me*, Mom. Maybe that will include becoming a top-notch genetic surgeon, and maybe it won't. Maybe I'll just go practice medicine in a tiny clinic somewhere, because the truth is that I care one *hell* of a lot more about my patients—the people—I can help than I do about family names or shiny plaques or big offices or research grants. I'm like Alfred, Mom. I'm a *doctor*, and I need to be a doctor on my own merits, not my family name, and on my own terms."

"No one's trying to tell you you have to be anything but—"

"Yes, you are!" Allison interrupted. "Maybe you don't *think* you are, but you *are*. You had my career mapped out about the time I learned to read, and up until college, I let you push me straight down that path. Maybe I should have started digging in sooner. Maybe then you'd understand it's truly not what *I* want. And it's not just what *you* want out of me—for me. It's all the rest of the expectations coming at me. All the assurances from my professors and advisors that I'll be such a credit to the family name. That I'll be a 'worthy upholder' of the Benton-Ramirez y Chou legacy. But we're not some sort of ruling dynasty. We're not supposed to be the 'gold standard' of Beowulf genetics. We're supposed to be *doctors*, and the whole time you talk about doctors and making a difference in people's lives, what you're really talking about is taking me out of that clinic, out of that hospital room—that patient practice. And it's about slotting a neat little Allison-shaped piece into the Benton-Ramirez y Chou mosaic. But I don't *want* to be fitted into that mosaic. And I don't intend for it to happen."

"Really?" Jennifer's eyes flashed. "So that's why you're running away?"

"You can call it 'running away' if you want. It may even be fair. But from where I sit, I'm running *toward* something I want more than anything else in the universe."

"Allison!" Jennifer blinked back an angry tear. "Sweetheart! I'm not trying to *make* you be anything. I'm just . . . I'm just trying to keep you from throwing away everything that you can be and do right here at home. Where people love you!"

"And where what I'll end up being *isn't* me," Allison said almost gently.

"I don't know what's gotten *into* you!" Jennifer threw up her hands. "You were never so . . . so . . . stubborn and touchy about this! Not before—"

She broke off, jaw tightening.

"Not before I was kidnapped and tortured by people who planned to kill me as agonizingly as possible?" Allison finished for her, and Jennifer flinched.

"Actually, I was exactly this stubborn before that happened, Mom," Allison continued. "I just hadn't drawn the line as openly as I have now. As I should have. Maybe that was because I knew how badly it would hurt you, or maybe because I just didn't want to fight over it. But something like that changes you. It was the most horrible thing that ever happened to me, but it also . . . clarified a great many things. And the fact that it was so terrible put other things into perspective. Including how hard I'd tried to avoid this confrontation with you. I didn't want it, and I still don't want it, but I won't avoid it any longer. I hope you can listen to me and understand that I mean what I'm saying and that you can't change my mind."

"But *Manticore*?" Jennifer almost wailed. "If you don't want to follow the career you say I 'mapped out' for you, then *don't*. But stay here, at home, where you can have all the other opportunities Beowulf offers. You don't need to go running off to a backwoods planet where no one even *knows* you and you don't have *any* family!"

"The Star Kingdom is scarcely the 'backwoods,' Mom. In fact, it's the wealthiest star nation in the galaxy, on a per-capita basis. And while there may not be any Benton-Ramirez y Chous on Sphinx, there are a *lot* of Harringtons."

"But they're—"

Jennifer stopped herself again, but Allison's eyes flashed.

"Yes, they are," she said in a deceptively pleasant tone. "You can go ahead and say it. They're 'not our sort.' They're yeomen. Common, garden variety, 'backwoods' bumpkins. They're not rich. Not famous. Not even related to anyone in the Star Kingdom's government. Just the sort of unsophisticated people who go into the Marines and get promoted to sergeant. Who learn how to protect other people from exactly what happened to me."

"No, that's not what I meant," Jennifer said, but she heard the truth in her own tone. "I only meant they aren't...they aren't the sort of people you grew up with. You don't *know* any of them, or how well such a drastic move would work out. You should at least go and spend some time on Sphinx before you make up your mind about something this drastic."

"In case you hadn't noticed, I've already been to visit Sphinx— several times—and I've met Alfred's family. It's only a one-day trip through the Junction, Mom."

"That's not what I mean. A daytrip's not the same thing as actually spending time there! And, let's be honest, Allison. I understand why you feel the way you do about Alfred, but you've known him less than a T-year! You can't just...just tear up your entire life for a man you've known such a short time."

"I know Alfred Harrington better than I've ever known anyone else in my entire life," Allison said flatly. "And before you say it, no, I'm not infatuated with the white knight who saved me from a fate worse than death, even though that's exactly what he did. They'd've killed me in the end, but not before they'd had their 'fun,' and I know exactly how horrific that would have been. How horrific it had *already* been. Mom, I'd have been *grateful* when they finally killed me. That's how terrible it was, and Alfred walked into the middle of that—alone, against *sixteen* men—and got me out alive."

"I know," Jennifer said softly. "And, believe me, I'll never be able to thank him enough for that. But I think you *are* a little 'infatuated' with him because of the way he came to save you."

"I'm not infatuated with him because he came. I'm in *love* with him because Hell itself couldn't have *stopped* him from coming. I know that, with absolute certainty. He'd have come for *anyone* in that situation, because that's who he is, but he came for *me*, and he came *knowing* he was a lot more likely to die with me than get me out. That's the man I love. The man who will always come for someone— *anyone*—who needs him. And that's also the man I've been incredibly lucky enough to know *loves* me. Please, Mom. Don't make me choose between him and you. Don't."

"I'm not trying to make you choose between—"

"Yes, you are. Maybe—no, certainly—because you think I'm making a terrible mistake. But you're trying to make me choose between a backwoods doctor's monogamous life with a nobody with no family history and no medical legacy, and a life here on Beowulf being who *you* need me to be, not who *I* need me to be. And much as I love you, and much as it would grieve me, if you force me to choose between those two lives, you'll lose."

Jennifer stared at her, cheekbones flushed, and Allison looked back unflinching.

"Is that really what you think I'm doing?" Jennifer snapped after a moment. "Do you *really* think I'm that *shallow*, Allison?"

"It's not a matter of 'shallow,' Mom. It's a matter of . . . flexibility. It's a matter of living up to the standard you *taught* me. The one that says people have the right to be what they aspire to be. Be anything they're willing to work to become. Whatever they choose to invest themselves and their lives in accomplishing. That's what you taught me. Are you saying it didn't apply to me?"

"I'm trying to prevent you from making a terrible, terrible mistake! One you may not see is a mistake now, but which will *haunt* you when you finally realize everything you've thrown away!"

"If it does, I'll live with it."

"Damn it, Allison!" Jennifer thrust up out of her chair to stalk around the sunny kitchen. "How can you be so stubborn, so *blind*! You need to . . . to step back. To clear your head! The one thing you don't need to do is to plunge headlong into this wonderful fairytale world you've imagined! It's not *real*, Allison. *This*"—she threw out her arms in a broad sweep that took in the entire Beowulf System—"is what's real. What you were born to be part of! What you're throwing away like it was *nothing*."

"Is this really concern for me, or is it about being pissed off because I refuse to see things your way?" For the first time there was genuine anger in Allison's tone. "I'm not throwing away anything 'like it was nothing,' Mom. I'm simply choosing what's most important to me. If you can't see that, if you can't understand that, I don't see any point to continuing this conversation."

"What?" Jennifer stared at her in consternation, and Allison pushed back her own chair and stood, eyes blazing with a fury hotter than anything Jennifer had ever before seen in them.

"I said there's no point continuing the conversation," she said flatly. "I've made up my mind, and that's obviously unacceptable to you. So I suppose I'll just have to live with that, won't I?"

"Sit back down!"

Jennifer realized her mistake almost before the barked command was out of her mouth. She half-raised one hand, but Allison's lips had turned into a straight, iron line.

"No, Mother." Her eyes were cold, now, and her voice was carved from a glacier's heart. "I won't sit back down. In fact, it's time for me to leave."

"No! I mean, you have to—"

"I don't 'have to' do anything, Mother," Allison told her in that same frozen voice. "I hope you come to the wedding next week. I'll miss you if you don't. Goodbye."

She strode from the kitchen, heels like tack hammers on the ceramic tile, and Jennifer watched her go.

⚒ ⚒ ⚒

"God, I'm sorry, Sweetheart," Alfred Harrington said quietly. "I never wanted anything like this to happen."

"Do you think I don't know that?" Allison lay with her head on his shoulder, one arm stretched as far across his deep, powerful chest as it would reach. "I still don't have a clue what this . . . thing between us is, but of course I know."

Alfred nodded. He could no more describe the bond between them than she could, but he knew it was there. He could literally feel her glowing in the back of his brain, just as he could in the center of his heart—a presence he could never walk away from, never mistrust. And never betray.

"I hate to say this," he stroked the column of her spine with feather-gentle fingers, "but she may not be entirely wrong." Allison stiffened and raised her head to look him in the eyes, and he grimaced. "I'm not saying she's *right*, Honey. I'm just saying she may have a point about the difference between Beowulf and the Star Kingdom. There's no point pretending you wouldn't be giving up one hell of a lot if we move to Sphinx."

"I realize she doesn't believe this, but I not only understand that I'd be 'giving up one hell of a lot,' I *want* to give up one hell of a lot. This isn't just about how you and I feel about each other. Oh, that's a huge part of it." She pressed a quick kiss against his bare chest. "And so is your commitment to the Navy. But she's simply constitutionally incapable of grasping that I don't want to be Allison Benton-Ramirez y Chou. Especially not here on Beowulf!"

She laid her head back on his shoulder and snorted.

"You know, every Beowulfer I know prides herself on how open-minded she is, how totally prepared she is to let everyone else live however they choose. And as far as I can tell, they all mean it. But only because they assume everyone with a working brain will choose from the same options *they* would. If you don't, then something's obviously very *wrong* with you."

Alfred considered disputing that point, but not very hard. After all, she was right. And until he'd come to know and love her, he'd never realized what a prison family expectations could become.

"So, what, exactly, do we want to do?" he asked, instead, and she hugged him tightly, because he'd meant that "we."

"We do what we've planned all along," she replied. "We get

married on the nineteenth. And, yes, Mom will be furious. She's going to think I'm deliberately putting a thumb in her eye by 'rushing ahead' with the very thing she warned me against doing. And much as I hate to admit it, there may be some truth to that." Alfred tasted the painful honesty of that last sentence. "But what's more important is that it's what I want—need—to do, and it's the first concrete step into building the life—the *shared* life, Alfred—that I want more than anything else in the galaxy."

"Hey, I'm an ex-Marine, and we're tough. If you're ready for the shit storm, so am I, Honey!" he told her with a chuckle.

"It really may be . . . spectacular. And the fact that we're declaring a monogamous bond will only reinforce her belief that I'm thinking with my heart and certain other body parts, rather than my brain!"

"Well, thank God for 'other body parts,'" he murmured, raising his head from the pillow to nuzzle the back of her neck, and she gurgled a laugh.

"And then, once we're married," she continued, "you finish your internship under Dr. Mwo-chi at ISUH while I finish at the university. And after that, we move to Sphinx."

"Are you sure?" he asked. "About the timing, I mean. I may not agree with your mother about everything, but there's a reason the Navy sent me *here*. Doing your own internship and residency at ISUH would put your credentials about a light-year ahead of anything on Sphinx or Manticore."

Ignaz Semmelweis University Hospital was the Solarian League's most prestigious medical school's teaching hospital. Doctors who'd interned there were the galaxy's medical elite.

"Two thirds of that's just name recognition," Allison said flatly. "In Dr. Mwo-chi's case, it's a valid distinction, but Queen Elizabeth's is as good as any hospital anywhere. I can 'make do' just fine in the Star Kingdom."

She was right about Queen Elizabeth's Hospital's quality, Alfred thought, although an internship and residency there wouldn't carry the cachet of a Semmelweis residency. But, he realized, that was part of her thinking, another step in her determination to escape the Benton-Ramirez y Chou niche into which everyone seemed so determined to cram her.

"All right, if that's the way you want it," he said simply. "Do you think your mother will ever speak to Jacques again when he stands up as my best man?"

"I'm sure she will...eventually." Allison shrugged. "She'll probably blame the entire wedding on your insidious influence on my poor, mushy, infatuated brain, not him. So I'm pretty sure she'll forgive him *sometime* before the energy death of the universe. Now, *you*, on the other hand—?"

Copperwall Mountains,
County Duvalier,
Duchy of Shadow Vale,
Planet Sphinx,
Manticore Binary System,
August 1847 PD.

Allison Harrington shivered ever so slightly, despite her warm jacket, as the chill wind plucked exuberantly at her hair. They stood at least a thousand meters above sea level, looking out across the endless sweep of the Tannerman Ocean until it merged with the distant horizon, and she drew the crisp air of her new homeworld deep into her lungs.

"It's gorgeous, Alfred," she said, leaning back against the comfort of her husband's towering bulk. "Way better than the video!"

"What? You thought I was stupid enough to show you the *good* video and spoil the real world comparison? *Please!*"

She giggled at that deep, resonant voice's affronted edge.

"It was plenty good enough to convince me to come up here with you," she told him. "But without the wind, without the air?" She inhaled again, even more deeply. "God. I understand exactly why you're a 'homeboy'!"

"You say that *now*," he told her with a chuckle. "But your mom had a point about Sphinx winters. Once you see snow drifted up over the eaves, you may rethink that."

Allison snorted, although he did have a point. They'd arrived in the Manticore Binary System only a T-month or so before the summer solstice in Sphinx's northern hemisphere. They had over a T-year of glorious summer to look forward to, before they got to the autumn equinox. And then they had over a T-year and a half of winter to survive. Even in summer, Sphinx was far cooler than Beowulf, especially this high in the Copperwall Mountains, and she had to acknowledge—very privately, and only to herself—that she anticipated her first Sphinx winter with a certain trepidation.

"Quit trying to impress me with your hardihood, Marine!" she growled. "I know the real reason you keep telling me how terrible winter is. You're just trying to impress me with the fact that you survived growing up here!"

"Actually, generations of Harringtons survived growing up here," Alfred pointed out, wrapping his arms around her.

"Sure. Despite the horrible privations they endured. Although, I have to admit, views like this one probably make up for a lot of ice and snow."

"I can't disagree there, and this spot's always been one of my favorite places. Sort of runs in the family, I guess. Stephanie Harrington *loved* it up here, although not for the same reasons I do."

"She did?" Allison turned in his arms to look up at him "Why?"

"Because of the updrafts."

"Updrafts?"

"Oh, yeah!" Alfred grinned. "Someone given to wild understatement might have called her an 'avid' hang glider. Apparently, she and Lionheart spent as much time in the air as they did on the ground! I've never been interested in the sport myself—somebody my size would make an ugly hole when he hit the ground—but I've been up here some days when the wind coming off the Tannerman was almost enough to pick me up without a glider." He shook his head. "For someone like her, this must've been a door into Heaven!"

"Really?" Allison smiled up at him in delight, then looked back out over the ocean as she filed that new factoid away.

As the newest member of the Harrington clan, she'd barely started learning her way around the family history, but the more she learned, the more she liked. The Harringtons were sturdily, one might say determinedly, yeomen, with none of her birth family's connections to inherited wealth and power. She liked that. She liked that a *lot*. In fact, she'd discovered she tended to *wallow* in that quiet, independent self-reliance that didn't give much of a damn about what the world expected out of them. Yet there'd been Harringtons on Sphinx almost from the beginning of the Star Kingdom, and they'd played a far larger role in shaping that kingdom than her mother would ever realize.

Despite Beowulf's proximity to the Star Kingdom, Allison had known precious little—as in virtually nothing—about Sphinxian treecats or their adoption bonds with humans. She certainly hadn't known that the very first Harrington to ever grow up on Sphinx had been the treecats' discoverer when she was only a child. Or that young Stephanie Harrington had been the first human adopted by a treecat. Or that she'd advocated fiercely, ferociously for them for the rest of her long life. Or that Dame Stephanie Harrington had risen to command the Sphinx Forestry Service *and* effectively drafted the Ninth Amendment to the Star Kingdom's Constitution, recognizing and protecting them as the indigenous sentient species of Sphinx.

Maybe she hadn't led an expedition to rescue Old Earth from the self-inflicted trauma of the Final War, and maybe she hadn't helped found the Solarian League, or write the Cherwell Convention. Allison was sure her mother would have pointed that out, anyway. But Stephanie *had* very possibly saved an intelligent species from extinction, and she'd certainly preserved that species' claim to its own homeworld. Allison took a strange, deep satisfaction from knowing she'd married into the family of that remarkable young woman.

Of course, she took an even deeper satisfaction from the fact that Allison Harrington wasn't Allison Carmena Inéz Elena Regina Benton-Ramirez y Chou. Or even Allison Chou-Harrington. Alfred had been completely comfortable with the Beowulf practice of hyphenated married surnames; Allison hadn't. The discovery that Stephanie Harrington's husband, the man from whom Alfred's first name descended, had changed his surname to Harrington because, as Stephanie had recorded in her journals, "He says there should always be Harringtons on Sphinx" struck another deep resonance with her, but she'd refused the hyphen before she knew a thing about Stephanie Harrington or Karl Zivonik.

Allison *Harrington*. She repeated the name in the depths of her own mind and almost purred in bone-deep satisfaction. If she had her way, no one in the Star Kingdom of Manticore would *ever* discover what her full maiden name had been. It was so glorious to be just "Dr. Harrington," the newest intern at Queen Elizabeth's Hospital, and not some avatar of centuries of inherited grandeur.

It bothered her—a little, sometimes—that Alfred's family name had become part of her...camouflage. She loved him deeply, and his parents had welcomed her as a fourth daughter, but she couldn't pretend that hiding behind the Harrington name wasn't part of her escape from Beowulf. Thank God whatever link they shared meant Alfred understood exactly how that worked and that it could never mean she loved him one iota less.

"So, if wasn't the wind that lured a younger Alfred up here, what did?" she asked, turning back to the ocean in the circle of his embrace.

"Partly the view." He bent far enough to rest his chin atop her head, which took some bending, given the height differential. "Partly because every Harrington grows up reading Stephanie's journals, and she describes this place in such loving detail. I think all of us come up here at some point as some rite of passage. And partly, because of how much I've always loved the Copperwalls. When I was a kid, I spent every hour I could either out in the bush hunting, or rock climbing. And this is a great place to come if something's on your mind. That—" he waved one arm at the spectacular panorama "—always puts things into perspective." He shrugged and wrapped both arms back around her. "So this was sort of a natural destination for me for a lot of reasons."

"I can see that." She nodded. "And I can't blame you for loving it up here, even if it is quite a hike."

"Well, next time, you can just crank the counter-grav and let me tow you, I suppose. Or, if you *really* want to cheat, we could fly. There's a clearing big enough set down an air car just south of here. Of course, all those past generations of Harringtons would glower down upon such an effete evasion of responsibility to the name!"

"Yeah, sure!" She elbowed him none too gently in the belly. "Listen, O Mountain, some of us didn't grow up in Sphinx's gravity. For that matter, *some* of us don't have the Meyerdahl mods, either. So don't you go looking down your nose at me for my counter-grav, Karl Alfred Harrington!"

"Fair enough, I guess," he acknowledged with a chuckle.

"Darned right."

They stood in a comfortable silence, gazing out over the ocean, and Allison felt the chill, severe beauty of her new home soaking into her pores.

She and Alfred had moved to the Star Kingdom three T-months ago, as soon as he'd finished his internship. He'd begin his formal residency at Bassingford Medical Center, the Royal Manticoran

Navy's primary hospital on Manticore, next month, and Allison wasn't entirely happy about that. Bassingford had a top-notch—and well-earned—reputation, and the Navy had always intended to assign Alfred to it, but while Allison might be a Navy spouse, she was very much a civilian. Which meant she would be beginning her internship at Queen Elizabeth's a month or so after Alfred reported to Bassingford. Bassingford and QEH were adjacent, but they were also entirely separate campuses, and she was the daughter of doctors. She knew what long hours would be demanded of any intern or resident, and with the two of them on two different campuses, they'd see precious little of one another during their working days.

At least they'd be together for any time they *could* steal. But they'd also be on Manticore, not Sphinx, which was one reason she'd wanted to come up here and drink in the beauty of Alfred's childhood mountains. And why she wanted to spend as much time as she possibly could with Alex and Rebecca Harrington.

She understood a lot more about Alfred's inner strength now that she'd met the remarkable man and woman who'd raised him. She knew Jennifer Benton-Ramirez y Chou loved her deeply, but she couldn't even imagine such a bitter clash of wills with Rebecca Harrington. It would never have occurred to Rebecca—not in a thousand years—to tell any of her children what he or she "had to be." Which was how Alfred had ended up a Marine and now a Navy doctor. His oldest sister Jessica was a doctor of obstetrics with a bustling practice in Yawata Crossing, given the size of Sphinxian families. Clarissa, the middle sister, was married to a merchant service ship's captain. She served as his ship's purser, accompanying him on his voyages, and she, too, lived in Yawata Crossing whenever she was home, while Dominique, the youngest girl—two T-years younger than Alfred—was the mayor of Yawata Crossing's chief of staff. Richard, the baby of the family, had followed in the footsteps of the first Harringtons on Sphinx, become a xeno-veterinarian, and joined the Sphinx Forestry Service. He was also the only one of Alfred's siblings who didn't live in Yawata Crossing, since he was currently stationed in Carson's Hollow, halfway around the planet. It was a vastly larger family than the Beowulfan norm, and all of them had taken her to their hearts from her very first visit.

She smiled at the memory, but then her smile faded. Alfred's parents were older than hers, and neither had received prolong. Age was paring away their strength, and it was bitterly unfair that she must lose her heart-parents so damnably young.

"You do know your mom wants grandchildren—or, rather, *more* grandchildren—don't you?" she asked now.

"Excuse me?" She felt Alfred's surprise through their link. "Exactly where did *that* come from? She hasn't said a word about that. Or not to *me*, anyway."

"She didn't really 'say it' to me, either," she admitted. "But she does. I can tell. Partly from watching her with your nieces and nephews. But she's spent a lot of time showing me *your* baby pictures, too."

"Oh, my God! Not *that*—please!"

"Hey, they're not that bad! Not once you let your hair grow down over the ears, anyway," she added judiciously.

"Oh thank you!"

"You're welcome." She patted one of the arms wrapped around her. "But she'd really, really like another little boy or girl to dote on. She'd never push us to *produce* said little boy or girl, but she wants one. And so do I."

"You do, don't you?" he said, leaning into their bond. "Then it's probably a good thing I do, too. But you'll be at Queen Elizabeth's for at least a couple of years, and we both know how demanding that's going to be. So, are you thinking about tubing a kid?"

"No." The sharpness of her own response surprised Allison just a bit.

"Why not?" he asked gently, and she scowled at the horizon.

It was a valid question. In fact, "tubing" a child—bringing the fertilized zygote to term in an artificial womb—was the norm on Beowulf. For that matter, it was a broadly accepted option on most Core Worlds, because it made so much sense. The child could be more closely monitored during the pregnancy; it decoupled the child physically from her mother, so there was no need to worry about accidental falls, diet, or any other maternal health issue; and it freed the mother not just from the discomfort and limitations of the pregnancy but also from any impact on her professional life.

But...

"Mother and I disagree on a lot of things," she said at last, "but not on this one. She carried Jacques and me to term the 'old-fashioned' way, and she told me she's never regretted it. Of course, the women in my family have always had easy pregnancies. She wasn't morning sick a single day! But she also told me something I've never forgotten."

"What?" His voice was even gentler, and she patted his arm again.

"She told me it's better for the baby, because whether we remember it later or not, what we experience in the womb is huge in shaping our ability to connect with the people around us and, especially, with our parents and family. We learn to recognize the voices of people who love us, who are waiting for us. Our mothers' movements, the secondhand motion we experience, are part of it, too. Oh, obviously it can be a *negative* experience, as well. If a mother's in a bad personal relationship, if the voices we hear are angry or stressed, that can mark us, too, and not for the better. And if a pregnant mother doesn't watch her own health, that can have all sorts of negative repercussions.

"I know the artificial wombs provide aural stimulus, and the better docs make sure they simulate the mother's normal movement, as well. But Mom was convinced—and I think she's right—that no simulation is as good as the reality. Maybe it's irrational but there it is. We both think that way. But the real reason she carried us to term?"

She turned her head, looked up at him again, her eyes soft.

"The real reason was that she refused to share the experience with a piece of hardware, however good it was. She could have made all the voice recordings, chosen the music we heard, controlled every aspect of our gestation and birth, and she wouldn't do it. It would've been a hell of a lot more convenient for her, but she didn't care. Because all those months *we* spent hearing her voice, *she* spent feeling us grow under her heart. Feeling us come into being. Waiting for the first moment she felt us move, the first time she pressed the stethoscope to her stomach and heard our hearts beat *inside* her. I want that, too, Alfred. Especially with our first child. And I want that child born *here*—on Sphinx."

"Honey, are you *sure* about that? I know I tease you about counter-grav, but Sphinx's gravity really is thirty percent higher than Beowulf's. That can be hard on pregnant mothers. Even those with the Meyerdahl mods."

"I'm *very* sure," she told him. "I'm a Sphinxian now, and my *child* will be a Sphinxian from the moment she's born." She smiled up at him with a glint of challenge. "Don't mess with me on this one, Harrington!"

"Do I *look* stupid, woman?" He shook his head. "If that's what you want, that's what you'll get. But we'll definitely have to wait till you've got your residency out of the way. Trust me, the hours'll be tough enough on someone who *isn't* pregnant!"

"Well, of course we'll have to wait. But the good news is that Queen Elizabeth's and Bassingford are both right there in Landing, so once we find an apartment, we'll have *lots* of opportunity to practice the preliminary phase, shall we say, of the procreative process!"

Emerald Heights Tower,
City of Landing,
Planet Manticore,
Star Kingdom of Manticore,
Manticore Binary System,
April 1851 PD.

For all their estrangement, Jacques Benton-Ramirez y Chou reflected, his sister was definitely their mother's daughter. They might have become the proverbial irresistible force and the immovable object, but under the skin...

He sat at the small table in the kitchen, watching Allison carefully check the oven. Like their mother, she disdained the top-of-the-line auto chef in one corner. No doubt she did use it... for breakfast, perhaps, or other times she and Alfred were too rushed to cook. But under more sedate circumstances? Never! For her, cooking was as much therapy as a means of actually feeding people, and Alfred was almost as bad. In fact, he'd spent the last couple of years introducing her—thoroughly—to the Star Kingdom's cuisine. Today, though, she'd opted for roasted Beowulf shellbuck in Jacques's honor, and he inhaled its fragrance appreciatively as she closed the oven door.

"That smells delicious, Alley!"

"It does, does it?" She smiled at him. "You know, if you came to visit more than once every, oh, nine or ten T-months, you might get to smell it more often."

"Guilty as charged," he acknowledged. "The schedule's just so damned crazy lately. That's not much of an excuse, I know, with Beowulf right on the other side of the Junction, but it's the best I've got."

"Tell us about 'crazy schedules'!" Alfred said, stepping in from the apartment balcony.

The crystoplast doors slid shut behind him, locking out the midday heat. Landing was right on Manticore's equator. It was far warmer than Grendel, back on Beowulf, at any time, and today's temperature was just over thirty-three degrees.

Alfred carried the four large, ripe tomatoes he'd taken from the balcony garden across to the sink, washed them, and began dicing them—with, Jacques observed, an old-fashioned knife, *not* the auto chef—to prepare fresh pico de gallo. Jack watched his brother-in-law's hands. For all Alfred's size, they moved with the precision of the surgeon he'd become.

"Your schedule is getting crazier?" Jacques asked, and Alfred snorted.

"No, it's *been* crazy. We thought it was going to get less crazy, now that Alley's finished her residency. But it's not."

"It's not?" Jacques's eyebrows rose. "I thought your last letter said the two of you were going to have more time together."

"We thought that, too," Allison said, beginning to peel potatoes while Alfred worked on the pico. "It appears we were in error, however, which is one reason we're so glad you found time to accept this invitation, Jacques. When we extended it, we thought it would just be a 'celebrating Alfred's promotion' party, but we were wrong." She grimaced. "Turns out it's a 'going away' party, too."

"Going away?" Jacques frowned, then looked at Alfred. "Should I assume the person doing the going happens to be extremely tall, male, newly promoted to lieutenant commander, and married to my baby sister?"

"You should, indeed." Alfred finished chopping tomatoes and started on the onion. "The only good news is that BuPers is a lot like the mills of the gods. It may not be overly concerned with justice, but it does grind exceedingly fine, and occasionally, at least, it also grinds slowly. Which means sometimes you get at least some warning before your new orders strike."

"I thought you were firmly ensconced at Bassingford."

"Alley's right. You really ought to drop in more often." Alfred scraped finely cut onion from the chopping board into a bowl. "You do realize we just celebrated our fifth anniversary? If you visited a little more often, we might be able to share our surprises while they're still surprises to *us*. It would appear I've been such a good little worker bee at Bassingford that they've decided to jump me ahead in the box-checking queue. You're looking at the chief surgeon (designate) for HMS *Scepter*. She's just begun a five-month overhaul, so the yard dogs have her right now, and the appointment doesn't become effective until October, when she recommissions."

"Really?" Jacques sat back in his chair. "She's ... what? A battlecruiser?"

"Yes, she is." Alfred looked over his shoulder at his brother-in-law. "Why?"

"Oh, nothing."

Jacques waved one hand, and Alfred turned completely around to fold his arms across his chest. Jacques looked at him innocently, then shrugged.

"Well, actually, I was thinking that chief surgeon aboard a battlecruiser on an independent deployment is something of a professional compliment. Even I know that!"

"I didn't say anything about independent deployments. In fact, nobody's said anything to *me* about independent deployments."

"Oh." Jacques looked a bit embarrassed. "Well, it's just that somebody mentioned she's supposed to be heading for Silesia once she gets out of the yard."

"Most of the Navy 'heads for Silesia' at one time or another," Alfred pointed out. "Well, most of the Navy smaller than a dreadnought. But should I feel more than usually suspicious over the fact that you know that's where *my* ship is deploying?"

"It's nothing devious!" Jacques held up both hands. "It's just that the BSC's sending a team to Silesia sometime in the next year or so. And we tend to coordinate ops like that with your Navy." He shrugged. "We don't have any official naval presence in the area, and we've always worked well with Manticore."

"Why would it happen that this particular team may be heading to the Confederacy in the not-too-distant?"

"The usual." Jacques shrugged again. "There are some ugly reports that need checking out. Admittedly, it's a little more ... complicated than usual." He shrugged again. "That's why there's so much lead time in the planning."

"And they picked you as their checker-outer?" Allison finished peeling the last of the potatoes and turned to face her brother, and her eyes were dark.

"It's what I do, Alley."

"No," his sister said repressively, "that's what Biological Survey

Corps *recon* teams do. What *you* do is take in an action team, shoot every slaver you can find, and load the slaves aboard transports bound for Beowulf."

"We do *not* 'shoot every slaver' we can find. Sometimes there are innocent bystanders in the way." Allison snorted, and Jacques grinned. But then his expression sobered. "And this really is basically a recon run, Alley. I'll admit my team and I will be along to ride shotgun, though. We'll be taking a look at the Gorlice System, and the governor there doesn't like us very much. Go figure." He shrugged. "She can't tell us to stay the hell home because of the treaty the Directors extorted out of the Confederacy twenty-five T-years ago, but she's not going to make things any easier than she can help. And she won't go out of her way to protect our teams if someone takes exception to them. Hence, your humble servant's presence as a member of said teams. And the reason I'm so happy *Scepter* might be in the neighborhood. When you're stuck on the wrong side of town, it never hurts to know a local cop."

Allison glowered at him, but he met her eyes with an expression of bland innocence.

"I know that's your story and you're sticking to it," she said finally, "but you be careful, Jacques! You're the only brother I've got."

And the only Beowulfan family I'm still speaking to, she did not add out loud, although he heard it anyway.

"I have no intention of being anything but careful. And, like I say, this is primarily a scouting run. Which doesn't mean it won't eventually lead to something else. That's why we do intel runs. But I'd be astonished if anything untoward were to occur this time around. Governor Schreiber's not stupid enough to let things get too out of hand."

Allison looked less than totally reassured, but she turned back to begin cutting the potatoes which would shortly become potato salad. Jacques gazed at her back for a moment, then glanced at Alfred. His brother-in-law looked less mollified than his sister was pretending to be, he observed, and shrugged ever so slightly.

Alfred snorted and returned his own attention to the pico de gallo.

※ ※ ※

"How is Alley? Really?" Jacques asked much later that evening.

He and Alfred sat on the balcony, chilled bottles of beer in hand, gazing out across the magnificent nightscape of Landing. The city was actually a tiny bit larger than Grendel, and Grendel didn't have Jason Bay and the pleasure craft out enjoying the cooler temperatures on its dark waters.

"She's . . . good," Alfred said after considering for a moment. "Not perfect. She's tireder than she pretends. Everybody over at Queen Elizabeth's knows her by now, but she's very much the new kid on the block in the Genetics Department. They're keeping her on the hop while she learns the ropes, and my mom managed to break a leg back on Sphinx. Alley's been worrying about that. Well, I have, too. She's not getting any younger, and fractures are no joke in Sphinx's gravity. And now, just when we thought we'd actually have time to settle into something approaching a sane schedule, we find out I'll be deployed off-planet for at least a couple of years. Alley's made a lot of friends, but she'll still be pretty lonely, whenever exhaustion gives her time to admit it."

Jacques nodded. In fact, Allison was at Queen Elizabeth's at that very moment. She hadn't been on the rotation, but one of her friends had a family emergency, and she'd volunteered to cover his shift.

"I hate it that she and Mom still aren't even speaking," he sighed after a moment. "It's been *five T-years!* I swear I never thought even the two of them could go this long without even exchanging *Christmas cards!* What was God *thinking* when He put the two stubbornest, most obstinate females in the entire galaxy into the same family?"

"He does seem to have dropped a stitch," Alfred acknowledged whimsically. "I think if your mother had accepted the wedding invitation, it might've helped, but Alley and I knew she wouldn't. Alley even said she'd probably take the fact that we'd gone ahead as a deliberate slap in the face. Of course, if we *hadn't* invited her, that would've made it even worse." He shook his head. "My sisters never went toe-to-toe with Mom, but I have tons of female cousins. It's not like I haven't seen plenty of other mother-daughter confrontations. But Alley and your mother take it to an entirely new level."

"I know. I know! Sometimes I want to strangle both of them." Jacques took a swallow of old Tillman. "But having said that, Mom can't have it both ways. Either her kids were going to be independent people who do what *they* believe is right, or they weren't. And she may not realize it, but I think she'd be even unhappier if Alley was some compliant little mouse."

"Allison? *Compliant*?" Alfred snorted. "The mind boggles!"

"Yep. And that's Mom and Dad's work, but especially Mom's. Dad would've spoiled Alley rotten, if it had been up to him. She had his heart in her grubby little hand before she learned to walk! In fact, he's the innocent third party who's hurting worst over this. And I know he's said as much to Mom. But that just pushes her deeper into the bunker. There's no way she can admit Alley hasn't made a horrible mistake 'turning her back on' her family heritage. I think she literally *can't* do it, and the longer this . . . mutual silence stretches out, the harder it gets to do anything about it."

"Jacques, to be totally honest, Alley doesn't *want* to do anything about it." Alfred's expression was profoundly unhappy. "She won't admit to herself how much this estrangement hurts. She *knows* how bad it hurts, but she just . . . puts that away in a mental pigeonhole and gets on with her life. And she's still pissed as hell at your mother's attitude towards Manticore. And me. If either of them could just bring herself to make the first move, they might get past it, but—"

"Never gonna happen," Jacques said sadly. "Mom can't admit Alley's the injured party. And Alley isn't about to make the first move until Mom *does* admit she was wrong, especially about you. Which also isn't going to happen. Mom can't—or *won't*, at least—believe *her* daughter could possibly 'tie herself down' in a monogamous relationship before she was even thirty unless some sort of sinister mind control was involved. And guess who the mind-controller-in-chief had to be?"

"Oh, I've got that part," Alfred said wryly. "And to be fair, I'd rather she put *all* the blame on me, if that stopped her from taking it out on Alley. But her attitude toward me *is* rather part of the problem, isn't it?"

"You can say that again," Jacques acknowledged.

They sat in silence for five or six minutes, then Jacques stirred in his chair.

"What about the nightmares?" he asked in a much softer tone.

"Still there." Alfred's nostrils flared. "They're not as frequent, and her therapist says we're making progress. But she *remembers*, Jacques.

That's one of the things that worries me about this deployment. I know Mom and Dad, Richard, the girls—hell, the entire clan!—will rally round if she needs them, but none of them were there. None of them really understands, not deep down inside, what those fucking bastards did to her."

His voice was harsh, and he looked away, staring out over the gorgeous cityscape without seeing it. What he saw was an exercise room on Beowulf, and Allison—*his* Allison—hanging from her wrists, three-quarters naked, while a Manpower thug tortured her.

"You and I know about PTSD," Jacques said quietly. "We've both had to deal with it. What you saw at Clematis was a hell of a lot worse than anything *I've* had to deal with, but I've seen too much aftermath of my own, too much of the wreckage Manpower leaves in its wake. I know *exactly* what they were doing to her. And I know you're the man who *stopped* it. If Mom could just really wrap her mind around that, if she had the kind of first-hand experience the three of us have, I don't think she'd find it hard at all to understand why Allison *had* to choose you when it came down to it."

Alfred looked back at him, then inhaled and nodded.

"Do you think it would make Alley feel any better if I told her every single one of the Manpower execs who authorized Manischewitz's operation is no longer with us?" Jacques asked after a moment. Alfred's eyes narrowed, and his brother-in-law gave him a shark's smile. "Caught up with the last one three T-months ago. Took us a while, because she knew exactly who we were after—and why—and crawled into the deepest hole she could find. I don't think Manpower will ever be stupid enough to mount that kind of op on Beowulf again."

"I don't know if it'll make her feel any better," Alfred said after a moment, "but it makes *me* feel one hell of a lot better."

"I thought it might." Jack leaned forward and patted his brother-in-law lightly on the knee, then sat back again. "So, you think I should tell her?"

"Yeah, and not just for 'closure,' which, by the way, I think is one of the more useless concepts where something like this is concerned. She hasn't wanted to talk about it, but I know she's still worried about the possibility of the BSC losing people 'avenging' her. She'll be glad to know no more good guys are likely to get hurt 'over her.'"

"Of for the love of—!" Jacques made himself draw a deep breath. "I've told her a dozen times that the Directors didn't sanction our response just to punish them for what happened to her. That kind of shit can't be allowed, and all of them understood that *that* was the real message to Manpower. Why the hell can't she?"

"Oh, I dunno. Maybe because that may have been the 'message,' but it sure as hell wasn't the *motive*, as far as you were concerned." Alfred chuckled harshly. "In case you hadn't noticed, my wife's very perceptive. And she suspects—as do I—that you were perfectly prepared to sell the op to the Directors as a message-sending exercise ...just as long as it let you collect the head of every single person who'd authorized your sister's abduction, torture, and murder."

He gazed at Jacques for thirty seconds or so, eyebrows raised in polite inquiry, but Jacques declined to respond.

"Anyway," Alfred continued, "do me a favor and *do* try to not get shot full of holes in Silesia. You'll probably be through here on your way back to Beowulf long before I get home with *Scepter*, and I'd really prefer for you to arrive intact for the visit. Got it?"

"Yeah," Jacques acknowledged with a crooked smile. "I got it, Alfred. I got it."

Queen Elizabeth's Hospital,
City of Landing,
Planet Manticore,
Manticore Binary System,
June 1853 PD.

"Dr. Benton-Ramirez y Chou! How nice to see you. Do you mind if I join you?"

Allison Harrington's jaw clenched as the cheery voice cut through the hum of background conversation that filled the QEH physicians' cafeteria.

Hard almond eyes, cored with fire, looked up from her minicomp at the fair-haired, slightly built physician standing behind the empty chair on the other side of her table. He was barely ten centimeters taller than she, with blue eyes, and she knew him entirely too well.

She thought very, very seriously about telling him that yes, she certainly *would* mind if he joined her. Unfortunately, that wasn't the behavior expected of a staff physician, and so she showed her teeth in something a particularly charitable soul might have called a smile, instead.

"Of course not, Dr. Illescue," she lied through those teeth.

"Thank you."

Illescue settled into the no-longer-empty chair and tapped the tabletop to open the menu. He scanned it quickly, then looked up at Allison.

"How's the *hóngshāo niúpá*?" He actually pronounced it properly, she noticed.

"It's fine," she replied.

"But not as good as back in Grendel, I'll bet!" he said brightly, and she made herself smile again. *Hóngshāo niúpá*, flank steak braised in red wine with Highland mushrooms, onions, and peppers, was a Beowulfan specialty, and any truly snobbish gourmet knew, rightly or wrongly, that Beowulfers prepared it better than anyone else in the universe.

"Actually," she told him, "allowing for the fact that this is a cafeteria, not a four- or five-star restaurant like Dempsey's, it's every bit as good as anything I ever had on Beowulf."

"Really?" He chuckled. "Well, I guess you have to be *polite* about it."

He clearly thought he was being witty, Allison reflected. It would have been nice if he'd been more than half right about that.

"I do try to be polite, but in this case, it's nothing but the truth," she said.

He gave her a knowing smile, but tapped the entrée on the menu, then selected an appetizer and beverage and closed the menu down.

"I was a little surprised to find you on the QEH staff," he said, sitting back in his chair. "I would've expected to see a Benton-Ramirez y Chou in one of the major hospitals back in Beowulf. Wasn't that what you'd planned to do?"

Allison contemplated homicide, and then put the temptation regretfully aside. She'd ended her brief relationship with Franz Illescue on Beowulf shortly after she set eyes on Alfred Harrington. Not because she'd immediately recognized him as her soulmate, but because of Illescue's contempt for a military Neanderthal who could have qualified for admission to Ignaz Semmelweis only because it permanently reserved a small number of slots for the Manticoran Navy. She hadn't realized until that moment just how shallow Illescue was, although "shallow" might not really be the correct word. She knew enough Beowulfers who felt only disdain for the uniformed men and women who kept them safe enough they could regard their protectors with contempt.

But it had still been an awakening. Illescue was a bright, occasionally charming conversationalist and above average lover, but Allison had known too many of those uniformed men and women. To his credit, she supposed, Illescue had taken her departure from his bed with at least outward grace.

"No," she said now. "That wasn't what I'd 'planned' to do. It might have been what happened, if I hadn't met Alfred, but it wasn't really what I wanted. For that matter, it's not *really* what I want here in the Star Kingdom. Not permanently, at least. I love the staff and challenges here at Queen Elizabeth's, but I plan on going into private practice once I've checked off all the boxes."

"Oh! Hanging out your shingle here in Landing?"

"Possibly. Or on Sphinx."

"Well, I hope your future patients are properly appreciative. It's not often we see someone with your skills in the Star Kingdom. Especially not someone who's also a Benton-Ramirez y Chou!"

"Personally," she said a bit repressively, "I'm more impressed by someone's competence than by her last name."

"Oh, of course. Of course!"

He waved a hand in what might have been apology, then looked away as the server bot floated up with his drink order. He sipped appreciatively, then returned his attention to Allison.

"So, you're in Genetics?" he asked, and Allison nodded. "Neonatal and Obstetrics for me," he said. "Like you, it's box-checking time."

"I'm not surprised," she replied. "And OB/GYN is really, really good. I've worked with a couple of the pediatric geneticists, and they're top-notch."

"So I hear. On the other hand, I probably got spoiled doing my residency back at Semmelweis."

Allison wondered if he actually thought no one could overhear the conversation. Of course, knowing him, he wouldn't have cared, anyway. She suspected he was going to prove less than popular with his fellow doctors.

"Well!" he took another sip. "I understand you went ahead and married Harrington and you've been stuck here in Manticore ever since, but would it happen you've heard what happened to Kleinman when he came home from Beowulf? I've only been back a few days myself, and I haven't been able to find him."

"George Kleinman?" Allison shrugged. "I understand he immigrated to Erewhon. He's got family there, I think."

"Really? I never knew that. What about Jeffers? I know she planned to go into private practice, and I was wondering—"

Allison had been looking forward to the cafeteria's lemon torte. Now, regretfully, she decided that if skipping dessert was the price of escaping Franz Illescue as quickly as possible, she would pay it without a whimper.

Harrington Freehold,
County Duvalier,
Duchy of Shadow Vale,
Planet Sphinx,
Manticore Binary System,
August 1853 PD.

"So, how are you and Dr. Illescue getting along, Alley?" Rebecca Harrington asked with a wicked smile, as she sliced the loaf of rye bread, still warm from the oven.

"Oh, God!" Allison looked up from stirring the clam chowder and rolled her eyes. "Did you really have to mention him just before we *eat*?"

"She has a low and inappropriate sense of humor," Alexander Harrington observed to no one in particular while he set the table.

At the moment, only he and Rebecca actually lived in the Harrington freehold's enormous house, although Richard made it a point to visit regularly. Upon occasion, however, the Harrington clan had actually needed all that space. Alexander Harrington was one of nine siblings, four of them twins. Which, according to him, was the reason he and Rebecca had stopped at five.

"Do you *really* want to talk about the low sense of humor of the woman who said yes when you proposed?" Rebecca shot back, and Alexander chuckled.

Alexander and Alfred could have been clones, Allison thought, whereas Richard had Rebecca's fair hair and green eyes. He was closer to merely mortal in height, as well. Some, anyway. Sometimes—all right, *usually*—Allison felt like a midget around her in-laws. Alfred's sisters favored their father more than mother, and the shortest of them was almost 178 centimeters tall. Even Rebecca was a good seven centimeters taller than her own 157 centimeters.

"All joking aside," Rebecca laid down the bread knife and carried the sliced bread out of the kitchen, "did your . . . counseling session bear fruit?"

"In a manner of speaking."

Allison lifted the kettle carefully and carried it, too, across to the crown oak dining room table Karl Zivonik Harrington had hand-built three T-centuries ago. She'd adapted better to Sphinx's heavier gravity than she'd really expected, but she still used her personal counter-grav a lot, and its area of effect was only 150 centimeters across. The moment when something the size of the kettle crossed the boundary into Sphinx's normal gravity and suddenly weighed a third again more than it ought to could be tricky.

And "tricky" was not a good thing for a Harrington-sized kettle of steaming hot clam chowder to become. Even after six T-years of watching Alfred put food away, Allison was awed by the calories required to stoke a Meyerdahl-mod metabolism. The splash if she dropped it would be extreme.

But she got it situated on the warming island down the center of the table without misadventure, and felt a small stir of pleasure that neither Rebecca nor Alex had offered to carry it for her or hovered watchfully.

"He's backed off on the stupid jokes, at least," she continued, settling into her chair. "I think he was convinced he was actually being funny."

"Really?" Rebecca smiled at her. "Funny. From Alfred's description, coupled with what you had to say about his idea of 'humor,' I would've said the problem was that he was an unmitigated prick with a bruised male ego."

Allison snorted a laugh.

"Alfred's not the best judge of Franz's 'bruised male ego,'" she said. "Mind you, his ego *is* one reason he can convince himself he has a sense of humor. He's undeniably envious of all those centimeters of Alfred's, too, and the fact that I wound up with Alfred instead of him chafes. For that matter, he's way too contemptuous of the military in general. But he also knows at least some of what happened to me, and he knows Alfred pulled me out of it." Her eyes darkened, but she'd reached a point where she could speak about it almost—almost—as if it had happened to someone else. "I doubt he and Alfred will ever like each other, but I honestly don't think there was any rejected ex-lover angst behind it."

Rebecca nodded, although it was obvious she cherished a few reservations.

"Anyway," Allison continued as Alex began ladling chowder into three bowls, "when I explained why I didn't find his continual comparisons between Manticore and all things Beowulfan humorous, he shut them down pretty quickly. I think he truly hadn't realized he might be putting me on the spot. He meant it as a joke and expected me to share the laugh with him and his audience. I doubt it ever occurred to him that he might cause anyone to think of me as one of *those* Beowulfers."

Rebecca nodded again, this time in understanding. Manticore saw a lot of Beowulfers, given the Junction, and Allison was scarcely the first Beowulfer to marry into a Manticoran family, or vice versa. Despite which, too many citizens of Beowulf had a towering awareness of their own star nation's antiquity and role in the Solarian League's creation and weren't shy about looking down their noses at the single-system polity that had the effrontery to call itself a Star *Kingdom*.

"You said your little talk helped with the jokes," Alex said. "Not so much with the other part, I take it?"

"No," Allison sighed. "Although, to be fair, I'm afraid that ship had already translated out by the time I sat him down."

Both Harringtons grimaced in understanding. Her own department head and some of the other senior physicians had always known about Allison's family connections. The rest of the hospital's staff had known only that she was a Beowulfan Semmelweis University graduate who'd been named *Chou* before she married.

Now the secret was out, and some people inevitably assumed family connections, not ability, explained her rapid rise in the QEH Department of Genetics, which was less than helpful in her determination to be Dr. *Harrington* and succeed or fail on her own merits.

"Well," she said, helping herself to a slice of bread before she passed the plate across to Alex, "if he's the worst of my problems, I'm luckier than a lot of people. And, on a happier note, I got a letter from Alfred just before I climbed onto the shuttle!"

"You did?" Rebecca laughed. "The boy's obviously still besotted with you." She rolled her eyes. "*We* were lucky to get a letter every six T-months!"

"I don't know about 'besotted,'" Allison replied with a demure smile, "but I do have a few sanctions denied to a mere parent. And I told him I wouldn't hesitate to apply them when he got home unless he wrote."

"Good for you!" Alex said with a chuckle.

"So, how is he?" Rebecca asked, reaching for her spoon.

"I think he misses us more than he wants to admit, but he seems really happy as *Scepter*'s surgeon. He says it's a little boring—as he puts it, *Scepter*'s basically just looming ominously while the lighter units do the actual commerce protection stuff—but I can tell he's enjoying the assignment. It's a lot more of a general practitioner slot than anything he had at Bassingford, but that's good for him. And he's so much happier to be keeping people healthy than he was as a Marine."

"Bless the boy." Rebecca's eyes might have been a bit misty. Allison knew Alfred had never discussed Clematis—or, for that matter, her own rescue—as fully with his mother as he had with her, but Rebecca knew her son too well not to have guessed what he hadn't told her.

"From your lips to God's ears," Allison said, smiling at her mother-in-law. "And, as if to refute your cruel and unnatural allegation that he was an irregular correspondent, he zipped his letter to me with one to you. I thought we might view mine together after dinner—I think you'll get a laugh or two from some of it. Then you guys can view yours."

**Carlton Locatelli Tower,
City of Landing,
Planet Manticore,
Star Kingdom of Manticore,
Manticore Binary System,
August 1858.**

"Something smells good!"

Commander Alfred Harrington inhaled deeply as he stepped into the apartment, and Dr. Allison Harrington, wearing an anachronistic white apron, poked her head out of the kitchen.

"Don't you dare set one foot into the dining room!"

"What?" Alfred blinked. "Why not?"

"Mostly because I'll hurt you," she said sweetly. "The reason that's true, I will leave to your imagination."

She disappeared back into the kitchen, and Alfred chuckled as he crossed the comfortable living room and looked out through the programmable crystoplast wall. His recent promotion to full commander, coupled with his appointment as the executive officer for Bassingford's Department of Neurology and Neurosurgery, entitled them to a very nice apartment on the hundred and twelfth floor of Carlton Locatelli Tower, overlooking the beautifully landscaped Bassingford campus. Since Bassingford was adjacent— sort of—to Queen Elizabeth's Hospital, the location was incredibly convenient for both of them.

He'd been assigned to Neurology and Neurosurgery as a senior staff physician immediately after HMS *Scepter*'s return from Silesia. In many ways, he'd hated to leave the ship, and he'd formed a dozen close friendships over the course of his four-T-year deployment. On the other hand, she'd returned to Manticore exactly six times during it, and his longest leave had been only three T-weeks. Coming home to Allison every night—well, every night when competing schedules permitted—was heaven, and BuPers had promised they wouldn't reassign him to shipboard duty anytime soon.

He'd discovered they meant that when Captain Dunlevy, Neurology and Neurosurgery's longtime CO, stepped down and Commander Isadora Machowska, Dunlevy's exec, was named to replace him. Everyone had seen that coming for a while. Dunlevy was one of the best doctors Alfred had ever met, but he was over seventy, and he'd never received prolong. And it had been equally obvious that Machowska would succeed him. What Alfred hadn't seen coming—hadn't even remotely expected—was that *he* might be named as Machowska's replacement. There were at least two other neurosurgeons at Bassingford senior to him . . . until they bumped him to full commander out of the zone, despite the glacial pace of peacetime promotions.

The only person who hadn't been surprised—or *claimed* she hadn't been, anyway—by the Navy's clear declaration that it approved of him was Allison.

The new apartment was a really nice perk, he thought, gazing down into the gathering evening as the lights came up in the green belts and water features around the Bassingford towers' feet, but the sheer satisfaction of his new duties was an even deeper one. The only true fly in his ointment was that he was a much better administrator than he'd thought he was, and he dreaded the day BuPers figured that out and tried to pull him out of the clinical side and turn him into another manager.

"What if I promise to keep my eyes closed?" he called through the arch to the kitchen. "I could just walk across to my chair—you could lead me by the hand, actually—and then I could just sit there, eyes closed, smelling all those delicious baking smells, until you told me to look."

"Suuuuuure you could."

Allison didn't even poke her head out this time, and he grinned.

"But I'm *hungry!*"

"You're *always* hungry. You're a *Harrington.*"

"So are you."

"But not genetically. Thank God. Trying to feed just one Meyerdahl metabolism's bad enough!"

"You didn't seem to think it would be so bad back on Beowulf."

"That was the optimism of ignorance. Now I know better."

Alfred laughed and plopped down in the big armchair. It adjusted smoothly under him and he tapped the armrest touchscreen to bring the smart wall online, then skipped through the menu to his favorite newsfeed.

"Don't get too buried in that," Allison said. "Dinner is almost ready."

"You know I'd be happy to help you finish it up," Alfred offered hopefully.

"Forget it."

He shook his head. Given their schedules—Allison had become Department Head in Genetics at Queen Elizabeth's two T-months ago—they found themselves using the auto chef a lot more than either of them liked. Jacques wasn't all that far wrong when he called them "foodie fanatics," Alfred supposed. On the other hand, there was an almost sensual pleasure in selecting ingredients and then turning them into a meal the old-fashioned way. Not that he had any desire to start building fires. Except for the occasional cookout, that was.

They'd made it a hard and fast rule to cater to their "fanaticism" and cook supper by hand at least twice a T-week. They alternated planning and preparing the meal, and whoever was cooking took pains to surprise the other with that night's menu. Despite which, it was unusual for even Allison to be as adamant about that as she was tonight.

"I know that's a triple chocolate torte I smell! Not going to surprise me with it. So why can't I come sit at the table where I can talk to you while you finish up?"

"You're talking to me just fine. Watch your news. I'll tell you when it's time."

"Tyrant."

"*You* were lots worse than this last week."

"But that was because I was fixing *hóngshāo niúpá* and I didn't want you figuring it out. I've already figured out what you're baking."

"Oh? And what other savory concoctions' aroma might I have concealed under the scent of your favorite dessert in all the world?"

"That's cheating!"

"Sue me."

Alfred laughed again and returned his attention to the smart wall. Allison, minus the apron, stepped into the living room barely fifteen minutes later. Even seated, he was almost as tall as she was, and she crossed to his chair and leaned close for a lingering kiss.

"All right," she said then, straightening and running one hand through his hair. "Come and get it, Spacer!"

"Do we really have to *eat* right now?" he asked with a smile. "I mean, after that kiss and all..."

"Supper first!" The twinkle in her eye undermined the sternness of her tone. "Besides, you'll need your strength."

"Ooooh! A challenge! I *love* challenges!"

"Shut up and come eat, doof!" she said with a giggle, and held out a helpful hand as he hauled himself out of the armchair's sinfully comfortable embrace.

She tucked her elbow through his, leaning her head against his upper arm, as they crossed to the dining room, and he paused, eyebrows rising, in the archway.

No wonder she hadn't wanted him seeing the table early, he thought, looking at the snowy tablecloth, glittering "special occasion" dishes, and the bottle of Delacorte in the traditional wine chiller.

Both his and Allison's plates were covered, and there was a single temperature-controlled covered platter at the center of the table, flanked by a bowl of tossed salad and one of baby potatoes in butter and herbs. His eyes lit at the sight, and she lifted the cover from the platter with a flourish.

"Ta-da!"

"You made *Beef Wellington* without using the auto chef?"

"Yep."

"That takes hours! I thought you were stuck in the office all afternoon."

"I had one appointment this morning, and after that, I said the hell with it and took the rest of the day off." She shrugged. "I've been putting in enough hours nobody at Queen Elizabeth's is going to complain."

He looked at her, then back at the table, and then back at her. That sort of attitude towards her professional schedule was very un-Allison-like.

"So what's the special occasion?" he asked a bit suspiciously.

"I can't just want to share one of my beloved husband's favorite meals with him?"

"Sure you can," he said in a very unconvinced sort of tone.

"Just go ahead and sit down," she scolded.

"It really does look delicious, Honey," he said as he obeyed her. "And you're right, without the baking smells to cover it up, I *would* have guessed what you were up to."

"You think so? What if you're wrong about that?" She gave him a lurking smile, and he raised an eyebrow. "Go ahead and check your plate," she told him.

He chuckled and lifted the cover from his plate. Then paused.

"What," he asked, "is *that?*"

"That, love of my life," Allison said, much more softly, "is a baby bottle."

"A baby bottle," he repeated very carefully as she put an arm around his neck and leaned against him.

"Yes." She pulled back enough to look into his eyes. "I did say I had an appointment this morning. I just didn't mention it was over in OB/GYN."

"You're *pregnant*?!"

"Why, yes," she told him. "As a matter of fact, I am."

And she leaned close to kiss him again.

❈ ❈ ❈

Several hours later, Alfred leaned back in the outsized recliner on the outdoor balcony. Allison lay curled beside him like a contented cat, and the breeze tickled his cheek with loose strands of her hair.

"You're pregnant," he said again, softly, in the tone of someone who couldn't quite believe what he was saying.

"Actually, I prefer to think of it as a case of *we're* pregnant," she replied with a dimpled smile. "You do realize I'm not going to be the *only* one changing diapers, Commander Harrington?"

"Trust me, that's one thing I *do* realize," he chuckled.

"I'm already scheduled to be off this Saturday. Do you think you could clear that day, too? I thought we'd make a quick hop to Sphinx to tell your mom and dad in person."

"Trust me, I will *make* that happen."

"Good. And we've got to tell Jacques, too. Although that's going to take a letter, assuming we can figure out where to send it."

"Well, right now he's back in Grendel. I understand he'll be heading back to Silesia through the Junction in a couple of T-months, though."

"Maybe we could just tell him in person, then," Allison said thoughtfully. "I mean, there's not that much rush. I'm second-generation prolong, so we're—or at least, *I'm*—looking at a fourteen-month pregnancy." She grimaced. "I have to say, that's the one aspect of this that doesn't fill me with total joy."

"I suppose even the worthless male responsible for your condition can understand that."

"I suppose the worthless male had *better* understand that. I intend to be totally unreasonable for the last, oh, three or four months, you understand. I'm positive I'll develop more than enough cravings to drive you absolutely crazy."

"I'm sure," he said dryly, wrapping his arms about her. But his expression had turned serious, and she turned her head to look at him as she sensed his mood shift.

"What?"

"I'm really looking forward to telling Mom and Dad," he said. "But what about *your* parents, Alley?"

Her lips tightened and he hugged her more tightly, as she stiffened in the circle of his arms.

"I'm sorry, Honey. But we're going to have to decide about that."

"I know."

Allison sighed and pressed her face into his shoulder.

She hadn't seen her mother, hadn't spoken to her, in over twelve T-years, and she really, really didn't want to revisit that. Reopen the wound.

"We have to tell them," Alfred said gently. "Both of them. It would kill your dad if we didn't tell him. You know that. And however tempting it might be, could we really justify *not* telling your mother?"

Allison's mouth tightened. She knew how painful Alfred found the breach between her and her mother. She could feel it over the link between them, just as she knew the reason he felt that way was the way that same link carried him her own deep, lingering pain. She could go days, weeks—even months—without admitting that pain to *herself*, yet she could never hide it from *him*, and he was hardwired to fix things. But this wasn't something he could fix. In fact, it wasn't something anyone could "fix."

"All right," she said finally. "We'll tell her. There's a part of me that's really tempted to let you record the letter, though, Alfred. I know it's cowardly, but..."

"That would be...a very bad idea," he observed, and she managed an actual giggle. It wasn't much of a giggle, but it still surprised her.

"Do you want to invite—" he began in a cautious tone.

"No."

She cut him off, firmly, far more flatly than she normally spoke to him, and shook her head against his shoulder.

"No," she repeated, and if her tone wasn't quite as flat, it was no more yielding. "Alfred, she's had a standing invitation to visit us any time she wanted to from the day we were married. Hell, we invited her to the *wedding*—remember? And we must have repeated that invitation a dozen times in the first five or six T-years! She never accepted it. She never even *acknowledged* it." She shook her head again. "I know—I *know*—how much you want to heal this breach, bridge the chasm, but there's only so far I can go. I mean, literally. I all but *begged* her to come to Manticore for a visit for the first couple of T-years. I'm not going to do it again. If *she* wants to come, if she wants to take advantage of those invitations—hell, they're still open!—that's one thing. But that's as far as I can go, Sweetheart. Really. It is."

"And your dad?" he asked softly.

"He's got the same standing invitation. I know why he hasn't accepted it, and I can't really blame him, I suppose. It hurts, but I don't think anyone could expect him to break that openly with Mom. It's probably painful enough that he and I send so many letters back and forth while Mom and I never do. If he decides to come, I'll be overjoyed to see him, but I won't put him in the position of having to choose between Mom and an explicit, new invitation from me."

"All right." He kissed the top of her head and squeezed her tightly. "All right. I wish I could find a way to fix this, Alley. I really, really do."

"I wish you could, too," she said sadly. "But you're a neurosurgeon, love. A very good one, but still a neurosurgeon and not a wizard."

Huang Hai's Bar and Grill,
Shadow Tree Tower,
City of Grendel,
Planet Beowulf,
September 1858 PD.

"You do realize this is probably the only establishment in Shadow Tree that allows smoking, don't you?" Caspar Benton-Ramirez y Chou asked.

"That's an exaggeration," his son replied, tamping fresh tobacco into the bowl of his pipe. "Three quarters of the restaurants and bars in Grendel let you smoke."

"Maybe, but not tobacco."

"Which is frigging ridiculous." Jacques Benton-Ramirez y Chou lit his pipe. "This isn't the pre-cancer vaccine Dark Ages, and secondhand smoke from most of those other products is a lot more likely to affect your judgment."

"I'm just saying that when I get home, your mom is going to take one sniff and know I've been out hobnobbing with you. And then she's going to ask me why."

"No," Jacques replied. "She's not going to ask why you've been hobnobbing with me. She's going to ask why she wasn't included. Or maybe she isn't. She'll know what we were hobnobbing *about*, Dad. Do you think she'll want to open that can of worms?"

"Probably not," Caspar sighed, looking down into his beer stein.

"Dad, this is *stupid*." Jacques's frustrated anger was evident. "It's bad enough that Mom won't even record a letter to Alley, but she says that since Alley and—of course!—Alfred 'went out of their way to not invite me' to visit even now that Alley's pregnant, they obviously don't *want* to hear from her, anyway. I pointed out that she's had a standing invitation for years, and her response was that if they don't care enough to specifically invite her again, now of all times, they obviously never meant it seriously in the first place. She says she won't 'go crawling' to them if that's the way they feel about it. And now she flat out refuses to even discuss Alley with me!"

"You expected anything else?" His father looked up. "You think she doesn't already know what you'd say? What you've already said more times than I can count?" He grimaced. "And I've agreed with you almost every time. But you've known your mother your entire life. Don't tell me you're *surprised* by any of this!"

"That it's lasted this long? Yes, honestly." Jacques shook his head. "I mean, I know she's stubborn, and I know Alley's stubborn. But *this*—!"

He looked like he wanted to spit on the floor, and Caspar snorted.

"Your mother and I have been consensually bonded for a long time, son, and I've never seen her this dug-in, either. But I've spent a lot of time thinking about it. You want *my* take on it?"

"Please," Jacques said.

"All right, first, she's genuinely unable to understand why Allison would have opted for monogamy, especially so early. But I doubt she'd have a problem with that if Alley had just stayed home and taken her proper place in the 'family business.' She didn't. She's not going to change her mind and *come* home, either, and your mom knows that. But she won't—can't—admit it to herself, and it's not just stubbornness. That's a big part of it, granted, but it's also hurt. In her own mind, every single thing she's ever said about Allison's 'mistakes' is motivated by love. So when Alley rejected her 'advice,' she also rejected *her*. She rejected her mother's love in favor of some yahoo from an upstart, *nouveau riche* star nation like Manticore."

"Dad—!"

"I didn't say Allison really did. I said that's how your mom sees it, and it's not something even I can discuss with her anymore. And because she blames Alfred for 'luring' Alley into monogamy and 'locking her up' off-world, she also blames him for Allison's rejection of her. To be honest, though, I think another big part of the reason she's dug in so strongly on this is fear."

"Fear?"

"Jacques, you know exactly what those bastards did to Allison," Caspar said grimly, "and I've been Planetary Vice President of the Anti-Slavery League for decades, so *I* know, too. We can't lie to ourselves about it, however much we want to, but your mom doesn't have our insight, and she's never really admitted how horrible it was. Or how terrified she is, deep inside, that it might happen again. She can't admit the fear without facing the reality, and without admitting the fear, she can't admit that at least half her genuine anger stems from Alley's refusal to stay home where the people who love her could keep her safe. Or that the real reason she's pissed at *you* is that you're one of the people who's supposed to protect Alley *here*, and instead, you're helping 'put her at risk' in the Star Kingdom!

"I've told her she needs counseling on this, but she just brushes me off, and she's never done that before. That's why I know how deep her refusal to grapple with it truly goes. And that's also why, irrational as you and I both know it is, she resents the hell out of Alfred. She can't accept Alley's love for him—the fact that she chose *him* when your mom forced the issue—without admitting to herself what Alfred pulled Alley out of. As far as she's concerned, you're the one who really rescued her, when you got there with the assault shuttle. Again, because if she ever admits what Alfred did, she'll have to truly confront what happened to Alley before he got there."

"I hadn't thought about it from that perspective," Jacques said slowly.

"Well, that makes two of you," Caspar said with a bitter smile. "Because *she* sure as hell hasn't, either. Not with that first-class brain we both know she has, anyway. And I'm not surprised you haven't thought about it, because the last thing your mother normally is is irrational, and this is as irrational as it gets."

"What about you?" Jacques asked, sitting back and relighting his pipe.

"As far as I'm concerned, Alfred Harrington has an unlimited credit balance," Caspar said simply. "I do know what he did, and that Alley's probably *safer* in Manticore than here. And she and I exchange letters every couple of T-weeks." His eyes were unhappy. "I really wish I'd accepted their invitation to visit, but it hurts your mom badly enough each time we just exchange letters. If I actually went, it'd be like she's been deserted—abandoned—and disapproved of by everyone who ought to love her."

"That's ridiculous. Nobody's 'abandoned' or 'deserted' her!"

"I didn't say they had. But that's exactly the way it feels to her. I hate it, almost as much as I hate her refusal to seek any counseling of her own, but I can't find a way to *change* it. There has to be one. Whether she's showing it right now or not, your mom loves Allison too much for there *not* to be a way. But I will be damned if I know what it is, Jacques."

Harrington Freehold,
County Duvalier,
Duchy of Shadow Vale,
Planet Sphinx,
Manticore Binary System,
October 1859 PD.

"So you're still sure this is a good idea?"

Alfred Harrington smiled as he used his right hand to blot sweat from Allison's forehead while she squeezed his left in a two-handed, white-knuckled grip. She gritted her teeth, panting hard until the contraction eased, then let her head fall back.

"I seem to recall *your* thinking this would be a good idea while we were doing all the prep work!" she said tartly.

"Oh, I still think it's a *fine* idea! After all, I'm the one doing the sweat-mopping and coaching, not the one out there on the field, so to speak."

"And I will *so* make you pay for that remark."

"Just giving you something to focus on beside the contractions. See how virtuous I am?"

Allison gurgled a somewhat breathless laugh and shook her head.

"Actually, if I haven't mentioned it before, for the sort of insufferable cad who gets an innocent and unsuspecting young woman pregnant, you're not too shabby."

"Be still my beating heart!" Alfred shook his head. "Not sure I can handle all this effusive praise."

She laughed again, then gave his fingers another, gentler squeeze before she released them. For the moment.

Both of their daughter-to-be's parents were physicians, and somewhere around two thirds or three quarters of their friends—and virtually all of their professional colleagues—were also physicians, who worked in the two finest hospitals in the Star Kingdom of Manticore. Arguably, two of the finest hospitals in the entire explored galaxy. So all the prenatal care any expectant parents could have desired had been readily available. And taken advantage of.

But Alfred hadn't stopped there. Given Allison's determination that her child would be born in the same house in which he'd been born, he'd gotten his parents' permission to install grav plates in the north wing. As Allison had already observed, the sprawling "farmhouse" which had shielded so many generations of Harringtons was definitely on the spacious side. Especially by the standards of a daughter of Beowulf.

Housing in a city like Grendel was usually constrained and tended to be... compact. Not because of expense, given that modern construction technology made building projects no Pharaoh would have touched relatively inexpensive in terms of both manpower and resources. No, the problem was simply physical space. Towers like the ones in which Allison had grown up—or like Carlton Locatelli, today—went straight up rather than spreading out because of the restricted footprint that allowed. A tower like Locatelli housed the population of a moderate-sized pre-space town or even small city in a structure whose base was barely two hundred meters on a side. It did that by stacking its inhabitants on top of one another, and interspacing commercial floors with shops, restaurants, libraries, nightclubs, and every other imaginable service provider that were all conveniently located for its tenants. But even a spacious apartment like Allison's and Alfred's seldom afforded more than a hundred and fifty or so square meters of actual floor space. There were exceptions, especially in the luxury towers, but by most standards, theirs was decidedly on the palatial side.

The Harrington freehold, on the other hand, was a perfect square, twenty-five kilometers on a side. Virtually all of those sixty-two thousand hectares remained in virgin forest, and the Harringtons meant to keep it that way. Despite which, there'd been ample space for the original house and its accompanying greenhouses to expand over the centuries. Even its tallest sections were no more than three stories, but it was at least ten times the size of their Locatelli Tower apartment. The north wing, which was actually the oldest part of the house, boasted only a single floor and around two hundred square meters of floor space. It had been converted into a guest wing a couple of generations back, since it still boasted its own kitchen, among other things, and Rebecca and Alexander had insisted on making it officially hers and Alfred's. The fact that it was only a single floor had simplified fitting the grav plates—although it had still required a *lot* of structural work—which meant Allison could leave her personal counter-grav unit in the closet without subjecting herself to the full, heavy grip of Sphinx's gravity.

That was a not-so-minor consideration for a woman who'd been pregnant for over a T-year.

She could forgive Alfred quite a lot, whenever she thought about that. Besides—

"Uh-oh! Hand!" she said, reaching up, and snatched at his left hand again as the fresh contraction started.

They hadn't been bad at all when her labor first began. In fact, she'd had worse discomfort from indigestion, and she'd gone for a walk—with Alfred riding shotgun—and then come home and taken a long shower to help herself stay relaxed. But that had been fifteen hours ago, which was quite long enough, in her opinion.

In fact, she was more than ready for their daughter to put in her appearance. She wouldn't have missed her pregnancy for anything. The moment she'd first felt the baby move would live in her memory forever. Listening to the baby's heartbeat. Feeling her move with greater and greater strength. Feeling her kick. Lying in bed beside Alfred, her head on his shoulder, while they both listened to the heartbeat. Even the days when their undutiful offspring had decided to dance a jig on her bladder. All of it—every single instant—was something she would treasure forever. She might have felt differently if she'd suffered from the morning sickness that was still too often a pregnant mother's lot, but she'd dodged that pulser dart.

But now—

She held Alfred's hand tightly, panting hard, then slumped back again as the contraction finally eased.

"Four minutes apart, Honey," he told her, then. "Last one was fifty-seven seconds. Time, you think?"

"Probably," she replied, still breathing hard. "I hope so, anyway! This is hard *work*!"

"I've been told that," he said cheerfully, activating his uni-link and entering a code.

"Yes?" a voice said.

"Four minutes apart, fifty-seven seconds' duration," he replied. "My impatient spouse suggests it might be time for you to put in an appearance, Jessica."

"On my way," Jessica Harrington replied. "Fifteen minutes."

"I'll tell her to be patient."

"If you do, she'll kill you. Which would leave me with only *one* brother. The smart one," Jessica said tartly. "Clear."

"Would you *really* kill me if I told you to be patient?" Alfred asked quizzically, smiling down at Allison while he wiped her face and throat with a cool cloth.

"Oh, in a heartbeat!" she assured him. "In a *heartbeat!*"

✖ ✖ ✖

"She's beautiful," Rebecca Harrington murmured five hours later, gazing down into the squinched-up face of the blanket-wrapped infant in her arms.

"Really?" Alfred stood looking over her shoulder. Now he reached out and brushed his daughter's cheek with an infinitely gentle finger. "More beautiful than Leah? Or Alice? Or Anson? Or—?"

"Jessica's right," Allison said wryly from the huge armchair. "Richard *is* the smart one, isn't he?"

"Well, I'm not sure he's actually *all* that smart," her mother-in-law told her, looking back and up over her shoulder at Alfred. "He's the *smarter* one, but considering the questions his older brother just asked, that's a lower bar than I'd thought."

"Hey! I resemble that remark!"

"Yes, you do," his mother said. "On the other hand, and bearing in mind that I would never play favorites among my grandchildren, I have to say young Honor here does have a couple of...inside advantages. First, of course, there's Allison's genetic contribution, which probably means she won't have your ears or your father's nose. Both of those are *definitely* points in her favor. And, secondly, she's the *newest* of my grandchildren, which means I'll get to spend more time spoiling her and that—for the moment—she enjoys Grandmother's Favorite status. Although I will, of course, deny I said that if you breathe a word of it to your sisters. After which, Alley won't have to kill you, because *I* will."

"I don't want to sound like I'm complaining or anything,"

Alexander Harrington said a bit plaintively, "but she's *my* granddaughter, too."

"And your point is?" his wife asked sweetly.

"My point is when do *I* get to hold her?"

"You? A mere *male*? Surely you jest! The instant I let you touch this child, you're going to start planning where to take her fishing and calculating how soon she'll qualify for a hunting license!"

"Will not."

"Will so," his wife said firmly. "And we'll just delay that catastrophic moment for as long as we can."

"I don't think that sounds very fair."

"Give it up, Dad." Alfred shook his head woefully. "The monstrous regiment of women is in charge, now." He sniffed. "We'll be lucky if we get to visit with her on alternate Wednesdays."

"Ha! You'll *wish* when it's feeding time," his father snorted. "Don't forget, Alley's DNA or not, Honor *does* have the Meyerdahl metabolism. And then there's all those diapers. Parenting's supposed to be a two-person job, and your mom and I always handled it that way. But there are going to be times when the two of you wish you were right here on Sphinx where you could call in the support troops."

"I intend to call in a *lot* of support troops," Allison said softly, holding out her own arms, and Rebecca smiled as she put the baby into them.

"Oh, trust me, Honey," she said softly. "You call, and we'll come running."

"I know." Allison smiled up at her a bit mistily as she held Honor close. "I know."

Alfred perched on one of the chair arms and leaned close to rest his cheek on the crown of her head as they gazed down at their daughter. He tasted Allison's deep, happy joy, reaching out across whatever linked them. Her happiness at the depth of his family's love, the way they'd all embraced her.

And underneath it, like arsenic in the heart of honey, her bitter, bitter regret that her own mother no longer could.

Bassingford Medical Center,
City of Landing,
Planet Manticore,
Manticore Binary System,
November 1859 PD.

"So, that's Dad's take," Jacques said.

He and his team were scheduled to continue their journey to Silesia the next day, but for now he and Alfred sat in a quiet corner of the officers' mess, across the remains of lunch. Allison would join them for dinner at Dempsey's, but she'd been unable to get away for lunch. Which was just as well, he thought.

"I can't say I'm surprised." Alfred sipped wine. "I always thought he was smart, and as irrational as it may be, it actually makes sense, I suppose. Given the participants' starting points, anyway. I don't think Caspar's making enough allowance for *Alley*'s irrationality, though."

"Really?"

"I didn't say she's being un*reasonable*, but her own strain of irrational response is woven into this, too." Alfred shrugged. "Your mom doesn't realize the extent to which Alley saw me as the last shuttle out of town to get away from being one of *those* Benton-Ramirez y Chous."

"Alfred, she *loves* you!"

"Oh, trust me, there's no sense of insecurity on my part. And I'm sure as hell not suggesting I'm only a means to an end. Trust me, if anyone in the galaxy knows that, I do! But it *is* a factor in her thinking, and you know it."

He held Jacques's eyes steadily until the other man nodded, then shrugged again.

"So there's a part of her that would've irrationally—as in unthinkingly—opposed any compromise that left us in Beowulf, even if my Navy obligations hadn't prevented it. And she's just as bunkered-down emotionally as your mother, now. She's so damned *hurt* by your mom's response to something so important—so clear—to her, that her own anger's driving her response. You should go ahead and tell her your mother's reaction to the fact that we didn't invite her again, but I'll tell you right now that it won't change her position. You said your mom's not going to 'crawl' to her? Well, guess what. She's your mother's daughter!"

"Shit."

"Oh, definitely." Alfred's crooked smile mingled frustration with deep, abiding regret. "But I'm with your dad. I don't see a way out, either. And the one thing I'm depressingly certain of is that if there is one, neither your mother nor Alley will go digging for it. Not now. Not after all these years."

Pankowski System,
Silesian Confederacy,
June 1859 PD.

Jeremy Tanner tapped his thrusters, braking his last few meters-per-second of velocity and grimaced as his shuttle nudged just a bit too solidly into the cargo bay buffers.

"Man, I hate these backwater, back-assward depots!" he growled, and Inga Mastroianni, his flight engineer, snorted.

"You say that every damned time," she pointed out.

"Because it's *true* every damned time. At least they could install a couple of traffic-handling tractor units!"

"And deprive you of the opportunity to show off your impeccable piloting?"

"Impeccable piloting's not worth a bucket of spit in vacuum if I misjudge an approach."

"Probably do more damage to the station than to us," Mastroianni said a bit more sourly, studying her own readouts. "They must've put this place together with your bucket of spit and maybe a little glue."

"Like I say, backwater, bare-bone, and back-assward."

"Not saying you're wrong, but on the other hand, backwater has its advantages," she pointed out.

"I guess you've got that right," Tanner conceded, and tapped the com panel. "Yo, Traffic Control," he said, with a grimace for Mastroianni. Calling the half-assed, casual voice that had greeted the merchantship *Joseph Francis* upon arrival "Traffic Control" constituted physical abuse of a perfectly respectable title. "We're here, in case you hadn't noticed. Somebody want to open the goddamned hatch?"

"Keep your vacsuit on," the female voice replied. "Our guys are on the way. You got your manifest ready?"

"Of course we do."

"Okay. Give us another couple of minutes."

Tanner rolled his eyes and hit the intercom button.

"Yeah?" a voice growled.

"Two minutes—they say. Better get 'em on their feet."

"Be easier if they weren't tranked so heavy."

"Bitch, bitch, bitch." Tanner shook his head. "The *Joey*'s never lost a shuttle yet, and we're not starting with mine, asshole."

"Then why don't you come back here and get them moving?"

"Because that's not *my* job," Tanner shot back, and closed down the intercom.

"He's got a point," Mastroianni said. Tanner looked at her, and she shrugged. "I didn't say it was a *good* one."

Tanner grimaced. After twelve T-years with Manpower, Incorporated, he was solidly in favor of tranking cargo to the gills during transit. His last ship before the *Joseph Francis* had lost two cargo shuttles when the slaves aboard them rioted. It hadn't done the cargo any good in the end. Slavers like the *Joey* might be merchant hulls, but most merchies—even *legitimate* merchies—out here in Silesia normally mounted at least some armament. On the other hand, none of the shuttles' crew members had survived the experience, and Jeremy Tanner had no desire to emulate them. Besides—

"So, here we are," a new voice said over the com. "You're so hot to unload, you want to go ahead and crack your hatch?"

"Sounds good to me," Tanner said, and nodded to Mastroianni.

"Thanks," the new voice said. "Oh, and one more thing," it added as the hatch opened.

"What?" Tanner demanded, then stiffened as the unmistakable "*chuff*" of a flechette gun came over the com. It coughed twice more even as his head snapped around to stare at Mastroianni.

"Just that you might want to open the flight deck hatch and come out with your hands where we can see them." The voice was more clipped and professional—and far, far colder—than it had been. "If you do, you'll probably live at least a little longer than your buddies in the cargo bay did."

※ ※ ※

"And yet another fly into the spiderweb," Captain Benyamin Shing announced over the com in tones of profound satisfaction. "Good job on the timing."

"Practice helps," Major Jacques Benton-Ramirez y Chou replied, tipping back in his chair aboard the freight platform. On the display before him, Shing's "workboat"—a beat up looking commercial craft whose "trash hauler" exterior concealed the armament of a light attack craft and personnel space for a full platoon of BSC commandos—had just docked with the *Joseph Francis*. Getting it into position to pounce before Jacques's station-side personnel grabbed the inbound shuttle had been a little trickier than usual, but Shing was right. The timing had worked out almost perfectly.

"So does the fact that most slavers are frigging idiots, Sir," Sergeant Major Brockmann observed from her place at the communications panel.

"Fair's fair, Miliko. Far as they know, this shithole of a station is still under Manpower management."

"All due respect, Sir, they're still dumber'n rocks."

"Sar' Major's right," Shing put in, and Jacques chuckled.

"Not arguing the point, Benny. Just pointing out that we're *helping* them be 'dumber than rocks' this time around." Jacques climbed out of his chair and stretched. "Get the bastards cuffed and moved to the platform. I want their ship out of here and headed for Beowulf ASAP. No telling when the next fly will be along."

"It's sort of a waste of time to bring them back with us," Shing pointed out, and Jacques snorted. Under the Cherwell Convention, the slave trade and piracy were the same thing. Which meant *Joseph Francis*'s crew would shortly follow God only knew how many slaves who'd been dumped into vacuum to get rid of incriminating evidence.

"Got to dot all the 'i's and cross all the 't's," he replied. "It's even possible one of them has something worth trading to keep his or her sorry ass alive."

"I can always hope they don't, can't I?"

Shing's voice was much bleaker than it had been, which didn't surprise Jacques. Private Benyamin Shing had been part of Jacques's team for over three T-years before he'd been direct-commissioned and assigned a team of his own. And like Brockmann, who'd piloted the shuttle the day of Allison's rescue, he was the child of an ex-slave. Brockmann's father had been "cargo" aboard a slaver which had encountered one of the rare Solarian League Navy cruisers actually enforcing the Cherwell Convention, while Shing's mother had been liberated from Manpower in an operation much like this one. A lot of the BSC's people came from very similar backgrounds.

And had very similar attitudes.

"Well, it shouldn't take us too long to find out," Jacques replied now. "And just between you and me, it won't break my heart, either, if they don't."

Bassingford Medical Center,
City of Landing,
Planet Manticore,
Manticore Binary System,
March 1860 PD.

The attention signal chimed, and Alfred looked up from the case file on his display. He frowned, then sat back and tapped the acceptance key, and the com system's computer-generated voice spoke.

"Incoming burst transmission from Captain Adelina Gomez," it said. "No two-way link established. Do you wish to view the transmission?"

His frown deepened. Adelina Gomez was the CO of HMS *Scepter*, and *Scepter* had returned to her old stomping ground in Silesia four T-months ago. She wasn't due back in the Star Kingdom for another five T-months.

"Display transmission," he said, and a trim, brown-eyed senior-grade captain appeared on the display. Back when Lieutenant Commander Harrington had been *Scepter*'s ship's surgeon, Adelina Gomez had been the battlecruiser's executive officer. Both of them had risen in the world since, and he'd attended her promotion party when she made senior-grade and took over the ship.

"Hello, Alfred," she said now. "This is in the nature of a heads up, because I knew you'd want to know. We got an emergency request for backup from the Biological Survey Corps team in Pankowski. I don't know how much Jacques told you about their op on his way out, but it turned . . . messy."

Alfred's jaw tightened. As it happened, Jacques had told him quite a lot, although all of it had been strictly unofficial. Technically, the Star Kingdom listed the Audubon Ballroom as a terrorist organization. Because of that, the fact that the BSC routinely operated on intelligence the Ballroom generated was one of those little things the Crown—and the Navy—aggressively knew nothing about. In this instance, some of that intel had led the BSC to a ramshackle, beat up freight station in a poorer-than-rocks Silesian star system that seemed to be doing quite a lot of business.

That tended to happen when Manpower took over a remote station.

Trying to step on every transfer point in the slave trade network would have been a Sisyphean task, at best, especially in the Confederacy, which had become one of the primary markets for Manpower's "goods" over the last several decades. But every little bit helped. Especially when said transfer point could be seized and used to mousetrap incoming slavers.

"Apparently, Manpower figured out something was wrong in Pankowski sooner than anyone expected," Gomez continued grimly. "They hired themselves a mercenary outfit, loaded it aboard a 'slaver,' and sent it to find out what the 'something' was. Jacques got a little warning, courtesy of those people we don't talk about, and called us in, but we couldn't get there before the mercs. The BSC took heavy casualties, Alfred, including over a dozen from neural disruptors. You people at Bassingford are at least as good as anyone in the galaxy for that kind of damage, so we're inbound with the worst of them." Her nostrils flared. "Doc Crowder's done his best to stabilize them, but it doesn't look good. We're still almost a full day out of Manticore orbit, but you probably want to go ahead and get the trauma unit spun up now."

Alfred's jaw tightened, and he reached for his com pad. But before he could enter a code, the system pinged again.

"Incoming burst transmission from Major Jacques Benton-Ramirez y Chou," it said. "No two-way link established. Do you wish to view the transmission?"

Shadow Tree Tower,
City of Grendel,
Planet Beowulf,
March 1860 PD.

Jennifer Benton-Ramirez y Chou reclined in the chaise lounge, gazing out across Grendel's nightscape. The city never slept. In fact, it scarcely even slowed down, but there was something restful about the darkness. About the rivers of light running around the towers' feet, the glittering air car bubbles moving purposefully between landing stages. The night breeze swept over the balcony, rich with the scent of spring, even at Jennifer's elevation, and she felt the relaxation sink into her soul.

She'd always enjoyed Grendel's nighttime respite, but tonight she didn't just enjoy it; she *needed* it. The day had been . . . hard. She'd done her best to bury herself in the lab's current research, but it hadn't worked. In fact, it hadn't really worked for the last six T-months.

She closed her eyes, and behind them she saw again Alfred Harrington's brief message, announcing the birth of her first grandchild. A grandchild she'd never seen. One she'd realized she probably never *would* see. Harrington hadn't been discourteous. Indeed, his tone had been painfully neutral . . . and she'd wanted to scream at him for that. But she'd throttled her rage, because she'd known even then that it was totally unreasonable. Yes, he'd lured Allison away to Manticore, yet much as it grieved Jennifer to acknowledge it, he could never have done it—never have fenced in Allison's life that way—if Allison hadn't *wanted* him to. He hadn't been the Pied Piper Jennifer had accused him in her own mind of being. No. He'd been something even worse than that.

He'd been Allison's *escape*.

How had they come to this, she wondered. How had she *let* it come to this? How could Allison not see everything she'd thrown away, rejected . . . and how could Jennifer have allowed the fact that

Allison *didn't* see that to poison their love this way? Was Caspar right? Had Jacques been right, when he'd warned her all those T-years ago? But she'd been *right*! She *knew* she'd been right. She'd *had* to try to stop Alley from embracing such a horrendous mistake!

And how is this better than just letting her go? Jennifer asked herself. *Maybe if I hadn't forced her to* choose, *she could have stepped back off the ledge when she realized I was right all along. But now . . . Now it's too late, we're both too deeply dug in, and she'll never,* ever *forgive me. Never.*

She'd made herself respond to Allison's letter announcing her pregnancy, but she knew she'd been curt. Cold. She hadn't *wanted* to be, but—

Was that the reason it had been left to Harrington to tell her about the actual birth? Had she finally managed to push Allison *that* far away?

A tear leaked from the corner of one closed eye, and she brushed it away angrily. Sitting here moping wasn't doing anyone any good. She knew that. In fact, she needed to climb out of the chaise lounge and pull up Dr. Heyder-MacLachlan's progress reports. If Heyder-MacLachlan's team was right, the answer to the locked sequence in the Jakarta modification was probably—

Her uni-link vibrated.

She glanced at it, and her eyes narrowed as the bright yellow icon of an incoming interstellar message blinked at her. There was no sender ID, but it had been sent with her personal identifier, which meant it wasn't junk mail, and she drew a deep breath.

"Accept," she said, then jerked upright as Alfred Harrington's face appeared on the tiny display.

"I'm sorry to disturb you," he said. "I thought you should know, though. Jacques's operation ended badly. His team took heavy casualties. A lot of them were from neural disruptors, so one of our battlecruisers transported them directly to Bassingford. It doesn't look good. Jacques—" He paused, inhaled deeply. "Jacques was wounded, too, and he asked me to message you. He thinks you'd better come to Bassingford. Com me when you clear the Junction. I'll have an official air car waiting at the shuttle platform."

Harrington Freehold,
County Duvalier,
Duchy of Shadow Vale,
Planet Sphinx,
Manticore Binary System,
March 1860 PD.

"And aren't you just the cutest little volcano!" Allison Harrington said as she laid young Honor back in the bassinet.

She removed the towel from her shoulder, congratulating herself on her foresight. Honor was an even-tempered baby, and indescribably cute. She also had her father's metabolism, and when she ate, she did it with...enthusiasm. Enough enthusiasm that she sometimes ingested significant amounts of air along with her nutrition.

It wasn't that big a problem when Allison was nursing, but *she* didn't have the Meyerdahl mods, and she couldn't possibly produce enough breastmilk to stay ahead of the adorable little black hole in the bassinet. And when it came to baby bottles—or, worse, to cereal—air got into the pipeline. And tended to come back up, accompanied by messy bubbles, when Honor was burped.

Of course, the messy bubbles coming up were less messy than what the other end of her alimentary canal produced. And with her appetite, she did a lot of producing.

Allison removed the soiled towel and bent over the bassinet, cooing to Honor, who gurgled happily and reached up with a tiny, perfect hand. Allison captured it and pressed a quick kiss to it, then tossed the towel into the laundry and checked the time.

Rebecca should be back from Yawata Crossing in another hour, at which point Allison would—regretfully—pass the Honor-watching duty off to her mother-in-law so that she could concentrate on some of the work she'd brought home from Queen Elizabeth's. She'd been here on Sphinx for two days now, and she'd conscientiously spent at least a couple of hours each day on work.

She felt a little guilty—but only a *very* little—over taking a long weekend, but Rebecca and Alex hadn't seen Honor in almost two T-weeks. Obviously it was Allison's *duty* to take the extra day—she had almost a solid month of comp time banked—to deliver their baby fix! And, she reminded herself with a pleasant glow of virtue, she *had* brought an entire folder of case files to review. It wasn't like—

"Incoming message from the tall guy," her uni-link's personalized AI announced, and she arched an eyebrow.

At the moment, Sphinx and Manticore were almost half a light-hour apart as they neared superior conjunction, and Alfred was supposed to join her here on Sphinx tomorrow. So what was important enough for him to burst-message her at this point? Unless something had come up at Bassingford and he'd be unable to get away after all.

"Play message," she told the uni-link, and Alfred appeared on the small display.

"Hi, Honey," he said, and her arched eyebrow came down as she frowned at his tone. "Look, I'm sorry I won't be able to get home to Mom and Dad after all. *Scepter* just got back from Silesia. She picked up Jacques's team from Pankowski. Manpower sent in a bunch of mercs, and there was an ugly firefight. We lost Lieutenant Shing, and Sergeant Major Brockmann doesn't look good."

He paused, and Allison's hand rose to cover her lips. She knew—she'd *known*—Shing for years, and Brockmann . . . Brockmann had been the pilot on the shuttle that saved her and Alfred!

"I think we'll pull Brockmann through," Alfred continued. "But Jacques—" He paused again, then inhaled deeply. "Jacques got hit, too. He wants you to come to Bassingford. He . . . needs to see you, Love. I think you should get here as soon as you can. And bring Honor. He wants to see her, too."

Bassingford Medical Center,
City of Landing,
Planet Manticore,
Manticore Binary System,
March 1860 PD.

Senior Chief Radchenko, Alfred's senior yeoman, met Allison at the shuttle pad. He was a big, red-haired bear of a man, only three centimeters shorter than Alfred, and he'd always struck Allison as a solid, unshakable rock.

She needed that now.

"Where's the Commander?" she asked as Radchenko cycled the air car hatch open.

"At the hospital with your brother, Ma'am," the senior chief said in a reassuringly calm tone. "They sent me to collect you and the baby." He paused to smile down at Honor, asleep in her soft carrier across Allison's chest. "If you'll climb aboard, I'll take you straight to them."

"How badly is Jacques hurt?"

"Ma'am, I haven't actually seen your brother, and I'm no doctor. I just work for one. So I think it'd be best if I just get you to the Commander as quick as I can and let him explain everything."

"You're right. You're right!" Allison put a small hand on his forearm and squeezed. "Sorry. I'm just . . . worried."

"I know." Radchenko nodded and laid one large paw gently across her hand for a moment. "I know. So, if you'll climb in . . ."

Allison did just that. She settled into the backseat, the air car's computer recognized the baby carrier and configured the safety harness to stay clear of it, and she told herself to relax as Radchenko cleared their departure with traffic control and lifted into the city's traffic flow.

Flight time to Bassingford was barely fifteen minutes, and Radchenko landed the air car on the parking belt. He took the diaper bag Allison handed him as she climbed back out of the vehicle, then tapped his ID against the parking belt's reader, and the belt trundled the air car off to its assigned stall.

"This way, Ma'am," he said.

He steered her respectfully toward the central lift bank, and Allison was more than willing to let him take the lead. She'd visited Bassingford scores of times, but she was just a bit distracted today. Better to let the local guide navigate.

They rode the lift shaft upward, then stepped out into one of Bassingford's airy corridors. It was one of the outer corridors, on the inside of the tower but with a crystoplast wall looking out across one of the three-story atriums at the tower's hollow core. There were over a dozen of those atriums, stacked vertically every fourteen floors, but Allison had little attention to spare for the greenery and water features today.

Radchenko led her down the hall, then pressed the button beside a closed door.

"Yes?" Alfred's voice said over the speaker.

"We're here, Sir."

"Thank you, Jayden," Alfred said, and the door slid open.

Radchenko waved Allison past him, and she stepped quickly through the door and—

"*Allison?!*" the small, exquisitely beautiful woman standing beside the empty bed said, wheeling toward the door.

"*Mom?!*"

Allison froze. They stared at one another in shock, and then, as one, wheeled to glare at Alfred.

He stood at the foot of the bed, memo board under one arm, and looked back calmly.

"What's the meaning of—?!" Jennifer began furiously.

"Where's Jacques?!" Allison demanded, her eyes glittering with mingled shock, disbelief, and anger as she felt Alfred at the other end of their link. His emotions were too complex to sort out—the link didn't carry enough bandwidth for that—but one thing he *wasn't* was surprised. In fact, she realized, he'd set this entire thing up. And he'd done it expressly to get her and—

Those glittering eyes swept back to her mother, and her thoughts paused as she found Jennifer looking back at her.

No. Not back at *her*. Her mother was staring at *Honor*, and there was no anger, no shock, in her eyes. Not now. There was only soul-deep longing, and Jennifer half-raised a hand, reaching out before she snatched it back and those longing eyes moved back to Allison's face.

Silence hung heavy between them, almost as if it were afraid of itself. Or as if the two women on the opposite sides of it were afraid. Seconds trickled away, and then Jennifer inhaled deeply.

"Oh, Allison," she said. "I'm sorry. I'm *so* sorry."

Allison's lips quivered as she tried to sort through her own emotional flood. Lingering shock. A sense of betrayal for the way Alfred had tricked her into coming. Anger at her mother for the breach between them . . . and a perversely sharper flare of that anger at the uselessness of apologies after so much hurt, so much pain. As if just *apologizing* could make it all go away. Make everything all right again. As if—

But under the shock, under the betrayal, and under the anger there was something else. There was . . . a sense of wonder. Of disbelief. And the sheer joy of seeing her mother again after so many T-years.

"I don't understand," she said. "Why—"

"That's my fault. Mine and Alfred's," a voice said from behind her, and she wheeled to see her brother in the doorway.

His left arm ended just below the shoulder, and a black patch covered his right eye. He looked terrible, a corner of Allison's brain thought, but he was on his own feet, standing unassisted. Clearly, *he* hadn't been hit by a disrupter, and from painful experience, she knew how well he responded to regeneration.

"I figured that in my current wounded condition," he continued, walking slowly and carefully across to settle into the bedside chair, "neither of you would wreak mayhem upon me. Alfred's big enough, I figure he can take care of himself."

His drawn, weary face smiled whimsically, and despite herself, Allison's lips quivered ever so slightly. She felt Alfred's answering amusement flowing into her, but then Jacques's expression sobered.

"We really did get shot up badly," he said, lifting the stub of his truncated arm. "We gave better than we got, and we took out all the mercs before Captain Gomez could get there, but it was ugly. And that brought me face to face with some of the . . . unfinished business in my life. Like the fact that two of the people I love most in the universe have dug themselves into a position neither of them has a clue how to un-dig."

"In fairness to Jacques," Alfred said quietly, "he's not the only one who's felt a lot of pain over this. Doctor," he looked at Jennifer, "I've tried to tell you before. The breach between you and Allison is the last thing I ever wanted. And, Alley," he looked back at his wife, "you already knew that. Just like I already knew it wasn't what *you* wanted, either. But Jacques was right years ago when he asked me what God could have been thinking to put the two most stubborn women in human history into the same family. I'll be damned if I have any better answer for that now than I had then, but I have figured out *one* thing since then."

"What?" Allison asked, when he paused.

"I've figured out that my daughter—*our* daughter—has *two* sets of grandparents, and there's no way in hell I'm letting anyone, *including the two of you*, take one of those sets away from her. I don't think there's any point digging into how we got where we are, or assigning blame for it. Trust me, there's blame on both sides. What matters here is that people make mistakes, and after they make them—if they're as smart as I know the two of you are, and if they love each other as much as I know the two of you do—they make *amends*.

"All the people who love both of you are waiting for you to do that. If you think the timing on this was easy to arrange, then you just think again. There's a reason I didn't tell you Jacques had been wounded until your mother's ship had been in-system for eighteen hours, Alley. And there was a reason he was 'in treatment' when you got here, Doctor! We didn't want either of you seeing him until you *both* got here. But the fact that we went to such lengths to engineer this—that we were willing to go to them—should tell you both how deeply loved you are. So, please—for our sake, if not yours—admit it to yourselves and to each other. The only thing either of you want at this point is for it to be *over*. It's not about counting coup or proving who was right. What you want is to look at each other again and admit how much you love each other. And how much you've missed each other."

Allison's mouth quivered as she felt his love, his passionate honesty, flow through her. But her mother didn't have that connection. She couldn't feel his sincerity, the intensity of his desire—his *need*—for the two of them to heal their breach.

Any more than she could know, as Allison did, that he didn't want that for himself at all. He wanted it for them.

For *both* of them.

She looked at her mother. Jennifer looked back, and then squared her shoulders, inhaled deeply, and looked at Alfred.

"You're wrong, Commander Harrington," she said. "That isn't the only thing *I* want. Not by a long chalk."

Allison's spine stiffened, but her mother wasn't done yet.

"I do want that. But what *I* want most in the universe at this moment"—she held out her arms, tears sparkled on her lashes, and her voice went husky—"is to hold my granddaughter at last."

Harrington Freehold,
County Duvalier,
Duchy of Shadow Vale,
Planet Sphinx,
Manticore Binary System,
December 1877 PD.

"Everything packed?"

Honor Harrington turned from the snow-buried landscape outside the window, cupping her hot chocolate in both hands, as her father stepped into the kitchen behind her.

"I think so," she said. "Which means I haven't. Got everything, I mean." She smiled crookedly, and Nimitz bleeked a laugh from where he lay curled in a patch of sunlight on the windowsill. Her father snorted.

"Trust me, the DIs will rectify any shortcomings in your kit in short order. Don't forget," he smiled back at her, "in my less reputable days I *was* one of those DIs. That was before I traded up to the senior service, of course."

"Oh, of course!"

Honor rolled her eyes. She'd turned seventeen only three T-months ago, but both her parents had supported her from the moment she announced that she wanted a naval career. Not without qualms, she knew, and especially given that she wanted starship command.

Her father had never really wanted to talk about his own combat service, and she understood why. Maybe even better than he realized she did. But whatever he'd *wanted*, he'd talked about it, anyway. He'd talked about it because she was his daughter, and he loved her, and he wanted her to know as much about—to be as thoroughly prepared as possible for—the sort of career she'd chosen. Neither of her parents could hide how much they worried about where that career might take her, but they'd never tried to dissuade her, either. As her mother had told her father across the breakfast table on the day their twelve-year-old daughter announced that she wanted to command starships, it wasn't as if Honor didn't understand what she was getting into. Not with Captain Harrington for a father and Major Benton-Ramirez y Chou (retired) for an uncle.

But her dad did like to rub in the fact that *he* hadn't been any namby-pamby midshipman! She knew how proud he was that she'd won one of the fiercely competitive appointments to Saganami Island without a single gram of political pull. But deep inside, he still cherished a certain tribal loyalty to the Royal Marines.

Now her smile faded, and he arched an eyebrow as her expression turned pensive.

"What is it, Bug?" he asked in a gentler tone, and she shrugged.

"It's just . . . just that I'm so excited, and so happy, and so nervous, and so anxious, and so confused," she said. "I've been working to get here for half my entire life, Daddy! I know half of my life is a lot shorter than half of *your* life, but it seems pretty darned long to *me*. And it's here now, or it will be next month when I report to the Island. And I'm . . . I guess I'm a little afraid."

"Afraid?" He chuckled softly and crossed to stand behind her and rest his chin on the top of her head as he folded her in his arms. He was tall enough he could do that, despite her own centimeters. "*My* daughter is *afraid* of a batch of drill instructors and teachers? I know better than that, Honey!"

"I don't mean afraid of the Island." She leaned back against him, treasuring the arms which had always enfolded her in safety. "Oh, I'm a little nervous about that, because I know it's going to be the hardest thing I've ever done. That it's *supposed* to be the hardest thing I've ever done. But that's not what I'm afraid of."

"Then what?"

"It's just . . . I've always wanted command, Daddy. Somehow, I've always felt like that's what I was born to do. But what if it turns out I was wrong? What if it turns out I'm a bad leader? Or that I suck at tactics? A commanding officer needs to *win*. If she can't do that, she shouldn't be commanding in the first place!"

He was silent for a moment. That was one of the things she most admired about him. The way he thought about her questions instead of just throwing off an answer. Then she felt him shrug ever so slightly.

"Bug, I can't tell you you'll be a good leader. I'm sure you will, because I've watched you growing up, and you've always *been* a leader. But the only one who can really tell you that is *you*. So my advice is to be patient. One thing any good DI knows is that the cream rises to the top. They're going to put you under a lot of pressure, Honey. The kind of pressure that finds weak links so they can be strengthened . . . or eased out of the way. And the kind of pressure that shows someone like you that, yes, you're not only a good leader, you're a natural one."

She listened intently, testing not simply his words but his tone, and then, finally, she nodded.

"As for sucking at *tactics*—!" A deep chuckle rumbled through his chest. "Honor Harrington, I'm totally confident you'll excel at *that*."

"How?" she challenged, turning her head to look up at him with a twinkle in her eye. "How can you be so sure?"

"Because you're my daughter, and your mother's, and your Uncle Jacques's niece. Besides, I'll have you know you won your very first victory before you could even talk. Heck, before you could *walk*!"

"What kind of 'victory'?" she demanded.

"Oh, a great and glorious one!" he told her, and beneath the laughter in his voice, she heard a serious note, as well. "You vanquished an implacable foe, a veritable dragon of animosity and anger, liberating and reuniting two people who'd been separated by an unbridgeable chasm for *years*."

"What are you *talking* about, Daddy?" she pressed around a gurgle of laughter, and he gave her a squeeze.

"Well," he said, "you know how insistent your mom's always been on being *Manticoran*, not Beowulfan. What you may not know, because I don't think we ever told you, is exactly how your grandmother responded to that."

"I've always known she didn't think it was . . . a great idea." The last three words came out in a slightly questioning tone, and her father laughed.

"I think you might call that a bit of an understatement," he told her. "Quite a bit, in fact. So, freshen that cup of hot chocolate, and let me tell you about your very first victory, young lady.

"It'll take a while."